HIGHLAND
JUSTICE

Larry Stuart

Penpress

First published in Great Britain by Pen Press
All paper used in the printing of this book has been
made from wood grown in managed, sustainable
forests.

ISBN13: 978-1-78003-048-7

Pen Press is an imprint of
Indepenpress Publishing Ltd
25 Eastern Place
Brighton
BN2 1GJ

Printed and bound in the UK

A catalogue record of this book is available from
the British Library

Cover design by Jacqueline Abromeit

Acknowledgments

There are so many to thank:

First and foremost, my family, who, with good grace, endured my flights of fantasy and tested the umpteenth "last" draft.

Along the way, one or two have provided encouragement, just when it was needed. To them goes my gratitude, and assurance that I will protect their anonymity – until at least the millionth sale!

And finally, I extend my appreciation to the hundreds of authors who, throughout my life, have drawn me into their journeys, and inspired me to set out on my own.

Author's note:

For the purposes of continuity, a few of the historical events in this novel have been taken slightly out of time frame. To those of you who detect these inaccuracies, I do apologize, and hope it does not detract from your enjoyment of the novel.

OATS: 'A grain, which in England is generally given to horses, but in Scotland supports the people.'

Samuel Johnson 1755

BOSWELL: 'I do indeed come from Scotland, but I cannot help it…'
JOHNSON: 'That, Sir, I find, is what a very great many of your countrymen cannot help.'

James Boswell 'Life of Samuel Johnson' 1763

One

The door rattled in its frame, its decrepit wooden panelling cracking as it strained to withstand the pummelling. A cloud of dust and particles of rotted timber spread into the room; and in the tranquillity of that early morning, the noise and confusion almost overwhelmed a young boy as he was driven from his slumber.

Cameron sat bolt upright, his eyes unwillingly open. Disorientated, he frantically searched his shadowy surroundings; but in the dreary light of daybreak, ill-defined shapes were all that were present.

'Morris Stewart! This be the police…open the door!'

The booming voice completed Cameron's rude arousal.

'Father…Father wake up!' cried out his panicky voice, his eyes desperately peering into the darkness on the far side of the room.

'Come on, Stewart! We know you're there!'

The loud hammering continued, and as there was no acknowledgement from his father Cameron accepted that it was left to him to get to the door.

His bed had been placed in a rear corner of the old crofter's cottage – at the opposite end from where a door led to his father's room. So, swinging his legs out from under his blanket, he got to his feet and slowly shuffled across the cold wooden floor, his hands groping for the edge of the table that he knew stood between himself and the cottage's entrance. Suddenly, he stumbled into something soft. He didn't need to look to know that it was his father's comatose body lying at his feet, reeking of alcohol and rotten fish. With barely a

1

hesitation, he stepped over the human obstacle and worked his way past the table and towards the front door.

The thin light of dawn outlined two huge shapes, and as they entered with their batons drawn Cameron recoiled, cowering behind the door.

The unmistakeable form of Sergeant Boyd was first through the entrance; and although Cameron had grinned when he'd overheard the older lads in town making fun of the sergeant's chinless face, large stomach, and even larger behind, in his current situation the policeman seemed a frightening colossus.

Following him in was a fairly new addition to Banffshire's Victorian police force; and despite the fact that he was of much smaller stature – and had a clean shaven and almost kindly face – from a ten year old's perspective he was still an intimidating figure of authority.

'Och! What a stink! Where is he then?'

Cameron crawled forwards, peering up from around the edge of the door at the two daunting figures – for the moment stationary, as their eyes adjusted to the gloomy interior.

'There he be Sergeant…there…in front of that table.'

'Aye…an what a fine lookin' specimen of Highland stock,' sneered the sergeant. 'He dinna look like he's changed his clothes since Ah last saw him, scuttlin' through the trees by Conval woods.'

The two policemen inched their way forwards in the wedge of light provided by the open doorway.

'Look at the state of that. Ah reckon even a common snipe wud no wish to nest in that mess on his heid! What an example he's settin' for his wee bairn. No doubt in a few years time we'll be doon here doin' the same thing ag'in… only this time it'll be the lad we're arrestin'. Come on then, Constable…Let's get him outside. Ah expect he'll sober up soon enough when he sees where he'll be spendin' his time waitin' for the Magistrate.'

Both men pocketed their truncheons – it being obvious that the only danger from this criminal was the possibility of him staining their uniforms with vomit as they dragged him from the shack. Then, each grabbing an arm, they hauled the inert form across the floor and out through the open doorway.

Cameron's teeth chattered from fear as well as the cold, so as soon as the duo had left, he scurried from behind the door, making his way towards his bed. Then, after donning the shirt he'd left lying on his bedside chair, he knelt on the floor, carrying out a frenzied search for his trousers.

'There they be,' he mumbled under his breath, hurriedly pulling them over his shivering legs, before jumping onto his bed and pressing himself into the corner – where he drew up his knees under his chin.

A few minutes later the two officers returned and then spent twenty minutes searching for proof of Morris's guilt.

'Och…there's nothin' in here. Let's have a wee gander out back. That may turn up somethin'. Bring the bairn, Constable. Ah'm certain that with a wee bit of persuasion we could get him to point us to where somethin' may be hidden.'

'Ah hope yer no plannin' anythin' physical …'cause Ah'm no havin' anythin' to do with that.'

'Dinna make a palaver. Ah'll no do anythin' to hurt him… Just bring him out.'

Having overheard what the sergeant had said, Cameron found it difficult to control his shaking while they led him from the cottage. It did cross his mind that maybe he should try to escape. After all, he didn't think he would have much trouble out-running the sergeant. But then, what was the point? They knew who he was. Where could he run?

Not long later a muted 'over 'ere' could be heard coming from inside the ramshackle shed near the bottom of the overgrown vegetable plot.

Cameron crept towards the front of the shack and cautiously peered around the doorframe.

Both Bobbies stood looking at the canvas sack propped up against the wall under the workbench – liberally strewn with dried slime and fish scales.

3

'Well…pick it up then, Constable. We've no got all day.'

'Och, greet.'

Cameron retreated, leaning against the outdoor privy at the side of the cottage, as the two Bobbies ambled back to their wagon – where the constable gladly pitched their evidence into the back, alongside his manacled father.

'What shall we do with the lad then? Do ye think we should take him with us, Sergeant?'

'Dinna bother yoursel' about him. Ah'm sure the wee rascal has family nearby he can run to. Besides, we'll no be wantin' him growin' up thinkin' we're some kinda public service…now do we?' sniggered the sergeant.

Climbing into their transport, the two policemen set off for town, chuckling at the sight of Morris bouncing around in the back of their rig, while at the same time totally disregarding the woeful-looking lad staring after them.

Two hours later, a young boy with red-rimmed eyes, filthy clothes and mud-spattered boots, wandered up Church Street into Dufftown. It was still early in the day, and the sun had yet to creep over the hills to the east to cheer up the drab stone buildings lining each side of the roadway.

Head down, eyes staring at the ground in front of his feet, Cameron passed the baker's front door – the distinctive aroma from within reawakening the craving in his empty stomach. His despair increased with each step, his thoughts returning to the memories of that day a year before when they had buried his mother, and his life as he had known it had disappeared.

Until then, he'd led what he assumed was a fairly normal life. His father had been bonded to the Duke of Richmond's estate, so, six days a week from dawn to dusk he laboured in the fields; his one treat being a day off to take the family to Summereves Fair, in Keith. And, although the winter days were shorter, this was more than offset by the bitter weather, as he toiled outside coppicing, collecting wood and mending fences.

At the same time, his mother had prepared their meals, tried her best to keep their home clean and, during the summer months, tended her vegetables. But there was no respite for her either in the long, dark days of winter. Because once she had completed her daytime burdens, she spent hours squinting in the shallow light of smoky, tallow candles, spinning for next year's clothes.

Upon reaching the intersection with Fife Street, a loud bang on Cameron's left startled him back to the present. Glancing towards the clock tower, he glimpsed the all too familiar sight of old Mr Ramsay being ejected from the police station, after spending another night in the cells sobering up from a few too many ales at the inn.

Making his way around the corner to his right, Cameron plodded down the wide street, passing the quiet, dark dressmakers and general store. In fact, the only sign of life in this part of town was the white cloud issuing from the stack at the Mortlach Distillery, down by the river, and the coach-and-four being harnessed-up outside the blacksmith's, in preparation for its morning departure to Huntly.

Cameron returned to his doleful state of mind, recalling with horror that moment, a few hours before, when his father had been dragged from the cottage and tossed into the back of the policemen's rig like some sack of rubbish.

If only his father hadn't lost his job on the Duke's estate. Then maybe, he and his father wouldn't have had to leave their previous home and move into the dilapidated, crofter's cottage sitting on the hillside below Dufftown.

At least his sister, Margaret, had been luckier. She had been wedded a few years before. And when her husband, Peter, had lost his job at the distillery, they had moved away to find employment; and from what he could remember, his mother had said they were 'settled in Elgin and doin' just fine'.

Finally, Cameron turned the corner into Cowie Avenue and trudged past the long row of terraced stone cottages. When he reached number eleven he stopped, lifted his arm,

5

and with the back of his sleeve rubbed the tears from his eyes. For a moment he hesitated, thinking that it might be a bit too early to be knocking on his granny's door. However, the doubt in his mind was soon put to rest, when the early morning stillness was broken by the clop, clop, clop, of *Robbie*, the milkman's horse, turning into the street.

Pushing open the tired, wooden gate set into the flint stone wall, the rusty hinges creaked – seemingly determined to announce his arrival to every house on the street. Easing it closed, Cameron then turned, edging his way along the path.

'Och, no,' he mumbled, spotting a curtain moving in next door's upstairs window. 'Old, Mrs Murray wud have to be peerin' out'.

But, before he had time to worry further the front door opened. And there, with her curly white hair, welcoming smile and arms opened wide stood his grandmother.

Two

Helen put her arm around her grandson's shoulders and ushered him into her kitchen. Then, after placing two cups of tea on the table, she moved to the pantry – retrieving a plate piled high with freshly made bannocks and a porcelain pot filled with honey.

'Here we are then, Cameron. Come an sit yourself down… an then tell me what be botherin' you.'

As he recounted the morning's dismal events Helen's heart was saddened – not only by what had taken place, but also by the sight before her.

Cameron's mother, Anne, would never have allowed her son to go anywhere looking like this; if necessary, dragging him down to the river with a bar of carbolic to make sure he didn't. And even though his clothes were nearly all hand-me-downs, she had always made sure they were clean and in good repair. However, since Anne's untimely death from winter fever, Cameron's upbringing had been anything but disciplined, and he now sat before her unwashed and in filthy rags, which had probably not seen soap since his mother's funeral.

Cameron's father was her only child. But she had long since passed the point where she might have any influence over what course he would follow; and she had known that it was only a matter of time before the law finally caught up with him.

Poaching on the Duke's estate had been going on for generations by families eager to supplement their meagre diet – the occasional fish from the River Spey or small game from the heath seemingly never missed, or possibly even tolerated. But after the death of Cameron's mother Morris had lost all restraint, and began to treat the surrounding countryside like his own personal, hunting estate. Inevitably, Malcolm Campbell, the Duke's estate manager, had been approached by his game keeper, and, after listening to the evidence, had confronted Morris. Within minutes, the age-old enmity between the Stewarts and Campbells had re-surfaced. Morris had become enraged, blaming the manager and his ancestors for destroying the Highlands by supporting the English and helping to carry out the Clearances. The encounter could only have had one outcome, and Morris was given three days notice to vacate his tied cottage.

By the time Cameron finished telling his tale, Helen knew what had to be done. A hot bath, fresh clothes and warm food were the most pressing needs; followed by a kindly ear, motherly love and the assurance of a warm home.

'Nan, Ah no understand. Why have they dragged father off? Ah know he takes one or two fish from the Spey… but…but 'tis only so we no go hungry.'

'I'm afraid it's a wee bit more than that Cameron. Since your mother passed he's been takin' a lot of salmon an trout from the Spey…then sellin' them on the sly. And, from what I've been hearin', he an that ruffian friend of his, Dougal, have been takin' deer from the Duke's estate as well, an then sharin' it out with some of their other ne'er-do-well friends.'

'Maybe 'tis ma fault,' Cameron sniffed. 'If it was no for me, he wudna have two people to feed…an…an maybe he no be in the hoose when they come lookin' for him.'

'Don't talk such foolishness. If he'd been lookin' after you proper you wouldn't be sittin' here in them clothes… an…he wouldn't have had time to be out doin' what he's been doin'. Now…I'll bring you a nice bowl of porridge an

8

then fetch in the tin tub from out back. You finish your meal an have a bath, while I go down to the police station an see what I can learn.'

'Stewart! Ye have a visitor,' yelled the jailer.

At first, Helen could see nothing but a dim space – the only illumination coming from one small barred window set high in the opposite wall. But, when her eyes did finally adjust to the lack of light, she was shocked. Never before had she seen such squalor; and the obnoxious smell emanating from the bucket on the far side of the cell was nearly overwhelming. Suddenly, she felt faint, and clung to the bars for support.

'My God,' she gasped. 'What kinda place be this?'

It was hard to believe that, from the outside, this building appeared to be just a smart clock tower and police station. And even though she had heard rumours about dark secrets hidden behind its pleasant façade, she had never imagined anything this ghastly.

Just then a rat scurried across the room, having been frightened by a pile of rags in the corner. And while Helen's attention was focused on that mound, to her amazement it also began to move.

'Morris…is it you?'

'For sure, it isnae the Duke of Richmond…now is it?'

Having now regained some of her composure, Helen relaxed her grip on the bars, while at the same time she glared at her son.

''Tis your fault Morris…and you know it!'

'Aye…anyway the Magistrate's due here tomorra… so Ah'll soon know what they be plannin' for me.'

'You know they'll put you away this time…don't you?'

'Aye…that they will.'

'Well, you canna say you don't deserve it. By the way… just in case you be wonderin',' Helen continued, sarcastically,

'Your lad is now at my hoose…an I think it's time you an I had a wee talk about his future.'

By the time she left, Helen had coerced her son into agreeing to her plan. Cameron would have to stay with her anyway, while his father was behind bars. But what she had really wanted was Morris's agreement to leave Cameron with her until the lad was old enough to look after himself. In the end, it hadn't been all that difficult. In his own way, Morris did love his son. And, of course, it was quite convenient to have someone at home to run errands and prepare meals. But in truth, he didn't really want the responsibility.

Helen hurried down Fife Street, desperately hoping that she wouldn't come across   anyone she knew – sure in her own mind that the unsavoury odours from the cells would still be clinging to her clothes. For the first time since the death of her husband, Andrew, she felt she had a purpose in life, and maybe in some way, a chance to make up for her lack of success in bringing up her own son.

Morris had been a difficult child, wanting to spend all of his time out in the wilds with his grandfather – where the old man had filled his head with tales of the Highlanders' glorious history. She had tried to keep him under control, but after Andrew had passed away she gave up, no longer having the strength to fight her son's disobedience or irrepressible obsession with the past.

Cameron, though, was another story. So far, he had not displayed any of his father's boisterous or ill-tempered nature, and with luck, might be persuaded to shrug off the Stewarts' insatiable desire to redress the past. She knew education was the key to enlightenment – having herself been lucky enough to be well-read thanks to her mother's encouragement – and with that in mind had already decided to talk to Reverend Logan, the Minister at Mortlach Church, whom she hoped could be persuaded to use his influence to get Cameron into the local school.

On her arrival home, Helen could see that Cameron had

Three

Cameron readily adjusted to his new way of life. For the first time, he discovered the enjoyment of socialising with people of his own age – once two bloodied noses had helped him to understand that, even at school, there was an established hierarchy. And although he sometimes found the discipline of schoolwork exasperating, with his grandmother's urging he soon began to make progress.

Each night Helen would help him with his reading, writing and arithmetic; and at the beginning he was happy to let her lead the way. But before long, his thirst for knowledge, and childlike desire to show off his newfound abilities, began to reverse their roles.

Cameron's second year at school began in much the same way as his first – the only difference being that it took just one bloody nose before he finally accepted that it would not be until his final years at school that he would command any respect outside the classroom.

Cameron still felt affection towards his father. So, when his father had asked if he would like to spend Sunday afternoons with him, Cameron had gone to Helen – badgering her all week until she agreed.

On the following Sunday, after the congregation had bade their goodbyes and set off for home, Cameron did his best to suppress a smile as his father doffed his hat, held his hand over his heart and, with the most contrite look that he could muster, promised Helen he would never involve his son in any of his illegal exploits.

Thereafter, each Sunday, Cameron would dash down the

church's front steps – and, after glancing over his shoulder and throwing a wave to his grandmother – would hurry after his father. The two of them spent their days exploring the glens, climbing the sheep-grazed hills until, out of breath, they'd reach another peak. Whereupon, finding a spring they would have a drink before following the water down – Cameron gazing in wonderment as, on occasion, it would grow into a burn, and then a meandering stream that eventually joined the mighty Spey.

The wonders of nature did not stop there either. His father spent hours teaching him how to read the signs left by footprints, droppings and broken grasses. And if they were lucky, the odd roe-deer, fox, or blue hare might stumble into view, before taking fright and once more vanishing into the shadows; whilst all around them, nature's feathered creatures would provide a continuous chorus of background music.

One night after supper, Cameron sat in the front room doing his homework, while Helen busied herself sewing.

'Did I tell you that father's got a new job?'

'Why no,' Helen replied rather hesitantly, her brows furrowing as she glanced up from her lap.

'He now works part-time down at the sawmill…fellin' trees an draggin' 'em back to the yard with the help of *Tiny*, the Shire horse.'

'Well…that's good, is it not?'

Cameron returned to his homework, while Helen got up and went to the kitchen. Returning five minutes later, she set down two cups of tea, before once more picking up her sewing.

'Nan…Why does father hate Mr Campbell so much?'

'Och…I don't think 'tis so much,' Helen replied, haltingly.

'I'm no too sure. I remember father cursing him plenty. After what happened at Culloden, I could understand him no likin' the Campbell family, if they be Sassenachs. But, they're no that, are they?'

Helen sighed.

'They've probably no told you this at school, Cameron… because doubtless, they're not allowed to. In the lead up to the battle at Culloden, the Campbell clan would have nothin' to do with the Jacobites, an like the Gordons, fought alongside the English – slaughterin' anybody that supported the Prince. After it were over, the English handed out huge tracts of land to the Gordons. In fact, most of the estates around here were given to the Third Duke of Gordon, and remained in his family until they all died out. After that, the land was granted to the Duke of Richmond. He handed over the running of his Scottish estates to Malcolm Campbell's family…who have carried out that task with ruthless efficiency…and a blatant disregard for the welfare of anyone they employed. That's why the Campbells have come to symbolize all that is wrong in these parts and are hated by all true Highlanders.'

Cameron's head nodded as his mind added these bits of information to his ever-increasing knowledge of Scotland's tragic history.

After a further twenty minutes, Cameron closed his book, before looking over at Helen – now dozing in her threadbare, old chair. It was the first time he'd taken any notice of her worn, arthritic-looking hands. And, as his eyes moved upwards they settled on her face – now tired and grey-looking with wrinkles spreading outwards from the corners of her eyes.

The following evening Cameron wandered into town, hoping to intercept his father on his nightly visit to the ale house. Sitting on the edge of the trough outside the Fife Arms Hotel, he looked down at the water, just as a gust of wind disturbed its surface. A shiver ran through his body, and he hoped he wouldn't have to wait too much longer as more gusts arrived;

reminding him that winter was once more in the offing. Moments later, he became aware of the squelching of muddy boots approaching from behind.

'Cameron...Whit're ye doin' out here so late? Are ye no well? Is Helen ill?'

'No, no, father...nothin' like that. We're both fine. I've just been thinkin'. I need to find some kind of job. I mean, well...I want to earn some money of ma own. So, I been thinkin', maybe you could ask at the sawmill for me?'

Over the next three years, Cameron's appetite for learning continued unabated; while at the same time his standing amongst his contemporaries heightened – it must be said, though, only in direct proportion to his increase in physical stature.

Mondays to Fridays were spent at school, while on Saturdays he worked alongside his father – stripping the newly felled trees of their branches, before helping to attach them to *Tiny's* harness for the trip back to the mill.

As time went by, the burden of his schoolwork, plus his desire to spend at least some of his time with his friends, meant that Cameron's Sunday outings with his father began to slip away. At first he felt somewhat guilty, but, as he was only a young lad, those thoughts were soon pushed to the back of his mind.

After five years, Cameron's formal education came to an end.

The school's doors closed June 20th, the day before the solstice, so that all could enjoy the summer fair. His final school report was on the whole complimentary – apart from a short comment concerning his inability to apply himself when it came to literature. His only observation to his grandmother about that criticism had been that, he had 'no intention of following in the footsteps of Robbie Burns anyway!'

The following Saturday, as Cameron prepared to go home

from the sawmill, the manager beckoned to him from the office doorway.

'Now what have I done?' he murmured under his breath, as he plodded his way towards the main building.

Five minutes later, he walked out of the office. Not only had he not been let go, but in fact had been offered a full time job. Apparently, the mill had just won a contract from a railway company requiring more sleepers, so the manager was desperate to find more wood-cutters.

Cameron headed home with his mind in turmoil. He appreciated the mill offering him full time employment – after all, jobs were difficult to come by. But coming home every day covered in sawdust, with aching muscles, was not the future he had envisaged. At the same time, though, he did owe it to his grandmother to provide her with an easier life.

Moving to one side to get past a tall, well-dressed man standing outside the post office, he noticed a flyer – which he assumed the man had just pinned to the notice board.

* * *

GREAT NORTH of SCOTLAND RAILWAY

Requires suitable employees to build line extension

Huntly to Keith and Dufftown

Apply at Town Hall – this Saturday, 28th June, 1870

* * *

The man in the dark suit turned and began to walk away, at which point Cameron took three quick steps to get ahead, and then turned to face him – at the same time, hesitantly raising his hand.

'Excuse me, sir. Would you be knowin' what time someone might be at the town hall on Saturday...'cause, I would like to be the first in line?'

'Well…you're certainly keen...and obviously you can read. Have you ever worked before?'

'Yes, Sir. For the last three years I've been workin' at the sawmill on Saturdays… I would have done more, but I were at school all week.'

'Well…you certainly sound like you've been educated,' the man said, raising his hand to his face – his thumb and curled fingers resting against his chin. 'Hmm…You seem a bit young, but I like your manner. Furthermore, with your education you never know…you might just have a future in this business. Tell you what. Be here next Monday morning at six o'clock for the coach to Huntly. We'll start you on track laying and see how you do.'

Cameron couldn't believe his luck. He didn't know anything about track laying, but in school they'd been told that a new industrial age was upon them and the railways were leading the way. Apparently, trains already connected all the major cities in England, and now a line even ran from Liverpool via Manchester all the way to Glasgow. In Scotland, a new company called the Scottish North Eastern Railway was taking passengers from Aberdeen to Edinburgh and, according to the local newspaper, the GNSR had plans to extend their route, currently running from Aberdeen to Huntly, all the way to Inverness. This was the line that would eventually connect to Dufftown – although it was beyond him why anyone would want to connect a railway to this little town.

On the following Monday, Cameron was overawed by his first sight of the gleaming steel locomotive, idly puffing away at the station in Huntly. Never in his life had he ever been near anything man-made that was so enormous. And, it was beyond his wildest imagination that people actually got to ride in those luxurious wooden coaches – which were even fitted with steam heating to keep the passengers warm during winter.

'All ye new men line up over 'ere,' ordered a lanky, stern-looking fellow. 'Ma name's Robert Stevens…an Ah be yer foreman…so listen up. The first thing we're gonny do is fill out some papers. Then, Ah will take ye over to the depot… where we will give ye some work clothes and boots. After ye've changed, we'll go out to where the track laying to Keith has already started…so ye can see what ye'll be doin'…an meet the rest of the crew.'

The day had been a real eye-opener. It didn't take much imagination to realize that working for the railway was going to be a back-breaking and filthy job. The pay was certainly more than Cameron could ever have earned at the mill, but the task sounded arduous. Twelve hour shifts starting at seven were the norm – which meant staying at a boarding house in Huntly during the week and then travelling home after work on Saturdays.

After returning to the depot, the new men had been given the rest of the day off to find themselves some accommodation and get settled in. So, once he'd cleaned up, Cameron wandered into town.

Huntly was built around a main square laid in bricks – in the centre of which stood the statue of some kilted Laird, set in a militaristic pose; and it wasn't long before he learned that the monument had been erected in recognition of the first Duke of Gordon, who had established the town and whose ancestors still lived nearby at Huntly Lodge.

Radiating out from Huntly's square, like the spokes on a wheel, were four main roads. One led to the North West and the village of Keith, and one to the South West, back to Dufftown. To the South East was the main coach route to Aberdeen, while the road to the North East went to Banff and the coast.

Cameron did have to admit, the buildings in Huntly were very pleasing to the eye. They were nearly all made from a light grey stone – which was quarried locally – and hopefully, he thought, would last longer than Huntly's once famous castle, which had been built from the same stone, but had now fallen completely into disrepair.

The town had all the usual shops necessary for life, and was – as some said – blessed, with two inns. Its increasing importance in the North East had been confirmed a few years earlier by the opening of the Scott hospital, and that, allied to the new railway line, was all that was required to bring in more investment.

Huntly was already much larger than Dufftown, and supported such businesses as a tinplate works – making lamps for ships – and a mill, alongside the River Deveron, which had the dubious distinction of being the main supplier of oatmeal to the north of Scotland's prisons. A boot and shoe factory had recently started production, and the town's latest new employer, the Gordon Arms Hotel, was soon to open its doors, just up the street from the station.

As he and the other new men got to know their fellow workers, they began to hear about the harsher elements of their new employment. It seemed that track laying was only carried-out from spring to late autumn due to the poor weather and lack of daylight during the rest of the year. And, thinking this didn't bode well for employment during the winter months, they were pleasantly surprised to hear that they were still kept busy in the winter, doing maintenance and emergency line clearance. However, that good news was tempered on discovering that maintenance was hardly ever required – which was a shame as it was the easy work – whereas line clearance was brutal, and kept them busy for most of the winter.

The seasoned crew seemed more than happy to chronicle their previous winters' trials, highlighting the rigours by calling attention to their scarred hands, missing fingertips and withered earlobes.

'An, if ye think that's no much fun…wait 'till spring,' grumbled one of the older men. 'Some years we get one landslide after t'other. An then spend days diggin' for the tracks beneath that sloppy mess.'

Having listened to their tales, Cameron decided he was

lucky to be starting his new job in the summer. But, by the end of his second week, he was no longer certain.

Each morning when he had awoken, the aching in his muscles seemed to be worse than the day before; and he had begun to wonder if his claw-like fingers would ever straighten again.

'Come on, Stewart…Ye, too, McPherson. Get that rail over 'ere,' the foreman yelled. 'At this rate railways'll be a thing of the past before we e'en come to Keith.'

Monday, the 7th of July, was the warmest day of the summer so far; and the only part of Cameron's shirt that wasn't soaked was the bit hanging out at the back of his trousers. He and the rest of the crew grunted and cursed as they toiled in the midday sun, hauling the sleepers and rails from the flat-bed wagons following along behind them.

'You know what, Duncan?… I thought winters sounded bad…but now, I'm no so sure. Just as ma back and arms were startin' to feel normal again, we get this bloody heat. Still, I'm thinkin' I know somethin' that might make us feel a wee bit better.'

'Oh, aye…an what might that be?'

'You see that over there,' Cameron said, pointing to his left. 'The Deveron may be somewhat fresh…but…as soon as we stop for lunch that's where I'm goin'.'

The cooling dip in the river provided only a short respite to the day's seemingly endless slog. There was never any let-up, as the men were forced to keep up a steady pace, sandwiched between the horses and ploughs carving out the track-bed alongside the river, and the wagons loaded with ballast, sleepers, fishplates and rails being slowly, but continuously, pushed up behind them. Finally, just as the agonising misery of their sun-broiled bodies had become almost unbearable, the sun fell behind the Cairngorms and the day began to cool.

But nature had one more misery in store for Cameron and his fellow workers. Because, just as the men began to look forward to the end of their day, hundreds of thousands of midges descended on them, sending everyone scurrying for the wagons – hands and hats beating the air about their heads in a vain attempt to drive off the voracious tormentors.

That evening, Cameron sat sipping a pint of ale at the Kings Head – a local hostelry near the depot.

'Those damn midges,' he cursed, scratching behind his ears.

At the same time, his new friend, Duncan, sat opposite him, doing the same – only under the table – to his ankles.

It was here that Cameron had first met Duncan, and it was during their first week on the job that their friendship had developed. He, like Cameron, was from out of town, and although Duncan was nearly two years older, they shared the same sense of humour and outlook on life. Within days of getting to know each other they had decided to cut their living costs by sharing a room, and by the end of that week had moved into Mrs McGee's.

Her boarding house had come highly recommended. Not necessarily because of the acceptable rent, or owner's pleasant disposition, but more likely due to its position – being only a short stagger from the Kings Head. And as time went by, Cameron and Duncan's appreciation of their choice increased, as they supported one another on their journeys home from the inn after an evening's "relaxation".

The only part of Cameron's education remaining to be mastered was the tricky business of relationships with the opposite sex – a situation with which he was becoming increasingly frustrated. Cameron had heard all the ribald remarks, and listened with some interest to the lustful bragging of some of his workmates. He knew all about Loose-Lottie, and what took place behind the station coal store, but had no intention of being schooled in that manner. He just couldn't understand why he and Duncan seemed to be languishing at the back of the queue when it came to meeting comely females. Duncan was tall and well-built, with a mop of straw-coloured hair – which Cameron knew drew appreciative glances from most of the local lassies. And as for himself, well, at no time had he ever got the impression that he was particularly unattractive.

Duncan suggested that maybe they were being too choosy, or just looking for girls in the wrong places. So, one night after a particularly long session at the inn, he coaxed Cameron to the rear of the hospital – having been reliably informed that this was where the young nurses lived. Unfortunately, their alcohol-impaired sneak attack was detected by a corpulent matron on her way home, who, flailing her rolled-up umbrella, and with threats of the police, saw off the two Romeos.

'Och…nae mind,' Duncan stammered, as they scampered for home. 'Ah heard a rumour the other day that a textile mill is gonny open next year…just out of Huntly on the Banff road. That should bring plenty of lassies for us to choose from.'

'Aye… well maybe our luck is set to change after all,' Cameron replied. 'The foreman told me that the Gordon Arms Hotel is havin' a big Hogmanay party this year. So… how about you an me buyin' tickets? You never know… maybe two likely-looking females will show up…an feel sorry for us?'

The following day, Cameron was sitting on the bench outside the front door of the depot. Duncan's head lay against his shoulder, and his anaemic-looking face would have suggested a near death experience to anyone not familiar with his over-indulgent evenings. Cameron's head still throbbed, and his hands shook ever so slightly as he endeavoured to hold up, and read, the front page of Huntly's "Highlands" newspaper.

The headline that morning went a long way to answering the question he'd had in his mind since the first day of his job.

* * *

MORTLACH TO EXPAND PRODUCTION

Dufftown's Mortlach Distillery has announced
further expansion plans, which by the year's end
will more than double their current production.

* * *

Clearly, the railway's intention from the beginning had been
to make their profits from freight. Glendronach had been
producing whisky near Huntly since 1826, and the Longmore
Distillery in Keith was renowned as the oldest distillery in the
north east of Scotland. Whisky from the Mortlach Distillery,
and these two other Companies, was in demand throughout
Scotland and England. And some even said it was about to be
shipped to North America.

Finally, more than thirty minutes late, the yard engine
steamed into sight, hauling the three wagons loaded with the
crew's materials for the day.

Putting on his cap Cameron turned to his friend, nudging
him in the ribs.

'Come on, Duncan. Our transport is here…And whatever
you do, don't you go throwin' up on me like you did last
week.'

'Shhush! Ah heard somethin',' Morris whispered.

Dougal, his partner in crime, who'd been helping Morris
in his exploits ever since losing his own croft, stopped, and
then threw his massive bulk as flat as possible behind the
gorse bush at his side. Initially, as he desperately tried to
control his breathing and make himself as small as possible,
the only sound he heard was the beating of his own heart.

The problem was the salmon didn't do as they were told.
They still flipped and flopped about in the gunny sack over

24

Morris's shoulder, sounding like the muted applause at the end of a town hall meeting. That, the lively chirps of sparrows and deep staccato g'hak, g'hak calls of grouse grubbing for food were the predominant noises in the dawn's misty light.

Suddenly, the loud drumming of galloping hooves broke through nature's chorus.

Dougal thought his heart would explode. In front of him, Morris dropped to the ground behind a fallen trunk, the fish-filled sack shooting upwards into the air before falling back down on top of his head. Both men held their breath, until a flash of brown hair– headed by antlers – thundered past their position.

Seconds later, Dougal began to giggle; his right eyelid drooping over its empty socket as his hands searched the gorse at his side for his wayward eye patch.

Morris stood up, picking up his cap from the dirt, while at the same time cursing the fish slime pasting his hair to his scalp. And serenity once more returned to the natural world as the spooked buck disappeared into the distance.

Dougal also began to rise, but got no further than one knee before Morris's body flew forwards as if yanked by some unseen force. At the same time, the sack containing their booty had flown through the air, and was now twenty yards away, disgorging its contents into the nearby bracken. As Dougal looked over at his friend's body lying face down on the ground, a red circle appeared on Morris's back – spreading outwards at an alarming rate.

It was at that moment that he heard the echo of the Snider-Enfield rifle booming off the hillsides, as it progressed down the glen. The .577 bore barrel was accurate to extreme distances; and he knew of only one man in these parts who owned one of those. Dougal was immediately back on all-fours, scrambling through the heather and bracken, scared out of his wits, knowing that he had very little time to make good his escape before the rifle was re-loaded.

Four

The row of silver birches guarding the graveyard's western boundary swayed like drunken skeletons in the freshening breeze, while nearer the ground their previously discarded leaves swirled about the churchyard, momentarily caressing anything in their path before being driven on their way. In an almost surreal way, the old Pictish stone cross, which had stood in this cemetery for over a thousand years, cast its shadow over the grave, as the sun peeked through a break in the cloud-filled sky.

Cameron stood statue-like in front of the cold, pitiless grave. Helen clung to his right arm, softly weeping under a veiled, large-brimmed hat, while to his left stood his elder sister, Margaret, dabbing at her eyes with a small, white handkerchief.

Even though Cameron forced his eyelids closed, it proved impossible to erase the picture in his mind of what lay before him. His head lifted as he tried looking beyond the coffin, but the imagery deteriorated even further, his eyes locking onto his mother's headstone – only partially obscured by Reverend Logan's billowing cassock. A shiver of emotion coursed through his body as he scanned the horizon, in a vain attempt to distance himself from the proceedings.

'… we therefore commit his body to the ground, earth to earth, ashes to ashes, dust to dust, in sure and certain hope of the resurrection to eternal life …'

A movement on the periphery of Cameron's vision drew his attention. Squinting into the scattered sunshine he glimpsed two blurred figures, standing in the doorway of the old watch-house – their heads bowed and their faces almost hidden by caps and ragged scarves.

A long time ago, the building now obscuring those two silent onlookers had been used by men whose job it was to guard against body-snatchers; and for a moment Cameron wondered if they thought his father needed protection from that same fate. But, in his heart he knew. Dougal and his new partner were only maintaining a respectable distance from the proceedings – unsure of their welcome by Morris's family.

The service ended with the recitation of the Lord's Prayer, followed by a few minutes silence. Then the piper engaged by Cameron struck up his melancholy lament. The haunting dirge overwhelmed all other sounds, sending shivers up everyone's spine, until the tune and bellows had been exhausted.

Moments later, Reverend Logan, Duncan and a few old friends of Helen moved forward to pay their respects, before quietly melting away.

'At least they be together now,' Helen sobbed, placing a small posy of flowers on Morris's coffin, and then turning to place another against Anne's headstone.

'Come away then, Nan…you must be getting cold,' Cameron said, reaching down to help her up. 'And I think we could all now do with a wee dram.'

Cameron set down his empty glass on the mantelpiece, and when he turned and looked down at his grandmother, sitting quietly sipping her tea – heartened by a goodly measure of the local distillery's medicine – he was appalled by what he saw. Staring, empty eyes and grim, puckered lips had replaced her well-known, cheery smile, while the skin on her face had taken on a waxy paleness, with tired flesh hanging from her cheeks.

'I'm going to walk Margaret to the post office to catch her coach back to Elgin. When I get back, Nan, I'll make us some supper. You just rest there till I come home.'

Cameron waited in the hallway by the front door as Margaret and Helen said their goodbyes. Then, after closing the door, he took his sister's arm as they set off for the post office. For the first few minutes they strolled along in silence – Cameron not quite sure whether Margaret was still emotionally overwrought by the day's events or preoccupied by other matters.

'Are you all right? You seem unnaturally quiet. I know today was no happy occasion but…'

'I'm fine, Cameron. I guess today just bothered me more than I be thinkin' it would.'

'Aye, I know what you mean… I certainly hope Nan gets better. She looks terrible.'

Again they lapsed into silence, and as they turned into Fife Street Cameron decided that the subject everyone had been skirting around all day had to be addressed.

'Where's Peter? How come he's no here today?'

He'd barely got the questions out before she stopped and turned to him.

'He's no well, Cameron. That's all,' she said, brusquely.

Taking her arm again, they crossed the street and soon reached the post office. He suspected she was hiding something, but could tell from the look on her face that maybe now was not the time to be pestering her.

Once Margaret's coach had departed Cameron slowly strolled back towards Cowie Avenue, his thoughts troubled by the ordeal of the last few days. It was only now that the reality of the death of his father had begun to take hold; and it wasn't only his grandmother and sister that had been affected by what had happened. A void now existed in his life where his mother and father should have been. Somehow, he had always taken it for granted that they would always be there but, as he now had to accept, that was not to be.

'I'm home, Nan. Is there anythin' I can fetch you?' he asked, sticking his head around the parlour door. 'How about a wee warm drink before supper?'

Helen's head went slowly back and forth, and then, with a fearsome look on her face, she hauled herself from the chair.

'Where was Peter today? He could have at least come for Morris's funeral. Och, never mind...I'm tired an I be goin' to bed.'

The following morning, as Cameron prepared to leave, he was quite surprised to find that his grandmother was not yet downstairs. Grabbing the post at the bottom of the stairs he turned and looked up.

'Nan...Nan, are you comin' down?'

Getting no reply, and now thinking the worst, he hurried up the stairs, rapped on her bedroom door, and without waiting for a reply walked in.

'Canna anyone get any privacy about here?' Helen exclaimed, half out of bed and reaching for her dressing gown.

'Sorry, Nan. I were just a wee bit worried about you. I'll fetch you a nice cup of tea before I leave. I'm goin' out to the old cottage to clean it up before I go back to Huntly.'

'Do somethin' for me, Cameron. Can you stop by the police station on your way an pick up your father's things... an then, just get rid of them.'

'All right, Nan...Oh, and I just remembered, I saw Constable Stevenson the other day and he said the accident report would be ready today...so, I'll pick up a copy while I'm there.'

For a moment an evil look passed over Helen's face as her eyes turned coal-black.

'Accident they say? Ha! That'll be the day any Stewart is accidentally shot by a Campbell!'

'Good morning, Mr Stewart. Ah did wonder when we might be seein' ye.'

It would be that fat slob of a sergeant on duty, Cameron thought, as he walked over to the reception desk – remembering him well, from that early morning wake-up all those years before.

'Sorry about yer father's terrible accident… Mind you, if he had no been trespassin' …'

'Thanks very much for your heartfelt sympathy. Just give me his belongin's.'

Grabbing the bag hoisted onto the desk by the sergeant, Cameron turned, and with undisguised loathing made his way out of the police station.

As he wandered along the rutted track winding its way down the hillside towards his old home, he was lost in thought. He had never seen his grandmother show such anger before, even if it was only fleeting; and the confrontation with the police sergeant had also unsettled him. He knew from his schooling – and from quiet conversations that he'd had with his friends at work – that there were still plenty of people in the Highlands who hated the English and their Scottish collaborators. But he was determined not to make the same mistakes as some of his ancestors had. There was no proof that his father's death had been anything but a tragic accident; and as far as he was concerned it was time to let the past fade into history.

After a while, his mind returned to his immediate task. He was certainly not looking forward to the memories – both good and bad – that he knew would be waiting to wreak havoc on his emotions; and worst of all, he now began to feel a deepening sense of guilt welling up inside of him.

In his last year at school he had only seen his father on Saturdays at work. And since joining the railway he'd been even more remiss, using up most of his spare time with Duncan, or on short trips to Dufftown to see Helen.

The door opened with an eerie creak. After stepping into the dilapidated old shack, he found it hard to believe that anyone could have lived in such a disgusting   hovel.

The stink of dead animals and rotten fish permeated the atmosphere, and the sight of years of filth and disorder saddened his heart. Once more, self-recrimination invaded his thoughts. Would it have helped if he'd seen more of his father? Or maybe if he had tried to intervene earlier, his father's death could have been avoided. But in his heart he knew that what had happened was probably inevitable, as his father, like many others, had made it their mission to harry, cheat – and where possible – exact their revenge.

Cameron spent the rest of the morning lugging everything that was moveable outside and stacking it in a huge pile in a clearing behind the cottage. Things that wouldn't burn such as his father's illegal traps – which he'd found still hidden behind the false panel in the back of the shed – he buried in a hole dug in a nearby copse.

A few hours later, he sat on a boulder near the warm glow of the fire. The pyre crackled and burned, quickly consuming the record of his father's transgressions and meagre lifestyle. Staring into the fire, he was absorbed by the tumbling, twisting flakes of ash carried heavenwards by the blaze. A smile spread across his face as he remembered those wonderful days spent together. And for a moment it seemed his imagination had overwhelmed him when, through tear-misted eyes, he was sure he saw his father's face smiling back at him from the flames.

Soon, the job of sweeping out the accumulated years of dust and dirt was nearly complete. A mask might have been a good idea, he mused, coughing for the umpteenth time as the broom's movement created an almost impenetrable fog of detritus. Moving through the doorway into his parents' old bedroom, he headed to the far corner where the bed had stood. Unexpectedly, with the first sweep of the broom a plank dislodged, coming to rest on the toe of his right boot. Bending over, Cameron picked it up, but in the process of replacing it his eye was drawn to what appeared to be some old bits of rag lying in the dirt below the floorboards.

'Nan…it's me,' Cameron yelled, as he came through the front door of her house.

In his right hand, pressed against his body, he carried a flat, rectangular-shaped object wrapped in some old tartan cloth, while in his left was a similarly covered article, but this time cylindrical in shape.

'Wait till you see what I discovered,' he exclaimed, strutting into the lounge and giving Helen a peck on the cheek. 'They be under the floorboards in the cabin.'

Helen sat up, her back rigid.

'Oh, no…not those,' she murmured, as with a gasp she sank back into her chair.

'What's the matter, Nan? 'Tis only some old bible and some kind of flag or other from the old days. I have no looked at them very careful, but I presume they be somethin' father must have found…or worse, stolen.'

'Och, Cameron…I only wish that be true.'

Setting the objects down in front of the hearth he then knelt beside Helen.

'Why do these old things bother you so?'

'More of that later, Cameron…but for now, I'm goin' upstairs to fetch ma shawl… then I'll prepare our meal. We be goin' to have mince an tatties for a change.'

It was getting dark outside and the wind was beginning to howl, bringing with it cold draughts from under the front door and through the gaps around the poorly fitting windows.

Cameron knelt in front of the hearth, prodding the burning logs with a twisted metal poker as he anxiously awaited Helen's appearance; all the while gazing at the fire dancing and flickering, as sparks, like miniature stars, were carried upward into the chimney. I wonder what could be so significant about those dusty old relics, he mused, as he listened to the rattling of dishes and cutlery coming from the kitchen.

The front room was warm and cosy as he and his grandmother finally settled into their chairs. Reaching down, she grasped the bible, and with some effort hoisted the large, leather-bound tome onto the table at her side. For the moment she left it closed; and then she began to recount the story that all true Scots would have heard in one form or another, since 1746.

For over an hour, Cameron listened as Helen relived the story of the aftermath of Culloden. She described in detail how "Butcher Cumberland" had chased Charles Edward Stuart – now affectionately known as Bonnie Prince Charlie – across Scotland, murdering the Prince's supporters as he went: how the young Prince had escaped to France with the help of a few loyal supporters; and how he had promised he would return with the French army and throw out the English.

'But, as I know you must be aware, Cameron, that oath was ne'er kept. Because soon after he fled, the English Parliament signed a peace treaty with the French. All we know for certain is that Bonnie Prince Charlie never returned to Scotland an died some forty years later, in Rome.'

'I still no see what this has to do with us, Nan…after all, we're descended from lowland Stewarts…are we no?'

Helen seemed to hesitate; and for a moment Cameron wondered if she was now too exhausted to continue.

Then, with a wistful sigh she carried on.

'In order to survive the massacre, the remainin' Highland Stuarts quickly changed their names to Stewart. And…well… look here.'

Helen opened the bible to its third page, where ornately scrolled and framed in gilt were the words Family Register. Directly below this title, the page was lined and handwritten in ink.

'These be your ancestors, Cameron, and your great-great-grandfather is here,' she said, pointing to the second name down from the top.

Cameron expected to see his great-great grandfather Donald's name, but what he was not expecting to see was his family name being spelt S.T.U.A.R.T.

'So…I guess I be a true Highlander then? But that's all history. Does it really matter now?'

'I'm afraid it does.'

Helen reached over, picking up the bright yellow cloth bearing a rampant red lion, which was rolled around a wooden staff.

'This rolled up old flag, as you call it, just happens to be the Royal Standard of the Stuarts, and was carried into battle by your great-great grandfather.'

'Well, surely that's just a wee keepsake then?'

'Oh, Cameron…that it certainly is not. To the Highlander families it's a reminder of all they suffered – and proof that your ancestor ran from the battlefield with the Prince – while to the English, it is a sign of the burning resentment still present today, and is somethin' that could be used to rally trouble in the future.'

Helen now looked completely exhausted. Her eyes were sullen and her face grey and drawn.

'I must be off to bed now,' she mumbled, as she struggled to pull herself from her chair. 'But before I do…I beg of you, Cameron…please…take those things away and get rid of them…once and for all.'

'I will, Nan…dinna you bother yourself. You'll never see them again.'

The crew battled on that year through pelting autumnal rain and early winter snow showers. Finally, as Christmas approached, track laying was halted. At the end of that week all the men were brought together in the depot for an announcement from the management.

'Men…As Ah'm sure ye be aware, there is no sufficient light during the day now to make track layin' practical. So, Ah be instructed by the company to tell ye that when ye come back from Christmas, the workin' day will start at eight o'clock an finish at four.'

34

Loud cheering erupted, accompanied by whistling and clapping. The foreman raised his right hand, slowly moving it back and forth as a signal for them to curb their enthusiasm.

'Before ye get too excited…Ah should warn ye that at the same time there'll be a reduction in pay to reflect the new workin' hours.'

As he stepped down from the coach in Dufftown, a blast of arctic-like air assaulted Cameron's body. At the same time, the glow from the gas streetlamp on the corner of Fife St. and Balvenie wavered, as if it too was feeling the attack from the north.

Cameron had three days off for Christmas, and he was determined that the weather was not going to spoil his time off. In the bag slung over his shoulder was a full bottle of whisky and a new coat he'd bought for his grandmother. And, as a special treat for their supper that night, he had ordered some bannocks from the baker to have with the piece of salmon that he'd bought – which now lay carefully wrapped in the bottom of his bag.

The extended Christmas weekend with Helen had been peaceful and enjoyable. She had loved her coat, but was dismayed that he had wasted all that money on her. Cameron had amused her with stories of the antics he got up to with his crew; and astounded her with the news that the mail from London now got to Aberdeen in just two days! For a lot of the weekend, though, Helen had seemed unusually quiet, until finally on Sunday evening she broke the news.

'I just thought you should know…I've had a letter from Margaret.'

'That's nice. Are she and Peter well?'

'No, they not be all that well. Peter lost his job a while back, and has no been able to find any other employment.'

'But…I thought Elgin was a prosperous town, with plenty of building work takin' place because of the imminent arrival of the railway?'

'Margaret asked me no to tell anyone but…I suppose it does no matter now. Peter has taken up with the evils of drink…and because of this he can no find any employment. So, last month they applied for government assisted passage to the Colonies… and it has just been approved. They be leavin' for Canada at the end of March.'

'Och…I'm sure a new start is probably just what they need,' Cameron said, trying to make light of the situation for Helen's sake.

'I suppose,' she replied, gazing forlornly into the fire.

Three days later, Cameron was jarred from his slumber by the loud crack of a whip and a sharp pain to the side of his head. With a jerk, the coach swayed back to the left as the driver recovered the carriage from another frozen rut in the road. Twenty minutes later they arrived at Huntly Station, and after grabbing his bag, Cameron jumped down from the coach – bidding farewell to the driver. Then, pulling up his collar and shoving his hands into his pockets, he headed for the depot.

That winter was brutal. And what made it worse was that it seemed to last for ever. Even in England people began to wonder if it would ever end; especially when in Nottinghamshire, on March 11th, the night time temperature fell to 13 degrees Fahrenheit. Still, there was one positive aspect arising from the populations' adversity. The English Government were spurred on to approve, and pay for, more assisted passages to the New World than ever before.

Margaret and Peter left Liverpool on March 28th, duly arriving in Quebec thirty days later. Unsurprisingly, those on government paid passage did not get accommodated on the newer steam-assisted ships, so were forced to endure a long, tiring voyage by sail.

It was with some relief that three months later, Helen received a letter from her granddaughter, confirming that all was well. Apparently, she and Peter had now moved on to some land given to them by a generous Canadian Government, and were moving ahead with the building of their new home.

Five

Another year had almost passed when, at the beginning of December, the line to Keith was completed. Celebrations took place welcoming the town's connection to the new industrial era; but Cameron and Duncan's participation was limited to viewing the proceedings from behind a five-foot high stone wall on the opposite side of the track to the station.

The promised opening of the new textile mill had been delayed, so the anticipated harvest of congenial young ladies had not taken place. However, during the last year, Duncan's pursuit of the opposite sex had been reasonably successful – although Cameron did have serious doubts as to the virtue of one or two of his conquests. As for Cameron, well, he did manage to go out with two different ladies, but they had both left him feeling dissatisfied.

When the next season began, the crew started on the 11 mile line from Keith to Dufftown. The Company's intention was to be in Dufftown by the end of September, so that they could transfer Cameron's crew to the more pressing task of extending the main line to Inverness.

But once more, nature conspired to make her presence felt, and exact her toll of misery.

Cameron was standing alongside Rob – one of the new men hired at the end of the previous season. Suddenly, his hands seemed to have a will of their own as they began to shake uncontrollably. He and Rob looked at each other, and then dropped the rail that they'd just begun to lift from the flat-car. Seconds later, Cameron became aware of his legs beginning to tremble; while at the same time a terrified voice cried out.

'Look out! Run!'

Cameron glanced to his left and froze. Suddenly, the whole mountain seemed to come alive. The hillside rumbled and groaned, the volume of noise magnifying by the second. With a deafening crack trees began to snap, and boulders bounced down the hillside, crushing everything in their paths. Fishplates were torn up like paper and, as Cameron continued to stare, part of the track that had just been laid was wrenched free from its adjacent rails. Metal spikes, which until moments ago attached rails to sleepers, were shot into the air like bullets, eventually falling back to earth to join the already cascading maelstrom of debris.

'Get doon,' Rob yelled, yanking on Cameron's arm.

Both men ducked behind the flat-car, spluttering and coughing as they were hit by a gale-force wind of dust, dirt, pieces of bark and pine needles. The tempest forced its way into every opening, making it temporarily impossible to see and nigh on impossible to breathe.

A minute or so later a new sound arose. The deafening roar of the monster, which had just hurtled down the mountain, was now replaced by the cries and moans of the injured men.

'Cameron! Are ye all right?'

'I think so. What about you, Rob?'

'Aye…Ah be fine, but we'd better look to the others.'

While they were talking, the engine driver and fireman, not requiring any further encouragement, had uncoupled the loco from the rest of the train and were already beginning to accelerate back to Keith to raise the alarm.

When the air finally cleared, the scene was one of total carnage. The section of newly laid track was gone. In its place a chaotic new hillside had been born consisting of dirt, boulders, tree trunks and branches. Amongst this confusion were human limbs, some still attached to screaming bodies, others bloodied and rootless.

Cameron and Rob did their best to help the injured. Strips of clothing were used as makeshift tourniquets and bandages. Assurances were given, promises were made, and lies were told, as they comforted the living. As time passed, the groans and wails of those suffering began to subside – and to some death was a welcome relief.

Cameron was on his knees. His hair was matted and grey with dust, his face streaked with dirt and lined with tension. His shirt lay in tatters around him, the sleeves having been used to try to stem the blood pumping from Duncan's pulverised legs – now lying screened from view by Rob's blood-soaked shirt. In his hand Cameron forcibly gripped Duncan's fingers, as if somehow this might transfer some of his strength to his injured friend; while in the distance, the shrill whistle of the yard engine announced the imminent arrival of help – but also served as a timely reminder of how long the suffering had lasted.

Rob tried to hold Duncan down as, even though he was unconscious, he thrashed from side to side. Suddenly, his dust-encrusted eyelashes fluttered and his eyes flew open.

'Get yer hands offa me, Rob…Let me get up!'

'Lay still, Duncan,' Cameron interrupted. 'There's been a landslide and you've injured your legs. The engine driver's gone for help…but he's almost back, so you just lay there, quietly.'

But…but Ah feel…fine,' Duncan stammered, his head jerking upwards as he started to cough and choke.

Using the only clean piece of shirt he had left, Cameron reached out, wiping the trickle of blood appearing from the corner of his friend's mouth.

'Help is nearly here. You'll be fine,' Cameron said, with a smile of encouragement masking his inner dread.

'But…but why canna…why canna no feel any pain if Ah'm hurt?'

40

'Don't bother yourself, Duncan…The two of us will no doubt be off chasing the lassies again by tomorrow night.'

The engine arrived, and within seconds nurses from the hospital and men carrying stretchers hurried to the scene of the catastrophe; but Cameron did not seem to notice.

Suddenly, Duncan's eyes opened wide again.

'Cameron…Ah'm frightened. Ah dinna want to die…Ah feel…Ah feel cold.'

'Don't b…be silly, Duncan. You'll be ff…fine,' stuttered Cameron, squeezing Duncan's hand.

'Thanks, Cameron…ye are a…a real…friend…'

Suddenly, a spasm passed through Duncan's body. His fingers clenched – claw-like – and then relaxed.

'Duncan…Duncan. Hang on!' Cameron cried. 'Please hang on…Help is coming.

The only response he got was the peaceful look appearing on Duncan's dirt-encrusted face as his life melted away. Cameron stayed kneeling, unmoving, as if frozen in time and place. He felt almost lifeless – the adrenaline having drained from his body – and still he didn't seem to notice the arrival of the train, or the crowd of people now milling about.

Rob, with the wave of his hand, silently directed the rescuers away from Cameron and his friend. Then, twenty minutes later, he softly squeezed Cameron's shoulder.

'Come away now, Cameron. Let's have a cup of tea an somethin' to eat. We'll come back for Duncan. Dinna fret yoursel'…we'll no leave him behind.'

With an aching heart, and tears streaming down his face, Cameron took off the remains of his tattered shirt – gently placing it over his best friend's face.

Six

The following Monday morning Cameron was subdued and lost in thought as he folded up his newspaper and stepped down from the coach. The extra days off provided by the company to all surviving crew members – and the mature counselling afforded by his grandmother – had gone some way in helping him recover from his emotional ordeal. But the headline in today's newspaper had brought reality back with a jolt.

THREE MORE BODIES RECOVERED
AFTER WORST SCOTTISH RAIL
DISASTER

The article had gone on to say that, with the addition of the two men who had died on Saturday from their injuries, and the presumed death of the two senior railway men who had been swept away down the hillside, the death toll stood at eight.

'Excuse me…Mr Stewart. It is Cameron Stewart, isn't it?'

Cameron turned, staring in the direction of the voice.

Appearing from around the far corner of the station building was a vaguely familiar man, hurrying in his direction.

'I'm sorry. Allow me to introduce myself. My name's Bruce McTavish. We did meet once before, I believe. Wasn't it outside the post office in Dufftown?'

'Of course … Please, excuse me,' Cameron said, holding out his hand as he recognised the Company's Personnel Manager.

'Nice to see you again…even if it is under such difficult circumstances. It must have been very distressing for you. Anyway, if you have a minute would you follow me up to the office?'

Passing through a door marked "Private" in the main hall of the station, they climbed the stairs leading to the second floor and then turned left, before walking to the end of the hallway. As Mr McTavish knocked on the door – inscribed G.J. Mathieson Regional Manager – Cameron gazed out of the window overlooking the yard. He was trying his best to look calm, even though inside he began to feel like a naughty schoolboy standing outside the headmaster's office. After a brusque 'Come in' the two men entered the room and advanced towards the man sitting behind a large oak desk.

'Good morning, Mr Mathieson. This is Cameron Stewart… the man I was talking to you about.'

The man glanced up from his work, and then half rose to offer his hand.

He was a tenacious looking character, with thick-lashed eyes and veined cheeks, bordered by a neatly trimmed beard flecked with grey. His pendulous double chin spilled over his high white collar, while his meaty right hand was damp to the touch. The worsted woollen suit probably cost more than a month of his wages, thought Cameron. But his fashionable look was rather spoiled by the flakes of dandruff sprinkled over his shoulders.

After settling back into his chair, he signalled to Cameron and the Personnel Manager to take a seat in front of his desk. Then, putting down his pen, he leaned back into his leather-trimmed chair.

'I'm afraid we seem to have a bit of a staff problem after that unfortunate accident last week…and we were rather hoping you might be able to help us, Mr Stewart.'

Cameron wasn't too sure where this was leading. But surely, he thought, the railway didn't need his input when it came to hiring people?

'Mr McTavish,' said Mr. Mathieson, angling his head towards the Personnel Manager. 'Would you be so kind?'

'The track laying crew need a new foreman and we're thinking of promoting Rob Pirie into that position. You've worked with him. What do you think of the idea?'

Cameron felt like he'd just taken a blow to the body. In the back of his mind he'd had thoughts of that job for himself, and he'd been here six months longer than Rob.

'I'm sure he would be great for the job, and the men really respect him...especially after last week.'

'Good...good.'   .

Mr Mathieson now half-raised his hand, indicating that he would carry on.

'We lost another good man last week. He was not only the depot manager, but also controlled our entire inventory. Mr McTavish, here, has been doing a little checking into your schooling, and it appears you were very highly thought of by your former headmaster. From what he tells us, you did particularly well in mathematics and grammar...is that so?'

'Well, I suppose I did all right in those subjects if you...'

'Yes, yes...well anyway, we're offering you the job. Let me just say, though...I thought you might be a bit young to be taking on those duties... but Mr McTavish seems to have a lot of faith in you, so I've decided to give you a chance. If you go with him now, he'll brief you on your new position.'

An hour or so later Cameron walked out of the Personnel Manager's office. His heart was still pounding – in his wildest dreams he could never have imagined being offered that promotion. Along with the job came a substantial increase in pay and shorter hours. His day would now start at eight and finish at five, and on Saturdays, assuming there were no major problems, his working day would end at noon. In addition to running the Huntly depot, he would also be doing a lot of travelling – to attend company meetings in Aberdeen, and to arrange contracts with their various suppliers for sleepers, rails and ballast.

Cameron's mind was elsewhere as he wandered across the marshalling yard. All he could think about at the moment was the pleasure of being able to tell his grandmother about his good fortune, and the sadness he felt at not being able to share his news with Duncan or his father.

An almost party-like atmosphere greeted him as he opened the door and wandered into the depot.

'Where ye bin?' shouted one of the track crew.

'Have ye heard the news?' another yelled. 'Rob's the new foreman. Is that no greet?'

Just then Rob appeared from behind the men, strutting over to Cameron with a stern look on his face.

'What time ye calling this to be showin' up for work?'

The room suddenly went quiet. Then Rob, unable to contain himself, burst into laughter, while at the same time giving Cameron a playful punch on the arm.

''Tis fantastic Rob…I'm really happy for you. You really deserve the job. My only concern is whether or no you'll be able to get any work out of this bunch.'

'Och! No problem. If they dinna do as Ah tell 'em, Ah'll just cut off their food at meal time…Now, come on ye lot. At least try to make it look like ye is doin' as Ah asked, on ma first day.'

Cameron remained where he was, shifting uncomfortably from one foot to the other as his cheeks got redder and redder.

'Come on, Cameron. What's yer problem?'

'Well…actually…I'll no be comin' with you. I've got a new job.'

'Och, so they finally realised yer worth…an given ye a broom to sweep the station floor?'

Suddenly, Rob's chuckling stopped and his mouth hung open.

'Bloody hell! Yer no tellin' me ye be the new depot manager…are ye?'

Cameron quickly settled into his new role, and soon discovered that the job required much more travelling than he'd imagined.

Within three days he was back in Dufftown, where the manager at the sawmill was a little bemused to be dealing with his ex-employee. However, a few days later his amusement turned to chagrin – and a little admiration – when he discovered that Cameron had altered the basis of the railway's contract. And by changing the payment for sleepers from unit price, to paying by the board-foot, he had in fact negotiated a better rate for the railway than they'd previously had.

Two days after that success Cameron was in Aberdeen, attending his first monthly board meeting. At first, the other directors and managers tended to disregard the "young upstart". But it didn't take long for them to discover that what he lacked in experience he soon made up for with perception and invention.

A few months later, after a particularly long and tiring meeting, the board unanimously approved two of Cameron's "fresh new ideas". And from that day on, he was fully accepted as a manager – even Mr Mathieson now referring to him as Mr Stewart, as opposed to his previous title of "Young Cameron".

His social life was inexorably changing as well. Although Cameron still met up with his friends at the Kings Head, his relationship with them was no longer the same. They still traded jokes and bought each other drinks, but he could tell the men had become more guarded. Cameron had suspected that this might happen, and so, gradually, began to reduce the number of nights he spent at the inn. As a consequence, going home on Saturdays became much more the norm as he now needed Helen's company as much as she wanted his.

One gloomy autumn afternoon Cameron stared out his office window, unable to concentrate on his work. Low, grey clouds raced across the sky piling up against the brooding crags to the east, while dust and decaying bits of vegetation swirled about the marshalling yard, rising higher and higher as the breeze strengthened. Soon, the large window beside his desk began to rattle in its frame and, for the third time in the last fifteen minutes, he looked up at the clock on the wall. 'That's it. I've had enough,' he announced to his empty office, stacking his papers and tidying his desk, before throwing on his coat and leaving the depot.

Head down against the wind, he made his way across the yard towards Bogie street – the main road leading from the station to the centre of town. Inside the station the stopping train from Keith to Aberdeen had just arrived. Like some shiny, great caterpillar, it lay alongside the platform disgorging its passengers, while at its head the loco idled – exhaling steam at the legs of the unwary. Porters with loud voices touted their services, while trainmen busied themselves refilling the locomotive's water tanks and bunkers in preparation for its onward journey.

All of a sudden the front doors of the station crashed open. A porter's trolley over-loaded with bags and boxes appeared, crudely being shoved out of the arrivals hall by a uniformed member of staff.

Cameron's heart suddenly felt as though it was pounding its way out of his chest. His body froze as his eyes fixated on the heavenly vision before him. Struggling through the doorway behind the trolley was the most beautiful girl he had ever set eyes on. She was smartly dressed in a long, fawn-coloured skirt – with matching buttoned jacket – while on her head she wore a cream-coloured bonnet, accentuated by a chocolate-brown ribbon above its brim. In her left hand was a holdall-style bag, whilst in her right she dragged a large, metal-edged chest along the station forecourt.

Cameron's legs finally responded to his urgings, and as he hurried over to offer his help, he took in her shapely neck, flushed rosy cheeks and the long, dark-brown curl, which had sprung from beneath her pretty bonnet.

'Can I help you with some of those?' he asked, before awkwardly coming to a halt directly in front of her.

'Oh…be you a porter? Them inside all seem to be taken.'

'No, I'm no a porter…but…but I do work for the railway,' he added, quickly. 'And I would be…ah…very pleased to help you.'

For the first time in his life Cameron was nearly at a loss for words; and he was sure he now looked and sounded like a complete idiot.

'That's very kind of you, but I'm afraid I have to get to Scott's Hospital… and I've no idea how far that may be. Maybe you could point me in the direction of where I could hire a hansom cab?'

'Och, you don't want to be wastin' your money on that. The hospital's no far…an…an I'd be happy to help you with them bags.'

'Well, if you're gonny help me with them, we should at least know each other's names. My name's Mary…Mary Fraser.'

'Of course…sorry. I'm Cameron Stewart….Anyway, give us them here and we can get goin'…oh…and I do hope you're no too ill.'

At this point she began to giggle.

'As a matter of fact, I be very well, thank you. I suppose I should explain. I'm a nurse…and I've just arrived to take up a new post at the hospital.'

That night when Cameron got home, along with a sore shoulder from carrying the heavy trunk, his chest ached and his head felt as though it were in the clouds. He couldn't stop thinking about that enchanting dark curl, those honey-coloured eyes, rosy cheeks and slightly-flared, pert little nose. Although he had little experience with women, he was sure he had just met the girl of his dreams. Now he just had to work out how to charm her.

The next day was typical of late autumn. The wind picked up in the morning, whistling through the trees and dispersing what was left of the leaves. By early afternoon the rain fell in sheets, and the clouds could be seen colliding with the nearby hillsides as they raced across the sky. Huntly was a madhouse. Everywhere you looked people were scurrying about the town with their heads down, buried under large hats held in place by cold, wet hands.

However, in Huntly that morning there was at least one person whose spirit was not dampened by the drenching Mother Nature was unleashing.

Unusually for Cameron, especially as it had taken him an eternity to get to sleep the night before, he had woken early. Leaping out of bed, he quickly got ready for work – humming some tune that magically came into his head. Having spent a little more time than was normal grooming, he now stood in front of his wardrobe, sorely regretting his lack of attention to his clothing. 'My God,' he murmured, 'Is this really all I have? Maybe this be why I no seem to get a second glance from the lassies. Whatever happens, I really must purchase some new clothing next time I'm in Aberdeen.'

Ten minutes later, Mrs McGee – unaware of what had taken place the previous day – assumed that Cameron's uncommon morning cheeriness was just another sign of his increasing maturity. Since Duncan McPherson's death, he seemed to have been propelled into manhood, she thought, smiling at him as she placed a bowl of porridge on the table in front of him. Why, almost overnight, lines had appeared around his eyes, and his boyish grin had now been replaced by a more cynical smile.

A rap at the door, followed by Matron's agitated voice demanding her presence in thirty minutes, was Mary's none-too-gentle awakening. She had overslept on her first day. What a disaster! Throwing herself out of bed, she dashed to the bathroom at the end of the corridor, nearly bowling over a young, freckle-faced nurse hurrying in the opposite direction.

In fifteen minutes she had washed, dressed in her new uniform and was now bustling down the hallway – pinning on her hat as she went.

The rest of the day went by so quickly that it wasn't until she returned to her room after her duties that she began to think about the reason for her tardiness. She, too, had experienced problems getting to sleep last night. Maybe it was just the excitement of the new job, or was it something else....?

A few days later, when Mary discovered from the other girls that Cameron had been hailed as some kind of hero after the rail disaster, and was a highly regarded manager for the GNSR, her interest grew even more.

Days went by, and then nearly a week had passed without further contact.

Hospital rules disallowed her from going out during her first week. However, she had hoped Cameron might at least have tried to communicate with her. Sadly, he had not, and she was forced to conclude that he wasn't interested.

Cameron had been called to a meeting in Aberdeen, which after his arrival, had subsequently been delayed three times. Finally, having being away for nearly the whole week, he got home; and the following morning hurried to the hospital, where he hesitantly approached the reception desk.

'May I help you?' the dour-looking nurse sighed, sounding as if she'd just been interrupted in the middle of a major operation.

'Yes, may I speak to Miss Mary Fraser, please?'

'She canna just come doon to talk to any Tom, Dick, or Harry durin' the middle of her shift, you know!'

Cameron put on his best smile, before softly asking, 'Then, would it be possible to leave her a message…Please?'

'All right. I'll pass on your note…but dinna you go makin' a habit of this.'

'Oh, thank you so much,' Cameron replied, his hands

fumbling in his pockets for something to write on.

Seconds later, with a dispirited look on his face, he turned back to the nurse.

'You no by chance have a pen and piece of paper I could borrow…do you?'

'You young ones…You be all the same,' the nurse said gruffly, and then with a hand guarding her smile, waited for Cameron to finish his note.

They met in a tearoom on Gordon Street. It was Friday evening and Cameron had just finished work. Mary on the other hand was about to go on duty, so their date would be necessarily short.

Cameron had arrived thirty minutes early; and had then sat nervously, fidgeting with the cutlery on the table, as the two matronly-looking ladies who ran the teashop stood behind the counter, discreetly whispering to each other behind raised palms. When Mary walked through the door, Cameron quickly stood up – knocking over his chair with a loud crash, causing two other ladies sitting behind him to jump and squeal. After which, the whole room descended into silence. Momentarily, Mary hesitated – finally moving forward towards the scene of the disaster whilst giggling behind her hand.

'Well…that be some entrance! Just as well this be no clandestine meetin',' chuckled Mary.

'I'm sorry. I not normally be so clumsy.'

For the next thirty or so minutes the conversation went back and forth, each revealing certain details of their past, and then questioning each other about their present employment. Soon, though, Mary began to take over the conversation; which really was just as well, because Cameron was smitten. He no longer knew what to say. He just stared, as his thoughts swirled about and her words passed him by.

In what to him seemed like only minutes, the clock in the square struck nine.

51

'I have to be gettin' back now.'

'What…Sorry, what did you say?'

'I have to go now or I'll be late for work.'

Where did the evening go, he wondered, as he pushed back his chair – drawing a sharp intake of breath from the other diners – and then carefully walked around the table to escort Mary from the tearoom.

As they made their way back to the hospital, Cameron's brain was working flat out as he tried to maintain a conversation and walk in a straight line without stepping on her feet, while at the same time striving to figure out how to broach the subject of another date. When they finally reached the back door of the hospital, and before he could open his mouth, Mary calmly turned and faced him.

'On Sunday…I'm no on duty until early evening. So, if you be in town, maybe you would care to show me around? I still don't know what there is to see in Huntly.'

'Yes…yes of course. That…that would be fine,' stammered a very relieved Cameron. 'I'll be by at about eleven o'clock… if that be all right?'

On Sunday morning, a leisurely stroll through town was followed by a meal at the Gordon Arms Hotel.

Once more Cameron found himself staring at his beautiful dinner partner.

'Haloo…Cameron…hello.'

'Sorry.'

'I know I be an enchantress. But I no as yet cast ma wicked spell.'

Then, with a smile on her face, she reached across the table, gently placing her hand on his before looking into his piercing, blue eyes.

'I no have much experience at this either, Cameron…so why don't we just try to relax and let things come, natural like?'

Later, as they passed through the front doors of the hotel, Mary's arm wormed its way through the crook of Cameron's elbow. Wandering north from the main street they soon came to the ruins of Huntly Castle.

Built in the 13th Century, it was now in a sorry state. The outbuildings had been totally carried off, and although some of the carvings in the stonework over the castle's main entrance still left an impression of its once opulent history, all that now remained of the rest were soulless walls penetrated by empty windows – towered over by castellated turrets and massive stone chimneys.

Leaving the castle grounds, Cameron and Mary ambled along the well-used path towards the River Deveron, and then followed its course towards the west, talking and laughing as they set about each other's hearts. Again the hours and minutes galloped ahead and, before long, the light began to fade.

Once more, Cameron found himself standing outside the nurse's entrance – hands at his sides – unsure of what to say or do. Taking her hands in his, he moved closer and stared into her sparkling eyes. As she returned his gaze, her lips began to quiver. Slowly, Cameron leaned forward, gently placing his hand behind her head. At first she resisted. But it was only a token display of her modesty and her resolve soon evaporated, allowing his mouth to cover hers. His other arm now moved slowly down her back, and after what seemed like only seconds, she quickly pulled back, turning towards the entrance.

'Thank you for the wonderful day,' she uttered over her shoulder, as she hurried through the doorway.

As the weeks went by Cameron began to begrudge the days that he had to spend away from Huntly. With increasing frequency, meetings were being scheduled in Aberdeen or Keith to resolve the details of the extension of the main line to Inverness. Between his meetings, and Mary's duty rota, he began to wonder if there might be a conspiracy afoot.

Finally, a weekend arrived when they had time-off together. Cameron arrived at the nurse's residence on Saturday, at 12:15. In an effort to impress Mary, and because there were no coaches to Dufftown at this time of the day anyway, he had hired a hansom cab – which was just as well, as the weather was the all too familiar late autumnal joy of icy, grey rain driven by buffeting winds.

Cameron met her at the door; and then the two of them ran up the path laughing and jumping from slab to slab, failing miserably in their attempts to miss the puddles along the way.

The crack of the horseman's whip split the air as they set off down the rough and muddy road towards Dufftown. For over an hour the cab bounced and slewed its way towards his grandmother's, but neither seemed to notice the uncomfortable ride – pre-occupied as they were with falling in love.

Soon after their arrival at Helen's the weather cleared, allowing the three of them to walk to the cemetery to lay a small bunch of flowers at Anne and Morris's graves. On their way back along Church Street, Helen never stopped talking, giving Mary the history of each house they passed – along with a shortened biography of its inhabitants and their immediate families. At Cameron's insistence, a quick stop was made at Jones's general store, to purchase some Crowdie (white cheese rolled in oats) to have with their supper that evening; after which they carried on to Helen's, both women talking and laughing non-stop, at times it must be said, even to the exclusion of Cameron.

That evening, after a meal of Helen's special Scotch pies made with offal and onion, followed by Cameron's cheese, the two ladies carried on in much the same manner as before. Cameron almost welcomed the moment when it was time to say goodnight, even though his bed for the night was two blankets and a pillow on the floor in front of the fire.

The following day, morning worship was followed by a second sermon from Reverend Logan – directed at Cameron from outside the front door of the church – extolling the virtues of regular appearances at God's house, 'in order to insure the cleansing of one's soul'.

Then after lunch, while Helen rested from the exertions of their morning trip to church, and her subsequent labours in the kitchen, Cameron showed Mary around Dufftown – pointing out his old schoolhouse, and then taking her to the sight of the new Dufftown railway station, due to be completed in the very near future.

On arrival back at Helen's there was only time for a quick cup of tea before their transport arrived to return them to Huntly.

'I think Mary's a very bonny lassie,' Helen whispered, as Cameron bent over to give her a hug and a kiss goodbye. 'Whatever you do, make sure you no lose her.'

As the cab moved off down Cowie Avenue, two pairs of hands cheerily waved goodbye from the door's window. Rounding the corner into Fife Street, Cameron sat back, nervously placing his arm along the back of the seat. Meanwhile, Mary re-arranged the travelling rug over their legs before gently leaning back; and on feeling Cameron's arm behind her, eased towards him, resting her head on his shoulder.

Very little was spoken on their way home. It was almost as if both were too frightened to destroy the blissful place to which their hearts and minds had retreated. All too soon a loud 'whoa' signalled the end of the journey, and the cab drew to a halt alongside the path at the rear of the hospital.

'Thank you for a marvellous weekend,' Mary said, reluctantly raising her head from Cameron's shoulder.

Cameron said nothing as he wrapped his arms around her, pressing his lips to her waiting mouth. Feeling a spark jump between their lips, his desire rose. But moments later, Mary gently pushed him away.

'No, Cameron. You know I'm no like that. Besides…,' she whispered, pointing upwards towards where the cab driver patiently waited.

Over the next month, their meetings were restricted by their respective work schedules to two quick suppers at the tearoom on Gordon Street, and a few snatched drinks at the Kings Head. Cameron again spent Christmas with his grandmother, whilst Mary, being the new girl at the hospital was obligated to work double shifts over the Christmas period, after which she travelled to Keith to be with her family.

By the time New Year's Eve finally arrived, they had not seen each other for nearly two weeks. When Mary came down to the rear entrance of the hospital, Cameron was stunned. She looked so beautiful that for a moment it seemed to him that he must be in a dream; and when she extended her arm, he took it with almost indecent haste, worried that she might have a serious look at him and have a change of heart.

The music coming from the ballroom could be heard from halfway down Duke Street, and as the hotel came into sight it looked delightful – its front aspect being covered in seasonal decorations. Approaching the entrance Cameron hesitated, his thoughts momentarily returning to the first time that he had been due to join in the celebrations at this hotel with Duncan. His friend should have been here, he brooded. But then, almost as quickly as that sad reflection had crossed his mind, it disappeared; and a sardonic grin spread across his face. I do miss him, he mused, but what a sight his face would have been if he had only been here now, to see me arrive with Mary on my arm.

'Cameron, are you all right? I'd like to go in if we may… it's really quite chilly out here.'

'Sorry, Mary…Yes, come on then, let's go in.'

When the two of them strolled into the ballroom, Cameron could feel the eyes in the room swing onto Mary. Her glistening, dark-brown hair was braided and twisted up on top of her head, while her eyes teased with their lustrous sparkle. Over her shoulders, and loosely fastened at her throat by two slim ribbons, was a silver-coloured shawl, beautifully complementing her matching long-sleeved dress, which hung provocatively low at the front.

She was without doubt the most beautiful woman in the room; and Cameron knew there wasn't a man here who wouldn't have gladly traded places with him.

Later that night, the crowd stood mesmerised as they listened to the piper play in the New Year; and with the encouragement of the band, joined in singing *Auld Lang Syne.* Then, as one, the throng jumped and screamed when a loud bang followed by sparkling multi-coloured flashes in the sky, signalled the beginning of a new year.

Cameron's heart also jumped, and stars flashed in his eyes, when he and Mary kissed. He knew, with certainty, that she was the one and that no better time or place would ever present itself.

'Mary, would you do me the honour of bein' ma wife?' he murmured, as they pulled apart.

Mary stood motionless. For a moment, she thought he'd asked her to marry him, but…but she must have misheard, she thought. Although she was now nineteen, he was her first real suitor, and they'd only been going out for what, a few months? Well, certainly much less than a year. I mean, was this even decent, she wondered. People might suspect that she had to get married!

'Mary…did you no hear me?' Cameron asked, gently holding her by the upper arm. 'I love you. Will you marry me?'

'Oh yes…please. I mean…I will,' she sighed.

Cameron wrapped her in his arms again, sealing his proposal with a long and passionate kiss.

Both were oblivious to the cold, and the other people milling about, continuing to embrace long after everyone else had drifted back to the ballroom. Cameron caressed her neck and cheek with small circular movements of his fingers, while at the same time Mary closed her eyes and her arms fell loosely at her sides. His lips now replaced his fingers, lightly touching her cheek and the nape of her neck. Then his hand travelled down her bodice, cupping her firm left breast through the shimmering, soft gown. Moments later his other hand also began to wander, drifting slowly down her spine and past her waist. And as he pulled her hips towards him, Mary smiled, before gently pulling from his grasp.

'Any more than that I'm afraid is reserved for our wedding night, ma darlin'. Otherwise, you would no have anythin' to look forward to...now would you?'

Seven

The wedding was to take place in June at Mortlach Church.

On that first day of January, when the engagement had been announced, the couple had been persuaded by Cameron's grandmother that it was only decent to have a proper engagement, 'to ensure the tongues in the village had no cause to start waggin''. And of course, Reverend Logan was more than happy with these arrangements, as it allowed him plenty of time to prepare the couple for 'this most sacred moment'.

In the end, the months passed quite quickly. In fact, in some ways they passed much more quickly than Cameron would have wished, because now that the new contracts were being awarded for the extension of the line to Inverness, he never seemed to have any spare time at all. Typical, he thought. Just when he wanted to spend more time with Mary, the railway seemed to be scheming to work him harder, and send him away as much as possible.

It all came to a head one cold February evening, while he and Mary were sitting having supper in a little cafe on Bogie street.

'You know, Mary. I'm beginnin' to think I'm the only one workin' for this railway. I've got to go to Aberdeen again next week, and then on to Inverness Saturday for four days!'

'Don't go be botherin' yourself over it, Cameron,' Mary said, reaching across the table and resting her hand on top of his tense forearm. 'It's no matter.'

'Well, it matters to me. I feel like I'm just becomin' their lackey. I'm sure the rest of the management are just sittin' at home with their feet up in front of a warm fire.'

Due to the landslide, the branch line to Dufftown had been delayed by more than six months. But, with the completion of the viaduct bridge over the River Fiddich, the eleven-mile stretch from Keith to Dufftown was finished. Final inspection took place during the last week of April, with the official opening of the branch line scheduled to take place on May 25th.

Cameron spent a lot of time organising the event – at the special request of the regional manager – and he could barely contain his almost child-like excitement at being included in the celebrations. And with that in mind, on his last trip to Aberdeen, he'd even splashed out on a new grey suit and matching waistcoat.

It was hard to believe, he thought, that his life had changed so much in just a few short years. From a family of down-on-their-luck unemployed crofters, he had emerged and climbed to a position in society unattainable to most people. Yesterday, Mr Mathieson had called him into his office, and what transpired had left him wandering down the hallway feeling guilty about his previous misgivings. Mary had been right. They really did recognize the hard work he'd put in for the GNSR, or why else would he have been told to present himself at the dignitary's platform, 'at twelve sharp tomorrow'?

The skies were blue, the air was warm, and only a zephyr of wind rustled the leaves on the silver birch trees lining the road to the station. Two flowering cherry trees, planted near the entrance to the main hall, had recently burst into bloom, framing the doorway with their pink and white blooms. And to complete the picturesque scene, pink and scarlet rhododendron bushes, which had been placed alongside the front aspect of the main waiting room, were now a riot of colour and proving a visual delight to the people flocking towards the station.

Cameron's chest was bursting with pride as he strode arm-in-arm with Mary and Helen into the new station, before leading them along the platform towards the area reserved for the local townsfolk.

'A wee bit over-dressed for the occasion aren't we, Mr Stewart? After all, you're not exactly a director…well not yet, anyhow,' chuckled his boss, on intercepting Cameron halfway along the platform.

'Anyway, when you're done here…be a good fellow and see to it that our guests find their seats.'

'Of course, Mr Mathieson,' Cameron replied, his face burning with embarrassment.

Having escorted his ladies to an advantageous position at the front of the growing crowd, he made his way to the other end of the concourse – where a raised seating area had been erected for the invited dignitaries.

Suddenly, striding into sight like some kind of bad dream came Malcolm Campbell – the man who had "accidentally" shot his father, and no doubt here to represent the interests of the Duke of Richmond, thought Cameron. Beside him, on his left, swaggered a lad of about fourteen years of age, who Cameron assumed must be his son; while to his right strolled Mr John Gordon, the owner of the Mortlach Distillery.

Cameron's lips compressed into a thin ragged line and his face turned red with anger. For a moment he stood dead still, the knuckles white on his clenched fists at his side.

'Och…what have we here?' sneered Malcolm Campbell. 'I do believe I'm seein' the young pup of our last great poacher. I did hear he'd gone and got himself some fancy job with the railway.'

Turning to his son, he put his hand on the boy's shoulder.

'You'll need to keep a wary eye on him when yer older, Donald…'cause sooner or later these people all seem to forget whose runnin' this country.'

In Cameron's mind, time stood still. But then he, like everyone else on the platform, became distracted by the distant wail of the locomotive's low-pitched whistle signalling the imminent arrival of the special train. Using this as cover to disappear, he turned and stole away to the back of the raised dais.

The train came into view, slowly chugging its way across the viaduct bridge. Rob's crew had spent the previous day polishing the loco and carriages, and they were truly a sight to behold. The engine's shiny black frame and undercarriage contrasted beautifully to its dark green body – enhanced by the company's initials painted in gold on its sides. And its three carriages sparkled as the blazing sun reflected off their newly varnished surfaces.

Rounding off this impressive spectacle were two flags – each one mounted on opposite front corners of the loco – snapping loudly as they fluttered in the warm spring air. On the left flew the red, white and blue of the Union, whilst on the right the new GNSR company flag made its first proud appearance.

The train screeched to a halt; at which time most of the crowd's view of the proceedings became temporarily obstructed by the cloud of steam released as the brakes were locked on. But the air soon cleared, and an orderly procession of company directors and guests began alighting from the carriages. This was truly a momentous occasion, as most local people had never before witnessed such an event. And as the dignitaries made their way, with great aplomb and grace, towards the raised platform, applause broke out.

'Stewart…Stewart, where are you?' barked a voice from the crowd.

Cameron immediately recognized the regional manager's distinctive tone.

'Here, Sir…Just over here.'

'Well come over here! You're supposed to be handin' the champagne around. These people are important and they no have all day.'

With an aching sense of dismay Cameron's dreams came crashing down. His presence here wasn't a sign of appreciation. He'd been right all along. He hadn't climbed out of his place in society. He'd just been temporarily allowed to sit at the top of the lowest class. Everything now became clear to him. He was just a flunkey for the middle class who ran the railway and the upper class who owned it. The indignity he felt was palpable, and if it hadn't been for Mary and Helen he would have walked away.

Life was a cruel mistress, and Cameron learned another lesson that day. Nobody in this country would ever be allowed to rise above the position into which they were born. He had gone as far as he was going and must now acquiesce, or, like his father, and his father before him, be consumed fighting against the establishment.

As the days went by the change in Cameron's attitude was there for all to see. His previous enthusiasm for the railway waned and, whenever he and Mary got together, the GNSR was never mentioned.

But Cameron was no fool. He knew very well that he still had a good job. As such, he diligently did his work, but no longer did he go out of his way to solve the railway's problems, or offer to perform any extra duties. As a consequence, he now seemed to find more time for himself, and as an added bonus began to regain the trust and friendship of all his old workmates.

The day of the wedding finally arrived. Helen had excelled herself, and the church looked beautiful. Foxgloves and irises adorned the altar and windowsills, their sweet fragrance manifesting itself throughout the church; while small posies of pink thistles, attached to the aisle end of each pew, outlined Mary's route towards her nuptials.

Cameron stood in the nave facing Reverend Logan – the fingers of his hands nervously fanning the pages of his prayer book – while beside him on his right, casually erect and wearing a cheeky grin, stood Rob.

Suddenly, the muffled hubbub was shattered as the piper

struck up the first few notes of "Laura's Wedding March". The congregation rose as one. Mary and her father started down the aisle, with Mary's nursing friend, Annie, in attendance.

When Cameron turned and first laid eyes upon his bride, his breath caught in his throat. She seemed to drift down the aisle, her feet hidden within the ivory gown billowing out around her. A veil shrouded her head, giving her an almost eerie appearance, until she drew nearer and he discerned the silhouette of her face.

Later that day, Cameron assumed that he must have murmured the correct responses at the correct time; because all he could remember was the moment he rolled back her veil. Her honey-coloured eyes had sparkled, and two dark-brown curls hung down each side of her face, resting peacefully against her tear-moistened cheeks. And, at the culmination of the ceremony, when his lips had lightly touched hers, he would never forget thinking that his desires had now been completely fulfilled.

To the piper's melodic strain of "Mist Covered Mountains", the service ended.

Cameron and Mary strolled down the aisle arm-in-arm, and as they exited through the pair of studded, cathedral-style doors the bells began to peel.

Typical Scottish summer weather graced the wedding party that day. A spirited wind from the east buffeted them, while rain drummed down from low grey skies. As one wry wit was overheard to have said, 'At least with this weather, there's no guessing as to where the wedding's at'!

A minimum of formalities were endured outside the church, before Cameron and Mary jumped into a hansom cab – specially decorated with lewd articles by Rob and the "boys" from work – and waved cheerily, as they were spirited away.

Shortly thereafter, the wedding party and guests arrived at the village hall, where drinking and reels went on well into the night. It was a party that would be recalled with delight by all the guests, and judged by some by the severity of their aching heads the following morning. The newly married couple remained at the hall for a "respectable" amount of time. Then with great fanfare, and many knowing winks and nudges from the younger crowd, waved goodbye and left.

Cameron whisked Mary up the stairs to their room at the Highlander Inn. After fumbling with the key for what seemed an eternity, he finally opened the door and carried her in. The room was dimly lit with scented candles; and on the table beside the bed lay a small saucer of sweets and a flask of cool water. A warm glow radiated from the dying embers of a fire set earlier in the evening, making the room's temperature perfect.

Cameron and Mary fell into each others arms, kissing with wild abandon. The last six months' restraint was finally dispensed with, as Cameron released the final hook constraining the bodice of her gown and eased it from her shoulders. His head bowed to her bosom, his lips encircling a rigid nipple. Mary gasped, as his tongue sent impulses to a warming place deep inside, while at the same time her hips involuntarily moved forward to meet his growing manhood. When he suddenly pulled back from her breast, she almost screamed in protest. But the loss of sensation was only momentary, for now his hands moved slowly downwards, his fingers tracing the curve of her breasts before following the outline of her body to her waist.

As Cameron knelt to remove her lower garments, Mary's eyes opened. The glow from the candle illuminated his face, and for a moment she almost laughed at the lecherous grin it exposed. Hooking his two index fingers into the waist of her skirts, Cameron yanked, disposing of them all in one downward movement. Rising again, his clothes seemed to melt away.

Mary couldn't help but stare at his loins. Although she

was a nurse, and had seen plenty of male organs, none had ever been as ample or vibrant as the one he now revealed; and without warning her legs began to tremble.

Cameron slipped one arm behind her back, while the other reached down to lift from behind her knees and gently place her on the bed.

Mary's heart fluttered uncontrollably, and when his mouth travelled down her body she thought she might faint. Surely she must be in heaven, she thought, as his tongue painted tiny wet circles from her forehead to her feet. And, as she lay writhing in ecstasy, and their lovemaking reached its climax, her only wish was that the night would somehow never turn to day.

Later that week, as she and Annie made up beds in the women's ward, Mary's mind drifted back over the last few days. After that wondrous first night, Cameron, with the connivance of Matron, had surprised her with a few days away. They had travelled to a pretty little guesthouse by the sea near Banff and, when the owners had discovered that they had just been married, they had been treated like royalty. Breakfast had been delivered to their room – but not until late in the morning – and for lunch, a basket had been provided, so that they could picnic amongst the dunes. Daylight hours had been spent wandering hand-in-hand along the shore, jumping and splashing like children on a day-trip with their parents; and lunch had been taken amongst the dunes, stretched-out on a blanket well out of sight of prying eyes. In the evening, supper had been served to them in a small alcove overlooking the ocean, on a table decorated with flowers carefully arranged around a lighted candle.

'Mary…Haloo…Mary…are ye there?'

'Sorry, Annie, I be thinkin' 'bout somethin' else.'

'Ah could see that,' Annie replied, a cheeky grin arrayed

across her face. 'Are ye gonny give me all the lurid details?'

'Certainly no! What do you take me for?'

'Och, ye be no fun...An how is married life?'

'Wonderful...Well, nearly. Unfortunately, we be havin' to stay at Mrs McGee's for a few more days, until the house we've rented is free. She's very nice and all that...but we're havin' to be awfully quiet 'cause the walls are paper thin and...Och, you know,' Mary said, turning her head away to hide her crimson cheeks.

Annie placed a hand over her mouth to cover her laugh, but couldn't quite suppress a loud snigger as they moved on to the next bed.

Since the wedding, Cameron's life had taken on a new dimension. He was now finding it more and more difficult to set aside enough hours in the day to accomplish all of his tasks. Work was the same, and required no more or less of his time than previously. But women! He never realised how complicated they could be, and how much of his time would be spent trying to adapt to his wife's wishes. Mary was beautiful, clever and lustful. She was caring, and he was sure would turn out to be a good wife. But she just didn't think like him. Now he understood why the church referred to marriage as a "lifetime commitment". Oh well, he reflected, she'll change.

During the first week of July, they moved in to their new home. The cute two-up and two-down was on Chapel Street, only a short walk from the hospital. Within days, Mary set about making it her own, and had soon coaxed Cameron into constructing a window box – which she placed outside the parlour windows at the front of the house and filled with red begonias and sky blue irises. While on the following Saturday, Cameron was dragged along to the market, from where he staggered home carrying two large clay pots and a container filled with yellow, pink and white freesias. By the morning of the following day, the pots were placed like sentries outside the front door, welcoming visitors with their wondrous scent.

Of course, not everyone was enamoured with the Stewarts' horticultural endeavours. Their neighbour, Mrs McDuff, who lived at number fifteen, had already been overheard in the local shop complaining about their flowers, and suggesting that 'too many flowers at the front was not really in keepin' wi' the rest of the street'. But the chagrin that Mary felt on hearing these comments soon evaporated upon meeting Mr & Mrs Leith. They were a lovely old couple, who lived across the road at number fourteen. And on their first meeting with Mary, had said how 'nice it be to have a young couple livin' on the street', but at the same time had warned her to 'just ignore the old busy-body at number fifteen. She's a miserable old you-know-what, an nobody pays her any mind'.

Two weeks after moving in, Mary was in the kitchen preparing dinner when the front door closed with a bang.

The jingling of Cameron's keys landing in the bowl on the hall table was soon replaced by the sound of his footsteps as he headed towards the kitchen.

'That smells good!'

'I hope you like it. 'Tis ma mother's recipe for mutton stew, and I no made it before.'

'Ouch,' he cried, after dipping his finger into the simmering pot.

Mary grinned at his stupidity.

'Can ye no see the heat risin'?'

Removing his now scalded finger from the pot, Cameron waved it about in the air before sticking it in his mouth.

'By the way,' he said, sighing with some relief, while at the same time looking at the offending digit as if it had a will of its own, 'I've invited Rob for dinner tomorrow. I hope you no mind.'

'No, that be just fine. Maybe I should ask Annie to come?

Who knows? They may just take to each other.'

In August the weather was unusually warm and dry, and Cameron and Mary spent idyllic days walking and picnicking in the glens surrounding Huntly. One Sunday, they lazed for hours by the river bank, listening to the music of the water as it tumbled over the rocks; and while gazing at the river were almost hypnotized by the sight of salmon leaping and fighting their way upstream to start the cycle again. By mid-afternoon it had become so hot that they furtively stripped off their clothes, jumping into the water and swimming and cavorting until their ardour overtook them. Then quietly slipping from the water, had made frenzied love amid the long grass at the river's edge.

But summer was now definitely over, thought Mary, as she wandered down the second floor corridor at the hospital. A sudden bolt of lightning illuminated the dull-grey picture outside the window, and a few seconds later a rumble of thunder could be heard reverberating down the valley leading from Huntly towards the east. Once more, Mary's mind drifted away, and her thoughts returned to Cameron.

That morning he had left at 6:00 a.m. to catch the first train to Aberdeen, and would not be home for three days. That, and the depressing weather outside, was undoubtedly fuelling her feelings of despondency. Still, at least she was on duty with Annie, she reflected, which normally was enough to ensure a little light-heartedness and humour to help her through the day.

Unexpectedly, Matron appeared from the first doorway on the left. Although she was short and almost frail looking, there was no more formidable person in this establishment. Her piercing, hawk-like eyes never missed a speck of dirt, and her quick, cutting remarks left the strongest of characters babbling in her wake.

'Mary Stewart…would you please join me in my office.'

Mary hurried along the hallway, trying her best to keep up, while at the same time wondering where she had stepped out of line. The last time she had been summoned it had been for a 'breach of etiquette'. One of the staff doctors had got just a little too friendly and she had vociferously put him in his place. As it transpired, 'this one does not do', and she had left Matron's office duly reprimanded.

Ten minutes later, she drifted out of Matron's office dumbstruck, having just been promoted to Ward Sister. The increase in salary was more than welcome – especially as she and Cameron were desperately trying to save up enough money to buy their own house – and the new position meant she would now have some control over her work patterns. Mary grinned, as she thought about the look of pleasure that would appear on Cameron's face when she told him about her advancement. But unfortunately, that would have to wait.

Never mind, she thought, hurrying back down the hallway to give Annie the news. At least now she would be able to arrange her work roster to be at home whenever he came back from a trip.

Cameron sat at his desk almost hidden behind a mass of paperwork. Since the Company had decided to join up with the Highland Railway in the construction of the line from Keith to Inverness, he was under enormous pressure. He knew the GNSR directors were only trying to impress their new partners by getting him to re-negotiate all their supply contracts. But what he couldn't comprehend was why all the orders from head office had to land on his desk on Friday afternoons – thus necessitating his presence at the depot every Saturday for most of the day. In the past, Mary had never complained. But last Friday, her acceptance of their lives being totally controlled by the railway had come to an end.

She had gone out of her way to arrange her work schedule, to allow the two of them to go to Dufftown on Saturday to spend the night with Helen. But, when he came home on

Friday, and informed her that he couldn't go, Mary had gone off to bed in a huff; and in the morning had picked up her holdall and slammed the front door on her way out.

By the time Mary arrived home the following day, she had calmed down, but she had made her point. Cameron listened without interruption, as she told him about her visit: how Helen had tried her best to seem chirpy and as usual claimed to be fine, 'apart from the usual aches and pains associated with age'. But Mary had not been convinced.

That, and his guilt at not being able to go with Mary, had gnawed away at him all week. It was now Friday again and he didn't care what landed on his desk, because nothing was going to stop him from getting on the train tomorrow to visit his grandmother.

Eight

Cameron walked briskly along Balvenie Street, leading from the station towards the centre of town. His face was numb and his ears began to sting – exposed as they were to the raw northerly wind. But he was determined that nothing was going to ruin his mood, or the day he had planned for him and his grandmother. He had already made arrangements for them to be picked up at 12:00 and driven to the Highlander Inn for lunch, and had also got a message through to the baker on Church Street, ordering a freshly baked loaf to have with their meal that evening.

The moment he entered the house, he knew that something was terribly wrong. It was cold – deathly cold. Shutting the front door, he anxiously called out his grandmother's name – but silence was all that greeted him. With increasing unease he hurried towards the parlour, where, upon entering, his legs froze and his brain attempted to block out what lay before his eyes.

'Nan, Nan…Oh, God, no,' he exclaimed, his legs hesitantly carrying him forward to kneel by her side.

Helen sat rigid in her tired old chair. Her head was thrown back, her eyes vacant and unblinking. The skin on her face was devoid of colour. Her lips were pale and unmoving. Her right hand was curled into a fist at her chest, while her left arm hung lifelessly over the arm of the chair.

Cameron lifted Helen's arm, placing the hand into her lap, and then reached down to pick up the crumpled pieces of paper lying on the floor alongside her chair.

The doctor said her heart had given out, and there was nothing anyone could have done to prevent it. Cameron already knew her heart had given up – but also knew the reason why.

Helen had spent her life resolutely overcoming all the burdens sent her way. But Cameron's sister's letter had been the final blow. Those creased up sheets of paper that he'd found lying on the floor had broken Helen's heart. The news from Margaret about the loss of her unborn baby, and Peter's death in a drunken brawl outside a bar in Montreal, had been more than she could take.

Looking back, Cameron now realised that he should have paid more attention to how frail she'd become since Morris's funeral. Work, and the never-ending progress of time had conspired to deflect her from his attention. Mary had recognized the symptoms and tried to warn him, but he hadn't grasped the significance until it was too late.

Two days later, Cameron and Mary once more found themselves standing in the cemetery at Mortlach Church. No rays of sunlight penetrated the drab, grey skies on this occasion. And the bare trees and cheerless, frozen ground were in stark contrast to the colourful autumnal scene present the last time they were here.

Reverend Logan stood stiffly, the top of his dark woollen cassock now hidden under a large black cape. Beneath his black hat, strands of long greying hair whisked about in front of his eyes as, with his usual solemnity, he carried out his duty. On this occasion the finishing touch was added by the Reverend, with his moving homily to 'Our dear friend Helen'; and for the first time, even he seemed to be having some difficulty disguising his feelings.

Once again, Cameron found himself trying to swallow his emotions, while his grip around Mary's waist tightened with each passing minute. Helen had been like a mother to him. And as she was lowered into the ground beside her

73

'dear Andrew', Cameron prayed that there truly was a God. Not because he had suddenly become overwhelmed by the presence of the heavenly host, but because she deserved so much better.

At the end of the service, Reverend Logan looked up at the assembled gathering.

All heads were bowed and most shoulders trembled with emotion.

'Mr Stewart would like you all to know that he and Mary would be pleased to see you for a warmin' drink at the Fife Arms Hotel, in about thirty minutes.'

It would have been difficult that day for any passers-by to ascertain who was supporting whom. Cameron and Mary, both nearly overcome with grief, remained at the graveside with their arms around each other – until finally they turned and hugged, before helping each other away from the sombre surroundings.

'Thank you so much for your wonderful oration,' Cameron said, as he shook hands with Reverend Logan on his arrival at the wake. 'It was very kind of you and, as I'm sure you were aware, I was no in any fit state to do one maself.'

'It were an honour, Cameron. Your grandmother was a wonderful lady and a tireless member of our congregation.'

The Reverend's normally humourless face then brightened, a half-smile crossing his lips.

'My wife be just sayin' to me the other day that…well… now that you be the last remainin' member of the Stewart family in these parts, that maybe you and Mary might soon be makin' an announcement confirmin' the temporary nature of that state of affairs?'

Mary's face turned beet red. Cameron on the other hand barely reacted, his mind clearly somewhere else.

Over the Vicar's shoulder, he'd caught sight of a face that somehow seemed familiar. The man had glanced up, before

74

almost guiltily looking down at his drink again. Moments later it came to Cameron. It was at another funeral – his father's – where he'd seen that face. And the face was that of Dougal, his father's old friend.

For Cameron, time slowed to a crawl. Suddenly, what his grandmother had told him about his ancestors' hatred of the interlopers from the south, and her allegations that his father's death had been no accident, flashed through his mind.

Later that evening, Cameron and Mary sat near the small peat fire in the waiting room at the station. The flames danced in the grate, spurred on by the wind whistling through the draughty windows, as it tried to eradicate what little warmth there was. Cameron could feel Mary shake, as a shiver flowed through her body causing her to lean towards him and put an arm through the crook of his elbow.

Cameron's mind was once more in turmoil. He was certain that, like his grandmother, Mary would want him to bury the past. But he still needed to know the truth behind the death of his father. He wasn't sure if it had something to do with his coming of age, or was connected to his increasing frustration at the way some people just accepted the manner in which they were treated. But whichever it was, he felt bound to discover the truth. He needed to talk to Dougal. If the shooting had not been accidental, then all his good intentions of not becoming involved in old feuds or reprisals might need to be reassessed. Apart from this newly-found desire to see justice prevail, it had now become blatantly obvious that nothing in this country was ever going to change as long as the upper class were allowed to run roughshod over the masses. One thing was for certain, though. He would not rush into action and make the same careless mistakes as had some of his ancestors.

The following Saturday evening Cameron and Dougal met in the kitchen at Helen's house. Six bottles of ale and a bottle of whisky sat on the kitchen table, as Cameron had been a little unsure of how much it would take to embolden his guest's courage.

Dougal stepped through the back door like a walking advertisement for the church's charity clothes market. The frayed white collar of his shirt showed above his dark-blue jersey – the elbows of which were completely worn-through. Old brown woollen trousers were held up by a cord around his waist. And on his feet he wore muddy calf-high boots – with the sock on his right foot visible through a hole at the toe. His face was ruddy and weather-beaten, while on his upper lip rested an untidy moustache – not quite the match of his bushy mane of dark-brown hair and dishevelled eyebrows.

Dougal sat down, scrutinizing Cameron with his one dark-blue eye.

Cameron could tell his guest was uneasy. But, after the ales had been downed and they settled into the whisky, Dougal began to relax; and what followed next was a complete history of every person, past and present, who'd ever lived within twenty miles of Dufftown. Cameron soon began to appreciate that sitting opposite him was another of life's likeable rogues, and he couldn't help but chuckle at many of his improbable insights.

Eventually, Dougal's words began to slur, and Cameron knew that the moment of truth had arrived.

'Tell me…what really happened that day?'

'Ye sure ye want to know?'

After a confirming nod from Cameron, Dougal proceeded to tell the story of Morris's final day.

'It were misty in the mornin' when we set off…but, about an hour later, when we'd only half filled our gunny sack, it began to clear. Yer father decided we should leave…in case we be spotted. But, before we'd even cleared the heath the mist burned off …an 'tis then he were murdered.'

'What makes you think it was no accident?'

'Ah know it wisnae. Yer father were killed by a single bullet from a Snider-Enfield Mark II rifle…fired from a good 1000 yards away. Ah were in the Argyll an Sutherland Highlanders…until our sergeant accidentally ran onto ma knuckles…an Ah know what that rifle sounds like.'

'But the police and doctor said it were an accident?'

'Were nae accident. Listen. Ah were there an Ah know what Ah heard. It were no fowling piece that done away wi' yer father.'

'Why did you no tell the police?'

'Och…They're all in Campbell's pockets. All that wud have done is make sure Ah met wi' an early accident. Ah'm no sure I shud be tellin' ye this…but if ye want more proof come by old Hamish Munro's place… tomorra after dark.'

As Dougal moved his chair back to get up and leave, Cameron held up his hand.

'Hold just one moment, Dougal. I've somethin' for you.'

Dougal left Cowie Avenue that night a happy man. Not only because of the whisky he'd drunk, but also because in his pocket was a map drawn by Cameron, with an X marking the spot where he'd buried his father's traps.

A pounding in his head like the drums of a highland marching band forced Cameron to open his eyes. Slowly, he rolled out of bed and tiptoed to the kitchen. Six empty bottles of ale and one empty bottle of whisky stared back at him, and the lingering smell made his stomach turn.

It was only as he drank his third glass of water that the freezing cold floor got through to his brain – encouraging him to retreat to the bedroom and put on his clothes.

Later that morning, while he nursed his second cup of tea, his mind returned to the previous evening. Like most people in town, he had assumed his father's death had been an accident. The fact that Helen had been certain from the outset that it wasn't, he'd originally put down to a mother's natural desire to have someone to blame for the death of her child. But, if what George had told him was true, then she'd been right all along. Maybe he should stay another night, he mused. After all, Mary was working again that night, and he could still be home before she returned Sunday morning.

When Cameron stepped out the front door, the air was frosty but windless, and the street glistened with the first snowfall of the year. Closing the door behind him, he carefully made his way up the path towards the rickety front gate.

He was certainly not in the best of moods. Apart from his headache, and the discovery that his father's death had not been an accident, he was dismayed by the note he'd just found on the floor inside the front door. His grandmother had only been dead for just over a week, and already Mrs Murray was asking about the sale of Helen's house.

His boots crunched with each step on the fresh white covering, until drowned out by the cries and laughter of children fighting street-wars with their new-found ammunition. Turning the corner into Fife Street, he stepped out of the shadows. Like the reflection from a mirror, the sunshine temporarily blinded him, sending a spike of pain to the centre of his throbbing head. Slowing momentarily, he peered through squinting eyes, desperately seeking protection from the glare. Spotting what he needed, he crossed the street and continued in the shade on his way to the post office.

The legal requirements of life and death, like taxes, never relented. The proving of Helen's will had been carried out by the church, and her house, plus the old cabin on the hillside, had been left to Cameron. This document, along with the Certificate of Death, needed to be transferred to the Sheriff's court in Elgin, where they would be legally notarised. So, all he had left to do now was send them off.

That evening, Cameron crept up the dark alley between the baker's and Mr Jones's general store. On reaching the end, he tapped on the frail-looking door situated between the darkened windows of the abandoned harness maker's. The warped door squeaked as it began to open, but only did so far enough to allow the weathered face of Hamish Munro to peer out from the darkened interior.

'Quick…go back there,' Hamish whispered, moving aside the filthy blanket hanging behind the doorway, and pointing towards another door at the back of the dimly lit room.

It would have been nearly impossible to find a group of rougher looking characters, thought Cameron, as his eyes grew accustomed to the dull interior. Life had not been easy for any of the seven men, quietly sitting at the back of the room on makeshift seats made of rough-hewn planks, supported by empty, old crates.

'Who be this, Hamish?' grunted one of the men, hunched over and almost invisible in the darkest corner of the room.

'Aye, what're ye doin' mon…lettin' him in here?' murmured another.

'Dinna make a palaver, Ian…'tis Morris Stewart's lad… Cameron,' replied Dougal.

'Oh…aye…an what he be doin' here?'

Dougal then proceeded to recite the same story he'd given Cameron the night before. And when he'd finished, a nodding of heads all around confirmed it was a tale with which they were all too familiar, as many of their friends and relatives had come close to suffering the same fate.

'Aye, that be that bastard, Campbell,' Hamish pronounced. 'Ah remember him weel from ma days in the Dragoons. He were our company sniper… an it were indecent how much he liked that job.'

The following morning, light snow was falling; and the high-pitched grinding of metal-on-metal, accompanied by the jerky movements of the train, bore witness to the difficulty the loco was experiencing getting any traction on the slippery rails. Eventually, as the sand released by the driver onto the tracks began to take effect, the movement of the train became more regular and its speed increased.

The fingertips on Cameron's right hand slowly rubbed his forehead, while the backs of the fingers on his other hand made circular motions on the frosted window beside him – gradually widening the aperture through which he could monitor their progress.

The clandestine meeting the night before had certainly given him cause to re-evaluate his attitude towards the state of affairs in the Highlands. All those who had spoken had a grievance, to some degree or another; but none had suffered the outrage of having one of their own hunted and shot down like an animal. He was now convinced Malcolm Campbell had murdered his father, and had made up his mind he would not allow that act to go unanswered.

As time went by, Cameron's thoughts kept returning to the same seemingly insoluble problem – how he could make Campbell's death look like an accident? He had no guns, so a shooting accident was out of the question...and besides, that would look suspicious to say the least.

The shrill blast of the engine's whistle rebounding off the surrounding hillsides nudged Cameron from his felonious musings. And he would never know why his eyes were drawn to his little window on the world at exactly that moment. But as they were, a blurred shape, standing proud against the snowy background, passed before him. The indistinct shape was in fact the memorial cross, which had been erected by the railway in memory of his best friend Duncan and the seven other men. For a moment he closed his eyes, and his mind drifted back to that hellish day. And he recalled the noise and destruction and death. But no sooner had he recovered from those doleful memories than, like the sun bursting forth from behind clouds on a rainy day, the solution to his problem was illuminated; and his face lit up with a smile.

Nine

For weeks Cameron had been barely communicative, and even now he just sat in front of the hearth, eyes glazed, staring into the flickering flames. Finally, Mary had had enough.

'Are we no gonny talk again, Cameron? I know we've had a few bad months, but this is becomin' unbearable. Christmas and New Year are no far away, so can we please try and get our lives movin' ahead again? Maybe we could invite Annie and Rob over for Christmas? She and I both be off this year, and I expect Rob be as well.'

In his mind, Cameron knew his plan was nearly complete. Of course he had doubts. He wasn't born to be a killer – far from it. His mother had been a gentle person and, although his father broke the law, as far as Cameron was aware, he had never resorted to violence against other people. And as for Mary, well, she would be horrified if she discovered what he was contemplating.

Education had taught him the folly of not learning from the past. But, this was not about bye-gone days. This was about justice, and maybe even about sending a small message to the arrogant few who perpetuated such hardship against the masses.

'You're right, Mary. I'm sorry 'bout the way I've been behavin'…so tomorrow I'll drop in at the hotel on ma way back from work and find out about this year's Hogmanay party. Maybe Rob and Annie would like to go as well?'

Christmas and New Year had now come and gone. Cameron sat in his office, his mind mulling over the last few weeks. They did have quite a good time at Christmas, even though the early season snow had been replaced by a muddy hotchpotch, curtailing any ideas they might have entertained of enjoying any winter fun. The Hogmanay party had been good fun; although by the end of the evening, Cameron got the distinct impression that Rob and Annie's friendship would remain just that.

The sale of Helen's house was speeding ahead. It turned out that Mrs Murray's son was the interested party and was keen to move in as soon as possible. Of course, this now suited Cameron, as the sooner he divested himself of any interest in the Dufftown area, the sooner, he hoped, the Stewarts would begin to fade from the minds of the local inhabitants. And the seventy-five pounds and fifteen shillings that he would be receiving from the sale would certainly come in handy when he and Mary began their new life.

Cameron's attention returned to the present, as his office door suddenly flew open, accompanied by a burst of cold air entering the room.

'Excuse me, Mr Stewart. Sorry to bother ye.'

Standing in the open doorway, nervously clasping his hands, was the young office boy from the station's second floor.

'Do come in…and hurry up an close the door before I lose what little heat there is!'

'Sorry, Sir... Mr Mathieson wud like to see ye in his office… straight away.'

'All right, John…Oh, and I dinna mean to sound so harsh. I just have a lot on ma mind right now.'

Cameron stood up, donning his coat and following the young lad down the stairs; and while they crossed the yard a gust of freezing wind ruffled Cameron's hair and turned his ears pink, as in the distance the clouds once again began to pile up against the craggy hilltops.

This fits in rather nicely with my plans, thought Cameron, as he sat in the front carriage of the evening train to Aberdeen. Apparently, some major complication with the building of the new line to Inverness had arisen, and an emergency meeting had been called at head office. Mr Mathieson hadn't yet received any details, but had just said it was 'imperative' he get there as soon as possible.

The carriage swayed as the gusty wind – now accompanied by swirling snow – buffeted the train. Thank goodness he'd had time to go home, leave Mary a note, and get some warm clothes, he mused, because the world outside his window was now beginning to disappear as the blizzard took hold.

For the next 24 hours the wind found new purpose. It blew from the north, bringing with it arctic air laden with snow. Conifer branches sagged under the weight of their white covering, as rocks and shrubs became giant pillows scattered on a snowy bed.

In the city the snow was only a momentary nuisance. Aberdeen was on the coast – its temperature moderated by the sea – so, soon after the blizzard had ended, the snow on the streets melted away, to be replaced by muddied puddles scattered amongst a cocktail of filth.

The following day's meeting finished by noon; the dire emergency averted. As Cameron had suspected it was not a catastrophe, merely a staffing issue. The solution to the problem was simple. He now added "surveyor's assistant" to his ever- increasing portfolio; and although the directors did not immediately agree to his request for an increase in his salary, they did promise to consider it 'in due course'. 'Oh I'm sure,' he mumbled, as he strolled down the hallway at the conclusion of the meeting, sporting a cynical grin on his face.

By mid-afternoon Cameron had found himself wandering through the middle of Aberdeen, with plenty of time to spare. The main line to Huntly was blocked by snow, and according to the Company was unlikely to re-open before the following day.

Aberdeen's main street was bustling. Whips cracked as drivers fought to control their steeds, and the cries of street vendors filled the air. The mixed aroma of spices, roasting chestnuts and maturing manure confused the senses; while at the same time one's eyes were drawn to the gaily-coloured posters hung in most windows proclaiming the superiority of that store's merchandise. Men's outfitters displayed the latest gentlemen's apparel on manikins in their windows, whilst in their entrances stood liveried doormen, expediting access to the "right type" of client. But, as might be expected, Cameron's eyes were lured to the beautifully attired ladies, stepping gingerly from their carriages on to the wooden walkways, before briskly entering the brightly decorated milliners and dressmakers.

Nearing the far end of the street, noticeable changes began to take place. The premises which Cameron now passed became tired-looking and smaller. While at the same time, the fragrance inveigling its way into his nose became one of rotting fish and seaweed. However, colourful posters did still drape the windows, but this time displayed enormous ships beckoning passengers to the New World.

Thanks to the crews spending all night clearing the line, Cameron finally boarded a train for home the following morning.

'Poor Rob,' he mused, staring out the carriage windows at the pristine, snow-covered scenery. It would have been he and his crew that had spent the last thirty-six hours shovelling snow in these freezing temperatures. It was at times like this that he felt quite smug. If only the board of directors had listened. Twice in the last year, he had suggested purchasing one of the new American snow-blades. But, both times he'd been rebuffed; and he was now certain that had they not done so, they could have easily avoided this major shut-down, which no doubt cost the railway more than the price of one or two of the ploughs.

Reaching into the inside pocket of his overcoat, he extracted today's "Aberdeen Mail" – purchased from the lad on the station platform while he was hurrying to catch the train.

Cameron almost gasped, as the enormity of what appeared on the front page jolted him to his boots.

* * *

SEVEN MEN ARRESTED AT SECRET MEETING!

* * *

According to the article, Dougal, Hamish, Ian and four others had been rounded up by the police at Hamish's old workplace. Someone had tipped off the constabulary, and once they had marshalled sufficient extra constables, they had surrounded the place and struck. The story went on to say that, according to an unnamed official in the Procurator's office, all the men could expect lengthy jail terms, especially as the English Government did not take kindly to any acts of subversion.

'My God,' Cameron murmured to himself. 'That could have been me. In fact, it would have been me if I hadn't rushed off to Aberdeen.'

The following day the snow began to thaw in earnest, and by the weekend, rain had washed away all signs of winter. Cameron was more than happy with this turn of events, as it now allowed him to pursue his new part-time job as assistant to Mr William Reid, the company surveyor, a position he had talked the directors into giving to him.

The surveying of the new line to Inverness had advanced to near Brodie Castle – halfway between Forres and Nairn – before Mr Reid and his assistant had had a falling out. So it was to Forres that Cameron proceeded on Monday morning to take up his new post.

As he arrived in the town, he was amazed by the amount of activity taking place in what had previously been just a small village in the county of Moray. The new station was almost finished, while at the same time a new mill for textiles was well on its way to being completed. The town's first ever hotel was at the planning stage, and the Parish Church was in the process of being rebuilt – for the second time.

Cameron could now truly see what effect the coming of a railway had to a town's growth and prosperity; and he began to realise how fortunes were made in property and industry by those with the wherewithal to make the investment. Of course, what he didn't as yet appreciate was that the wherewithal was useless without timely inside knowledge of the impending route of the railway.

All too soon, he became aware that the job of surveying was not quite as simple as just sticking some stakes in the ground in as straight a line as possible. Generally speaking, there was no road or path to follow, so a lot of time was spent hacking their way through forests and dense underbrush.

Each night as he went to bed, it was William Reid's monotonous litany that finally lulled him off to sleep: 'Gradient and Radius…Gradient and Radius. If you don't get this right, you'll either have a nasty accident or a permanently unprofitable route. Speed is of the essence. But speed with safety is critical'.

At the end of his first week, Cameron arrived home scratched in places he didn't want to think about, and exhausted from scrambling up and down hills, wading through streams, and clambering over fallen trees.

The line crawled forward.

Apart from deep snow, the only hold-ups occurred in the springtime, when, as he was sadly aware, water-logged ground could create mudslides. Occasionally, their weekly progress was notable. But more often than not, a mile or two was the norm. The track had to be laid around hills – when the gradient would be too steep to climb over – and rivers and streams had to be spanned. Specialist bridging crews were left behind to complete the water crossings, while the men laying track were just moved to the other bank to continue on from there. Teams of horses strained – with heavily re-enforced harnesses attached to deep iron ploughs – to carve out track beds from the hillsides. But even they were no match for the almost impregnable veins of granite, which nature had seen fit to use as a foundation for some of the higher slopes. This was the time of greatest danger, because this was the time when the blasters were summoned.

'In the old days, we used black powder,' the chief surveyor said to Cameron one day as the blasting team's wagon neared. 'But a few years back, some Swedish guy called Alfred Nobel came up with this new stuff, he called *Nobel's Blasting Powder* …which they now call dynamite.'

Just then, the blaster's wagon drew to a halt alongside the two surveyors.

'How goes it, Fergus? Here…chuck us one of them wee sticks, will ye?'

'What the hell…!' exclaimed Cameron, turning to run as the man in the wagon reached into a wooden crate behind him, picked up one of the eight inch long sticks, and literally threw it to Mr Reid.

Fergus grinned, and then climbed down from the wagon and turned towards Cameron.

'Tis nae a problem, Mr Stewart. That be one of the great things about them sticks. They is pretty well harmless…till ye light the fuse. An then 'tis only a matter of makin' sure ye have a long enough fuse.'

'I can no believe you can just haul them things around in a wooden box, bouncin' around in the back of the wagon like that.'

'Och, aye. Mind ye 'tis sure different to bygone days. Only problem now is some people think the whole process is safe…an can be done by just anyone.'

'Well, if you no mind…for the next few days I'd like to watch how an expert like yourself uses these things. I think it might be good for me to learn somethin' about 'em… especially as I'm havin' to store 'em at the depot in Huntly.'

Over the last two years, Mary and Annie had become the closest of friends, and would quite often get together when Cameron was away. Annie was one of life's characters. Her permanently curly auburn hair, set on top of her round freckled face, gave her a whimsical appearance. But her pale-blue eyes, set far apart, and her large, firm breasts, added something exotic to her appeal. In the evenings, when the two of them got together, they talked about almost everything. Annie was quite capable of revealing all the "nasty details" of her love life, but became quite frustrated when Mary drew the line on what she considered to be her private life – she being all too aware that her friend sometimes blurted out certain intimate details to others when she'd had a few too many drinks.

'So, when are we gonny hear the patter of wee feet in the Stewart household?' Annie asked one evening, as the two of them sat in Mary's front room.

'Cameron thinks it best we be waitin' until we move into our own house.'

'Och, that sounds daft to me. What difference does it make? Ye've plenty of space here.'

Mary's mind drifted back to the conversation she'd had with Cameron when he was home the previous weekend. She'd said almost the same thing to him when feeling frustrated at his having, once again, cut short their lovemaking.

'What's the matter, Cameron?' she had said. 'Why are you worried…are we no married now?'

'Aye, I know,' he'd replied. 'But if you are with child you're no goin' to be able to work.'

'Aye, but do you no want a family?'

88

'Of course I do…but…I was just thinkin' that maybe it be better if you worked a wee while longer…so…so we can put a bit more away for our future.'

'But…but how long is a wee while longer?…Och, never mind,' she had said petulantly, before giving him a quick peck on the cheek and turning over.

That night, her thoughts wouldn't allow her to easily drift off to sleep. She just didn't understand him any more. Not long before, he'd done nothing but complain about the Company. But now, even though he was away more than ever, he never protested. Until Helen's death, Cameron had still had moments when his boyish inexperience or lack of commitment had been exhibited. But, since her passing he appeared to have matured, almost overnight, and now seemed driven to advance in his new field as quickly as possible.

The sale of Helen's house went through during the first week of February. Surely now, we can get on with finding our own place, Mary reflected, as she hurried along Bogie Street chased by a biting northerly wind. Cameron was due home at any time, so she had stopped at McCarthy's store on her way home to pick up a few things to make him a special supper.

'Oh greet, just what I needed,' she mumbled, when five minutes from the house the rain started to fall in torrents. Arriving at their front porch, soaked through and covered in splashes from her ankles to her knees, she put her key in the lock and kicked open the door.

Her heart skipped a beat, while at the same time she screamed and dropped her provisions on the floor, as a figure shot out from behind the door.

'I hate you! You done scared the life out of me,' Mary yelled, her fists pummelling Cameron's chest.

Bursting into tears, she then buried her face in his shoulder as she sobbed and gasped for breath.

Cameron wrapped his arms around her, and for a moment

they just stood in the hallway saying nothing as Mary quivered and dripped onto the floor. Then, placing a hand on each side of her head, he gently drew her away.

'Oh, come on. I'm sorry. I no mean to scare you.'

''Tis no so much that you scared me. I were just wantin' everythin' to be perfect when you got home. Now look at me. My hair's hangin' down like some wet puppy and I'm so cold ma teeth are chatterin'. I was going to cook you a surprise supper… and even bought you the last newspaper in the shop to read while I'm preparin' your meal.'

'What you be doin'?' Mary exclaimed, as he suddenly lifted her up and threw her over his shoulder.

'I'm takin' you upstairs to warm you up. After that you can have a wash, dry your hair and make my surprise meal. Then, when we've eaten, you're goin' to come and sit on ma lap in front of the fire…'cause I have somethin' to tell you.'

Ten

Over the next few days, Mary wandered the wards in a trance, her mind totally preoccupied with absorbing what Cameron had told her. Australia! She couldn't decide whether he was out of his mind, or it was just some kind of cruel joke. But then it couldn't be. He had shown her the tickets for a ship called the "Lady Elgin", leaving from Campbeltown on April 21st; and for the rest of the evening she had sat there, stunned, as he explained the reason behind his decision.

Cameron was convinced there was no future for him or his family in Scotland. He accepted that his present job was better than most, but was certain that once the line to Inverness was complete more than half of the employees would no longer be required. And no amount of persuasion by her could convince him otherwise.

When Mary told Annie, to say she was shocked was an understatement. Her mouth hung open, gulping like a fish out of water. And before long, moisture gathered in the corners of her eyes.

'Och, that's wonderful, ye be so lucky,' she'd said, flinging her arms around Mary and holding her tight.

Mary knew it was devastating news for her best friend, but there was little she could do to soften the blow.

'I know it be upsettin' for you, Annie…and in many ways 'tis for me too.'

'But I no understand why he wants to leave? I thought Cameron was happier now than ever before.'

'He is…but there's more to it than that. He just thinks there will be a better future for us in Australia. I guess I never really appreciated what he felt after Helen passed…I mean… now he's no got any family in this country.'

'But he has ye.'

'Aye…that he does…and now he needs ma support more than ever. Hopefully, one day Cameron and I will have our own bairns…and then we'll become their roots, and the foundation from which they can grow. If that must be in Australia…then so be it.'

Annie's eyes were downcast, as she reached into the pocket of her uniform for her handkerchief.

'Never you mind, Annie. Maybe you can save up and come out later. I'm sure they will always have need of nurses.'

But in her heart, Mary knew it would probably never happen.

With just over six weeks to go, Cameron decided it was time to let the Company know that he was leaving. He didn't really care what the GNSR thought, but he did want to put Rob's name forward as his replacement. Initially, Mr Mathieson did have some misgivings because of Rob's lack of formal education, but, with Cameron's strong recommendation on the table he relented, agreeing to a trial period.

A replacement foreman was quickly appointed, followed by Rob being released into Cameron's capable hands. As expected, his friend did have some initial difficulties wrestling with the maths involved in inventory control. But, with perseverance, and the odd evening spent at Cameron's with pen and paper, Rob overcame his lack of formal education.

Phase two of the training was then put into effect. It was essential that Rob quickly develop the ability to handle suppliers, and arrange contracts. In the Company's eyes this skill was more important than controlling inventory, because mistakes made in this part of his job could have enormous effects on the profitability of the whole railway.

Rob joined Cameron on trips throughout the Northeast,

meeting the individuals with whom he would be dealing. As it turned out, Rob's buoyant personality more than made up for his lack of experience. And strangely enough, it was this obvious lack of experience that disarmed their suppliers, allowing Rob to stamp his own kind of control over their negotiations.

It was during one of these journeys that Cameron bought three steamer trunks, dragging them home to Mary one Friday night. And it was these same three trunks that led to their first major argument.

'Here we be then, Mary. We each have one of these for our hold baggage, and then there be one large trunk for the both of us to use during the journey. '

'Surely you jest?'

'No...Why...Be there a problem?'

'Aye, there sure is. I'll no be able to fit all I'll be takin' in those trunks.'

'Well, that be all we can take... so it will have to do,' he said, rather impatiently.

'I'll be tellin' you right now...I have no intention of leavin' half of ma clothes and other things behind...so you'd better be thinkin' ag'in.'

With that Mary stomped off to the kitchen and slammed the door.

For a moment, Cameron stood in the hallway, hands on hips staring at the closed kitchen door. Och, she'll come around, he thought, walking into the front room and dropping into his chair.

An hour later he had cooled down, but there was still no sign of Mary. So, throwing yesterday's paper on the floor he got up and headed for the kitchen.

'Och, come on then, Mary. It's no ma fault we be restricted to them three pieces.'

Mary swung away from the sink, her eyes dark and foreboding, her manner still incensed.

'Are you tellin' me that with the size of those ships there

be no room for extra baggage? What about all the mail and cargo they carry? 'Tis bad enough you expect me to follow you to the other side of the world…and probably never see ma family or friends again…but, now you be tellin' me I have to leave behind all the things I been collectin' since I was a wee girl?'

'All right…I'll look into it a bit further when I get back to work on Monday.'

'Well, you'd better,' Mary said, turning her head away as tears began to appear in the corners of her eyes.

Monday morning, after leaving the regional manager's office, Cameron's face broke into a wide grin. Due to heavier than normal snowfalls that winter the hills had become very unstable, and over the weekend a mudslide had swept away a large section of newly-laid track. Thankfully, no one had been working in the area at the time; and the company now accepted that it was too dangerous for men to be in the hills, so surveying and track laying was suspended until further notice.

There was a spring in Cameron's step as he strolled home that day. He no longer had to be away all week surveying, and with any luck would probably see out what time he had left with Rob at the depot in Huntly. With his mood ebullient, he stopped at McCarthy's shop to pick up a bag of Mary's favourite candied fruits.

'Mary, 'tis me.'

He could tell from the aroma that Mary was making supper, so, sheepishly, stuck his head around the kitchen door.

'Mary…I'm sorry about the other day. It's just that… well…I were told that we be restricted to three pieces of baggage and I didn't really give it much thought after that.'

'No you didn't, did you?'

'Well, I talked to the shipping agent today, and there be

no bother bringin' extra luggage…We just need to pay a wee bit extra. So, I'll be buyin' us two more chests.'

Delving into his pocket, Cameron then extracted the small paper bag containing his peace offering.

'Truce?'

That night, for the first time since Cameron's shock announcement, their relationship once more became peaceful and tender. And to Mary's surprise – and exquisite pleasure – Cameron did not interrupt their lovemaking.

Satiated, Mary fell asleep, one hand loosely covering her flushed right breast, while the other lay limp at her side. The fringe of her love-moistened hair stuck to her brow, while the rest lay unrestrained in long strands across the pillow. Leaning on his elbow, with his head propped up by his hand, Cameron gazed at the sight of her naked body, revealed to him in the glow of the burning candle at their bedside. She was strong and capable, and yet looked so vulnerable laying there beside him. She trusted him implicitly and, not for the first time, his stomach twisted into a knot as the guilt of his deception swept over him.

Cameron crouched behind a large Rhododendron bush on the hillside, with moisture trickling down his spine. It didn't seem to matter that he was wearing a wide-brimmed hat, with his collar pulled up as far as it would go. The rain always managed to find a way through – adding its measure of misery to his already freezing hands and feet.

In the beginning, he had been in a dilemma, as he struggled to find an unobtrusive way of observing the comings and goings of Malcolm Campbell. But, eventually he worked out that on Sundays the man always went to the evening service at Mortlach Church, and subsequently, could easily be monitored on his way home from good cover on the hillside adjacent to the Balvenie road – two miles north of Dufftown. From then on Cameron's only other problem was finding an excuse to get away from Mary – unless, like tonight, she was on duty.

The snap of a cracking whip and the thundering of hooves disturbed the evening's tranquillity. From Cameron's left an almost apparition-like coach and horses came galloping through the misty darkness along the empty road. The phaeton sped to a point directly abreast of where he remained concealed, its passing marked by the disappearance of the dim carriage lights. Once again, Cameron began to count, and when he reached forty-five the noise stopped, as the rig rounded the curve in the road cut from the steep hillside. From here it was at least four miles to the estate house, so there would be plenty of time for him to get away before anyone noticed that Malcolm Campbell was late.

As far as he was aware, no one had seen him sneak back into town that night – nor for that matter on any other of the Sunday nights he'd been skulking around Dufftown. He had picked his route to and from the station carefully, ensuring he was always on the darkest side of any streets, well away from the loom of any gas lamps. And his return to the railway yard was always made from the opposite side of the tracks to the station, having first waited in the long grass on the embankment to ensure the trainman had completed his final check.

A piercing blast from the guard's whistle, followed by the cascading clanging of the couplers taking up the strain, signalled their departure to Huntly.

Cameron sat hemmed in by barrels of whisky on the floor of the last freight car, idly gazing through the crack in the open door beside him. Two weeks to go, he mused, and then it would all be over. Or would it? Once more, doubts began to cloud his mind. 'Am I just starting another cycle of revenge?' he muttered, under his breath. Don't be stupid, he thought, of course I'm not. Bloody Campbell murdered my father, and will never stand trial! On top of that there are seven more men in jail, just because they wanted a little better life for themselves and their families. No, this is not just revenge. Nothing will ever change in this country until enough people make the point that they've had enough!

Eleven

April 17th, 1874, started out like so many other Scottish spring days, with blue skies in the early morning, which by lunchtime were overwhelmed by cloud, wind and rain.

'Are you ready yet?'

'Almost...I'll be down shortly.'

Five minutes later Mary appeared on the landing gripping a small holdall.

'Sorry, Cameron. I had to pack a few things for tonight, and everythin' I needed were at the bottom of one of ma trunks.'

'All right...but hurry up or we be missin' the train. God forbid we be late for dinner at you Mother's.'

Later that day Cameron rode in another train, but this time not as a passenger in one of its coaches. The light was fading fast as the eight-car goods train slowed for its arrival into Dufftown. From experience, Cameron knew that only the first two cars contained goods to be off-loaded. The rest, including the one he was riding in, would remain untouched until later that evening.

So far, today had gone like clockwork. After dinner at Mary's parents' house in Keith, he had said his goodbyes and headed for the station. As far as Mary and her family were concerned, he was heading back to Huntly for a meeting with Mr Mathieson, followed by a boisterous evening with Rob and a few of his other friends at the Kings Head. Mary, meanwhile, stayed on in Keith to bid farewell to her friends and relatives and then spend the night with her mother and father.

A shiver ran through Cameron's body, and his hands shook as he reached up to lift the collar of his coat. Thankfully it wasn't raining, although water from the saturated floor of the woodland still seeped into his boots. While at the same time, the musty smell of the damp, decaying vegetation pervaded his senses, injecting its own measure of grimness to the already chilling atmosphere.

Where the hell are they? I'm sure they should have been here by now, he thought, as he crouched behind the bush. A sickly feeling began to claw its way upwards from the pit of his stomach, as his mind began to grapple with the consequences of failure.

Suddenly, his ears singled out the muffled drumming of hooves, and adrenaline surged through his body. Cameron reached into his jacket pocket and retrieved the small tin box containing his matches. Without taking his eyes off the road, his hand rummaged about near his feet – finding and then picking up the safety fuse. The wait seemed interminable; but then the horse and carriage passed by and he lit the fuse and ran.

'Och…Cameron…'tis about time ye showed up! We bin beginnin' to think ye had already left the country,' Rob shouted, when Cameron casually strolled through the door into the Kings Head.

'You all must know what it be like when you're dealin' with the in-laws. I been thinkin' I would never get away… and I ended up havin' to take the later train. Still, I be here now …and best of all… there be no one at home to give me an earful if I come home late…or drunk.'

Two hours later the door of the inn banged open, as a wet, dishevelled and out of breath regular stumbled into the room.

'Och…did ye hear the news! There be a landslide on the Balvenie road north of Dufftown. Apparently, it happened just as Malcolm Campbell's son were headin' home from the church. From what Ah been hearin', the coach and horses got swept down the hill into the Spey…an both Donald Campbell an the rig's driver are missin'.'

Cameron was stunned. Initially, the room went quiet as the news sank in. But, before long, the previous noise and commotion returned – the general feeling seeming to be that they were sorry for the boy, but it was nothing to do with them. However, in Cameron's mind the questions and concerns were not so easily dispelled. Why wasn't Malcolm Campbell in the carriage? What the hell was his son doing in it? If the rumours were correct then it had all gone horribly wrong.

'Come on, Cameron…have another. We no gonny make ye pay for all the drinks, ye know,' chuckled Rob.

Cameron forced a sheepish grin across his face, but deep down inside he felt bile beginning to rise in his throat. The situation he'd put himself into was now much more serious than he'd contemplated. Malcolm Campbell would leave no stone unturned as he tried to discover what happened to his son. More than ever, the rest of his plan must work flawlessly, as now it was the only thing keeping him from the hangman's noose.

An intense ray of sunshine found its way through the crack in the curtains, warming the right side of Cameron's face. At the same time, the savoury aroma of frying bacon found its way up the stairs and into his nostrils. As his eyes slowly opened, they scanned the wall at the foot of the bed, eventually focusing on Mary's favourite painting of the Cairngorms at Aviemore. From that moment on, he knew this wasn't a dream, as he prepared himself for the pain which he knew must surely come.

Having crept gently down the stairs, Cameron snuck up behind Mary, slipping his hands around her waist before kissing her on the back of the neck.

'Cameron…no, or I might be burnin' maself!'

Gazing over her shoulder, his juices began to flow at the sight of the two thick rashers of bacon sharing a sizzling pan of fat with an egg and a huge chunk of bread.

'Mary, you be too good to me. But, can we afford all this?'

'Well…I bought you the egg as a treat for being so nice to ma parents, and the bacon was a leavin' present from Mr McCarthy at the shop.'

'Greet…Anyway, how come you be home so early? I thought you be catchin' the late morning train?'

'I did,' Mary said, with a grin on her face.

'I suppose you been hearin' 'bout the landslide over near Dufftown yesterday? The news is all over the village. Kind of sad for Malcolm Campbell. Mind you…it would have been him if he'd no been home in bed with some illness or other.'

'Aye…well it wouldn't exactly have broken my heart if it had been him.'

'Shush, Cameron. You should no say things like that… Mr Leith said they were startin' to clear the road today… but most people think it will be some time before they get it open.'

For Cameron, the next two days couldn't pass quickly enough. He was terrified of being found out, but at the same time knew how important it was for him to look and act as normal as possible. Each day more news filtered through from the site of the disaster. As expected, the authorities' immediate concern was to clear the road and recover the bodies. But, so much of the hillside had come down that a dam had been created, extending halfway across the River Spey. Owing to this, nearly a hundred extra men had been drafted in from all over the area to try and remove the impediment to the river's normal flow.

The longest three days of Cameron's life finally ended. Just after sunrise on the 20th of April, he and Mary loaded their worldly possessions in a horse-drawn cart for the short trip to the station. Although they hadn't lived on Chapel Street for all that long, a crowd of well wishers turned out to see them off – with some men even crowding forward to shake Cameron's hand. Once the crowd finally dispersed, Mr Leith stepped forward.

'Do ye know why so many people turned out today, Cameron? Sure, they be wantin' to say goodbye…but 'tis also 'cause of what ye two are doin'. Nearly everyone here wishes they had the bottle, or the years left, to take advantage of the opportunity to start a new life. So, make the most of it, Cameron…because not only are ye takin' our best wishes, but ye are also takin' our dreams as well.'

The Stewarts did not look back, nor did they speak as they were slowly driven away towards the station; and as Mary's two small hands anxiously balled into fists in her lap, Cameron's strong right hand reached over and gently encompassed them.

Upon reaching the station, the two slowly followed the porter and their baggage. As they strolled out onto platform one, Mary's stalwart appearance finally cracked – for standing on the platform, with tears streaming down her face, was Annie.

The two rushed forward, wrapping their arms around each other and openly weeping – both seemingly oblivious to the furtive looks of the other people around them, who quickly turned away.

Cameron and Rob stood awkwardly to one side. But then, as the departure time drew near, Rob solemnly turned to Cameron to shake his hand.

'Thanks for everythin', Cameron. I'll ne'er forget what ye did for me. Let me know when ye be runnin' yer own railroad out there…an maybe Ah will come out an give ye a hand.'

The guard's whistle blew, followed by his loud beckoning

announcement; after which, Cameron took Mary's arm and encouraged her towards the waiting train.

Soon, they had settled themselves into facing seats alongside a window on the platform side of the carriage. As Mary waved goodbye with one hand, the other, containing a small white handkerchief, dabbed at the corners of her eyes. And as the train began to move, she mouthed the words *I'll write to you* through the glass.

Annie, now supported around the waist by one of Rob's arms, looked inconsolable, as her shoulders shuddered and tears cascaded down her face.

On Tuesday the 21st April, Detective Inspector Jamieson sat behind the desk he'd commandeered in the police station in Dufftown. He'd arrived two days before, having been sent from Edinburgh to run the inquiry into the two deaths.

Although he had just passed his first half-century, most people assumed the Inspector was much younger. He was of medium height and very fit – not surprising really, as he believed in a daily exercise routine, which included a three mile run each morning; and he was endowed with a full head of dark-brown hair, whose slight greying where it met his temple was the only hint of his actual age.

The Inspector's right thumb and index finger slowly twisted the end of his handlebar moustache, while his other hand turned the pages of the file on his desk. Within twenty-four hours of his arrival, he had already decided that the theory of this being an accident was highly unlikely.

'Very questionable,' he murmured, before his concentration was broken by a knock on the door.

'Och…come in.'

A nervous looking Constable Stevenson stood in the open doorway, holding a small cloth sack in his right hand.

'Begin' yer pardon, Sir. Ah was asked to bring ye this.'

'Bring it here, then…Now…what have we here?' he said,

upending the bag onto his paper strewn desk.

A cylindrical object about eight inches in length tumbled out in front of him.

'Thank you, constable...just wait outside. Ah'll be there shortly.'

The constable seemed blissfully unaware of what he'd been asked to carry, but D.I. Jamieson knew exactly what it was – it was the proof he'd been waiting for to confirm his suspicions.

Within a short time of his arrival at the scene of the landslide, the Inspector had had his doubts about Nature's involvement. To start with, the area had been rocky, with very little over-lying earth, and the trees that had been ripped from the ground were mainly of the deep-rooted variety, such as ash, birch and oak – which should have made the earth more stable, not less. The other detail striking the D.I. as being rather odd was that the road itself had not collapsed when inundated from above by tons of rubble.

However, his suspicions had now been confirmed. The unexploded stick of dynamite was the final piece of the evidence. He now knew this was no accident. All that was left to do was catch the perpetrator; and so far, his investigations had led him in the direction of only one man.

In most cases of homicide, the person responsible came from a fairly close group of antagonists, or was in fact a close relative of the deceased. He had found no evidence suggesting that a family member was involved, but there was no shortage of well-documented ill will between Morris Stewart and Malcolm Campbell. His recent review of Morris Stewart's death suggested foul play may well have taken place. So the oldest motive for murder – namely revenge – fitted rather neatly into this case, leaving Morris Stewart's son as the most obvious suspect.

It hadn't taken long to discover that Cameron Stewart worked for the railway – giving him easy access to transportation between Dufftown and Huntly. His enquiries soon confirmed that the GNSR were the only company using explosives in this area – which, as it turned out, Mr Stewart would have had unfettered access to. Add to these facts the information that Mr Stewart and his wife just happened to have left yesterday to emigrate to Australia, and the case looked pretty conclusive.

The Inspector rose from his desk and hurried from his office. Sitting behind the reception desk was the portly sergeant – who at just that moment was placing a rather large oatcake into his mouth.

'Sergeant Boyd...when you've finished stuffing yer mouth...I'd like you and the constable to get on a train and go to Campbeltown. There's a ship there called the "Lady Elgin", sailing for Australia some time today. On board you should find the two Stewarts...Cameron and Mary. I want them arrested and brought back, immediately!'

'Ah doubt we be gettin' there before it sails, Inspector,' replied the sergeant, sweeping the crumbs off his tunic with the back of his fingers.

'Well, if you don't shift yer fat arse you probably won't... now move it!'

Twenty minutes later, Sergeant Boyd and Constable Stevenson stood at the ticket window in the station.

'Let me see...now,' the agent murmured, running his finger up and down the pages of three different books of timetables. 'It appears ye may just be lucky. That train outside is leavin' in five minutes for Aberdeen. On arrival there ye will have about fifteen minutes to catch the express to Glasgow. Then...let me see...aye ...then there be a good connection for ye to Tarbert.'

'But we be goin' to Campbeltown,' Sergeant Boyd insisted, rather brusquely.

'Ah know...but, there be no train service to Campbeltown. At Tarbert ye catch the mail coach to Campbeltown. If yer trains are all on time ye shud just catch the last coach of the day.'

Sergeant Boyd was not a happy man. Ahead of him lay a long day with no guarantee of a good result at the end. His impatience increased and his mood darkened, as it now seemed to take an eternity to issue the required tickets.

'There ye be then, sergeant. These tickets will take ye both to Tarbert – courtesy of the railway. Then, just produce yer badges at t'other end for the return.'

'Tell me,' the sergeant said, as he reached forward to grasp the tickets. 'Ah bin hearin' there may be a restaurant car on the express from Aberdeen to Glasgow. Do ye know if they serve ale as well?'

'Ah'm sorry, Sergeant. But Ah'm afraid that carriage is only available to first class passengers,' the agent replied, placing a hand in front of his face to hide his mirth.

The trip from Dufftown to Tarbert traversed some of the most beautiful scenery in Scotland. Starting in the Highlands, the line wound its way down to the coast at Aberdeen. Then, exiting the city, it followed the coastline to Dundee and Perth, before turning southwest towards Glasgow. After another change of trains, the final leg of the journey was via a new line, running northwest from the Clyde to Tarbert.

Constable Stevenson was enthralled, having never been further than fifty miles from his birthplace in Rothiemay. The line descended from the Highlands using the river valleys. Icy streams – just awakened from their long winter sleep – tumbled through wooded glens, whilst higher up, crumbling crofts and ruined castles competed with mammals and birds to catch the eye. Approaching Aberdeen, the vista changed to one of dark, decrepit buildings, and a seemingly endless number of vulnerable human beings, huddled beside small fires in the waste ground alongside the tracks – their only possessions appearing to be the filthy blankets around their shoulders and the few bits of wood shaped into some kind of shelter.

Soon they were on their way again. The express train sped on its way, paralleling the eastern shoreline of

Scotland. Breathtaking seascapes of windblown dunes, and tiny fishing boats pitching and rolling as they hauled their nets, accompanied them to Perth. Then, once more turning inland, they weaved their way through the spring-awakened lowlands, the colours becoming brighter the further south they ventured. But, it was the last part of their journey that, to Constable Stevenson, was the most memorable. The West Highland Line, from Glasgow to Tarbert, took them through 'the garden of Scotland', where nature was already in full bloom due to the wondrous influence of the warming Gulf Stream.

Inevitably in life, a kind of equilibrium is usually maintained, and to the dismay of the Constable, competing with all this beauty was the nausea of having to listen to Sergeant Boyd's litany of complaints. His main displeasure was the unavailability of the restaurant car to lowly second-class passengers like themselves. But as the journey wore on even he tired of those complaints, so he turned his vitriol to the train itself; and the purported damage being done to his spine, and rather large posterior, by the least forgiving seats he'd ever had the displeasure to sit on.

Finally, after five and a half hours of enchanting scenery – and never-ending whining – the two policemen arrived in Tarbert.

With only minutes to spare, they hurried from the station, rounding the corner at the post office to where they had been told the mail coach normally waited. In front of them stood the strangest transport either of them had ever set eyes on. Four wheels, two small at the front and two large at the rear, supported a large, gaily-painted, wooden carriage. Like most normal coaches, a passenger door was fitted to each side, but what made this coach so strange was its roof, which, although correctly sloping upwards from front to back, had built onto it two rows of bench seats – each fitted with curved metal arm rests at either end. On approaching the contraption, it became readily apparent the coach was about to depart, as the driver was already seated at the right end of the front seat – reins in his hands.

The lead pair of horses snorted, and shook their heads with impatience, as Constable Stevenson jumped in front of them and raised his hand.

'Excuse me, driver. Be this the coach to Campbeltown?'

'Aye…that it be,' the driver responded, 'and if ye want a lift ye had better get up here…'cause Ah have a schedule to keep.'

Twelve

Mary stood on the quarterdeck, her cold hands grasping the teak rail with such force that her knuckles were white; while at the same time, two moist trails on her pale, quivering cheeks revealed the state of her emotions. In her heart she was determined to stay in Scotland, but in her mind she knew it was too late. She still couldn't believe he had betrayed her so, and failed to understand how she could have so badly misread the man she loved.

The gusty wind suddenly abated. Mary sensed movement beside her, and then tensed, as she became aware of Cameron's encircling arm. Neither spoke. Mary wrestled with alien emotions; while Cameron struggled with an increasing sense of anxiety the longer they remained attached to the shore. .

The frenetic life around them seemed to pass unnoticed, as both appeared oblivious to the cacophony of noise. Dozens of small boats scurried about the harbour, while at the same time hundreds of people hurried in every direction on the worn and rubbish-strewn quay – amazingly, none stumbling or falling over the ropes, boxes and other obstacles lying in their way. Amidst all this mayhem, goods of all descriptions weaved their way to their destinations on donkey-carts and all other manner of two-wheeled conveyances, while hansom cabs and coaches stopped at various ships' gangways to discharge their human cargo.

Both Stewarts' thoughts were suddenly interrupted by the appearance beside them of a bearded, ruddy-faced seaman.

'Beggin' you're pardon. Captain would like all 'tween-deck passengers to proceed to the fo'c'sle as we'll be getting underway soon. Please follow me.'

Mary's shock and fervent desire that the last few days were all some kind of bad dream had been futile. Finally, her thoughts returned to the present, and the reality of her situation took over. For the first time, she noticed the overwhelming odour of rotting fish and seaweed, and the continuous background din of halyards banging on masts. Seabirds shrieked overhead, while hawkers on the quayside yelled at everyone in sight, in their last ditch attempts to sell fresh fruit, *for the scurvy*, whisky, *for medicinal purposes only*, and firearms, *for protection against savages and wild animals*.

Cameron was not impervious to all this, but his main sense was still of anxiousness. Had he planned well enough? Would they get away in time? Had his subterfuge worked and how long would it last?

Making their way up the starboard side of the ship, they passed the stairwell descending to the second-class passengers' living quarters – a place they would get to know all too well over the next few weeks. Continuing forward, they moved through the amidships area where they had first stepped on board. To their left was the roped-off section signposted – *Private Deck - Cabin Class Passengers only* – and both could only imagine what comfort was afforded the well-heeled occupants of that part of the ship. In due course they arrived at the spacious raised area at the bow, now filled to overflowing with their companions for the voyage.

'All hands on deck! Make ready for sea!' boomed a voice, from somewhere aft.

Men appeared, almost magically, from hidden steps, hatches and doors, each one proceeding to a different location before busying himself retrieving and coiling large hemp ropes.

Unexpectedly, a small, damp cloud rose over the bow of the ship, indicating the position of a steam tug, as it took up its towing station under the bowsprit.

'Single up,' cried the same deep voice.

The lines at the middle of the ship dropped into the water, to be pulled on to the quayside by willing dockhands.

'Secure the gang plank!'

For the first time, the reality of what the passengers were about to embark on was brought home, as their bridge to the shore was swung away.

'Let go aft!' followed ten seconds later by, 'Let go for'ard!' – the deck then canting slightly as a second tug yanked them away from the quayside.

The cloud of steam at the bow now belched skywards, as the tug at their head took up the strain and began to haul the huge ship out into the current of the river; the hubbub on shore quickly fading astern, to be replaced by more bellowed commands and the muffled drumming of the crews' feet hurrying to complete their tasks.

The emigrants crowded towards the right side of the ship, silently staring at the docks and buildings on shore as they began to merge into one – most realising this would probably be the last time they would ever see their birthplace.

'Stand by port mooring line!'

A large yellow buoy now appeared slightly ahead and to the left of the bow. A line arced over the rail, to be instantly grabbed by a member of the tug's crew. With practiced ease he looped it through a ring on the buoy, and then threw it back to one of the seamen on board. Without hesitation, it was fastened off around a large metal cleat on the deck; and after a quick wave from one of the crewman, the tug was sent on its way. The ship now began a slow turn to the left, and once the line to the buoy had straightened and the current took hold, the ship stopped moving – facing up the Mersey.

Like most passengers, Cameron knew very little about ships or how they left port. But it did seem a bit odd to be tied up again in the middle of the river. As he pondered this latest development, two crewmen appeared carrying a large table between them. Placing this at the edge of the raised forecastle, they then moved off to be replaced by various other crewmen – who between them arrived with three chairs and two large boxes of paperwork.

The loud din created by hundreds of people aimlessly milling about in a confined area suddenly ceased. Cameron gazed to his left, and to his consternation, not ten feet away, the bosun could be seen, quietly giving instructions to six armed men. To make matters worse, Cameron could now see a large pinnace, containing two uniformed men, making towards the right side of the ship.

'Ow! ... Cameron, stop it!'

Mary's sudden cry drew his attention, as unknowingly, he had begun to squeeze her arm harder and harder.

With a sigh of resignation, Cameron turned to Mary, wrapping his arms tightly around her and giving her a kiss on the cheek.

'I'm sorry I put you through all of this. I will try to make sure you be taken care of…and I hope one day you may find a way to forgive me.'

'Here it comes,' he murmured, as over Mary's shoulder he watched the armed men beginning to spread out in all directions.

'Would you give me your attention please? My name is Fisher…and I'm the First Mate on this ship. I'm sure you're probably wondering what's happening.'

Cameron stiffened in anticipation.

'As part of our preparations for departure, we shall now be making a final search of the ship for stowaways. While this takes place, the purser will be calling out the names of those who have not yet paid their full fares. On hearing your name, please line up by the table to make the necessary settlement. On completion of this task, all passengers have to be assessed by the port medical officer. Any persons not deemed to be fit, or failing to clear their account, will be immediately escorted ashore.'

Mary pushed Cameron away.

'What you be doin'? People be lookin' at us!'

'Sorry.'

'So you should be... And I expect you to be lookin' after me...no somebody else. As for forgiveness, we shall just have to see.'

Ten minutes later, a commotion towards the rear of the ship drew everyone's attention. A man and woman appeared, being roughly herded in manacles towards the accommodation ladder on the right hand side near the bow. Both wore shabby clothing and were impossibly thin – their hollow cheeks and dark, sunken eyes a testament to their desperation. Undoubtedly, most of the people watching this sorry sight felt an affinity towards these two, knowing full well that they were themselves only one step removed from this selfsame plight.

Without further ado, the poor souls were manhandled over the side and into the waiting boat.

'Stuart...Cameron and Mary!'

'Here...just here,' Cameron announced, easing Mary by the arm towards the table.

'Would you just spell your name please?'

'Certainly...S.T.U.A.R.T.,' Cameron replied, at the same time applying gentle pressure to Mary's elbow.

'There's four pounds and ten shillings still to pay on each ticket.'

Cameron reached into the inner pocket of his jacket and extracted some notes.

'Paid in full, thank you... Move along please.'

While Cameron and Mary waited their turn to see the doctor, the wind freshened and swung around to the North West. At the same time, the beautiful blue sky was now under-cut by thin, wispy streaks of white cloud. Cameron sensed a change in the weather would soon be making its presence felt. And with any luck, he thought, might just help to speed them on their way.

All at once, everyone's attention was drawn towards the head of the queue.

'It's not possible. It's just a cold,' said the obviously agitated man standing at the head of the line.

The doctor listened again to the chest of the young girl standing beside the man, then peered down her throat before placing a hand on her forehead.

'I'm sorry, but we have to be certain. If it's measles it will spread like wildfire.'

In a rage, the father turned to the purser. 'I've paid our fares! I'm not getting off this ship! He doesn't know what he's talking about.'

'Master-at-Arms!' yelled the purser. 'Remove these three as well.'

Once the commotion settled down, the line slowly began to move forward again; and not long after, Cameron and Mary reached the head of the queue. Their medical examination took only a few minutes, and shortly after, the pre-departure checks had been completed. The table and chairs were removed, and the passengers were once more left to their own devices.

'Why has the spellin' of our name suddenly changed? Is this another of your big secrets that you're tryin' to hide from me?'

'Shush. Keep it down, Mary…'tis nothin'. I'll explain it to you later.'

A subtle vibration in the deck – like some giant heart beginning to beat – announced the firing of the ship's boilers, and seconds later smoke spewed from the exhaust stack mounted just behind the forward mast. Once more seamen began to move purposely about, unmistakably well versed in what was required. And this time, nobody could misjudge the fact that they were actually about to get underway.

The bosun's voice boomed out once more.

'Hoist the Blue Peter!'

At that moment, the question likely foremost in the minds of most of the passengers was suddenly answered by a loud crack, as a blue and white flag unfurled on its way to the top of the forward mast. It was only later that Cameron discovered, from talking to a member of the crew, that it was a signal required by nautical convention, to warn ships nearby that they were about to set sail.

The ship slowly swung around, before starting to move down the river towards the open sea. The three hundred or so people on board spread out all over the ship, gazing over the rail and excitedly pointing out various landmarks; while at the stern, the ship's wake began to mark their passage from the old world to the new.

After a bone-jarring, cold, and what felt like interminably long ride, the two policemen's journey finally came to an end outside the post office in Campbeltown. Having been reliably informed by the driver that the harbourmaster would have the information they required, they hopped down from the coach and hurried along the rutted road leading towards the town's wharf.

The harbour master was a man who looked exactly as one would have imagined. He wore an old, dark-blue, double-breasted jacket, with six brass buttons down the front. His head was covered in a mass of white, straggly hair, matching his bushy white beard. His face was old, and looked tough as leather, while his hands were wrinkled and worn. As he moved out from behind his desk, he donned a tired-looking, peaked sailor's cap, and then, shoving a pipe in his mouth, briskly headed towards the door.

'Come outside,' he said, leading the sergeant out the door of the harbour office and along the quay. On reaching the end of the pier, the cold north westerly breeze whipped the harbour master's hair about under his cap as he extended his right arm and pointed with his finger.

'Can ye see that there lighthouse o'er yonder? Just to the left of it, if ye look real careful, ye will be able to make out some sails about to pass behind the Mull of Kintyre. That be the "Lady Elgin". She weighed anchor wi' the tide some four hours ago an 'tis headed down-under so, Ah reckon we no be seein' her ag'in for at least six months.'

'How can Ah get a passenger list of them on board?'

'Ye could go an ask the Eastern Star Line's agent. But, he normally goes home as soon as the ship sails...so he no be here ag'in until tomorrow...when their next ship is due.'

The following morning, after a pleasant night at the Swallow Inn, the two Bobbies stood at the front desk in the Eastern Star Line's office. Having ascertained that Cameron and Mary Stewarts names were indeed on the passenger list, and as far as the agent was aware, they had sailed with the ship, Sergeant Boyd started to put away his notebook when another thought struck him.

'Ah don't suppose ye know of any other ships that may be departin' for Australia, soon?'

'In fact, Ah do. The "Eastern Flyer's" due in later today... an she leaves ag'in in three days' time. She's a clipper and our fastest ship, an will no doubt beat the "Lady Elgin" to Sydney.'

'Greet,' the Sergeant said under his breath, writing down the details.

Later that afternoon, two rather subdued looking policemen stood in front of D.I. Jamieson's desk. They had again spent all day travelling, and had just walked in the door ten minutes before. Having related the details of their failed mission, they now awaited the reaction of their rather over-bearing superior.

'Well, men...Needless to say, I be very upset that you missed them. However, you did show a certain amount of initiative in finding out about the next sailing, so I've decided there will be no further action taken against you. You be both

116

dismissed and can go home…as soon as you've written out a full report that is. In the meantime, I shall try to work out how we be going to get our two suspects returned to us.'

It took two hours for the two men to write out their individual reports, and both were totally fed up by the time they got home. But that was nothing compared to the indignation Sergeant Boyd felt the following day. In his absence, D.I. Jamieson had written his report to the Chief Constable of Scotland. In it he had taken full credit for sending a request via the "Eastern Flyer" to the Australian authorities requesting the immediate detention of the Stewarts on their arrival, and their return to Scotland on the next available ship.

Thirteen

The orders from the bosun had become just background noise as the ship took on a sound of its own. Spars swung as their sheets were loosened until, with a resounding crack, the billowing canvass filled. More and more sails were hoisted, and as the pressure on the masts increased, they too began to creak and groan in protest.

Underlying these intermittent, but nonetheless startling sounds, a continuous low hum – like the sound of a poorly played bass fiddle – encompassed the ship, as the upwind shrouds supporting the masts vibrated under their ever increasing strain.

The Isle of Man passed quickly down the right-hand side to be replaced by the coast of Ireland, just visible as a brown, wavy smudge on the horizon. On the left the coast of Wales, which only a moment ago was jagged, and frothing at its base, rapidly withdrew, as if yanked away by some leviathan just out of sight. As more sails cracked open the ship's speed increased. A sizeable bow wave now accompanied their progress, doing its best to swamp any small boats daring to stray into their path. The colour of the sea changed from a dull, brownish colour to dark blue, marking their progress into deeper waters; while at the same time, the previous straight line of the wake now seemed off-set towards the north, as the invisible force of the wind attempted to push them from their desired course.

Cameron and Mary stood gripping the rail on the starboard foredeck – both unconsciously licking their drying lips as the salt in the air made its presence felt. Cameron put his arm around her – as the temperature began to noticeably decrease – and then lowered his mouth close to her ear.

'I do love you Mary, and I'm sure our new home will prove to be good to us.'

Mary was not convinced she shared his confidence, but nonetheless snuggled closer as her mind drifted back over the previous twenty-four hours.

The first part of their journey had been a revelation, as Mary had never even been to Aberdeen, let alone any further. They had left the snow-capped mountains behind, winding their way down the descending landscape, blooming with patches of pink-flowered heather. Before long, the rough, rolling landscape became grassy hills, which, as they descended lower, transformed into fertile green dales.

At the start, sheep, still sporting their thick winter coats, were the predominant animal in sight, but were soon joined by shaggy, long-horned Highland cattle. Then, as the terrain became less formidable, so too did the animals – and the fierce-looking, shaggy, brown steers were replaced by black Aberdeen Angus, with shorter, less dangerous-looking projections on their heads.

Once more, Cameron reverted to long silences, as he stared, almost forlornly, out the panoramic windows. Mary assumed that he, like her, was having second thoughts, so left him to his musings.

Her first surprise, and in hindsight the first indication of the lies that were to unfold, occurred when they stepped off the train in Glasgow and Cameron enlisted the help of a porter.

'Which gate be ye goin' to?'

'Whichever platform the two o'clock to Liverpool leaves from,' Cameron replied, taking Mary's arm and turning to follow their luggage.

'What do you mean Liverpool? I thought we be goin' to Campbeltown?'

'Och...did I no tell you?' They changed our port of departure.'

Mary had thought that a little strange, but in the end she shrugged it off, assuming he had simply forgotten to mention it.

Five hours later, they duly arrived at Liverpool's Lime Street Station, and what an amazing place it was. Five sets of tracks led in and out of the station, converging onto three separate platforms, beneath a huge, curved roof covering the station like some giant armadillo.

Upon leaving the station, Cameron led Mary across the street to the nearest hotel for her second surprise of the day – an overnight stay prior to their departure.

Having plied Mary with a good meal and a few gins at a nice little restaurant up the street from their hotel, he then led her back to their room; where he proceeded to stun her with his confession. Of course, he still lacked the courage to be direct, and so, slowly worked his way towards the shocking truth.

'We're on a fantastic ship called the "Allepo". She's over 350 feet long and 35 feet wide. As well as sails, the ship is fitted with a coal-fired steam engine, drivin' a single propeller...and although she dinna carry enough coal to power us all the way, it does allow us to get in an out of ports under our own power, and apparently helps our ship to maintain speed in the right direction...even when the winds are light or contrary. Oh...and she's made out of steel, so is really safe...and apparently is so fast we should get there in about fourteen or fifteen days.'

At this point his voice faded away as he realised he'd just put his foot well and truly into his mouth.

'Did you say fifteen days? But surely that no be possible?'

As the night wore on, Mary became even more dumfounded. Cameron told her about his family's purported history, telling her about the bible and royal standard – now safely tucked away at the bottom of one of their trunks.

'And do you remember, Dougal, ma father's old friend?'

Mary replied with a blank look, and then imperceptible nod.

'Well, I met him the night I went back to Dufftown to sort out Helen's things. He told me about what happened on the day ma father was killed…and it were no accident.'

'Sure…and what proof did he have?' Mary murmured.

'Well…only that he knew from his fightin' days what kind of rifle killed ma father…and who owns one of them. So, the followin' night after I left the meetin', I was left in no doubt that what he'd told me were the truth.'

'Meetin'…what meetin'?'

This was not going the way Cameron had planned. Originally, he had hoped to only tell her enough to explain the change in their destination, leaving the rest to disclose gradually, over time. But, he now realised that wasn't going to work. Mary was no fool, and he could tell by the look in her eyes that she would now not let up until she had the whole sorry tale.

'All right,' Cameron sighed, lifting both hands in the air as a gesture of surrender.

So, over the next hour he told her everything: from his clandestine meeting with the other disgruntled Highlanders; to talking the Company into giving him the new job so that he could learn how to use dynamite, and then finally to his setting off the landslide that had killed Malcolm Campbell's son and his coachman.

As he told the story, Mary's face went from scarlet to white.

After he finished, for what seemed like an eternity she said nothing. Then, with undisguised revulsion and ire, she turned to him.

'My God!…Not only have you lied to me for months… but now it seems you're a murderer as well!'

'But, Mary I…'

'I no want to hear any more,' she said brusquely, as she then silently prepared to go to bed.

Getting under the covers, she turned onto her side, her back forming an impenetrable wall between herself and Cameron. Who on earth did I marry, she wondered, before quietly crying herself to sleep.

'Och, come on, Mary. I'm sure Canada can no be all that bad. After all, thousands of people be goin' there…and besides, ma sister's there as well.'

'Well, we no really have much choice now…do we?'

For the first few hours the passengers were left to their own devices. The majority stood silently by the rail, staring out as if in a trance at the rapidly receding shoreline. With some unease, most women grasped the salt encrusted rail with one hand, while bravely clinging to their bonnets with the other. Their husbands, on the other hand, seemed to quickly get to grips with leaning against the heel of the ship, using their hands to steady their wives. In the meantime, the children did what children always do. The young ones ran amok all over the decks getting in everyone's way, while the older ones stole furtive glances at the opposite sex, all the while doing their best to appear completely uninterested.

The Captain and crew knew from their experience that the present holiday atmosphere would soon change, so for the moment were willing to ignore the disorder on the ship.

None of the passengers noticed the slight shift in wind direction, nor its increase in speed; and even if they had would not have realised its significance. But the crew certainly did, and were well aware of what was about to take place. The ship had just moved out from behind the calming influence of the land, and the real crossing was about to begin.

The sedate progress of the ship abruptly changed as she put her shoulder into the first green, curling Atlantic swell. A slight rolling motion ensued, and the ship began to shudder each time they plunged into a white-crested roller. Spray from the bow was thrown higher than the hull, before once more settling back into the confused water adjoining them. And as the sails began to flap, the crew once more sprang into action, scrambling about the rigging like monkeys in the jungle.

Within minutes, the voyagers began to drift towards their accommodation – having for some reason lost their enthusiasm for the sea. Cameron and Mary followed the others, descending the staircase into the second-class passengers' living quarters. The moment their faces cleared the deck, the previous overwhelming sound of wind moaning through the rigging, and halyards beating against masts, almost vanished, to be replaced by a sound that would become all too familiar.

Throughout the compartment people became ill, violently ill, and hard as one tried it was impossible to block out the moaning and retching of the afflicted. However, thankfully, most had the decency to suffer in the privacy of their curtained-off berths, or were now hurrying topside to find the nearest unoccupied section of railing.

The area that they were to call home for the next two weeks was surprisingly large. Immediately adjacent to the staircase was a semi-enclosed area, topped by a waist high counter – under which numerous deep drawers had been fitted. These drawers, along with the larger cupboards fitted to the hull side of the enclosure, contained the cutlery, crockery and all manner of pots and pans needed to feed the passengers. And finally, attached to a bulkhead at the bow end of the enclosed space was a large metallic vessel containing hot water, heated from below by an iron firebox.

Down the centre of the compartment, stretching from nearly one end to the other, was an enormous table, provided with benches on either side. To the right of the table was a cleared area including a few chairs and settees – allowing somewhere for the travellers to relax and socialize during inclement weather – whilst to the left, against. the port hull, were the curtained-off sleeping areas for married couples and their families.

Fitted below the deck head were port holes to allow the movement of air in and out of the interior, lockable from the inside by large wing nuts, whilst overhead were two large hatches, which when open provided extra light and more fresh air.

Cameron and Mary's little cubicle was not exactly grand. Under their lower berth the space was just sufficient to allow them to stow away their steamer trunk, while alongside their bunks there was just enough space in which to get dressed. The hull made up one side of their little compartment, and heavy curtaining enclosed the other three. The berths themselves, although just of planked wood, did at least have a clean straw mattress, with two folded blankets provided for each occupant.

'I think we need to put on some warm clothes and find somewhere on deck to relax until supper time,' Cameron said in hushed tones. 'I don't know about you…I felt fine until I came down here…but I'm no sure how long that will last if I have to endure this smell.'

A few minutes later, Cameron and Mary had put on some warmer clothing and were now standing at the bottom of the staircase reading the "RULES FOR PASSENGERS" posted on the notice board.

MEALS & BED-TIME
- Every passenger to rise at 7 a.m. unless ill.
- Breakfast 8 to 9 a.m., Dinner 1 p.m., Supper 6 p.m.
- Passengers to be in their berths at 11 p.m.

FIRES & ILLUMINATION
- Fires will be lighted by one of the ship's cooks at 7 a.m. and will be extinguished at 7 p.m. unless otherwise directed by the Master.
- Two safety lamps, hanging in the compartment, will be lit at dusk.

CLEANING – BERTHS AND CLOTHING
- All passengers to roll up their beds and sweep their spaces on a daily basis.
- After breakfast, the main compartment area will be completely swept and the dirt thrown overboard. A rota will be posted, to carry out these duties.
- Weather permitting, all beds to be well shaken on deck each day.
- Mondays and Thursdays are appointed as washing days. All washing and drying to be done on the main deck.

VENTILATION
- Portholes and hatches (where fitted) to be kept open (weather permitting) from 7 a.m. to 10 p.m.
- Main hatch to be left open at all times.

MISCELLANEOUS
- Sundays (weather permitting) all passengers to muster on main deck at 10 a.m. in clean and decent clothes for Services – to be conducted by the Master.
- Any spirits or firearms brought on board must be given into the custody of the Master until the termination of the voyage.
- No gambling, fighting or swearing is allowed on board.
- No sailors are allowed on the passenger decks, without permission from the Master, and no passengers are permitted in or near the crew's quarters in the forecastle at any time.

BY ORDER OF THE MASTER

'Well I guess that just about covers everything. I wonder if we'll have to walk the plank if we step out of line. Och, and maybe we're supposed to salute the crew as well,' joked

Cameron, as they climbed up the staircase leading towards the deck.

Supper that night was a sombre affair. At 6.00 p.m. sharp, the second-class passengers' cook and three other seamen began to shuttle back-and-forth from the main galley, carrying iron pots of stew and baskets of freshly baked bread. From the fitted counter, plates of food were handed out to those partaking of supper – the baskets of bread having already been secured in holes cut into the table at regular intervals for just that purpose. Less than half of the passengers showed any interest in food, and of those, many downed only a few spoonfuls before sprinting topside. Cameron decided not to tempt fate, and remained sitting on deck drinking a cup of tea. Mary, on the other hand, was hungry and had a full helping; although she did take her plate of food up top to sit with her husband.

After supper, Cameron and Mary strolled hand-in-hand around the ship as the wound in their relationship, slowly, continued to heal.

'By the way,' Mary said, as they stared out at the sea from the quarterdeck. 'What be all that palaver over the spellin' of our name?'

'I needed to lay a false trail, in case the police figured everythin' out and came lookin' for us.'

'But why still use the name Stuart? Why not use somethin' totally different?'

'When I bought the tickets for the "Lady Elgin", I gave them our correct names and paid in full, so there be a record of us going to Australia on that ship. Then, when I was about to put down a deposit for the reservation on this ship using a completely false name, they asked for some proof of identity. All I had in my pocket was my railway pass, which were in my real name. The only thing that I could think to do was tell them the railway had spelt my name incorrectly, and that they should have spelt it S.T.U.A.R.T. Not a great false name, I know, but better than nothin'.'

Both silently watched the final smudge that was Ireland disappear astern, as the last few greyish-white gulls wheeled away to the east – seemingly bored with the chase. With nothing left to look at, Cameron and Mary turned back towards the bow. Ten feet in front of them stood the two men manning the ship's wheel. Both were stonily silent and stared straight ahead. The lower ranked seaman stood directly behind the wheel with both of his hands resting on the spokes. Occasionally, his eyes would look down at what Cameron assumed must be the compass, before slowly lifting again to gaze towards the bow. Beside him on his right was the First Mate, palms together behind his back, looking to all as if he was completely relaxed. What most people failed to notice were his eyes, which continuously scanned from side-to-side and front-to-back, monitoring all parts of the ship.

'Good evening…gentlemen. Sorry… but I'm no actually sure how we're supposed to address you,' Cameron said.

'Beggin' your pardon, sir,' replied the First Mate. 'Passengers are not allowed to talk to the helming crew at any time.'

'Oh, sorry,' Cameron said, taking Mary's arm and continuing their stroll back towards the front of the ship.

Mary sniggered as they descended the short steps from the quarterdeck to the passageway on the right side of the main deck.

'My God, Cameron, you really may end up walking the plank.'

'I hope all the crew are no goin' to be as unsociable as those two. It's beginnin' to feel like we all be prisoners…and they be the guards!'

Cameron and Mary continued their stroll and exploration of their temporary new home, as neither of them wished to return below decks. But both knew that moment would soon be upon them, as passengers were forbidden on deck once darkness fell. Stopping to stare over the bow at the slowly sinking sun, they were almost hypnotised watching it change from yellow to orange and then blood red as it fell shimmering into the distant ocean.

Twilight followed, and with it the wind began to abate. Once more the crew sprang into action, attaching larger sails to the rigging to make up for the loss of speed.

Slowly wandering aft, but now on the port side of the ship, they passed another wide stairwell, leading down to the divided accommodation for single men and women; while just up ahead, a soft red glow was cast over the deck by the port running light, firmly attached to the foremast's shrouds.

Once again, Cameron and Mary stopped and leaned against the railing, staring out at the vast, darkening void; as the horizon rushed towards them and their world became the ship.

Before long a bell rang out; and with the change of watch a member of the crew was dispatched to clear the decks of unauthorised persons. Arm-in-arm, Cameron and Mary turned, heading back to their nether world, knowing that this was surely to be a night they would not soon forget.

'Take this,' Mary said, handing Cameron a small vial of liquid from her pocket.

'What's…?'

''Tis eucalyptus oil. Put some on your top lip…just under your nose. Believe me…it'll smell a lot better than tonight's alternative.'

Cameron lost track of how many times he was awakened by the dry retching of some poor soul, or the screaming of a baby whose mother could do nothing – she being just so ill. Mary didn't get much rest either. But each time she threw back her blankets to go and help, Cameron's firm hand stopped her.

'Don't,' he whispered. 'There's nothin' you can do. You'll just make yourself ill. Besides, if you're no careful, they'll all be expectin' you to clean up their mess… and that's just not fair.'

Over the next few days, everyone recovered from what they all feared was a near death experience. In the meantime, the weather was now perfect; and the ship pushed on at a good rate, carrying every stitch of canvass she possessed. Shipboard life took on a routine – just like life ashore – except now the ship became their village, and the sea out to the horizon their surrounding countryside. The mornings were occupied with cleaning and washing – cleaning of the ship coming first, followed by cleaning of one's body. Twice a week, the washing of clothes was carried out in huge tubs on deck, followed by drying on lines strung up in the more sheltered areas.

After their main meal, most passengers spent their afternoons on deck socialising with their fellow travellers; and because they were now isolated from the rest of the world, the passengers became intensively involved with each other. People, who only two days before were strangers, now became the best of friends – in fact almost part of the family – and worries and fears were expressed and shared, somehow making them easier to deal with.

Because of Mary's nursing experience, she unwittingly became the person to whom everyone brought their ailments – both physical and mental – and once her supposed healing abilities became known, even the ship's crew began to consult her.

Children played board games, and were generally kept entertained by the more energetic adults. While the crew arranged treasure hunts and deck sports to help keep them occupied.

Cameron spent most of his day talking to other men, soon striking up a friendship with a man from near Kilmarnock, called James McRae. He and his wife Fiona had been working for over ten years on an estate that raised dairy cattle, and now hoped to establish a farm of their own.

'It can't be an easy life then...runnin' a farm...I suppose?'

'No, Cameron, 'tis a lot of hard work,' James said. 'But then, at least ye be workin' for yoursel', an when the profits come they be all yer own. Apart from that…Ah can't wait till the day comes when Ah can gaze out over the countryside an all Ah can see is mine…an there be no one 'round who can throw me off.'

'I guess it would take a lot of money to be startin' a farm when we get to Canada?'

'Och, no…'tis what be greet about Canada. It has more land than almost anywhere else in the world…and right now they're givin' it away to get people to settle there.'

Even though he had very little experience in farming, Cameron began to give this serious thought. After all, land owners in England and Scotland lived very well, so, why shouldn't it be the same in Canada? He really must talk to Mary he decided as he said goodnight to James.

As he wandered back towards the stairwell, Cameron looked out to sea, and noticed a line of ragged clouds loitering on the horizon; while at the same time a cold gust of wind touched his face, sending shivers down his spine.

Fourteen

Sometime during the night the motion of the ship began to change, and their previously calm little existence disintegrated. Instead of the rhythmic plunging of the ship, a twisting movement developed as the ship now met the swell at an angle. Before long, a clap of thunder reverberated throughout the compartment, rousing Cameron from his slumber. And soon he realised that he wasn't the only one awake, as the heart rending sound of vomiting and retching returned with a vengeance.

Slipping from under his blankets, he eased down from his bunk.

A loud scraping noise accompanied Cameron's vain attempt to quietly extract the trunk from beneath Mary's berth.

'What are you doin'?'

'Sorry if I woke you. I be searchin' for the eucalyptus oil. The weather has taken a turn for the worse.'

'Why don't you just go back to bed? It'll probably be fine in the morning,' she muttered, before rolling back the other way and dropping off to sleep.

Now wide awake, Cameron slipped on some clothes and, barefooted, headed for the staircase; while at the same time the ship did its best to throw him from his feet. Three steps from the deck his head emerged into the open, and what he saw almost defied description. It was black, pitch black, and the wind was screaming through the rigging driving the salt-water infused air horizontally across the decks. Almost immediately his eyes began to sting, and within seconds he was soaked from head to foot. Suddenly, lightning flared, illuminating some of the drenched crew struggling to control flailing lines, and reduce the amount of sail the ship was carrying.

'Hey!…You at compartment "C" hatch…get below decks! It's too dangerous out here!' yelled the bosun, from somewhere in the dark.

Duly chastised, Cameron carefully descended the wet steps; the dull-white glow from the night lantern now casting strange, evil looking shadows throughout the under deck area as it swung madly about on its chain. A patch of water, spreading out in all directions from the foot of the stairs, now added to the danger of moving about, and as he stepped down onto the floor the ship lurched to the right, trying once more to propel him across the compartment.

Using the centrally placed dining table for support, Cameron carefully edged his way back towards his berth, having now decided that maybe bed would be the safest option. But as he climbed up into his bunk – eucalyptus oil in hand – he knew sleep would not come easy.

Throughout the following day, the frightened passengers huddled below decks. Their world was a terrifying, dimly-lit cavern, seemingly being shaken to pieces each time a roller punched into the hull. At first, terrified screams accompanied each downward plunge from the top of the towering swells, but, as time wore on, their protests faded away – either because they had become inured to their home's wild gyrations, or because they were just numb with fear. Amidst all this chaos, Mary did her best to nurse the sick with quiet reassurance, and attended to the injuries of those ignoring the suggestion to stay in bed.

Sometime during the afternoon, two crew members broke limbs after being swept into solid objects fitted to the deck. Not long after, a crewman arrived at the bottom of the steps in compartment "C".

'Mrs Stuart…is Mrs Mary Stuart here?' he yelled, trying to make himself heard over the commotion outside.

'I'm here,' Mary replied, lurching out from behind one of the injured passenger's heavy curtains.

The ship once again heaved to the right, and Mary's hand reached out – just managing to grip the edge of the table.

'Captain Rosseau sends his compliments, and requests your presence in the ship's infirmary to help with two injured crewmen.'

'Tell him I'll be along presently. I just be finishin' the bandage on Mr McCauley's arm.'

'All right...but I'll wait for you at the bottom of the stairwell. It's much too dangerous topside for you to be on your own.'

The journey from below decks, down the right side of the ship to the amidships cargo door, and then down to the infirmary, was to be the most frightening three or four minutes of Mary's life. The crewman tied a length of rope fitted with a metal clasp around her waist, and then led her up the steps to the deck. As soon as she emerged from the hatchway, she was almost knocked off her feet by the force of the wind. The seaman steadied her, and then led her towards the starboard passageway – hurrying from one handhold to the next during the lull between the gusts of wind and torrential rain. On reaching the safety line, but before Mary could be attached, a monstrous wave curled over the ship's side, and had the seaman not been there to hang on to her, she would surely have been thrown across the ship – and either disappeared over the far gunwale or suffered horrific injuries. Over the next few minutes, as they made their way down the starboard passageway attached to the safety line, she was pummelled by blasts of wind, and deluged by walls of water until finally reaching the doorway leading down to the infirmary.

After what seemed an eternity to Cameron, Mary returned, and after changing into dry clothing, painted a picture for him of the world outside.

'I've never been so scared in ma life. The air is so full of water that when you breathe it almost feels like you're drownin'. The ship…well…it doesn't even look like a ship. All you can see are blurred images of various sized wooden partitions and dark vibratin' ropes disappearin' into a wet blanket a few feet above your head. There were times, when I was strugglin' through water up to my knees, that I wasn't even sure we were afloat any more. God forbid there's another ship out there, 'cause we'll never see it before it's too late.'

All day the ship lurched drunkenly from one side to the other, and at times all on board held their breaths as they fell off the top of another massive roller. But somehow the ship always survived the impact, and once more began its slow climb out of the trough.

Night came early that day, as very little light was able to penetrate the slate-grey sky visible through breaks in the low, scudding clouds. No attempt was made to serve hot food, but containers of dry biscuits and plenty of fresh water were provided in all compartments. In the end, very few risked the trip from their berths to retrieve what was on offer – especially as the floor was now covered in a mixture of seawater and human excretions of all kinds. Most passengers were just happy to be alive – the exception being those that were so ill that they were beginning to wish they were dead!

Mary finally collapsed from fatigue into a deep sleep, while Cameron lay in his bunk reassessing his beliefs about God, and wondering if this might not be the Almighty's retribution for the sins that he'd committed.

Cameron awoke to a new and much more pungent fragrance, and if he wasn't mistaken it was the acrid odours of carbolic soap now assailing his nose and making his eyes feel sticky. Climbing down from his berth, he gingerly put his feet on the floor, and prepared to dodge the soiled parts of their saloon. Then, pulling aside the curtain, he walked towards the bow.

All at once his brain registered two facts. First, the ship was no longer trying to cripple him by launching him across the compartment, and second, the floor was as clean as the day they had first stepped aboard.

'Good afternoon, Mr Stuart. How is Mrs Stuart this fine day?'

Cameron couldn't believe what he was seeing. Behind the counter in their little galley stood a smiling seaman in a clean white jacket. And, if he wasn't mistaken, the man was preparing to serve dinner.

'I hope she enjoyed her sleep…because she certainly deserved it after all the help she gave us. When you speak to her, please tell her the two men she fixed up yesterday are much better and send their thanks.'

From experience, the Captain had known what state the passengers would be in. So, he had ordered the crew not to disturb them until one o'clock. In the meantime, he had ordered a deep clean to be carried out in all compartments, as quietly as possible.

As Cameron's eyes took in their spotless accommodation, they were drawn to a new instruction, recently posted on the notice board. Not more rules, he thought, wandering over to read the latest orders.

NOTICE TO ALL PASSENGERS

- Passenger bedding to be aired on deck as soon as possible
- Any soiled bedding to be replaced from ship stores
- Curtained-off areas will be provided on deck, with sufficient hot water and soap, to enable all passengers to bathe
- After bathing, an extra clothes washing day will commence and operate until sun down
- This evening, weather permitting, supper will be served on deck, followed by dancing and entertainment
- Note: would any passengers able to play a musical instrument please contact the purser?

BY ORDER OF THE MASTER

What Cameron wasn't aware of was that Mary had requested the first four items as she knew only too well what dangers lurked when people lived in close proximity to each other and hygiene was not given top priority.

Not surprisingly, most people appeared from their berths soon after the pots of stew arrived below decks – their nausea having vanished with the retreating storm. And no adverse comments were heard during dinner concerning the new work details, as once their stomachs had been filled, their spirits had become completely rejuvenated.

For the next ten days the voyage took on a festival atmosphere. The normal routine was re-established – except now, during tranquil evenings, dancing and socialising took place on deck, accompanied by a violin, two flutes, and even one Irish bagpipe. The weather remained settled and good progress was made towards the west. Each morning, the hazy eastern horizon gave birth to a new blazing glory. And as evening approached, the sun painted the sky red and then, like a compass, indicated the way before extinguishing itself in the darkening sea.

Yet, just as nature's blessings were not always bountiful, it seems God's benevolence was not everlasting; as once more, the little world of ship, crew and passengers were about to be tested.

Fifteen

Sunday morning's well-attended service had just drawn to a close. The passengers and crew had sung with relish; and even the Captain's sermon had received favourable comment.

Mary completed her examination of the two McLean sisters, and then closed the curtain tightly, before leaving their berth area. The girls' parents waited outside, and Mary could almost smell the fear that they exuded.

'Keep cold wet cloths on their foreheads and try to have them sip some water. I'll be back very soon.'

With that, Mary hurried past some of her fellow travellers – enjoying a cup of tea in the lounging area – and ascended the stairs towards the deck. With mounting anxiety, she went over in her mind the symptoms she'd observed: fever; headache, muscle weakness, abdominal pain and diarrhoea. The irrefutable evidence, though, was the rash of small, rose-coloured spots on the girls' lower chests.

Hurrying along the deck, she quickly reached the aft steps leading to the officer quarters. Ignoring the "Crew Only" placard, Mary descended the gangway, strode towards the Captain's cabin and knocked on the door.

'I'm sorry Captain, but I must inform you that you have two cases of typhoid in compartment "C".'

'Are you certain?'

'Yes…I'm afraid I am.'

'All right,' he sighed. 'What do you recommend?'

'First, we need to get the girls moved to the infirmary as quickly as possible…then you'd better move their parents in with them. Do you have anyone in there at the moment?'

'No…the two crewmen went back to their quarters this morning.'

'Good…Once the family are out of their compartment I suggest you destroy all their bedding and clothing…oh…and the curtains as well.'

'Tell me, Mrs Stuart, what is the prognosis for the girls? Do they have any chance at all?'

'The youngest lassie will probably die in the next few days. As for her sister…I'm no sure. She seems a wee bit stronger…and because of her age, she has a slightly better chance of survival. Unfortunately, the disease was initially masked by seasickness and now they both be well into the second stage. Tell me, Captain, how far be we from medical help?'

'We are four or five days from Grosse Isle…the quarantine island maintained by the Canadian Authorities in the Gulf of St. Lawrence. Obviously, we have no choice but to go there now…Tell me, what are the chances of the typhoid spreading?'

'I can no really tell. It depends on how much contact the family have had with the rest of the passengers, but I must warn you…you should prepare yourself for the worst. At the very least, their mother and father will be infected, and there may be a few cases from people who have been in direct contact with the lassies. I'll talk to the mother and father… and then make up a list of them they be socialisin' with.'

Over the next few hours, the mood on board the ship changed dramatically. At least a dozen passengers had seen the poor little souls being taken from their berths and accompanied by their weeping mother to the infirmary – supported around her waist by an arm from her fearful-looking husband.

No sooner had the sad progression disappeared, than two crewmen rushed below. Within minutes, they arrived back on deck carrying the family's bedding and belongings – which they unceremoniously pitched over the side. All passengers below decks were then asked to go topside, before another deep clean was carried out to the compartment.

Cameron was not at all happy. He had tried his best to dissuade Mary from putting herself at risk with the typhoid-infected travellers, but she had insisted that it was her duty. Of course, it now meant she also was quarantined, and Cameron would see very little of her for the foreseeable future.

During their first night in sickbay both parents began to show signs of the disease, and by the end of the next day two more passengers exhibited the initial symptoms. The ship's carpenter was summoned by the Captain and ordered to come up with plans for quickly extending the infirmary, if it became necessary. While at the same time, the purser was instructed to draw up a new accommodation list, in case the need arose to rearrange the passengers' sleeping quarters.

On day three, both little girls passed away.

A mournful gathering jammed into the mid-ship deck. With great solemnity, the Captain carried out what he described as one of his 'saddest duties'. Most women wept openly, and even some men's eyes were seen to fill with moisture as the two small, canvass-shrouded bodies were positioned at right-angles to the railing. The service was kept as short as was decently possible; and thankfully, no sermon was called for, as it would have been impossible for the Captain to justify God's reason for taking two such innocent lives.

Thank goodness their parents weren't here to see this, thought Cameron, as Captain Rosseau stoically read out the invocation '...we commend to almighty God our two sisters, and we commit their bodies to the sea...earth to earth, ashes to ashes...'

To Cameron, the rest was a blur, although the misty picture of the two little white bundles falling into the ocean would be forever etched into the back of his mind.

The following days were harrowing for all on board. The emotion of the deaths, and the fear of more to come, kept everyone on edge. The Captain risked everything to get to medical help as soon as possible. The ship raced through the night with full canvass, even though the area was well known for icebergs. Extra lookouts were posted aloft, and for the first time on the voyage a man was posted at the end of the bowsprit to give as much warning as possible of any ice. Two days later, while the Captain stood on the quarterdeck taking the noon sextant reading, the cry went out.

'Land ho! Fine on the starboard quarter.'

Belle Isle, an island off the northern tip of Newfoundland, had finally been spotted.

Captain Rosseau decided he would personally deliver the good news to Mrs Stuart, so ten minutes later he knocked on the infirmary door.

'Mrs Stuart...it's the Captain. I've some good news for you.'

Worryingly there was no immediate response. So, turning the handle, he pushed open the door. Lying on the floor beside her small dispensary table was Mary – her face pale and her clothing in disarray.

When Fiona McCrae heard about Mary, she volunteered to help, and immediately took over the needs of the infirmary. Mary was placed in the last spare bed; while at the same time, Cameron had to be forcibly restrained from entering the medical facility. Meanwhile, Captain Rosseau, having first established that they had sufficient coal for the rest of the journey, ordered full steam to be raised – thus adding the propulsion of the engine to the power of the sails – after which, the ship's speed gradually rose to an impressive fifteen knots. Twelve hours later, they rounded up into the lagoon on the south western side of Grosse Isle and, with a yellow quarantine flag fluttering at her masthead, dropped anchor.

A longboat soon set out from the dock. Two men in seamen's uniforms handled the oars, while a middle-aged man with thick, pepper-grey hair and matching moustache, sat in the stern.

'How many casualties and what ailment?' yelled the Doctor-in-charge, as they came alongside.

'Two buried at sea and five in sick bay,' the Captain replied. 'One of our émigrés is a young nurse and she's been looking after them. She reckons it's typhoid. But sadly, she's not well now either.'

'Right…we'll take the sick ones ashore with us now. The rest of you are quarantined on board for the next week. After seven days we'll bring you ashore for a final medical check, after which you may proceed. In the meantime, we'll do our best to provide you with some fresh provisions. Good day to you Captain.'

Cameron was beside himself with worry. He knew from his discussions with Mary that the survival chances for those with typhoid was very poor. Over the next few days, every time a boat approached the ship with supplies, Cameron was certain it would be delivering the message he most feared. On the third day of their incarceration, he was still below decks finishing his dinner, when a seaman approached.

'Captain's compliments, Mr Stuart. Would you please accompany me to his quarters?'

Cameron stumbled after the crewman, his heart pounding and his stomach beginning to churn as it threatened to bring up his recent meal. Looking towards the stern, Cameron noticed the longboat, its oarsman patiently waiting on deck with the boat's painter in his hand. This confirmed it to be a message from ashore; and the bile rose higher in his throat.

On entering the Captain's cabin, the same bearded man who had met them on their arrival stood beside the Captain. With a pleasant demeanour, he stepped forward and offered his hand to Cameron.

'Hello… Mr Stuart, I presume. My name's Doctor Sterling.

Cameron's hand shook with fear as he leaned forward to return the greeting. With increasing anxiety, and now barely able to speak, he mumbled, 'Mary…How be Mary?'

'She's just fine,' beamed the doctor. 'She was just completely worn out from working so hard for those four days…and, of course, morning sickness doesn't help.'

This time it was Cameron who almost collapsed. His mouth began to move – albeit without any words being issued.

'You'll be able to see her in a few days' time – when the quarantine's lifted. All I can say is that your wife is some lady. She's even insisted on giving us a hand, now that she's up and about. I only wish that all new people who come to our country were as conscientious and hard working as your Mary. If there's ever anything I can do for you two…please let me know.'

No further cases of sickness developed over the next four days. So, on the morning of day eight, a small flotilla of boats left the shore and headed to the "Allepo". A uniformed official was first to clamber on board, and was immediately directed to the Master's cabin. Within thirty minutes, all passengers were gathered on the quarterdeck.

'May I have your attention please?' bellowed the First Mate. 'You are now all to disembark the ship. The Canadian staff on the island will meet you on shore, at which time you will be directed to your quarters for the next two days. While you're ashore, the ship will be completely fumigated and then made ready to sail. I do apologise for this further inconvenience, and assure you that we will get underway again as soon as possible.'

The cabin class passengers were the first to get off – with a separate boat provided for each family – and on arrival ashore, were immediately directed to their private accommodation. Soon, the off-loading of the second-class passengers began. This was to be carried out in alphabetical order; and they were to be jammed into the boats until all empty spaces were filled.

Cameron stood beside the gently swaying accommodation ladder, his hands buried in his pockets. Try as he may, he was finding it very difficult to conceal his frustration at having to wait. As he watched the first boatload of passengers beginning to descend the precarious steps, the ship's purser quietly approached him.

'Beggin' your pardon, Mr Stuart…but the Captain asks if you wouldn't mind going ashore on the first boat, to help get the party ashore. For some reason there seems to be a shortage of staff on the main dock.'

'Why…of…of course,' Cameron stammered.

Turning to join the queue of people preparing to descend the accommodation ladder, Cameron looked across towards the ship's wheel, nodding to the Captain, who for the first time in days, sported a smile on his face.

Twenty minutes later, after a choppy and cold ride from the ship, the longboat drew near the main dock, where a lone figure in a nurse's uniform could be seen standing on the quayside.

'Hey, look who it is!' exclaimed one of the female passengers. 'It's Mary Stuart. Thank God she's all right.'

Indeed, thought Cameron.

The crew quickly tied up the boat, and within minutes the first load of passengers was on dry land. Mary indicated the group's destination to the assembled gathering, before turning back towards the end of the pier.

For a few seconds they just stared at each other.

Mary slowly ambled towards Cameron, but then, as he raised his arms, she ran the last few steps.

'Don't you ever do that to me again,' Cameron said, squeezing her until she was almost breathless. Then suddenly he stopped. 'Oh my, God! I forgot about the baby.'

'Don't be silly, the baby's fine…and so am I. Now come with me,' she said, grabbing his hand and leading him away. 'We've got a lot to talk about…which we can do while I show you 'round.'

The island was split into three sections. The eastern part was approached through a gate. In this fenced compound, laid out in rows of three, were single-storey huts.

This was the infirmary for the sick and dying; and what couldn't be seen from the dock area was the huge cemetery, located just beyond a stand of trees on the far side of the compound. According to Mary, it was one of the saddest places on earth. Under the protection of a single huge cross were the graves of over three thousand people. Most of those buried there were Irish, with the exception of a small number of Scots, English and other Europeans. Nearly all of those interred there had died from typhoid, cholera or measles; and sadly, two new graves had been added in the last week – those of the parents of the two little girls.

In the centre of the island were the buildings containing the administration offices and staff accommodation, and to the west was the temporary housing for the passengers awaiting onward transportation. It was to this area Cameron and Mary slowly wandered, as they both came to terms with just how lucky they had been.

Two days later, they finally departed.

So many hopes and dreams lay dead and rotting in the ground on that remote Canadian island. Thousands had wrenched themselves away from family and friends, suffered numerous physical and mental privations crossing that vile ocean, only to fail within sight of their new home.

So, an almost audible sigh of relief could be heard, as the sails once more filled with air, and they distanced themselves from the horror of the last fourteen days. Twelve hours later, the mouth of the majestic St. Lawrence River was reached, and the ship turned on to a south-westerly heading for the final leg of their journey.

Before long, it became apparent the Captain had relaxed some of the rules, because the crew now ignored passengers remaining on deck after dark. Some huddled together on the fo'c'sle, breathing in the heady smell of seaweed and dead fish; which every now and then was replaced by wafts of pine and wood-smoke, signifying the invisible presence of man.

In days gone by, this last leg could have taken many days, as ships were forced to tack back and forth due to unhelpful winds. But with the advent of the steam engine an almost direct course could be maintained, ensuring an arrival at their destination in just over a day.

Eventually, the cold got the better of most and they headed down below. Thank God, it was their last night sleeping in their little curtained area, thought Cameron, on finding that all of their bedding, including their mattresses, had been removed during the fumigation process. He and Mary joined their fellow travellers in the lounging area until well past midnight – most people having decided that the prospects of getting much sleep on the hard wooden slats did not seem very likely. The general conversation was about farming and crops; and Mary listened carefully, questioning James and Fiona sitting alongside them, if anything was mentioned that she didn't understand. By the time Cameron and Mary did go to bed, they had both come to the conclusion that maybe farming was an inviting prospect. However, both agreed that if they were to pursue this option, they must try to get land near Cameron's sister, as her experience would be invaluable to the two novice settlers.

'You know what, Mary? I'm really lookin' forward to seein' Margaret now…and I can't wait to see the look of surprise on her face when we be gettin' there.'

And as the night wore on, the shores of the mighty river crept ever closer, as if the ship was now being swept into some mammoth funnel.

Sixteen

The next day, a party like atmosphere greeted Cameron and Mary when they joined their fellow émigrés in the main saloon. Men slapped each other on the back in congratulations, as if they had just survived some test of their daring, while women gaily chatted to each other, like old friends or family meeting each other on the street. When breakfast was finished, the previous daily ritual of cleaning up was ignored, and everyone hurried to the upper decks.

During the night the mighty river had become a much smaller passageway. Green forests, occasionally broken by cleared areas sloping down to the water, now bound the ship on either side. At first, the excited voices heard over breakfast had become somewhat subdued when, as far as the eye could see, there appeared to be nothing but desolation. But as time passed, the cleared areas grew larger, and then became ploughed fields being readied for this year's crop. Eventually, further signs of habitation appeared, as wisps of smoke came into view, lazily rising into the still morning air.

The river continued to narrow, and as it did, the previous small blemishes on the landscape turned into houses and barns, while at the same time, the ant-like forms moving about became people and animals.

The Allepo's passengers now became more animated. Fingers pointed and arms were raised in salute, until, on rounding a bend in the river, the city of Quebec came into view. A cheer followed, accompanied by the waving of caps – some would say more as a sign of relief than a rousing sound of welcome.

A massive fort stood on the cliff guarding the city – some canons pointing directly at them, while others warned off invaders from across the river to the south – and to the right of this citadel, the spire of some enormous church or cathedral rose into the welcoming, azure sky.

Below the lofty cliffs stood the port, made up of numerous low buildings and three piers projecting out into the river like some giant letter "E" lying on its side. Several ships lay alongside the jetties, and from this distance Cameron could just make out the swinging booms of the large steam cranes, busily unloading baggage and cargo. Near the eastern edge of the harbour the cliff became a sharply sloping hill, terminating at the point where another river joined the St. Lawrence from the north; and it was only as they drew near that the access road to the port came into view, snaking its way back and forth down the hill.

Cameron and Mary stood alongside the rail on the starboard side of the ship, watching as a tug took up its position. Towlines were secured, after which the slow, deliberate procedure of docking the ship commenced.

Apart from the shouted commands of the bosun, and the background noise of a working port, a hushed atmosphere enveloped the ship, as once again the passengers gathered in small family units to stare at the approaching shore.

How strange, Cameron thought. The scene was so reminiscent of their departure from Liverpool; and no doubt some of the passengers were once more entertaining the same nagging questions. The big difference this time, though, was that they had already made the jump, and there was no turning back. The gulf between here and their home country was now an ocean, which most accepted they would never cross again.

With a light thump, and a judder felt throughout the ship, they were nudged alongside one of the piers. Loops, previously spliced into the ends of hemp ropes the size of men's wrists, were thrown over the waiting steel bollards, and then made fast with figure-of-eights onto the onboard cleats. Within minutes, a wooden gangway was swung into place, creating a pathway to their new lives.

'May we have your attention please? The Quebec Port Authority requires you to remain on board until cleared by the Health Department. This will be carried out as quickly as possible. After the medical checks you will be escorted to the immigration building to be processed. Once these formalities are complete, and you have cleared the hall, you will find desks manned by various groups of people willing to help you with onward travel, or to answer any questions that you might have. Thank you for your attention…and best of luck in your new country.'

This was the beginning of what was to become a very long and trying day. The cabin-class passengers were the first to be led off the ship. None of them had been exposed to any illnesses, so their medical check was only a formality. The rest of the immigrants then lined up in alphabetical order.

After standing in line for what seemed like ages, Cameron and Mary were approached by a member of the crew.

'Beggin' your pardon, Mr Stuart. Captain Rosseau would like to see you and Mrs Stuart in his quarters…if you'll just follow me.'

'Now, what!'

'Oh, Cameron, just relax. I'm sure it's nothin' to worry about,' Mary said, her hand reaching out to rest on his arm.

'I know. I'm just a wee bit tired of all this waitin' 'round.'

Captain Rosseau met them at his cabin door, ushering them to a settee adjacent to a low coffee table. Once they were seated, he lowered himself into the armchair opposite and then reached for the china teapot sitting on the tray in the middle of the table.

'Can I offer you a cup of tea and a biscuit?'

'No thanks…We'd just like to get goin',' Cameron said, rather tersely.

148

'I am sorry about your delay, but we have to be seen to be fair. Anyway…I asked you to come here because I've been in touch with our office in the city…and we'd like to extend our gratitude for all the help given to us by Mrs Stuart.'

'Oh…that's no really necessary,' Mary replied.

'All the same…I don't know where we would have been without you…So… as a gesture of our appreciation, the company would like to refund you your fares…'

'But that be…'

Captain Rosseau raised his hand. 'And as a further token of our indebtedness, I've been authorised to give you two tickets on the steamer "Laurentian", leaving for Montreal later this afternoon.

'I…I don't know what to say,' Mary stuttered.

For a moment Cameron was speechless. Then, looking very contrite, he stood up and offered his hand.

'Captain Rosseau, I'd like to apologise for my attitude earlier…and on behalf of Mary and myself say thank you.'

'You're more than welcome. And before you go, may I just add my personal good wishes to you both.'

As they wandered back towards the queue, Cameron was flabbergasted. They'd like to 'extend their gratitude', show their 'appreciation', their 'indebtedness'. Incredible! If this was how people treated each other in Canada, then the future really did look promising.

Cameron stopped and turned towards Mary, wrapped his arms around her, and gave her a quick kiss.

'Cameron, stop that! We're in public! This may be the new world…but I'm sure they still must conform to some rules of decorum.'

'We'll see,' he said, with a grin on his face, turning to lead her back to the disembarkation area.

After a further hour of watching the ship's cargo and baggage being off-loaded, and tons of lumber being on-loaded, Cameron and Mary were finally cleared by the port health authority. The doctor-in-charge quickly stamped their paperwork, after which he also passed on his appreciation to Mary for her help at Grosse Isle – it seemed the news about Mrs Stuart's help had already reached Quebec City as well.

Processing with Immigration was soon taken care of. The Canadian Government were still keen to receive settlers, and therefore kept the formalities to a minimum. Having cleared their final hurdle, Cameron and Mary moved towards the government information desk set up adjacent to the exit doors.

'Well, Mary, I guess that be it. We now be officially residents. Doesn't it feel good to know your wanted?'

Before she could answer, two familiar faces appeared, making their way through the crowd towards them. James and Fiona had obviously been waiting for a while, as they'd already reclaimed their baggage.

'Hello, Cameron. Hello, Mary...How's everythin' goin'?'

'Pretty good, so far,' replied Cameron.

'That's greet. Listen...we be catchin' the steamer up to Montreal later on, so why not join us?'

'Sure...that we'll do. We already have tickets. And just so you know, I think you and everyone else on board have talked us into takin' up farmin', so, we be just about to join the line over there to find out what we can about the land grants. We'll see you on board later.'

However, as Cameron and Mary soon discovered, even in the New World, bureaucracy still existed. Due to their not having pre-registered for a land grant from overseas, they now had to apply at the Ministry of Agriculture in the city, before moving on to the district administration office in Montreal. And, as it was now 4:00 p.m., the office was closed until the following day.

As Cameron threw off the covers, and swung out his legs to sit on the edge of the bed, the room began to sway. For a moment he wondered if this was all a dream, and he was still onboard the ship, but, after quickly taking in his surroundings, it all came back to him.

After the disappointment of the delay in their travel plans, he had arranged for most of their baggage to be put into storage in the arrivals hall. Then, with the help of the information desk, had located a room for the night at the Hotel Manoir – situated beside the old main gate into the city. Once settled in, he and Mary had left the hotel and strolled into the city, soon finding a cute little café for their supper. Two hours and a few drinks later, they had hurried back to their hotel, where a long night of passion ensued – their first since Cameron's shocking revelations.

Cameron's ardour now re-ignited. Then, seemingly with almost a mind of its own, his hand moved deftly under the covers, coming to rest on Mary's right breast. Taking her lack of response as a sign of approval, he rolled onto his side, sliding down the covers to reveal her slim, naked body.

'All right, Cameron…that's as far as ye go!' Mary said, quickly sitting up. We be havin' a lot to do before we catch the next steamer to Montreal.'

A little while later, Cameron and Mary stood motionless in front of the hotel's reception desk, their eyes fixed on the headline on the front page of the "Quebec Star".

STEAMER LAURENTIAN CATCHES FIRE
AND BURNS TO THE WATERLINE

It has been reported that out of the possible 300 passengers on board, at least 280 are feared dead or missing. The ship departed Quebec City yesterday afternoon for the 180-mile trip up the St. Lawrence to Montreal. At about 7 p.m., when passing Cap Rouge 12 miles west of Quebec, a fire took hold in the boiler room, which could not be brought under control. Apparently, during the Captain's attempt to beach the ship, it struck a reef, well offshore, and subsequently burned to the waterline. Most passengers drowned whilst attempting to swim ashore. A list of the victims will be published as soon as possible.

The Stuarts were speechless; and then, while Cameron stood at the desk settling their account, Mary rushed out the front door.

A few minutes later, Cameron's concern mounted, when on leaving the hotel, Mary was nowhere in sight.

'Excuse me,' he said, interrupting a couple strolling arm-in-arm past the front of the hotel. 'You haven't by chance seen a lass, dressed in a brown hat and coat, come rushing out of here…?'

'As a matter of fact, we have. She almost knocked down my wife. I think you'll find that's her…sitting over there on the park bench,' the man said, pointing over the road.

Darting across the street, Cameron sat down beside Mary, placing his arm around her and squeezing her to his chest.

'My God,' Mary sobbed, burying her face into his shoulder. 'Why is it so hard for people to build a better life? I thought the danger would be passed once we'd crossed the Atlantic. It's just no fair.'

There were times when she was so strong, thought Cameron, holding her tightly. But then, there were moments like this, when she was just another vulnerable young girl struggling to make sense of life's misfortunes. He had to admit, he'd never been much of a believer, but maybe at times like this faith did help people to come to terms with disasters, or at least give them someone to blame.

Eventually their shock gave way to numbness, and they both got up and slowly made their way towards the government's offices. One thing was for certain, thought Cameron. He had no intention of setting foot in another boat for a very, very long time.

As it turned out, the meeting with the land grant department was more than just a formality. It was a complicated process, and Cameron soon found that his lack of experience in farming put him at a distinct disadvantage. Thankfully, Mr LeBlanc, the civil servant dealing with their case, was very patient, and quickly summarised the options that were available.

'If you agree to settle to de west of Winnipeg, and can prove to us dat you have erected a permanent residence with at least one ancillary building, within 24 months, den you are entitled to a quarter-section of land…which equates to 160 acres. However, if you do not fulfil dis requirement, den you will be required to vacate de land, or buy it from de Government at a cost of $2.00 per acre.'

'But what if we settle in Quebec? My sister lives in the Eastern Townships and we would like to settle in that area… if possible.'

'Well, de rules are different for Quebec. De grant only provides for ten free acres, with an option to buy further land at a cost of $2.00 per acre.'

Cameron and Mary had already decided that they didn't really have much choice. After all, they would need all the help that they could get, and living near Margaret really was their best option.

Therefore, a little while later, with a stamped and signed "Requisition for Land" safely stored in Cameron's inside jacket pocket, the new settlers left the government building – flagging down the first empty carriage that came into sight.

Their first stop was at the arrivals hall in the port, to retrieve their personal belongings, after which Cameron directed their driver to the offices of The Quebec Steamships Lines – where he was hoping to refund their steamer tickets. As they rounded the corner of Main Street onto Pont-Neuf Road, their rig pulled up with a jolt, having nearly collided with a seething mass of people. Near riot conditions prevailed, as a half a dozen policemen struggled to control the crowd in front of the steamship line's offices. While their driver slowly manoeuvred forward, Cameron saw a man exit the office door and proceed to a notice board on the outside wall of the ticket hall. The man quickly retreated, and when he did the crowd surged forward. Moments later cries of anguish soon turned into screams of abuse.

'They're all dead!' someone yelled.

Suddenly, the crowd became hysterical, and Cameron heard the sound of breaking glass.

'We certainly no want to get mixed up in this' Cameron said, leaning forward to talk to their driver. 'Take us to the station, will you?'

As they drew away from the area, Mary visibly relaxed, her shoulders easing and her white fists unclenching.

'Don't fret yourself, Mary, we be safe now. I'll try and cash in our tickets at the company's head office in Montreal… assuming they still be in business when we get there.'

Ten minutes later they pulled up outside the railway station – their horse puffing like a steam engine and shaking his head, as if he, too, couldn't believe what they'd just been through.

It took a while for Mary's frayed nerves to calm down. However, after purchasing their tickets, checking in their luggage, and finding a place to sit down and have a drink, she began to relax.

All trains were running late that day – due to the railway's sudden increase in popularity. But, eventually, a locomotive bearing the livery of the Q.M. & O., and pulling six carriages, chugged into the station and screeched to a halt in a cloud of steam.

'Hey, Mary, look at that! 'Tis an 'American' 4-4-0!'

'All right, Cameron. Calm down. That be in the past now…remember…we're farmers now.'

In less than twenty minutes, the carriages were filled, and the Quebec Montreal and Ottawa Railway service pulled out of the station.

They barely seemed to get up a full head of steam before

the train began to slow for its stop at Cap Rouge. Suddenly, the good-humoured banter and jaunty laughter stopped. At this point on the route the tracks passed very close to the shore, and there, for all to see, was the price some had paid to try and improve their lives. Out in the river, stuck on a rock only a few hundred yards from shore, was the smoking shell of the paddle steamer "Laurentian".

What a terrible irony, thought Cameron. After leaving behind all their friends and family, putting up with deplorable mental and physical conditions, and then safely travelling thousands of miles, their lives had been extinguished by fate, and 300 yards of water.

Mary's long fingers sought the comfort and assurance of Cameron's hands, as her emotions once more overwhelmed her, and tears trickled down her face. All the while, her soulful eyes stared out the window at the smouldering monument to so many people's hopes and dreams. And when the train eventually accelerated away from the horror, her lips could be seen to move as she silently uttered a prayer.

Seventeen

Four and a half hours later, the train crossed the iron bridge on the eastern side of the island, and began to decelerate for its stop at Montreal's Bonaventure Station.

Most of the people in Cameron and Mary's carriage had long ago given up chattering, and those not staring out the windows were snoozing – sitting upright in their seats with their heads hanging down and their arms folded across their chests.

Soon, the peace was cut short, as the door between their carriage and the one ahead banged open, and in walked the uniformed ticket inspector.

'Next stop Bonaventure Station. All passengers for Ottawa remain on board. Those passengers leaving the train in Montreal please be sure to have your baggage claims ready to give to the porters on arrival.'

With the high-pitched grinding of pinched metal, and the lingering hiss of escaping air, the train came to a standstill adjacent to a long, covered platform.

Cameron and Mary didn't have long to wait for help. The moment they disembarked, uniformed porters vying for their custom assailed them. Picking one out of the melee, Cameron handed over his baggage claims. And, after the porter had retrieved their baggage, he and Mary followed him to the main concourse.

'Carriage, Monsieur?' their porter enquired, while, with great dexterity, he manoeuvred his trolley through the mad throng heading for the station's main doors.

'I'm not sure,' Cameron replied, while hoping the man

spoke more English than he did French. 'We don't really want to take all of this with us just yet. I don't suppose there be some kind of storage around here?'

'Oui, bien sur. Just down 'ere on de right.'

In no time at all, they had checked in most of their belongings at a left-luggage office, and then followed their porter to the carriage pick up point.

'Do you know where we might get a reasonable hotel for the night?' Cameron asked, as he handed over the porter's 25-cent fee.

'Most of de 'otels are on Rue St. Paul. Bien sur your driver can find you what you need.'

The early morning sun sneaking through a narrow crack in the curtains managed to find its way directly into Mary's eyes. Rolling over, she gazed for a moment at Cameron, softly snoring beside her.

I guess he isn't all bad, she thought, staring at his strong chin, rugged unshaven face and tousled, dark hair. And hopefully, he's left all that stupid Stewart family nonsense behind us.

'Come on you layabout! We've got a new life to get started,' she said, digging him in the ribs.

'Huh…what…Christ, Mary, can a person no get any rest around here?'

He never did get an answer, as Mary had already leapt out of bed and was heading for the bathroom. For the first time in their lives they had the luxury of an en-suite bathroom – as it was the only room left in the hotel by the time they'd checked in – and Mary was obviously determined to make the most of the extra 40 cents per night that it had cost them.

What Cameron didn't as yet know was that Mary had some ideas of her own, when it came to the next few days' schedule. She had never been to a big city before, and now couldn't wait to get out and some exploring.

For the next hour, Cameron listened as from the bath she told him what she had decided they were going to do that day. Although he huffed and puffed, deep down inside he was actually relieved that he'd gotten off so lightly. There were really only two matters he wanted to deal with, and as far as he was concerned the rest of their time in the city was just part of a relationship mending exercise – so he was quite happy to accede to her wishes.

After a stop in the brightly decorated café in the lobby, for their morning cup of tea, they left the Hotel Blanc. Both laughed like children as, together, they tried to shuffle through the strange revolving door; and after finally being ejected onto the sidewalk, Cameron took Mary's arm, leading her towards the left down the Rue Rivoli. One of his necessary stops was not far from the hotel, so arm-in-arm they headed for the offices of the Quebec Steamship Lines.

Thirty minutes later, they strode cheerily towards Rue St. Jacques – the main street in Montreal – three dollars richer. It seemed the steamship company, not wishing to have any more adverse publicity, was more than happy to refund their tickets.

The rest of the day was spent gazing in wonder at the goods on display, and marvelling at the architecture of the huge buildings. It was quite normal nowadays to see four and five story buildings, but here in Montreal, interspersed amongst these were other huge structures – some eight storeys high! Nearly all their facades were stone, with their windows ornately arched and divided into sections by wrought iron.

The roads looked familiar, with their springtime mixture of mud and puddles. But they were wide and neatly bordered by wooden sidewalks – at least twice the width of any they'd ever seen before. Rue St. Jacques, or as the English called it, St James Street, was now turning into the country's main financial district. Banks from Canada, England and the United States all had major branches on this street, and various insurance companies were now making this their home as well.

Cameron and Mary stopped to have lunch at a small French restaurant – sitting outside in the warm, spring sunshine. At the far end of the street, they could just make out workmen in the middle of the road, swinging their pickaxes and filling their carts; and on almost every street corner boys in flat caps stood yelling out the headlines, as they tried to persuade each passer-by to part with a few coins. Beautifully dressed ladies, sporting colourful parasols, hurried from shop-to-shop, while at the same time men in dark suits strolled purposely along, stepping aside and tipping their hats to the pressed women.

'You know, Mary? I can't get over how different this is to how I thought it would be. All I used to hear was how wild and undeveloped the Colonies were. At school, we were taught that North America was a mainly barren continent, roamed over by Indians and bison. Anytime Canada was talked about, all it seemed to be famous for was its bad weather, and dangerous natives lurking behind every bush and tree. Remember those men at the docks in Liverpool trying to sell us guns and ammo for our protection? Wouldn't you just love to send everyone a picture of us now, sitting outside a French-style restaurant, sipping lemonade and eating pastries in this wild and dangerous kingdom?'

'Let's just wait and see, shall we?'

Mid-morning the following day, Cameron and Mary sat in front of a large desk in the drab building housing the Quebec Provincial Headquarters of the Ministry of Agriculture. They were both surprised that a government department would occupy such an austere and obviously old property, but, as Cameron had whispered to Mary when their advisor left the room, 'at least they no waste the taxpayer's money on a lot of fancy buildings'.

So far, everything seemed in order, and all that was now required was the final authorisation and signature from a senior civil servant. Once this approval had been attained, their next step was to proceed to the registry office in the region in which they wished to settle, to pick out a plot.

159

'Voila...der we are. All signed and sealed,' said Mr Carvelle, on his return.

Taking his seat, he then handed Cameron the official looking document with its big red seal in the upper left-hand corner.

'Now...do you know where you'd like to live?'

'Yes...My sister and her late husband moved onto land near a place called Grenon, which I think is somewhere near the Richelieu River. We'd like to look in that area if it's possible.'

'Grenon...I t'ink dat's near Fort Lennox on de Isle aux Noix. Let me see...Yes. de local registry office is in a town called Lacolle. I'm afraid I don't have any information about de availability of land in dat area, but I hope you find what you want.'

Standing up from behind his desk, Mr Caravelle signalled the end of the meeting by offering his hand to Cameron.

'Monsieur...Madame...It's been a pleasure to meet you both, and I 'ope you find our country is what you 'ave been looking for.'

As the carriage wound its way back to their hotel, they were both astonished by the ease with which they had just become landowners. Only a month ago, they had left a country where 95% of the people could never have owned any land, and yet here they were giving it away!

'I can't believe it was that simple,' Mary said, turning to Cameron. 'I keep thinkin' I should pinch maself to see if it's real.'

'I know what you mean. Let's just hope we be able to find Margaret...and when we do, she be all right. After all, anything could have happened since she sent that letter to Helen...what ...nine months ago?'

Up until this moment, the problems of his sister had barely crossed Cameron's mind and it was only now that he was beginning to realise just how selfish he'd been. Poor Margaret, he thought. She'd been through hell with her marriage, and yet all along he'd just taken it for granted that he and Mary could descend on her and expect her help. He didn't even know if she was still in Canada, let alone in Grenon. Suddenly, for the first time in weeks, serious doubts began to cross his mind.

'Mary…if we no can find her, I think we should come back to Montreal and re-think our situation. After all, we no have to stay in that area if we no like it…and there's always the railway to fall back on.'

'Don't tell me after all we've been through you're beginnin' to have second thoughts? We're havin' a baby in six or seven months and we need to be settled!'

'No…no…it's not that. I just want you to be happy… and I'm sure that whatever we find over the next few days… well…everythin' will be fine.'

When Cameron and Mary arrived at Bonaventure Station the next morning, it was again bursting at the seams. Confidence in the shipping lines had not yet been restored, so most travellers were still opting for train travel along the St. Lawrence.

'Thank goodness we no be goin' to Quebec,' Cameron said, as they weaved their way through the crowds on the main station concourse. 'Just look at that line.'

The ticket counter for their train to New York was at the other end of the station, and, by the looks of it, not many people were travelling south.

'Where did you say you want to go?' asked the ticket agent behind the ornate glass window.

'I think it's called Cantic. I was told it's a small place near the border…just before the train crosses into the U.S.A.'

'Ah…yes…'ere it is. I don't t'ink you're going to find much of a station der. In fact, they call it a "'alt", which means de train only stops if de crew know der are passengers or freight waiting to get on or off. If you're lucky der might

161

be some cargo on board for Cantic, and somebody will be der when you arrive. If not, de nearest town is a place called Lacolle, which, I'm afraid, is a few miles down de road from de station.'

The New York Express departed on schedule, leaving the city via the Victoria Railway Bridge, spanning the St. Lawrence River at the western end of the island.

One hour later, they found themselves standing on a deserted platform surrounded by their worldly possessions.

'Well…this be a great welcome,' Mary said, rather sarcastically. 'No many cafés with pastries out here…be there?'

'All right…maybe 'tis a bit desolate. If nobody shows up in the next thirty minutes, then I'll walk down the road and see if I can find anyone.'

Thankfully, there was only a wisp of a breeze that day, because the station was in a very bleak position – devoid of any shelter from trees or shrubs. Cameron placed two of their trunks side-by-side to use as seats, and then he and Mary sat staring towards the west and the slowly descending sun. The countryside was beautiful. The green fields already planted with this year's vegetable crops alternated with golden-brown rectangles of newly sown wheat and hay. Rows of poplar and beech lined some of the fields and roads, providing windbreaks for the growing produce; while smoke drifted lazily into the windless air, from homesteads visible only as dark smudges against the rolling hills.

Without warning, their idyllic peace was shattered by the thundering of hooves. From around the bend of the road to the east, a horse and wagon suddenly appeared ahead of a wall of dust. Moments later, a wild looking individual with dirty, stringy hair sticking out from under a floppy hat, stepped down from a four wheeled wagon, and saunteed over to where they were sitting.

'Bonjour! Attendez-vous quelqu'un?'

After realizing that their mystified looks signified that they

162

didn't understand French, he quickly switched to English.

'Sorry…I just assumed you were French as most people who come 'ere are…Anyway, I'll start again…are you waiting for someone, or can I help? I'm sort of de stationmaster in dis booming city. I would have been 'ere to meet de train, but one of my cows held me up when it decided to give birth an hour ago. For dis I apologize.'

'Oh, please…'tis not a problem. Besides, we've been enjoying the peace and the scenery. My name's Cameron, Cameron Stuart, an this is ma wife, Mary.'

'How do you do? I'm Raymond Dupoint.'

'We were told in Montreal that there was always transport available here…but I'm beginnin' to think they may have exaggerated a little. We could certainly use a ride into Lacolle if that's possible… and of course, we'll pay.'

'No problem at all…and der's no charge. I 'ave to be 'ere anyway to pick up any mail and cargo dat might arrive. So, just give me a minute while I check de office, den we can load up your baggage and be on our way.'

Soon, they were on the road heading east, and sitting in the only place available – a sprung, bench type seat, just long enough for the three of them to sit on. Mary was in the middle, with Raymond in control on the right and Cameron hanging on for dear life on the left. Behind them were all their possessions, plus two mailbags and two other boxes. In deference to Mary's comfort, the pace this time was much more sedate. And, although still not exactly comfortable, the ride was pleasant enough for them to enjoy the countryside, while still maintaining a conversation with Raymond.

'I'm sorry about de lack of comfort, Mrs Stuart. Had I known you were coming I would 'ave brought something more suitable. By the way, why would you choose dis part of Canada in which to settle? From what we've 'eard most immigrants are going to Toronto…or even out west to de prairies.'

'Actually, Cameron's family knows someone who lives

near here, in a place called Grenon. So, it seemed the obvious choice to make.'

'Ah…now I see. What's der name? Maybe I know dem.'

'Her name is Margaret Grant. Unfortunately, her husband died last year, but we're hopin' she still be here… somewhere.'

'No…it's not a name I recognize. Not surprising really, because I live in de opposite direction to Grenon. Anyway, where would you like to go in Lacolle?'

'We be hopin' to stop at the Land Registry office,' Cameron replied, 'and then maybe get some information from them about where I might find Mrs Grant.'

'I'm afraid you're out of luck der, because der only open in the morning. Do you 'ave anywhere to stay?…because, if not, Madame Bouchard sometimes 'as rooms available. I could take you der if you like…although I must warn you…she is a widow and knows 'ow to talk. Den again, she might be of some 'elp to you, because she knows everybody around 'ere…and probably in de whole of Quebec as well,' Raymond chuckled.

Cameron did manage to stay on board for the rest of the trip, as he soon learned the knack of bracing the outside of his foot against the bottom of the springs, thereby counteracting the tendency to fall out. Along the way, he also discovered that this wagon was called a buckboard; and according to Mr Dupoint, it was the most useful piece of equipment one could own – and not surprisingly, he just happened to know where there was one was for sale.

That evening, over a delicious dinner served by Madame Bouchard's daughter, Evelynne, they spoke at some length. Or should one say, Madame Bouchard spoke at some length, about the history of nearly every family in the area. Thankfully, it appeared that the Stuart's would not be required to reveal much about their history; and when their chance to speak finally did arrive, they only needed to mention Margaret and Peter's name before Madam, once more, assumed control of the conversation.

'Oh...I know all about dat Mrs Grant and 'er husband. She was a nice lady and seemed to really enjoy de new way of life. But 'e was not satisfied being a farmer, and soon became involved in smuggling alcohol across de open border with de U.S.A. De poor woman was left to single-handedly take care of der farm, which in de end, t'roo no fault of 'er own, lost money.'

'We did hear that Margaret lost a child. Maybe that affected Peter an was why he got in with the wrong people?'

''e was an 'ard drinker...and de more 'e drank de more violent 'e became, until one day 'e almost killed Margaret. Dat is why she lost 'er baby.'

Mary reached across the table, casually placing her hand on Cameron's now rigid arm. 'So what happened to him, then?'

'One day last year 'e crossed de wrong people in Montreal, and de following night paid de ultimate price.'

'So where is ma sister? Is she still on their farm?'

'Non...I'm afraid not. 'er husband left 'er in terrible debt and she 'ad to sell off everything dey 'ad. After dat, the government took back de land and passed it on to somebody else.'

Cameron hung his head. All his doubts and worries resurfaced. Having come all this way, it now looked like they were on their own again. Reaching across the table, he grasped Mary's hand. Both their faces now bore a grim, sad look of resignation.

'Well... never mind,' Madame Bouchard said cheerily. 'Everyt'ing is now fine.'

Cameron and Mary looked at each other with furrowed brows.

'What...what do you mean?' Mary asked.

'Of course, you wouldn't know would you? She met a local man called John Williams, who 'ad lost 'is wife de year before last...Anyway, dey fell in love. And last month dey got married. Dey now live in a nice 'ouse dat 'e recently

165

built on 'is family's old farm. You'll be able to visit dem tomorrow. It's only a few miles from 'ere…near a town called Clarenceville.'

Eighteen

They both felt uneasy walking up to the house; and the smell of freshly cut timber and newly applied paint hung in the air as they climbed the three steps onto the verandah. With some trepidation, Cameron stepped up to the recently painted door and, using the metal knocker, announced their arrival.

The shadow of a tall, fit-looking man could be seen striding towards them through the lightly curtained panes of glass at the side of the door.

'Hello…can I help you?'

'Good Mornin'…You must be, John. I'm Cameron… Margaret's brother...and this be, Mary. Is Margaret in?'

For a moment, John just stood there with his mouth agape; then, taking a step back opened the door.

'I…ah…I think you'd better come in,' he stammered, before turning his head towards the back of the house. 'Margaret…can you come to the front door?'

What happened next caught everyone by surprise, but for vastly different reasons. Margaret appeared from the doorway directly ahead of them. Her head was down, as she walked towards them, while wiping her hands on a multi-patterned cloth. When she looked up, she took one more faltering step, placed her left hand on the rising handrail beside her; and then, her face turned ashen, her eyes rolled up, and without uttering a word, she collapsed to the floor.

Cameron and John froze. Mary immediately switched into nursing mode and hurried to Margaret's side. Kneeling beside the prostrate form, she immediately turned Margaret's body onto her side and started issuing orders to the dumfounded men.

'Someone get a cushion and place it beneath Margaret's feet. John…can you get me a wet cloth from the kitchen…but before you do, tell Cameron where he might find a blanket to keep Margaret warm.'

Both men scampered away to complete their assigned tasks, and within minutes returned – standing rigid beside Margaret's prone body.

'Stand back and give her some air! John, do you have any Salt of Hartshorn…or Sal Volatile?'

John stared at her with a blank look on his face, so Mary tried again.

'Ammonia, John. It might be called ammonia over here.'

John immediately rushed upstairs. Seconds later the sound of doors opening and slamming shut, interspersed with the creaking of floorboards, kept those below posted as to his progress. Finally, with a gleeful shout of 'Here it is!' he raced down the stairs – almost falling over his poor wife's motionless body in his haste to hand over the small corked bottle.

'Can you two just calm down a wee bit? She's only fainted. If you carry on like this it'll be one of you that'll be needin' serious medical attention.'

Pouring a small amount of the liquid onto a cloth, she slowly passed it under Margaret's nose. Almost immediately, Margaret's head moved away from the foul odour, and her hand came up to push away the offensive solution: followed by a sneeze and a cough, before her head slowly began to rise from the floor.

'Oh my goodness…what happened?'

For the second time that morning, Margaret's eyes took in the sight of her brother standing in the hallway.

'But…but you're dead!'

'I assure you I'm no dead, Maggie. Far from it in fact! Oh…and by the way…this kind lady who just took care of you is Mary, my wife…and she's quite alive as well.'

When Margaret had fully recovered, they all followed her

into the kitchen – a unanimous decision having been taken to have a cup of tea before any more surprises were produced.

'Why don't the three of you just sit down while I fill up the kettle? I have a feeling this might turn into a rather lengthy discussion,' John said, moving towards the sink.

Before Cameron could pull out a chair, Margaret rushed over, throwing her arms around him. And, even though tears streamed down her face, her eyes were warm and her smile seemed to light up the room.

'Oh, Cameron…I'm so happy to see you. But before we go any further, I'll just go and get something that might help to explain what just happened in there.'

Margaret was gone for ten minutes; and while John poured the boiling water into the china pot on the table, they could all hear the sounds of drawers opening and closing upstairs. Margaret soon reappeared, walking towards them while unfolding a newspaper. Smoothing the winkles from the front page, she carefully set it down on the table in front of her brother.

Cameron and Mary's eyes bulged from their sockets, as they took in the headline on the front page of the Montreal Star.

LADY ELGIN LOST AT SEA!
All Presumed Lost as Ship Founders
During Storm in the Bay of Biscay'

No wonder Margaret had fainted, thought Cameron. She must have thought she'd seen a ghost. He'd known all along that their showing up in Canada would be a shock to Margaret, especially as he'd told her in a letter that he and Mary were emigrating to Australia, on the "Lady Elgin", April the 21st. But all of his careful planning could never have foreseen this. What he couldn't quite understand, though, was why he and Mary had not heard about the sinking.

As he read on, it all began to make sense. The "Lady Elgin" had left Campbeltown the day before their departure from Liverpool, but would have still been well to the north of them when the "Allepo" passed the southern tip of Ireland heading out into the Atlantic. Therefore, the storm he and Mary had had to endure must have been the same one that hit the "Lady Elgin", only a few days later when she was in the Bay of Biscay. And by the time he and Mary had finally reached Quebec, the loss would already have been old news and no longer on the front pages – particularly in light of the burning of the paddle steamer "Laurentian".

Cameron looked at his sister. He could tell from her questioning expression that he had a lot of explaining to do, and was now beginning to regret he'd even considered involving Maggie in his escapade. Although she was only six years older, her face told a different story. The wrinkles at the corners of her eyes were those of a much older woman and, even though her hair was well brushed and neatly drawn back into a bun on the back of her head, the first wisps of grey could already be seen creeping from the edges of her temple. My God, what have I done? She's already been to hell and back and now I'm starting it all over again.

'I think you'd better sit down Maggie. I've got a long story to tell, and I'm afraid some of it's no very pleasant. Before I start, though, I just want you both to know that I'm really sorry I've involved you in this…and when I'm finished, I'll understand if you decide we'd better move on. And one last thing...Mary had nothing to do with what I'm about to tell you. In fact, I didn't even tell her until the night before we sailed from Liverpool.'

For the next hour, nobody interrupted as Cameron recounted the story. He glossed over his early years, and began at the point where Helen had told him about his family's history; and then finished by laying bare his soul – leaving out nothing, as he tried to justify his actions.

'I'm sorry if what I've been doin' seems wrong to you… and just so as you know…I do feel a terrible guilt about the lad bein' killed. But I still think I was right to try and avenge

170

my father…and will no apologise for gettin' involved with some other people who were just looking for a way to better their lives.'

Mary carefully listened in case she had got something wrong, or somehow over-reacted. But the confession had been the same; and now two more people knew of his family's chequered history, and Cameron's unspeakable deeds.

To Cameron's surprise, when he'd finished, Margaret's first words were not of condemnation, but questions of detail. It was almost as if she had made herself judge and jury, and she alone would be the one to decide his innocence or guilt.

'I understand if you be shocked and aggrieved by what I've done. All I ask is that you never repeat any of this to anyone else… and if you ever be questioned about us…please just say as far as you know, Mary and I were lost at sea on the "Lady Elgin".'

Cameron got up from the table, and turning to Mary, held out his hand.

'Let's you and I go and have a look 'round. I'm sure John and Margaret would probably like to be alone now.'

As they stepped out the kitchen door and made their way towards the steps leading to the back garden, Cameron took Mary's hand and turned her to face him.

'Well…there be one good thing to come out of this…at least the authorities, and old man Campbell, should no longer be lookin' for us.'

'I just hope you be right.'

To their surprise, Cameron and Mary discovered that the verandah they had so admired at the front of the house actually extended all the way around to the back. Leaning against the rail, they gazed out in admiration at what Margaret and John had accomplished. On each side of the path leading from the back steps to the outbuildings, there was a large chestnut tree, providing ample shade from the afternoon sun. And, running parallel to the verandah were flowerbeds – planted with bright yellow daffodils and flowering shrubs festooned with small pink buds. At the far end of each bed small conifer trees had been planted, marking out the corners of the house, which at the same time provided a fresh pine fragrance to the summer breeze when carried in through the windows.

The backyard itself was enclosed by post and rail fencing – accessed by three five-bar gates. On the right side of the yard a gate gave entry to two small outbuildings, while the one on the left led to a well-worn track meandering off through some planted fields towards a forest in the distance.

Directly ahead of Cameron and Mary was the gate giving access to the corral. On its far side stood a stone and timber barn, while on its right, part of the enclosure was taken up by a stable. The upper part of the stable door was open, and standing with its head and neck through this gap was a large black horse – returning their gaze with one large, round eye, and shaking its head as if daring them to approach.

'Isn't it beautiful here, Cameron? Do you think we could have a farm like this one day…and maybe a nice house as well? '

'I don't see why not. Of course, we have a lot to learn first. As it stands right now, I barely know the back end of a cow from the front.'

At that moment the kitchen door opened. Margaret went over to Mary, wrapping her arms around her, while John – with a smile on his face – put out his hand as he approached Cameron.

'I know I haven't said much since you two got here…but as Margaret will probably tell you…I like to listen and think awhile, before opening my mouth. Now, it seems to me, the story I've just heard is about a man who just wants justice, and a little better life for his family. What you did might be wrong in the eyes of the law, but in my mind, you were trying to make a point that should have been made a long time ago. All right, it went wrong, but if enough people took a similar stand maybe the bloody English would learn a lesson…and everyone would be better off.'

Cameron raised his finger.

'I know…I know,' John said, putting up both his hands. 'Yes…I'm English. But believe me…we people south of the border suffered almost as much as you. Dare I say…if Bonnie Prince Charlie had got to London things might well have been a whole lot different…and Canada might not be getting twenty thousand people a month arriving on its shores. Let me just finish by saying that Margaret and I will help you as much as we can…and you're welcome to stay with us until you're settled. We can't condone what you did, but we do understand why you did it.'

Nineteen

The dim light of sunrise brought a knock at the door – followed by Margaret breezing into the room.

'Good morning,' she said cheerily, placing two cups of tea on the bedside table before throwing open the curtains. 'Just so you know… makin' a success in this type of life means out of bed at sun up, and doin' chores until mid-morning. Then it's breakfast, followed by field work…then….'

'All right…all right, I get it,' Cameron grumbled.

'Oh…and just so you know. This is the first and last cup of anythin' that you'll be gettin' in bed…so make the most of it,' she chuckled. 'I'm always up first…and downstairs you'll find coffee in the pot and water on the boil for tea and a wash.'

By the end of that first day every muscle in Cameron's body was complaining, and he was seriously beginning to have doubts about his change in career. The day had been a blur: trying to learn how to control a horse as it pulled a plough; wielding an axe to restock the kitchen woodpile, lifting and bracing wagons and hayricks, as John removed, repaired and refitted wheels to ensure the equipment was ready when needed, and finally, repairing fencing. It had been a while since Cameron had been outdoors doing manual labour, but even when he had started out track laying, they hadn't done it from sun up to sun down with barely a break.

What Cameron and Mary hadn't appreciated was that certain jobs – like feeding animals, milking cows and collecting eggs – had to be done every day, irrespective of weather, illness, tiredness or relatives just happening to drop by!

Mary found the change in lifestyle quite invigorating, although at times she did wonder if Margaret had once been trained as a matron by the ease with which she gave orders. But what she didn't as yet know was that the really hard work hadn't even started.

It was during their second evening that John sat down in his easy chair with a pen and some paper, and began the first of many long evenings planning Cameron and Mary's new venture.

'Right…now that we've caught up, tomorrow after breakfast we're going to the registry office in Lacolle, to make enquiries about land availability in the area. Now, the first thing you're going to need is…let me see….'

It soon became apparent to Cameron that they wouldn't have stood any chance of doing this on their own. To start with, it had never dawned on him that the most important consideration was access to good water, while at the same time ensuring they weren't so close to a major water source that flooding could become a problem during the spring thaw. Next on John's list of essentials was a sizeable amount of woodland. Trees were obviously necessary to provide buildings, fuel and fencing. But what Cameron hadn't appreciated was that their location was just as important, as one of their primary roles was to act as a buffer against the wind – which if left unchecked could destroy nearly any crop.

Lastly, if at all possible, the land needed to be on rolling hills so the house and outbuildings could be set high and dry – well above the cold, damp valleys.

'But how am I supposed to achieve all this on just ten acres of land?' Cameron asked, as frustration began to creep into his voice.

'You're not. What we have to do is find a suitable ten acre plot surrounded by this type of land. Then, you buy as much land as you can afford around your initial plot. If you don't have enough money you can sign for the land, and then make

175

annual payments – with interest – to the government. The only requirement is the payments must start within one year of the date of the agreement, and that you must clear the debt within ten years. I believe the current price to purchase land is $2.00 per acre for arable, and $1.50 for woodland, so, over the next few days you want to be thinking about how much land you can actually afford.'

The following morning, Cameron sat up in bed with a start. Moments later, it became obvious what had woken him, as he listened to John and Margaret's roosters trying to out-crow each other. One thing was for sure. The sun did not rise peacefully in this part of the world.

Beside him, Mary yawned, and then reached out for a hug – smiling at his grumpy face.

'Oh…dear. Someone's no very happy.'

'You know what Mary? I think I've almost gotten used to this early rising. And I can't wait until I be first up…so I can go and scream in those bloody birds' ears!'

'You were late last night. How did you get on yesterday?'

'Great! I can barely walk and I can't lift my arms above my head…apart from that, just great.'

'Well, I really enjoyed my day. I fed the chickens and collected the eggs. Then we went off to the barn…where I learned how to milk a cow. After breakfast, Margaret and I went down to the root cellar, where we picked out the vegetables that be startin' to rot and took them out to feed the pigs. Muckin' out came next, which were no much fun, followed by back to the kitchen for cookin' and bread makin'.'

While they both got dressed Mary carried on, excitedly talking about the rest of the previous day. Cameron listened without comment, but each time she turned, and he caught sight of her face, her cheeks were glowing and her eyes sparkled. Pregnancy must suit her, he decided. She seems to become more beautiful each day. And, if this life really does make her happy then, after what I've put her through, the least I can do is try to make sure that we make a success of this.

It was a lovely late spring morning as Cameron sat with John in the buckboard, heading to Lacolle for their meeting with the land registry. Although the rig jolted and swayed each time they caught a rut, Cameron was now beginning to feel much more secure. As John occupied himself trying to miss the worst of the potholes, Cameron's mind went back over the previous night's conversation.

'So, tell me, John…how much land do you think we need?'

'Well, to start with, you need to have enough pasture for a cow, a couple of horses and an ox…which is about four acres. Then you'll need another four acres to grow winter feed. Now let's see…the house, barn and a couple of other buildings will take up about two acres…and Mary will want about half an acre for kitchen vegetables. Oh…and you'll need at least an acre for a couple of hogs.

'Well that sounds o.k.'

'Hang on a minute, Cameron. That's just what you need to feed yourselves and your animals. We now have to figure out what crops you're going to grow for market. I would suggest you plant maybe 10 acres of wheat, 5 acres of oats, 2 acres of peas and maybe an acre of potatoes. As I told you before, woodland is where people make their biggest mistake. They just don't buy enough…and don't forget, some of it can always be cleared in the future if you need more growing land. If I had my time again I'd try to get at least 30 acres of woodland. Oh, and keep in mind, you need to allow for more pasture and hay if you plan to increase the number of animals you own. So, what it boils down to is this. If you can afford to carry the loan for a couple of years…I'd say you want to be looking for about 65-75 acres. Ten of that's free...so the rest will cost you about $115.00.'

'That be fine. Mary and I can afford that... So I don't think I'll need to go into debt with the government.'

'Wait a minute, Cameron. You've got to buy livestock, farming equipment and seed, not to mention a house, barn and other buildings...and keep in mind, you won't have any income for nearly a year.'

'Get on Blackie,' bellowed John, as he snapped the reins, dragging Cameron back to the present. Ten minutes later they arrived in Lacolle.

John took over the meeting with the registrar, and thanks to his knowledge of the area, managed to narrow down the available plots to two. The registrar was happy to reserve both lots for Cameron, for a seven-day period; and after promising to return with a decision within a week, he and John left.

'I'll tell you what we should do,' John said, as they headed for home. If it's a nice day on Sunday, why don't we get the girls to make us a picnic? Then, after church, the four of us can go and have a look at those two plots, and have lunch down by the river.'

'I guess that would be nice,' Cameron said, rather hesitantly, after glancing over his shoulder at the bouncing buckboard.

Sunday soon arrived. Cameron and Mary were now both aware that cows, hens, pigs and horses did not have a day of rest; but, as it turned out, with four people in the house to share the chores, the livestock's needs were easily taken care of by mid-morning.

After a filling breakfast of bacon and eggs, followed by oatmeal topped with John's own maple syrup, the ladies retired upstairs to change into their Sunday best. In the meantime, the two men headed out to the stables to harness up the buckboard – or so Cameron thought.

'Cameron…can you go to the stable and bring Blackie over to the small barn for me? I've just got to get the harness sorted out. I'll meet you there.'

Cameron did as told, even though he was still a little uncomfortable handling the stallion. Ten minutes later, he led Blackie by his bridle towards the front doors of the small barn. On his arrival, the doors swung open, and as they did Cameron's mouth hung open. In the doorway stood John, with a grin on his face; while behind him was a pretty little trap – ready to be harnessed up. Two padded bench-type seats, mounted on curved steel supports, spanned the carriage from side to side. Above the seating area was a white canvass top – with sides extending down about a foot to protect the passengers from rain or too much sun. The carriage sat on four equal-sized wheels, whose axles were mounted on sprung-steel suspension – thereby ensuring a comfortable ride for all the passengers.

'You didn't think we'd go to church in that old buckboard, did you?' John chuckled.

The local church was Catholic, but its service was fairly close to the Scottish Presbyterian form of prayer – so the newcomers did not feel completely out of place.

After the service, the parishioners stood around in small groups passing the time of day. If it hadn't sunk in before, then Cameron and Mary were now left in no doubt that the whole community's life revolved around the seasons. The men mainly talked about which crops seemed to be coming on best, and what price a bushel of spring wheat would probably fetch at the market in two weeks' time; whereas the women gathered in two small groups: in one passing tips back and forth about new methods for filtering water to increase their yield of lye for soap making, whilst in the other, one woman excitedly passed on rumours that she'd heard about a new type of clothes wringer, which apparently could be fitted to their washing barrels and significantly reduce their hardship.

The weather did co-operate, and an hour after church they approached the small village of Noyan – a few miles to the south of Lacolle.

The first plot that John had recommended was just east of the village alongside a small stream emptying into the Richelieu River. A minor road ran parallel to the river, and ten minutes after passing through the village they reached the spot where a bridge crossed over the small stream.

Cameron helped the ladies down, while John tied off Blackie's bridle on the branch of a nearby elm tree.

'Come on…let's see if there's any kind of path or animal trail around here that might give us an easy way up. I'm sure we'll get the best view from up there,' John said, as he crossed the road and pointed towards the top of a grassy hill in the distance.

When they finally reached the summit, they were all puffing a little. Cameron and Mary were both bent over at the waist, their hands resting on their knees. Neither was yet accustomed to such a vigorous life; and after they recovered, Cameron took Mary aside, quietly talking to her for a few minutes before once more re-joining John and Margaret.

The land surrounding them looked perfect to Cameron, but he now knew better than to voice any opinion until John had made up his mind. In the meantime, Margaret grasped Mary's arm and the two wandered off, animatedly talking and pointing to places where a house would be perfect, and a garden protected from the wind. John slowly wandered about at the crest of the hill, checking on the land's access to water, and its suitability for buildings and roads. Having spent more than an hour marching here and there, and bending over to check the grass and type of soil, John's only comment was 'we'll see'.

As the sun began its descent, all four lay stretched-out on a blanket beside the river, basking in the warm spring sunshine. The location was idyllic, and for the time being everyone seemed absorbed watching the fluttering butterflies in the meadow beside them, and gazing at small fish leaping for their lunch – or possibly leaping to not become lunch – at the junction of the stream and the fast flowing river.

The few remaining titbits had already been packed away, and in the end it was John who suggested doing the same with the home-brewed cider, before the rest of the day was a total loss. Cameron rolled over on his side, winking at Mary, while the other two looked on with quizzical expressions on their faces.

'Mary and I have something to tell you. I suppose we should have mentioned it before…but…well anyway, now's as good a time as any.'

Mary had wanted to put off the announcement, because only last week Margaret had told her the harrowing story of her life with Peter, and the loss of her baby; and as if that wasn't bad enough, it emerged that she would never again be able to have a child. However, Mary knew her own body would soon reveal her condition, so silence was no longer an option.

With a suitably long pause, to allow Margaret and John's minds to conjure up all manner of shocking developments, Cameron continued.

'You two are goin' to become an Aunt and Uncle!'

The Monday morning chorus came all too soon – especially as more cider had been uncorked Sunday evening to celebrate the Stuarts' forthcoming arrival. Margaret and John had appeared to be really excited and insisted on spending the evening toasting every notion that entered their well-lubricated minds. At times during the evening, Margaret's eyes took on a far-away look, but then within minutes, her self-assured character took over once more and she re-joined the party with gusto.

Cameron's head pounded as he entered the kitchen. Even the habitually cheerful Margaret seemed somewhat subdued, murmuring a much quieter 'good morning' than was usual. Cameron grunted in reply, before sitting at the table to cradle his mug of tea. Five minutes later Mary entered the kitchen, and with a bright and cheery 'hello' joined the others.

'You shouldn't be down here yet. Nothing is so important that you need to get out of bed so early,' protested Margaret.

'Oh, come on, Margaret. I only be havin' a baby…no dyin' from some terrible disease. I'm able to do ma jobs around here…just like everybody else.'

Arguably, the farm wife's most onerous tasks took place each Monday and Tuesday. Washing was first, and its steps were many: water had to be drawn from the well and then heated on the stove; after which it was poured into a wooden tub; clothes and lye were then added before being agitated by a five pronged piece of wood known as a dolly stick; more buckets of water followed, until all the lye was rinsed from the clothes; and then finally all items were wrung out by hand before being hung out to dry.

Mondays were bad, but Tuesday just compounded the torment, as it was the day normally reserved for ironing. Although irons were relatively small, they were extremely heavy, and had to be continually re-heated on the stovetop. This job again took nearly all day, by the end of which most women were exhausted.

Of course, the saving grace for Cameron and Mary was that they were afforded a gentle introduction into this way of life. Living with Cameron's sister not only allowed them to learn how to run a farm, but at the same time absolved them from having to find a roof for their heads and food for their bellies.

Both were pleasantly surprised by the quantity and variety of food they ate on the farm. There never seemed to be a shortage of vegetables, and meat was in abundance. Biscuits, cakes and bread were also a staple in their diets – one or more of these being cooked every day. Of course, all of this cooking required a ready supply of wood for the ovens, and Mary soon learned that the hard work of hauling wood to keep the fires going was another of the women's jobs.

Cameron had never worked so hard in his life. Harvesting the spring wheat was immediately followed by ploughing the fields to prepare them for a summer crop. In the past, John had always done this by himself, but with the extra help, he was now able to plant more crops and look forward to a larger income if the harvest was good.

Twenty

The land they had chosen was the second plot they had looked at on that Sunday. Cameron had gone to Lacolle the following day to register the plot, and at the same time had put down their names for seventy adjoining acres.

Both properties had been on similar types of rolling countryside, and both had comparable access to water and roads. But the second property had one main advantage. The section of forest attached to the land was larger and on its western side, thereby providing better shelter from the prevailing wind – this being particularly important when the snow-laden winds of winter blew for weeks at a time.

From the day of registration onwards, the only topic of discussion became the Stuarts' new property. Hours were spent discussing everyone's ideas, and making countless drawings of the house and its outbuildings. The pros and cons of various crops were endlessly considered, until a final decision was made and an outline map drawn up, separating the acreages into workable fields. By the end of the summer only one major decision was left – namely the size and type of farmhouse. Of course, the Stuarts would love to build as near a replica of John and Margaret's house as possible. But in the end common sense prevailed, and a single storey log house was agreed upon.

'Listen, Cameron. I know it's not what you two really want, but for now it will be fine. Look at the advantages. They're easy to build, and you've got all the wood you'll need on your own land. Also, because they're a simple design, you and Mary can have the interior layout any way you like. And besides…after a couple of decent harvests, you should have all the money you'll need to build whatever you like and still have somewhere to live while your new house is being built.'

During their spare time, Mary and Margaret threw all their enthusiasm into designing the interior of the new home. Cameron was more than happy to let the girls get on with it, especially as Mary needed something to help occupy her mind. She was now finding it more and more difficult to help with some of the more physical work, and "matron" Margaret was seriously beginning to restrict Mary's jobs.

Cameron lay with his head propped up against two pillows, desperately trying to keep his eyes open as Mary exuberantly explained the layout she and Margaret had come up with.

'We think the baby's room can be just there,' she said, pointing to a spot on the paper. 'And our room will be right next door. The fire in the stove will be burnin' all night in the winter, so I'll have a chair over there…and that way I'll be warm when I'm feedin' the baby.'

''Tis a great idea,' Cameron mumbled, trying to put on his best "that's really interesting" look on his face. 'Do you know somethin'?'

'What?'

'You look even more beautiful now than when we first met.'

'No, I don't. I'm fat and horrible…and besides…I hate you,' she replied, playfully hitting him with a balled up fist. 'You're no payin' any attention to what I be showin' you, are you?'

'Of course I am.'

Having said that, he picked up the papers and threw them on the floor, then placed his right hand on her shoulder, forcing her back onto the pillow. Just as she was about to rebuke him he leaned forward, placing his mouth over hers.

185

As he ran his tongue over her lips, she began to sigh, so he eased his hand into the bodice of her nightdress.

'Don't you be gettin' any funny ideas,' Mary whispered, pushing him away. 'They be right through that wall and can hear every noise we make.'

'All right, I know,' he said, rolling back onto his side of the bed. 'I guess I'll just have to ravish you outside one of these days…when nobody's lookin'.'

The autumn came, and with it arrived the most hectic time of the year. John kept a wary eye on the weather as a judgement had to be made about when to begin the harvest.

One morning, when Cameron entered the kitchen for his morning cup of tea, he sensed something was unusual.

'What is it? Has something happened?'

'Nope…everything's fine,' John replied. 'But when you're finished that tea we're starting the harvest. The wind has changed…and I'm pretty sure rain will be here by the end of the week.'

The next three days were like nothing Cameron had ever witnessed, as he and John worked non-stop from sunrise to sunset. The women brought out breakfast, dinner, supper and drinks to whichever field they were working in. And, as the light began to fade, they brought in and fed the animals: followed by the men returning to the house for a quick wash before going to bed. The job was backbreaking for both men and animals, with the routine continuing until just before sunset on day three – when the task was finally completed. Two exhausted men staggered into the kitchen, collapsing into chairs at the kitchen table.

'Well, I'm glad that be over,' Cameron remarked.

'Kind of….'

Cameron looked over at John, his eyebrows raised inquisitively.

'Well, we're finished here, Cameron…but I told some of

our neighbours we'd give them a hand once we were done. You see, I knew we'd get our harvest in first, because most of our friends are on their own. And I was sure you wouldn't mind helping them once we were finished, seeing as how they're the ones who'll be helping us build your house and barns this winter.'

The farmers living in the Eastern Townships were lucky that year. The rain held off for two more days, allowing all of them to get in their harvests; and with the ever increasing population in Canada creating an ever burgeoning demand, the price of all produce was high.

I guess this is a profitable occupation, Cameron thought, after returning from the market with John. But you sure do have to work to make it pay.

Once John's fields had been turned over in preparation for winter, and all their winter vegetables had been put away in the cold cellar, work was finally switched to Cameron and Mary's new property. John borrowed a straight-faced plough from one of his neighbours, and with this implement attached to his ox, the first task of creating access into the property began. Within a week a lane had been cut in, and the property staked out for the house and buildings. Another road was then excavated towards the forest – great care being taken in its construction, as it would be the most frequently travelled track over the next year. And then finally, the area was levelled where all the buildings were to be sited.

As they completed the last of the groundwork, the days were getting noticeably shorter. The beautiful autumn festival of colour was now over; and according to John early morning frosts would soon be upon them. The ox had already been returned to John's pasture, and work now switched to the gruelling toil of felling trees.

One late November afternoon, the sun was nearly down as Cameron and John arrived back from the new homestead.

187

'I'll put Blackie away...I've still got a few things to do in the barn,' John said, removing the wagon's harness and leading the horse towards the stable.

'All right...I'll be seein' if the girls need a hand with anythin' inside.'

Cameron headed for the house and on opening the back door the first thing he saw was Mary slumped over the kitchen table.

Slamming the door, he hurried across the kitchen, quickly dropping to one knee and putting his arm around her.

'Mary...Mary, what is it? Are you sick?'

Mary slowly raised her head, greeting Cameron with a weak and sickly smile.

'I'm all right...I'm just a wee bit tired.'

At that point Margaret arrived in the kitchen carrying a huge pile of clothes.

'What's going on here? Mary, you look dreadful...Come on, Cameron, let's get her up to bed, then I'm going for the doctor. And, Mary...before you even think about it...I don't want to hear any of this 'I'm fine' nonsense.'

Later that night, the three of them sat in the front room, with looks of impending doom upon their faces. After what seemed like ages, the clumping of boots could be heard descending the stairs, and they all looked up, expectantly.

'You can all stop looking like there's been some death in the family,' said Dr. Fitzpatrick. 'Mrs Stuart's going to be fine. She's just a bit tired...and needs to take it a bit easier... especially as there's only a few weeks to go now. I'll stop by again tomorrow, to check up on her.'

Then, as he put on his coat and prepared to leave, he turned to Cameron.

'Oh, and if you want to see her, Mr Stuart, you best hurry, as I've given her something to help her sleep.'

Once they'd all thanked the doctor and said goodbye, Cameron bounded up the stairs.

'Are you okay, Mary? You've had us all worried, you know?'

She was obviously very groggy, and as Cameron leaned forward to kiss her cheek, she began to mumble.

'I'm s...sorry Cameron. I've got somethin' to tell...'

She never finished before falling asleep. Cameron kissed her on the forehead, before pulling the covers up to her chin. Then, blowing out the candle, he quietly crept from the room.

The following morning, Mary awoke bright and cheerful, obviously feeling few ill-effects from the night before. As they relaxed in bed, she gaily chatted to Cameron – grilling him about the progress of their new home, while at the same time carefully avoiding any reference to the night before.

Over the next few weeks a new routine was established, and much to Mary's disgust, her role had been reduced to an absolute minimum. All the morning chores were now completed by the other three before the men set off for the new farm. Cameron and John would then arrive back well before sunset, to carry out the afternoon milking and settle the animals down for the night. Margaret now took care of nearly all the household chores, including the most onerous – ensuring Mary did very little. She was allowed to help with the cooking and baking, but only after first promising she would have an hour's rest during the afternoon.

November rolled into December; and with it the temperatures plummeted. Cameron and Mary had thought they were used to cold weather, but never had they experienced it so early in the winter, or for weeks at a time.

'You'd better get used to it,' John commented one evening, as they all sat around a roaring fire in the front room. 'In this part of Canada we have long, cold winters. Just be thankful the snow hasn't started yet.'

Twenty One

A glimmer of light was peaking through the curtains as Mary tugged on Cameron's arm.

'Cameron…Listen…Can you hear that?'

'Hear what?' he replied, his eyes slowly opening.

'Exactly…it's so quiet. It's like the end of the world.'

Rolling out of bed, Cameron hopped across the cold floor to the window. As he threw back the curtains, the reason for the silence became all too apparent.

'Wait till you see this. Everythin' is white. There must be two feet of snow out there…and 'tis still comin' down…in great big flakes.'

Mary threw off the covers, and as quickly as her condition would allow, walked over to the window.

'Oh, isn't it beautiful? It looks like everythin' is wrapped up in cotton wool.'

Mary put her arm around Cameron's waist, pulling him closer.

'One thing's for sure…I don't think you and John will be goin' anywhere today...which means I can have you all to maself.'

By mid morning, the men had finished the outdoor chores, and then hurried in to the kitchen to stand by the stove – stamping their feet and rubbing their hands. Although the snow had stopped falling, the wind had picked up, and outside was fast becoming a place to avoid. Gusts whipped the snow across the yard, and drifts began to build wherever the blasts of air were deflected from their course. Cameron stared out the window at the tempest, suddenly appreciating why the house was surrounded by a verandah – set three feet off the ground. There was nothing else needing to be done, so the men retired to the living room, and settled in to their now daily discussions about Cameron and Mary's enterprise, and their plans for the future.

In the meantime, the training continued in the kitchen. Today the secret of how to preserve fruits and jams was disclosed, and Margaret demonstrated how to seal in the contents of the jars with beeswax.

The wind continued to howl all day; and the visibility was now so poor that when Cameron made another quick trip to the back porch to collect more wood, it was impossible for him to tell whether or not it was still snowing. Hopefully, that will be the last trip outside today, he thought, kicking the back door shut and dumping his armful of wood into the basket beside the stove.

'When you're done, Cameron, can you go and get John for me?'

Margaret seemed a bit tense, he thought. And then, as he started to walk out of the kitchen, he noticed the puddle spreading out from beneath Mary's chair.

'What is it, Mary? What's happening?'

'I'm sure she'll be fine,' Margaret said. 'Her waters have broken and the baby's on the way.'

'Oh no, it cannot be…not on a day like this!' Cameron exclaimed.

'Just calm down,' said Mary. 'Everythin' will be fine. If we no can get Dr. Fitzpatrick then I'll talk Margaret through the birth.'

Cameron hurried down the hall, calling out for John. Even though Mary had assured him all would be well, he was still worried. This just wasn't fair, he thought. After everything that he'd put Mary through, he'd just wanted this to be easy for her.

'I'll go for the doctor, John. After all she is my wife, and if anyone has to take any chances then it should be me.'

'Cameron, you need to be here with Mary, and Margaret will need your help as well…Besides…I know the way a lot better than you do.'

'Listen, John. I couldn't live with the guilt if anythin' were to happen to you. Margaret has already gone through too much pain in her life.'

It was an argument Cameron was never going to win.

Under normal circumstances, John could have been there and back in less than an hour. But in this weather, it was impossible to say how long it would take – assuming he could get there at all.

Margaret helped Mary up the stairs, while Cameron remained in the kitchen, in charge of supplies. The instructions from Mary had been simple: get two big pots of water and keep them simmering on the stove; then go to the airing cupboard and get three old white sheets from the stack on the top shelf, and cut them into four foot squares; and finally, make some coffee, and sit down and drink it until you're called.

Cameron knew labour could sometimes go on for a long time, so he sat down and made a conscious effort to relax. After all, as Margaret had said, the doctor would probably be here long before the baby was born anyway.

Two hours later, as Cameron sipped his third cup of coffee, the call he had hoped not to hear until after the doctor arrived, came from upstairs.

'Cameron! Bring me some of that water and the cloths…now!'

'I thought this went on for hours,' he said, after setting down the two bowls of hot water.

'Sometimes it does,' Mary replied, 'but I guess our wee bairn is in a hurry to come into the world…now sit down and hold ma hand. I want you here with me.'

'Now, Margaret, listen carefully…'

'Oh, Mary…I'm not sure I can do this.'

'Of course you can. You've helped deliver a calf, haven't you?'

192

'Yes…'

'Well, it be nearly the same…so pay attention.'

Mary's intermittent cries of pain did very little to reassure Cameron. His mind was now in such a state that he no longer heard the flow of instructions being issued by his wife; while at times he squeezed her hand so hard that Mary's cries were directed at him. His eyes remained riveted on hers, as his mouth babbled a continuous stream of superfluous encouragement.

Finally, after an hour of unimaginable distress for both mother and father, the baby made its appearance; and immediately wailed to announce its presence.

Margaret quickly cleaned up the squirming infant, and wrapped him in a blanket before handing the little red-headed boy back to his mother.

'I'll leave you three alone for a while. If you need anything just call,' Margaret said, with tears beginning to show in the corners of her eyes.

'I can't thank you enough…you've been wonderful,' Mary replied cheerfully, knowing full well that Maggie's tears were partly of longing as well as joy.

For the next little while, the new parents took turns holding and cradling their son. Smiles of relief and tears of joy accompanied their childish giggling; and soon the name of Alex was chosen for their son. Cameron pondered a time over the choice for a second name, but when Mary suggested Morris, Cameron truly believed he had married the most wonderful girl in the world.

A little while later, Mary interrupted Cameron's light-hearted frolicking with Alex.

'Cameron…just call down to Margaret and ask her to bring me up a glass of water.'

Cameron walked over to the door of the bedroom and shouted out her request.

Then, after returning to Mary's bedside, put his arm around her as she began to feed Alex.

'Here you go, dear,' Margaret said, putting the glass of water on the table beside the head of the bed. 'Why don't we just sit you up a bit? You might find it a bit more comfortable.'

Margaret fluffed up the pillows and eased Mary back. But within seconds, Mary's face began to pale and beads of sweat appeared on her forehead.

'No, Maggie! I think it be better if I lay back down.'

Margaret gently lowered her back down, before placing two of her fingers across Mary's wrist.

'Your pulse seems awfully high to me. Is that normal?'

'I'm sure it's no anythin'. I just feel a little dizzy and nauseous. Sorry, Cameron… but could you just go down and refill the glass?' she said, quickly swallowing the last of the water. 'I be really thirsty.'

After he left, Mary asked Margaret to have a quick look under the covers; and the subsequent expression on her sister-in-law's face was enough to confirm what Mary had feared.

'I do hope John gets home all right,' Mary said, gently squeezing Margaret's hand. 'Maybe you should wait for him downstairs. Then you can bring him up to see Alex when he returns.'

'But…shouldn't I…?'

'No…it's all right Maggie. There's nothin' you can do. Before you go, though, I just want you to know that you and John have been wonderful…and thank you again for everythin' you've done to make us welcome. Go on then… I'll be fine.'

The pounding of Cameron's feet on the stairs could then be heard; and it was only Margaret's strength of character, forged through years of mental and physical abuse, that allowed her to turn and leave the room without bursting into tears. Her two soulless eyes stared straight ahead as she passed Cameron in the doorway; and then gripping the handrail, she slowly descended the stairs, before turning at the bottom and running into the kitchen – where she collapsed into a chair.

194

Mary's pale face and colourless lips formed a half smile, as she took the glass from Cameron's hands.

'Come here and lie down with me and your lovely son,' she said, patting the bed beside her.

Cameron laid his arm behind Mary's head, while she placed Alex between them.

'Are you sure you be all right? You look awfully pale.'

'Cameron, just listen for a minute. I'm beginnin' to feel a wee bit tired and I want to tell you a few things before I fall asleep. I know I shouldn't have done it, but I sent a letter to Annie. I couldn't bear the thought of what she must have been goin' through, thinkin' we was dead. I'm sorry Cameron… but I did warn her never to tell anyone about the letter.'

'Don't worry. I'm sure she'll no be sayin' anythin'.'

'Listen, if somethin' were to happen to me, I'd like Margaret…'

'Wait a minute. What do you mean if …'

'Cameron, please…I don't know how much longer… I'll…I'll be awake.'

Margaret's heart ached, as she cried her eyes out. She had no idea of the passage of time; but some time later, when all she had left were dry sobs of sadness, she knew it was over. Cameron's harrowing cry of anguish could easily be heard over the rattling of the windows, as the blizzard continued to vent its wrath long into the night.

Sometime later, the back door crashed open. Margaret raised her head from the tear-soaked arms of her dress, as a mini storm of swirling snow and freezing cold air penetrated the kitchen ahead of two staggering figures.

Dr. Fitzpatrick quickly removed his snow-encrusted coat, at the same time kicking off his boots.

'How is she doing? Has she had the baby yet?'

It was only then he noticed Margaret's tear-streaked, mournful face, and realised it had all been for nothing.

As she recited the sombre events of the last few hours, John's strength finally melted away. Pulling up a chair beside his wife, he looked into her sunken, red-rimmed eyes; and with sighs of wretchedness, they fell into each other's arms.

The doctor stayed with them that night, as it would have been more than foolhardy for him to try to leave. Thankfully, after consuming a cocktail of drugs and alcohol, Cameron finally passed out on the couch, allowing the Doctor to steal upstairs and confirm that Mary had died from an internal haemorrhage.

By the next morning, the storm had abated. Cameron and Dr. Fitzpatrick spent an hour in private conversation, before joining John and Margaret for breakfast.

After a time, Dr. Fitzpatrick put down his knife and fork, looking up at the others.

'She was a remarkable person. I don't know many women who could have talked somebody else through the delivery of her own baby…and then given birth to such a perfect child. I understand that Mr and Mrs Stuart would like you, Margaret, to be considered the mother of little Alex…and if you and John are willing to accept that undertaking, then I shall not stand in your way. For my part, if asked, I shall just confirm that Mrs Stuart died in childbirth. God have mercy on her soul.'

Spring came early the following year, after one of the hardest winters on record. Most of the snow had now melted, as John finished hauling the last of the freshly cut trees from his woodland to the log shed.

'Well, it looks like the end of the sleigh for this year. Hopefully we'll get some dry weather now and get rid of some of the moisture from the ground. And I'd like to get the new fence line up before the ploughing season starts.'

'I guess we'll just have to wait and see,' Margaret replied, shaking the baby's bottle onto her arm to check the temperature of the milk.

196

No adverse comments had been heard in the community concerning the sudden appearance of a baby in the Williams' household. It was quite possible Margaret had given birth during the winter, as people were often cut-off from each other for months when the snowfall was particularly heavy; besides which, it was nobody else's business, and family issues were always kept to oneself. A pleasant 'congratulations' and 'What's his name?' was as far as the discussions went when their neighbours first saw Margaret with the child. And, even when Madame Bouchard had mentioned to the doctor that she had seen Mrs Williams with a baby, his only reply had been, 'Yes…she has a baby'.

Similarly, there were no raised eyebrows when the young wife of the Williams' good friends – who had passed away during the winter – was buried in a small church way over at Clarenceville. After all, most local people were French – and therefore Roman Catholic – whereas they all knew the young woman had been Scottish Presbyterian, and would therefore have wished to be interred in a Protestant graveyard.

At first, the minister had thought it slightly odd when only three people were present for the funeral. Of course, it was a freezing cold day and they were forced to stand in deep snow at the graveside. But in the end, it was probably just as well, he decided. Because never had he seen a man so inconsolable that he needed to be nearly dragged away from the graveside at the end of the internment.

It also seemed a little strange to the minister, when a few months later the headstone arrived, and the inscription had said Mother and Child. But then, he did recall reading on the death certificate that Mrs Stuart had died during childbirth.

After the funeral, Cameron disappeared, his parting words being, 'I'll be back when I can'.

Two weeks later, he arrived back at the house, sober and surprisingly neat in appearance. John and Margaret said nothing about his absence, knowing full well the anguish he'd been suffering.

Over supper that night, Cameron confirmed that, for Alex's safety, he wished to abide by Mary's last wishes. And the following day he packed and left.

John and Margaret never knew where Cameron had gone after the funeral, until some years later.

At a corn roast one summer's day at one of their friends' farms, a new villager who'd just been posted to Lacolle as the local constable, was recounting a story from his training days in Montreal.

'Our teetotal sergeant thought 'e would teach us new recruits all about de evils of drink. So, one day 'e told us a story about some guy with a funny accent 'e'd 'ad to deal with at 'is headquarters in Montreal. Apparently, dis drunk 'ad been t'rown into jail t'ree times in one week. Each time 'e was found on a street near de docks… almost frozen to death. But de man didn't seem to care whether 'e lived or died. Den, after de t'ird occasion 'e just disappeared and was never 'eard from again.'

'Did this guy end up murdered? Because Margaret Williams' first husband was killed in some drunken brawl in the city…and he had a funny accent,' remarked one of the local farmers.

'No, I don't t'ink so,' Pierre replied. 'According to de sergeant, dis guy just vanished…so 'e assumed 'e'd probably fallen in de river and drowned.'

Thankfully, the talk soon reverted to the price of a bushel of this autumn's wheat; and John sloped away from the back of the group surrounding the constable.

Twenty Two

It was a beautiful summers evening in July of 1880. Margaret was in the kitchen drying up the last of the supper dishes as she gazed through the window at Alex, playing in the back yard. He was growing into a fine young boy, she thought, grinning at his vain attempt to corner one of the hens.

Her hand flew to her mouth to cover a giggle, as one of the birds, once again, waited until the last minute before flying over the fence – just out of reach of Alex's grasping hand. All he has to learn now is how to give in gracefully, she decided, as she listened to him cursing the bird.

'Alex…don't you dare! Leave the poor thing alone,' she yelled through the open window, when he bent down to pick up a stone. 'Anyway…it's time for you to get ready for bed… so go and say goodnight to your father and then come in for a wash.'

As she was about to close the window, her ears pricked up on hearing the drum of horse's hooves approaching from down the lane. Drying her hands on her apron, she walked towards the front of the house. Opening the door, she stared up the track, but with the haze in the air, and the dust being thrown by the horse and buggy, it was impossible to tell who it was.

Alex sidled up to her, placing his arm around her waist.

'Who's that, mother?'

'I'm not sure yet…but you go in and get washed and ready for bed. I'll come up in a minute and read you a story.'

When the approaching horse and buggy finally slowed to a walk, Margaret was taken aback.

Driving the rig, and wearing what appeared to be some kind of cowboy hat, was Cameron – sporting a huge grin across his face. It had been five and a half years since they had last seen him, and in all that time they'd not heard from him once. So, at that moment, Margaret was unsure whether to be happy or annoyed with his sudden appearance.

After coming to a halt, Cameron tied off the reins. Then, gazing at his sister and noticing the blank look on her face, he remained seated – unsure of what to do next. Maybe it had been presumptuous of him to assume their relationship would be the same as when he'd left? But, he was here now. So, making up his mind, he jumped down from the rig; while at the same time, Margaret hesitantly began to descend the front steps.

Time momentarily seemed to stop; but then, like water bursting through the breach in a dam, tears flowed down his sister's face and she ran the last few steps to greet him. He'd barely had a chance to take a step forward, when his sister threw her arms around him and nestled her tear-soaked face against his shoulder.

'Hi, Maggie…my goodness…is everything all right?'

'Oh, Cameron…we've missed you so much. Where have you been? What have you been doing? What…'

'Hey…slow down. I've got a lot to tell you…that is, if I'm still welcome.'

'Don't be so foolish, of course you are.'

'Listen, before we go any further…is Alex going to know who I am?'

'Of course he is. We told him he had an uncle called Cameron…and that one day he might get to see him.'

As the two of them walked into the house arm-in-arm, Margaret shouted up the stairs.

'Alex! Come down here and meet your uncle Cameron.'

'Wow,' Alex exclaimed, bounding down the stairs. 'Are you a real cowboy?'

'Ah sure am young fella',' replied Cameron, with his best western drawl.

Margaret grinned, digging Cameron in the ribs.

'Listen, Cameron...John's out in the barn. Why don't you go out and surprise him, while I get Alex ready for bed. Then you can come up and maybe tell him a story, while I'm out finishing the chores.'

The men sounded as though they were on their second or third drink by the time Margaret joined them in the kitchen. Vanishing for a moment into the larder, she soon re-appeared carrying a huge ham on a wooden platter. And by the end of a further two trips, the makings of a feast adorned the large kitchen table. Once Margaret was settled John stood up from the table, returning a few minutes later with four more bottles of cider.

'Just one thing I need to ask before we start,' said Cameron, raising a finger to emphasise the point. 'Has anyone been around here asking any awkward questions during the last five years?'

Having been reassured by two shaking heads, Cameron visibly relaxed.

In the beginning, Cameron's only interest was in the progress of 'little Alex'. He laughed as they regaled him with some of Alex's antics, and was pleased to hear that his son was starting school at the end of this summer. At times during the evening Cameron's eyes took on a far-away look; and had it not been for John's intervention with a timely quip – and top-up of his glass – Margaret feared the emotion of the past might well have returned.

Eventually, the time came for Cameron to tell his story; and what he chronicled was so unlike their predictable, almost boring lifestyle that it kept Margaret and John transfixed until the small hours of the morning.

His narration began with an account of the dark days after the funeral, and even though John and Margaret suspected they knew about his escapades in Montreal, they never let on.

'After I left you for the last time, I went back to Montreal, and then the following day...'

Cameron had left the city by train, with the intention of travelling to Texas. The first leg to Detroit, via Toronto, had gone as planned; but he soon discovered that America's fledgling rail network still had a lot to learn. The onward service had only gone a further two hundred miles when they became stranded by a severe winter storm, and had been left to fend for themselves for nearly thirty hours. Teams of horses pulling sleighs loaded with food, blankets and men to clear the tracks, finally reached them, and after a further twenty-four hours, they were underway again.

The following night as he slept, a thief stole his canvass travelling bag, containing most of his money. The robber had waited until the train had begun to pull away from the station at Kansas City, hoping that Cameron would not wake up until it was much too late. However, when the train jerked during its acceleration, he was jolted from his slumber, and then noticing the theft, leapt from the slowly moving train.

Later that evening, he sat in a local saloon, consoling himself with whisky.

'You're new in town.'

'Well, to be honest…until half an hour ago…I no had any intention of being here,' Cameron replied, to the man now sitting on the stool beside him.

Soon, the two struck up a conversation, and after a few more rounds of the "water of life", Cameron told his new found Irish drinking partner about his earlier escapades on the train.

'Well, I'll be damned,' Cameron muttered sometime later, when who should wander into the bar but a very happy looking vagrant, carrying an all too familiar dark canvass holdall.

With Sean's support, he "thanked" the man for "finding" his bag, while at the same time suggested that he might like to leave town – quickly.

It was almost daylight by the time the two buddies staggered back to Sean's rented accommodation – where Cameron collapsed for 'just the night'.

During the time Cameron stayed in that wild, mid-western town, he and Sean became the best of friends. Although, after his arrival, he hadn't planned on staying in Kansas City for longer than was necessary to plan out his future, the Great Sioux War broke out. And when a few months later, Sitting Bull defeated the seventh cavalry at the Battle of the Little Bighorn, Cameron conceded that further westward travel might be a little unwise.

'When I was there, Kansas City was a boomtown. It had sprung up at the junction of the Kansas and Missouri rivers, and was the last major supply station for pioneers setting off on the Santa Fe Trail to New Mexico, or heading north to connect with the Oregon Trail to the Pacific North West. Year after year thousands arrived...travelling by train from the east or paddle steamer up the Mississippi. Sean talked me into learning to ride. 'After all,' as he said to me more than once, while we sat propping up the bar after work, 'you'll not be able to get a job anywhere west of here if you can't handle a horse'. And you know something, Maggie? That was the smartest thing I've done since leaving Scotland.'

'So, is that where you've been since you left?'

'No. I worked for Sean in his hardware store until finally, in the spring of 1877, the Indians surrendered. For the next three years I just kept on the move, picking up work wherever I could. In the spring, I'd help round up cattle and brand the new calves, while in the fall I'd join huge cattle drives – moving the steers down off the high ground for the winter, or pushing them to the railhead to be taken back east to be slaughtered. I never stayed at any one ranch, or in any one area, for more than a season. And in that way, I hoped to remain pretty well anonymous and completely forgettable.'

'So what's changed? Why have you come back?'

'Well...I never planned on spending my life in the U.S.A. I still think Canada is where I'd like to settle down. And, before you ask...no...I don't plan on settling in this area, because that letter Mary sent to Annie could, one day, still bring trouble. One thing I did decide is that I don't think farming is the life for me. Much as I appreciate what you two did for us, I think at the time I was probably doing it more for Mary…you know…to make up for what I'd done to her.'

'So…what are you going to do now?'

'Well…I've been reading that they're planning to build a railway, all the way across Canada. So, I'm going to head up to Montreal and try to find some part time work, just to tide me over until this new railway company gets going.'

Cameron didn't get much sleep that night, and the next morning he was up early.

'Listen…before I go, I just want you to know that what I said five years ago still stands. I must admit, there have been moments in the last twenty-four hours when I almost broke down and risked telling Alex the truth. But when I looked at how happy you three were…and remembered how dangerous it could be…especially for you and Alex… I knew I mustn't do it. I'll always love you…and there's no need for Alex to know anything until he's a man. John, you asked what's changed. Well…it's taken me five years to get over Mary. And when I leave here, I'm going over to Clarenceville to make my peace before moving on. I'll let you know how I am from time to time, but for your sake and Alex's, I won't tell you where I am.'

Cameron shook John's hand, before giving his sister a long and tender hug.

'When Alex gets up, just tell him his uncle's sorry he missed him this morning… oh, and I got this for him,' Cameron said, handing Margaret a small, white Stetson.

Cameron didn't look back as he strode from the house, nor did he turn or wave when, with the crack of a whip, he hastened away towards the final moment of his previous life.

Twenty Three

The grass was long, and still damp with the summer's morning dew. Cameron knelt beside Mary's grave arranging a posy of summer flowers against the cold granite headstone. He still felt the guilt of what he had put her through, but was sure that after five years of mourning she would have forgiven him.

'There will always be a place for you in my heart, Mary,' he whispered, before leaning forward and placing his lips against her name.

Later that day, he drove up to a stable yard on the south side of the St. Lawrence River. It was here, just off the end of the Victoria Bridge, that he had hired the horse and buggy.

Lugging his one large duffle bag, and under the pretence that he had to get to a meeting in the city, he quickly strode away from Mr Ducard. Although the owner of the yard was a pleasant enough fellow, he seemed determined to tell Cameron the history of the area: starting with how many people had been shot and killed by troops trying to disperse the striking workers building the locks, 'over der at Lachine'; to how many had died building Montreal's first bridge over the St. Lawrence River. Luckily for Cameron, the streetcar had just arrived from over the bridge, and was presently going around the loop in preparation for its return journey to the city. Jumping on board, he settled into a seat in the almost empty car, for the one-hour ride into the centre of the city.

Picking up a newspaper – kindly left behind by the previous occupant – he turned to the employment pages.

At one time, he had considered becoming a lumberjack, to earn enough money to set up a cattle ranch. But, the more he'd thought about it, the more he'd realised that working in mosquito-infested forests seven days a week – while at the same time living in a tent with three other misfits – was not really the life he craved. Not long after he'd heard about the plans to build a new railway, stretching from one side of Canada to the other; and now that he'd established no one had been making any enquiries about his whereabouts, felt it might well be safe enough to contemplate living in Canada.

Cameron whistled, as he strolled down Tupper Street on his way towards the docks, and his temporary job at Joe Beef's Tavern. The bar was owned by a big Irishman called Charles McKiernan – an ex quartermaster with the British Army. He proudly advertised that he 'refused service to no one' and, strangely for an Irishman, was an atheist – so put up with 'no religious squabbles' in his establishment. The beer was cheap and the food even cheaper; while entertainment was provided by his menagerie of animals – including a live black bear, kept in a cage in the saloon. Every night there was at least one fracas – with glasses flying along with the fists – so those of a weaker constitution did not remain in employment very long. Cameron had only remained there as long as he had because the turnover of bar staff was high, and nobody really got to know, or care, about anyone else.

Every day on his way home, he stopped in at the local general store to buy the Montreal Gazette. He was now convinced that his best chance of a decent life was to return to what he knew, so spent hours each day scanning the paper for possible opportunities.

In parliament, the acrimonious debate about the new railway had been going on for months, and barely a day passed without reports concerning the arguments lasting long into the night.

Finally, on a cold February morning, the headline he'd been waiting for was displayed from every news stand.

* * *

CANADIAN PACIFIC RAILWAY INCORPORATED!

Last night at midnight, 16th February 1881, a final agreement was reached between all parties. A new company, hereafter known as the C.P.R., has been formed to connect Canada from coast to coast.

* * *

The story went on to say that the Canadian Pacific Railway intended to buy up all the current railway companies operating services in Quebec and Ontario, and amalgamate them with the C.P.R. The rest of the road was to be newly built, starting in Winnipeg, and then proceeding from there in both directions.

That was all Cameron needed to know. So, after his shift that day, he hurried home – packing his few belongings into his well-travelled holdall, and paying off his landlord.

The following morning, he was on the first train heading west.

The initial part of his journey passed along the same route as did his journey almost six years before. But this time after Detroit, he headed west-northwest to Chicago, and then on to St. Paul. From there it was a relatively short hop, proceeding due north through Minnesota, until crossing the Canadian border – and shortly thereafter arriving at Winnipeg.

Sitting in the second class carriage, as it clickety clacked and swayed its way across Ontario, he was completely absorbed reading the follow-up stories concerning the new railway. Apparently, once built, the new line would make it possible to get on a train in Halifax, on the east coast of Canada, and not get off again until reaching Vancouver – over three thousand miles away. Along the way, stops would be made at all major towns and cities, with branch lines radiating out from them in all directions. The figures quoted concerning the miles of track, tonnage of supplies and manpower required were astounding. Could this really be achieved, he wondered? And if so, how long would it take to accomplish?

The C.P.R.'s main competition was the Grand Trunk Railroad, who had spent years trying to dissuade the Canadian Government, and various other financial backers, from investing in a new railway company. Well, they had lost. But there was no doubt, they were doing all within their means to try to disrupt the all-Canadian railway; as almost every other article in the newspaper claimed proof of the dirty tricks uncovered, followed by denials and counter-claims.

Eventually, Cameron's eyes began to tire. Neatly folding the paper, he tucked it away, determined to complete it later in the trip. Staring out the window at the bleak white landscape, his mind wandered as he tried to imagine what life might have in store for him. Was he finally about to see the real Canada? The country he'd previously been warned was wild and full of savages, with bandits behind every rock. Somehow he doubted it, and from the little he'd read about the prairies, the actual building of the track should be much easier than what they'd had to deal with in Scotland. Finally, his eyes began to droop and he fell into a shallow sleep; and as the day turned to night, the train sped ever westwards towards his destiny.

Following an overnight stop in Chicago, and another change of trains in St. Paul, Cameron finally boarded the train which was to take him on the last leg to Winnipeg. The service from St. Paul to Winnipeg had been running for two years. But, by the looks of what he could see as he boarded, this railway's main concern was hauling freight – as there were only two passenger carriages available at the end of a long line of ten freight wagons. As it turned out, he had been wise to board early, because by departure time not only were all the seats occupied, but the aisles were fully taken up with men and their belongings. Again, the seats were somewhat unforgiving, but were now looked on with envy by late-comers, who would be spending the rest of their journey on the floor.

The news had certainly gotten out quickly. From the snatches of conversations Cameron picked up, all the men in his carriage were unskilled labourers intent on getting any job available. And, although they seemed cheerful and full of confidence, their weathered faces, hollow cheeks and sunken eyes told a very different story; a tale of men who, nearly at their wits end, were desperate to find any kind of work to survive.

Cameron's head was supported by his hand, with his elbow resting on his knee, as he stared out the window at the passing landscape. Initially, the world outside changed very little. St. Paul had been a dour, dismal-looking place. But once they had cleared the last of the inhabited areas, the view became one of clean white fields separated by dirty brown hedgerows and lines of leafless oaks and poplars. Their route paralleled a fast flowing river, which in places tumbled over ice-covered rocks sparkling in the midday sun. But as time passed the rocks became huge boulders, with snow-covered tops and dark uneven bottoms – looking like iced cakes sitting on a wrinkled blue tablecloth. The river continued to grow in stature until finally, as they drew near their destination, its flow disappeared beneath a sheet of snow and ice, covering it from shore to shore.

Cameron was soon to discover that this waterway's name was the Red River, and it ran for almost five hundred miles, before pouring its contents into a massive lake named after the city to which they were bound. Winnipeg stood at the confluence of this river and the mighty Assiniboine, which joined from the west and added its power and soil-enriched flow to the union.

The gradual deceleration of the train announced their imminent arrival. Men, who for hours had been lying on their bags, sitting on boxes, or squeezing into any floor space available, now began to stir. Cameron watched their antics as they tripped over each other's possessions in a mad scramble to recover their belongings. No doubt, they would all try to get out the door at the same time, he mused, as he sat back and decided to linger. After all, there was plenty of time. He had his whole life ahead of him.

When Cameron stepped down from the carriage, what he saw was not so much a train station as a huge marshalling yard. A small shunting engine could be seen manoeuvring into position to detach each freight wagon in turn, and tow it to its required off-loading site. And the two Mogul engines that had powered the train from St. Paul were already detached, and moving onto the turntable to be repositioned for their return journey. All around him were men yelling orders, or hurrying to respond, while horses and wagons were being positioned to receive their cargoes.

'Hey you! Look out! You wanna get killed?'

A ruddy-faced man, with long, dark hair sticking out from under a filthy, dark hat, and wearing a woollen scarf around his neck and ears, strutted towards Cameron. And it was only then that Cameron realised he was the only one left alongside the inbound train.

Suddenly, with a reverberating clang, the carriage from which he'd just descended jerked, and then moved off down the yard.

'Sorry…I was just kind of fascinated by all the comings and goings. Can you tell me where the C.P.R. offices are?'

'Other side of the river. Take that bridge over there,' he said, pointing off to the left. 'And then follow the crowd. That's where they'll all be headed.'

Throwing his bag over his shoulder, Cameron carefully looked up and down the tracks before heading off in the suggested direction. Light snow began to fall, and for the first time he noticed the cold. In Quebec, the air was moist, and as soon as the temperature dropped below freezing you knew it

– and how! However, here, the air was much drier, and apart from the stinging in his ears, it was only now that he realised he'd been licking his lips ever since getting off the train.

On reaching the so-called bridge Cameron pulled up short, gaping at the crossing.

He couldn't believe what he was looking at! Not only was it not made of steel, but it wasn't even stone, the next best thing. In fact, it wasn't even a permanent structure. The actual surface of the bridge was made up from rough, wooden planks held together by strips of wood nailed at right angles. These sections were then laid across the river on floating barges anchored in the stream. In other words, the only thing appearing to connect Winnipeg to its main supply line was a temporary pontoon bridge. With the experience Cameron had gained working for the GNSR, he knew this couldn't possibly work. There was no possibility of this rickety thoroughfare being used to successfully supply the needs of an ever-expanding rail network. To him, the bridge already looked to be dangerously overloaded, as huge wagons and carts jockeyed with myriads of foot passengers to cross the river; and he was certain it was only a matter of time before disaster struck.

Deciding it probably wasn't going to get any safer, the longer he stood there, Cameron moved off, quickly picking his way across the swaying structure.

What had started out as a small fur-trading outpost known as the Red River Colony, had turned into a chaotic, flourishing city, bustling with humanity. All that was left of the old settlement were the remains of Upper Fort Garry – the previous headquarters of the Hudson's Bay Company. And even this was now diminishing in size daily, as workmen demolished what was left to allow the city's expansion to the west.

Winnipeg was designed around two main thoroughfares – Main Street and Portage Avenue. Along these two streets non-stop construction was taking place as, on a daily basis, new businesses moved in. The signing of the agreement to build the railway had been like a gold rush, and had turned Winnipeg into the fastest growing city in North America; and it appeared that everyone was after a piece of the action.

Cameron wandered up the sidewalk on Main Street, soaking up the atmosphere. Most people moved about with a spring in their step, as if they all felt a sense of being part of some great new beginning. The air was pungent with the fragrance of freshly-cut lumber, and resounded to the din of construction. Sawdust was everywhere, and half finished buildings lined both sides of the street. A new courthouse, new police station and new legislative buildings, were all being raised. The Bank of Montreal was erecting a four storey building at the corner of Main Street and Portage Avenue, which would eventually house the new headquarters of the C.P.R.

Finally, further along the street, he came to the building that most interested him – namely, the current offices of the new railroad. No sign was needed to advertise its whereabouts, as the queue of men waiting to enter its door disappeared around the next corner.

Cameron kept walking. He was already feeling the effects of the extreme cold and quickly came to the conclusion that he didn't wish to spend the rest of the day getting frostbitten in that line. A few minutes later, he spotted a sign for the Davis Hotel, and decided to follow the suggestion from his feet that now might be a good time to get inside.

The following morning at eight o'clock, Cameron briskly rounded the corner, hoping to be the first in line at the C.P.R. headquarters. To his dismay, the line of men already snaked down the street, nearly as far as the day before. Realising that he had no choice, he began to make his way towards the back of the queue. Before he'd gone more than a few steps, a stocky, black-bearded man wearing a smart three-piece suit exited from the front door of the building. Turning towards the notice board at the side of the main entrance, he pinned-up a sheet of paper. The line automatically began to surge forward, at which point the company's representative held up his hand.

'I'm sorry, gentlemen, but there will be no labouring jobs available for at least another month...and all the other unskilled posts have been filled.'

The sound of grumbling gradually faded away as the men shuffled off towards a café down the street. Cameron waited until most had gone, and then approached the bearded man as he was about to re-enter the building.

'Excuse me. Did I hear you correctly? You did say all the unskilled jobs have been filled, I believe. Does that mean there are vacancies for experienced people?'

'Oh, yes...and what kind of experience would that be then?'

'Well…I did work as a surveyor and depot manager for a Scottish Railway, for the best part of three years.'

The rest of the morning was surreal. After being hustled into the building, he was taken to an office for further questioning, and then led down a corridor to where he was asked to wait outside a door – on which was printed the name A. B. Stickney.

'Come in, he'll see you now,' said a rather plain-looking woman, holding the door open for him.

Leading Cameron past her desk to the far side of the room she knocked on another door, which when opened revealed a large wood panelled office. Sitting behind a gargantuan desk, placed across the furthest corner of the room, was a man well suited to its size. What hair he lacked on the top of his head was more than made up for by his thick, sprouting eyebrows – giving him an almost permanent look of surprise – while on his face mutton chop whiskers failed to cover his heavy jowls. His chest was enormous, and his waistcoat appeared ready to explode.

'So, young man…I hear you claim to have some knowledge of railway inventory,' he said, his obvious misgivings manifesting themselves in the slightly scornful tone of his voice.

'Yes, Sir…I believe I do.'

'In that case, you wouldn't mind telling me how many rails, fish plates and sleepers are required per mile of track then, would you?'

'Of course not. That would be 136 rails, 132 fishplates and 1760 sleepers.'

Seemingly surprised by the speed with which Cameron had answered the question, Mr Stickney was momentarily silent, before thanking Cameron for coming in and terminating the interview.

Well, I guess that didn't go very well, thought Cameron, as he waited near the reception desk at the entrance to the building.

'Can you tell me who Mr A.B. Stickney is?'

'Certainly, Sir,' replied the girl behind the desk. 'He's the man in charge of the western division of the C.P.R.'

'Hmm…maybe that's why it didn't go so well,' he thought to himself.

But, to his surprise, five minutes later, he was taken to another office, where coffee was offered – along with a contract.

'But, excuse me,' Cameron said to the bearded, portly man – who, it seemed, was the Company's Personnel Manager.

'What is the job? Nobody's told me what it is I'm supposed to be doing.'

'Oh…sorry,' he replied. 'You're to be the new supply manager…and you'll be responsible for the inventory for the nine hundred miles from here to the Rockies.'

Cameron was aghast. In Scotland, he'd been responsible for the control and supply of maybe fifty miles of track at a time. This was way beyond his experience. When he told the Personnel Manager about his concerns, the portly man's only comment had been, 'Well, of course you don't have any experience of this magnitude…but then…neither does anyone else'.

Cameron arrived at work the following day determined to somehow get to grips with the mammoth task that lay ahead. Still, at least he didn't have to start from scratch. C.P.R. management had been planning this for over a year, and had already signed contracts for an enormous amount of stock. Half a million sleepers, five thousand telegraph poles and sixty thousand feet of pilings were already either in yards on the outskirts of the city, or in the process of being delivered.

In the main depot, west of Winnipeg, hundreds of miles of rails, thousands of fishplates and hundreds of boxes of spikes awaited the spring thaw. Triple-decker construction cars, to be used as bunkhouses for the workers, were waiting to move out, and hundreds of teams of horses had already been hired to move the necessary supplies. Two dozen teams of oxen had been bought to pull the great flat-bladed ploughs, which would be used to build up the track bed to four feet above the prairie – thus ensuring the movement of trains would not be impeded by snow during the long winter months.

When the writing on the paperwork in front of Cameron eyes began to blur, he looked up and rubbed his eyes. It was now dark outside. His first day had raced by, and it was only now that he had begun to make some kind of sense of the stack of papers in front of him. The scale of the undertaking was enormous, making his previous Scottish company look like a toy railway in comparison. Forcing his shoulders back, he twisted his upper body from side-to-side in an attempt to ease the ache he felt in his lower back. Then, deciding that that was enough for today, he pushed back his chair and tidied up his desk.

Even though it was Sunday morning the streets were still bustling. Cameron looked left and right, moved forward and stopped, and then ran forward again, as he dodged the horses, carts, wagons and sleighs on his way across Main Street. Having just found a quite acceptable room, at a reasonable monthly rate, all he had left to do now was retrieve his bag from the hotel, and then risk life and limb again, re-crossing this street on his way back to Mrs Baker's boarding house.

Twenty minutes later, his head momentarily down watching the placement of his feet on the slippery surface, he started back across Main Street. Just then, the muffled thundering of hooves drew his attention. On his left, appearing from almost nowhere and about to cross in front was a coach and four, galloping down the street at an idiotic speed. Suddenly, a cry went up directly in front of him, as a woman slipped and fell on the icy surface. His brain instantly foresaw the impending disaster, and without a moment's hesitation, he dropped his holdall and launched himself towards her – grabbing her with both his arms, and holding her to his chest, whilst throwing himself forwards and rolling as quickly as momentum would allow. Ice chips propelled by the hammering hooves struck his face and bare hands; but it was only after the wheels grinding on the ice and snow had passed him by that he knew they were safe.

Quickly standing up, he reached down to offer the woman his hand, and as he did he became aware of the cheering and applauding ringing out from up and down the street. Everywhere he looked men were waving their hats in the air and yelling their approval; and even the drivers of the carriages and drays crowding the street had stopped and tipped their hats to acknowledge his daring performance.

'I hope you haven't been injured. That idiot should be arrested for driving in such a reckless manner. May I help you to the sidewalk?'

'Thank you…thank you…so…so much,' the woman stammered, breathlessly.

By the time they stepped onto the boarded sidewalk, the milling crowd of onlookers had dispersed, and the non-stop

216

hustle and bustle continued.

Turning to say goodbye, Cameron was suddenly struck by how enticing his "damsel in distress" truly was. Her hair was reddish-brown, and her hazel eyes were set alluringly far apart. Her nose was pert, with a slight flare to its base, and rested charmingly between high cheeks.

'Thank you again for what you did,' she said, putting out a small, gloved hand to say goodbye. 'I'm sure you probably saved my life.'

Cameron gently grasped her hand, inadvertently holding it for longer than was probably necessary.

'Oh, excuse me,' he said, releasing her hand. 'By the way, my name's Cameron Stuart. Maybe we'll see each other around town some time.'

'Yes, that would be nice.'

At that point she turned to leave, but then abruptly swung back.

'Oh…I do apologise for being so rude. I'm afraid I'm still rather shocked. My name is Catherine…Catherine Phillips.'

Cameron watched her move off towards the main part of the city, before he turned and headed up the street towards his new lodgings; and as he wandered up Cumberland Avenue, his thoughts returned to what had just happened.

It had certainly been an exciting moment. His heart was only now returning to its normal beat. Good fortune had smiled upon them, because death or serious injury had been only inches away. He smiled as he recalled the ovation from the surrounding crowd, but as Catherine's lingering fragrance accompanied him along the street, a long forgotten yearning began to encroach into his thoughts.

The noise destroyed any ideas Cameron might have had for peace and quiet, and the smoke from half a dozen pipes made his eyes water, as he walked through the front door of his new lodgings. The other guests were all in Mrs Baker's front room waiting for their Sunday dinner, and not one of them could have been over twenty-five years old.

One thing was for sure. In the early spring of 1881, two thirds of all people seen on the streets of Winnipeg were men, and most of them were young or middle-aged. The ones doing the real work could easily be identified by their rough dress, while most of the rest were just trying to make a fast buck selling real estate. The railway had started a boom in property prices, and everyone seemed determined to make a killing. The moment any news leaked out about a new section of the route, men would rush to stake claims on any land they believed would be adjacent to the route. These lots then began to change hands at ever increasing prices, making a number of people very rich indeed. Nearly every other building along Main Street now accommodated a real estate agent; and the general consensus was that the property boom would go on forever.

Twenty Four

By the end of the following week, Cameron had solved the question of the C.P.R.'s inventory. All that was now required was Mr Stickney's approval; and the small matter of hiring and training four people for his department.

It was early Sunday morning, as Cameron strolled down Anderson Avenue. According to Mrs Baker, this street had been named after the first bishop to be consecrated in what was Western Canada's only cathedral, and if he remained on this road he would pass it on his way down towards the river.

As he crossed Main Street the bells began to peel, scattering the crows from the bare branches of the nearby trees, whilst up ahead, carriages could be seen momentarily halting at the steps of the cathedral to drop off their well-heeled believers.

At that moment, Cameron's eyes were drawn to a flash of reddish-brown hair showing beneath the cream-coloured bonnet of a woman stepping down from a shiny, black carriage. Realising it was Catherine his pulse quickened. But then, to his dismay, she turned to help a young, dark-haired girl and smartly dressed boy alight from the carriage. His illusions were dashed, and he immediately increased his walking pace in a bid to get by without being noticed.

'Oh, hello, Cameron! How nice to see you. Are you coming to church as well?'

Halted in his tracks, he now struggled to respond.

'Oh…Good Morning, Catherine…Ah…yes…yes, I am.'

'Well then…would you like to sit with us?'

Now he was totally confused.

While he pondered his dilemma, and before he could reply, a landau pulled up behind Catherine's carriage.

'Wait just a minute...I'll be right back,'

Cameron's bewilderment then increased, as Catherine took both children's hands and walked over to greet the landau's occupants.

With undisguised discomfort Cameron waited beside the carriage, his hands clasping and unclasping before returning to his sides.

Catherine spoke quietly to the couple from the carriage, and then they and the children proceeded towards the main doors of the cathedral.

'Come on then, Cameron. The service is about to start.'

Once inside, Cameron followed Catherine into the pew behind the two people with the children; after which followed one of the longest hours of Cameron's life.

From the start, he tried his best not to appear totally out of place – although Catherine's occasional grins from behind her raised hand dispelled any ideas he might have had that he was fitting in. But, when his solemn 'Amens' began to crop up in the strangest of places, she squeezed his hand – which he took as a suggestion that it might be time for him just to be quiet.

The service finally ended. Cameron joined the procession of worshippers leaving the building, his thoughts focusing on how to escape from his current situation. And when he slipped away from behind the throng milling about outside the church, for a moment he'd actually thought he might have gotten away unnoticed.

'Ah...there you are, Cameron. We began to think you might have stayed behind to pray for a bit more guidance,' chuckled Catherine. 'Anyway, I'd like to introduce you to Mr and Mrs Sifton and their two children, Amelia and John Junior.'

'Pleased to meet you, Cameron. My name's John and this is Diane... We've been hearing a lot about you lately. It seems we owe you a great deal of gratitude for saving the life of our dear Catherine.'

'Oh…it was nothing really.'

'All the same, if there's ever anything we can do for you please let us know. In the meantime, I'm sure you two would like to go off somewhere, so we'll take the children home with us.'

What had started out as just a quick cup of tea at the Winnipeg Hotel, turned into an all day outing. After leaving the cathedral, they had wandered along the riverbank, watching the colourfully dressed skaters taking advantage of the frozen waterway. Then, as they began to feel a bit chilled, they ducked into a small café near the ferry dock for a warming cup of coffee. Both felt quite at ease with each other, so before long, Catherine told Cameron about her employment as a tutor and nanny to the Sifton's children. She giggled when Cameron confessed his initial suspicions that she was married, and the two Sifton children were her own, and then laughed when he recalled their initial meeting and suggested that maybe they should have taken a bow in response to the applause from the onlookers.

Catherine accepted his invitation to lunch and, having been asked her opinion on a suitable venue, informed Cameron that the Queens Hotel was by all accounts the place to be "seen" in Winnipeg.

Their leisurely stroll continued after lunch, but as late afternoon approached, the temperature plummeted. The day ended with another risky crossing of Main Street, but this time there was no danger of another crisis, as Catherine's arm was held firmly in the crook of Cameron's elbow. A few minutes later, they entered the offices of the local transport company, and were soon on their way to where Catherine lived, on the northern outskirts of the city.

'Wow…is this where you live? You must be rich,' Cameron teased.

'Don't be silly,' Catherine chuckled. 'This is the Sifton's house, and my room is that one… right at the top of the house.'

Cameron got out first, offering his hand to steady her as she stepped from the rig – and again, seemingly unintentionally, he was a little slow at releasing her hand.

'Would you like to go out again next Sunday?'

'I'd really like that, Cameron, but I'm afraid I won't be able to as Mr and Mrs Sifton have already mentioned they're going to be away all day.'

'Oh well, how about Saturday afternoon?'

'I'm so sorry…I have to take the children to a party then.'

Cameron now felt that perhaps he was pushing too hard.

'Well, never mind. Anyway, I really enjoyed today and maybe we'll see each other again around town.'

'I don't know if you'd be interested,' said Catherine. 'But I just remembered… there's a concert in aid of the new General Hospital at the City Hall Theatre next Saturday night. It's already sold out…but the Siftons have two tickets which they offered to me because they have dinner guests that night. Would you like to go?'

By Monday afternoon, Cameron's new system had been approved; and by Thursday he'd hired the required four extra staff. It took two weeks to train them to a level with which he was happy, and that being done, it allowed him to concentrate on the more pressing need of sourcing and contracting the ever increasing demand for materials.

Within a month the snow had melted, and track building recommenced; and by the end of the following week, Cameron's system was proving to be eminently capable of maintaining control over the supply chain. In fact, his new procedures were working so well that the construction crews were now having trouble using up the inventory quickly enough, as it arrived at the head of the line.

The steel road moved west at a rate of about two miles a day. To some this sounded good: however, the building season was short, and at this rate it would take seven years to cross the prairies. Something had to give, and it wasn't long before it did.

Cameron arrived at work to find the whole office buzzing. The Company had just announced the "retirement" of Mr Stickney, and rumour had it that an American called Cornelius Van Horne was replacing him.

To most people's concern, Van Horne came with a reputation. A reputation of being a man of great physical and mental strength, who did not tolerate drunkenness, slackers, slowpokes or labour organizers; and as a consequence, even before he arrived, most office staff suddenly seemed to prefer their lunch at their desks!

Within three weeks of his arrival, the daily westward march of steel increased to three and a half miles, and by the end of the first week of August, a one-day record of five miles had been attained.

Cameron's system easily handled the increased productivity, and by autumn the railway's relentless push had already spawned two new towns – Portage La Prairie and Brandon. The new General Manager had achieved what was thought to be impossible by doubling the daily mileage within three months of his arrival.

The summer of 1881 also proved memorable for reasons other than the expansion of the C.P.R. Cameron and Catherine's evening at the concert had ended with a quick kiss on the cheek, and his promise to contact her during the following week. But with a new boss had come increased pressure, and Cameron realised that for the time being his job must take preference over his social life. He did get a message to Catherine, but for the next three weeks was forced to work through the weekends.

It was a beautiful summer's day. Cameron stepped out the front door of the office on his way to the nearby café for a quick lunch, and as he did almost fell over Catherine.

'Oh…hello…Cameron,' Catherine stammered.

This time it was Catherine who had begun to suspect their relationship was not to be.

'Catherine…How are you? I'm sorry I haven't gotten in touch with you. Things have been crazy around here since we got the new manager.'

Looking into her downcast eyes, Cameron's resolve to put work ahead of everything else dissolved.

'Can I see you on Sunday, Catherine?'

'Well…I…'

'Tell you what…I'm supposed to go up to Brandon to check up on a small problem we've been having with our distribution. So, how would you like to come along? I'm sure I can get you a pass for the train…and then, when we get back, we could have supper at the Queens Hotel.'

Sunday was a revelation for Catherine. When Cameron had mentioned passes, it had never crossed her mind that he meant in first class, with lunch served at their seats by a waiter in a white jacket; and because there were no other passengers in the whole of the first class carriage, it was almost as if they were in their own intimate dining room, in their own grand house.

Once the problems at the depot had been dealt with, they wandered about Brandon – at the end of which they both came to the same conclusion.

For the time being, Brandon had very little to offer. Most of its inhabitants lived in soiled tents alongside muddy, pot-holed roads. Construction was beginning to gather pace, but for the moment all that had been erected were a few partly-built frame structures scattered haphazardly up and down the main street.

On their arrival back in Winnipeg, Catherine was pleasantly surprised to find that Cameron had booked a table in a dimly lit alcove in the restaurant at the Queens Hotel – hardly the act of a man who was not very interested, she thought. And later that night, as she lay in her bed, with her mind going over the special moments of the day, what stood out the most was their long goodnight kiss, and his promise to see her again in the next few days.

During the following week Cameron's thoughts were in turmoil. Much as he tried to concentrate on his work, it was proving impossible. He was captivated by Catherine.

One warm Sunday afternoon in mid August, they picnicked on a blanket laid on the banks of the Assiniboine River. The sun was perched high in a cloudless sky, and the mixed fragrances of the nearby swathes of wild flowers filled the air. Cameron and Catherine laughed as their fingers turned blue from picking the bugs and bits of leaves off the wild blueberries. And later, like the petals of a lily opening as a new day dawns, Catherine's life unfolded.

She had been born on a storm-tossed ship in the Indian Ocean. Her father was a civil servant, and had been seconded to fill a post at the British Embassy in Bombay; while her mother was a teacher – sorely needed overseas, in those burgeoning days of Victoria's Commonwealth. Her childhood had been magical. Schooling had been provided in an English school – attended only by the colony's principal families. And while living in a huge colonial home, she had been fed, washed and dressed by exotic nannies in colourful wrap-around saris.

At fourteen years of age, it had all come to and end when her father had been posted to the new commonwealth country of Canada.

The difference could not have been more profound. Her environment changed from one of cosseted, upper-class stuffiness to classless, do-it-yourself bourgeois. But somehow, she had been drawn to this way of life, which seemed to her to be honest and meaningful. Her parents, on the other hand, did not adjust to the frontier spirit. And when she got wind they had applied to return home to England, she replied to an advertisement placed in the paper by the Siftons of Winnipeg.

Her parents duly returned to England, appalled at how

their daughter could have betrayed them by staying in that 'country of plebeians and savages'.

The following Sunday, Cameron and Catherine once more laid out their picnic beside the river, but this time it was Cameron who revealed a "carefully considered" history of himself and his family. He didn't actually lie about his past, just failed to mention certain particulars – such as the fact that he had a son called Alex.

And when he eventually fell silent, he wrapped his arms around Catherine, kissing her with unrestrained longing and passion.

Indian summer blessed the day, when on the third Sunday in September, Cameron and Catherine were wed. The marriage took place at St John's Cathedral. Of course, they were not so notable as to automatically deserve their marriage in such a magnificent place. But Mr and Mrs Sifton had arranged their wedding day – ostensibly in recognition of their fondness for Catherine. In truth, the reason was probably much more mundane. Good staff was almost impossible to find west of the major Canadian cities. So, Catherine was pretty sure that, by providing her and Cameron with such a memorable day, they hoped she would look kindly on continuing in their employment. And proof of her suspicion was provided on their departure from the ceremony, when a key was pressed into her hand.

'Please…use this cabin for as long as you like,' whispered Diane Sifton. 'You two deserve a place of your own… Besides…John and I never use it any more.'

The normal background noise of muted conversations and shuffling paper was suddenly overwhelmed by Mr Van Horne's raised voice.

'What do you mean he's quit? He can't do that! We're just approaching winter.

226

Who's going to lay out the lines for next spring? Get out and find me another surveyor…and do it quickly!'

Major Tom Rosser, the chief engineer, stood in front of Cornelius Van Horne's desk, nervously holding his hat in his trembling right hand.

'I'm sorry, Mr Van Horne. I've been trying to do just that, but nobody seems to be available…or let me put it this way… nobody wants to be out on the prairies with the winter coming.'

'Double the salary! Do whatever it takes! I must have that line surveyed for at least another hundred miles before we start next spring. Somebody must be willing to endure a bit of hardship for that amount of money?'

With his boss's rants still ringing in his ears, the chief engineer hurried from the office – no doubt feeling dozens of pairs of eyes boring into his back as he retreated down the hallway. Once the room returned to its previous business-like environment, Cameron quietly pushed back his chair, and then purposefully strolled towards the General Manager's office.

His initial knock at the door drew no response, but after a slightly louder rap, a curt 'come in' was heard.

Cornelius Van Horne stood behind his littered desk, replacing a book on its shelf. As he turned back, he reminded Cameron of a bulldog. His head was low-browed and large, supported on huge, powerful shoulders by a short, thick neck. His nose was broad and nearly lost in the mass of wrinkled flesh making up his cheeks, while his barrel-like chest was immense, and completely failed to hide his rather extensive waistline.

'Yes, what is it?'

'Excuse me, Mr Van Horne. I'm sorry to bother you.'

'Oh yes…Mr Stuart,' said the General Manager, seeing Cameron as he turned back towards his desk. 'Please come in and take a seat. Forgive me for not taking the time to see you before, but as I'm sure you're aware, things have been rather hectic around here for the last few months. Anyway…I'm very impressed with your work. I don't believe I've ever seen such a clever supply system. Well done…Now, what can I do for you?' he said, as he settled back down behind his desk.

'Well, sir… I couldn't help but hear that you require a surveyor…and now that my new system is working, I'd like to apply for the job. I spent quite some time surveying for the railway in Scotland, and I'm sure laying out the line on a basically flat prairie shouldn't pose much of a problem… not compared to our mountain routes back home, that is. As for the weather …well…we have plenty of cold and snow to contend with in Scotland, and I can't imagine it can be much worse on the prairies than it is in the Highlands in a good blow…now can it?'

Twenty Five

The first snowstorm of the season hit Winnipeg on the third weekend of October. Cameron was just stepping up to the rear platform of the private car attached to the supply train, when the big flakes of snow started swirling about. Oh great, he thought, that's just what I need! Snow and freezing winds to help me on my way!

Opening the door, he stepped into the railway carriage, and was immediately taken aback by the lavish interior. Then his eyes fell upon the chief engineer sitting behind a large mahogany desk, welcoming him in with the wave of his hand.

'Come in, Mr Stuart. How do you like our lovely weather? Not exactly what either of us wanted, I suspect?'

Cameron made his way towards the desk, while at the same time taking in more of the private car's interior.

The warmth in the car was sustained by a pot-bellied stove, standing midway up the right-hand side between two comfortable looking armchairs, while a three-seat settee, covered in the same chintz material as the two armchairs, was positioned behind a long, low coffee-table – liberally spread with current newspapers and periodicals. The walls were panelled in a honey-coloured maple, and hung with paintings by Canadian artists such as Kane and Verner, while finishing off this opulent interior were polished wooden floors, scattered with colourful rugs imported from the Far East.

Not a bad way to rough it on the prairies, thought Cameron, as the carriage jerked forward.

'I don't suppose you can leave this car at the end of the track for me?' Cameron asked cheekily.

'I'd be more than happy to…but I think Mr Van Horne might have something to say. He likes to think this is his personal railway carriage. I was lucky to appropriate it for our little trip…but I'm afraid I had to promise to bring it back as soon as possible.'

For the next two hours, Cameron sat listening to the briefing given to him by the Chief Engineer. The Major was a dynamic looking person, with deep probing eyes, and a manner to match. He displayed a full head of white hair, with matching bushy whiskers – effectively masking any clue of his facial expressions – and his personality was one that took over a room, except possibly when in the presence of one Cornelius Van Horne.

As time went by, the Major's manservant kept them liberally supplied with hot and cold drinks, and then at midday served them dinner, prepared in the small galley kitchen at the other end of the carriage.

Without doubt, Cameron was suitably impressed. It was certainly agreeable to be treated like someone of substance. But he was not a fool, and knew full well this was all part of a softening up exercise aimed at keeping him from quitting the moment he saw what he was up against.

In what seemed like no time at all the train arrived in Brandon, where it began to off-load some of its cargo. It was then Cameron noticed that a few large snowflakes in Winnipeg had turned into a full-blown blizzard, with visibility down to less than a hundred yards.

When they finally got underway again, the train crawled forward at a speed not much greater than walking pace. The driver couldn't possibly see more then a few carriage lengths ahead, and so was not taking any chances.

'Well, we're almost there now,' said the Major, peering out the window. 'The day after tomorrow, the last of the construction gang will be travelling back on this train…then, all we'll have left out here will be the six men maintaining security at the yard.'

'That sounds like an awful lot of security for out here in the middle of nowhere.'

'I'm afraid we've learned the hard way that unattended inventory tends to disappear. The Métis, who've been trading in this area for the last hundred years, and the local Indian tribes, both look on anything unguarded as trade goods...to be exchanged for food and bullets...or worse, alcohol.'

The shrill sound of the engine's whistle interrupted the two men's conversation. In all likelihood, the blizzard would have muffled the normal approach of a train, but there could be no mistaking that ear-splitting sound. The rest of the goods on the train needed to be off-loaded, so the sooner the men got on with the job, then the sooner they would be able to get back to their accommodation and out of the weather.

Looking out the windows from the warm carriage, Cameron did begin to wonder how successful a tent was going to be at providing a place of comfort in this kind of weather; and he was now beginning to suspect that he knew why the company had had such difficulty in finding a replacement surveyor.

As their private carriage was shunted to a solitary position ten feet short of the end of the rails, the snowstorm finally abated. Major Rosser still sat at his desk, carefully studying maps, drawing lines and pointing out various locations, while Cameron stood quietly by his side, making notes and voicing his own observations about the route over the next few hundred miles.

The light outside the windows began to fade, and so too did Cameron's concentration. Before long his mind returned to his departure that morning, and the tears in Catherine's eyes.

She had been in a foul mood since the announcement of his new job. And, as the day for his departure had drawn nearer, and her displeasure had grown, he accepted that what he'd done was wrong. Unfortunately, he'd been fixated on

231

the new challenge, and the large increase in salary, without any consideration whatsoever of Catherine's feelings. Within days, he knew it had been a mistake to accept the job without consulting her, but by then it was too late. He couldn't go back on the promise he'd made to the General Manager, even though he now knew his decision had been hasty, and totally selfish.

In the last few days he'd tried to mollify her, promising he'd be back before Christmas, and would then have a week off. But it had not been enough, and she'd still cried her heart out when he left.

'I shall be laying out the table for supper in five minutes. Can I get you two gentlemen a drink?' the Major's steward asked.

'Whisky and water for me, Abraham.'

Never again, thought Cameron. I always did what I wanted in the past and look where that got me.

'Mr Stuart...Excuse me, Mr Stuart. Would you like a drink?'

'Oh sorry…I was somewhere else. Yes, I'll have a whisky, thanks.'

The following morning, Cameron watched as Major Rosser donned two sweaters, heavy woollen pants, two pairs of socks, boots, a heavy parka and lined deerskin gloves.

'Do you really think it's going to be that cold, Major? I mean…I certainly hope not, because I don't have anywhere near that amount of clothing with me.'

'Don't worry about that. We'll outfit you from stores.'

A few minutes later, as the two men trudged their way through the snow towards the depot, Cameron looked on with some trepidation, as his breath puffed into the air like clouds of steam from a loco.

'Keep in mind, Cameron, this is only October. If this was January or February you'd have to cover your face as well to protect yourself from frostbite.'

On Cameron's right, smoke poured from the chimneys at the top of the triple bunk cars, as they were shunted into line at the head of some empty freight cars, in preparation for the next day's departure, whilst directly ahead of him stood two substantial wooden buildings – surrounded on all sides by cut logs stacked at least six feet high. One of these buildings was obviously the main office to which they were headed, while the other, he assumed, must be the accommodation building for the men over-wintering in the yard.

When he and Major Rosser rounded the corner of the office, another much larger structure loomed into view on the opposite side of the road. Large double doors, held shut by two iron bars, fronted this building, and high on its walls were rows of small windows – well out of reach of any curious onlooker.

The front door of the office suddenly swung open to reveal a tall figure dressed from head to foot in sealskins and furs.

'Sergeant MacDonald, nice to see you again,' said the Major, as he removed his glove to shake the man's hand. 'I'd like you to meet Cameron Stuart. He'll be spending the next little while west of here surveying the line. You'll probably run in to each other from time to time over the next few years, so why don't you come back into the office, have a cup of coffee and get to know each other?'

The last thing Cameron wanted to do was become acquainted with a member of the North West Mounted Police. Although he doubted anyone was looking for him, he was still a little wary of being questioned – particularly by someone with a Highland name.

Thankfully, he soon discovered the Mountie was second generation Canadian and had never set foot in Scotland; and although he did seem a likeable fellow, and appeared only to be interested in hearing about whisky smugglers, Cameron was still a little unsettled in his presence.

After the Sergeant departed, the volume of conversation once more returned to its previous level, with abundant good humour and raucous laughter.

233

Unexpectedly, the door opened again, and into the room came one of the oddest-looking human beings Cameron had ever set eyes on. He was covered from his shoulders to below the knee with a dark-brown shaggy coat – which Cameron surmised must be one of those that he'd heard were made from buffalo skins. On his feet was some type of moccasin boot, encompassing his leather leggings and reaching halfway up his calf. While on his head was what could only be described as a sort of flat turban, made from what looked like colossal handkerchiefs and secured to his head by a band of tooled leather.

Although Cameron was still a relative newcomer to the "wilds" of western Canada, there was no doubting this man's race, with his high-cheeked face, long hooked nose, and hair which hung in two braids down to his chest.

Major Rosser was the first man in the room to move.

'Come on over, Mr Stuart. I'd like you to meet your new assistant.'

'This is Spotted Bear,' he said, placing his hand on the Native's shoulder. 'He's a Blackfoot Indian...and knows these prairies better than any else in these parts.'

From the start, Cameron was a little unsure as to how this relationship was supposed to work. After a brief introduction – during which, the most Cameron got out of his new assistant was a few grunts – they were led by one of the depot staff to the large warehouse's doors; and once opened were left there on their own.

Inside the building were a couple of strange-looking wagons, numerous horses and various leather harnesses and bridles. Spotted Bear immediately looked over the horses and picked out two that he deemed suitable. Next, he signalled Cameron to join him near the front of one of the wagons.

These must be the infamous Red River Carts that Cameron had heard had been in use in Canada and the U.S.A. for years. They had two huge wheels, approximately five feet in diameter, which were set almost in the middle of the cart.

These big wheels kept the body of the wagon high off the ground – thus ensuring it would easily clear stumps and rocks – and if a river ever had to be crossed, they could easily be removed, allowing the cart to be floated across. The axles were never greased, as it would only have absorbed dirt, thereby wearing them down; the only problem with this being they were terribly noisy, and could be heard coming from miles away.

The wagon's body was made from rough softwood, and was held together by wooden pegs and strips of rawhide. And although the carts regularly broke down, there was no metal in their construction, so they could easily be fixed with the materials at hand.

Having ascertained that all was in order, Spotted Bear harnessed up two of the horses before mating each with a cart.

'You bring other horse…we take outside…make ready for tomorrow.'

So, he does actually speak then, thought Cameron, grasping the reins of the dark mare and following the native out of the building.

A few minutes later, the horses were secured near the open door of one of the two freight wagons sitting on a nearby siding. In these wagons were the goods required to sustain them for their upcoming journey, so, without further discussion, Spotted Bear vaulted inside and started passing out their stores. The list of supplies – had it been written down – would have taken up at least two pages. But Spotted Bear needed no written inventory.

First to be loaded were their food supplies. Now, to Cameron, this seemed a little strange as, surely, they would want to get at these fairly soon? Next to be packed were their sleeping bags and extra blankets – by which time Cameron was totally perplexed. These were followed by lanterns and kerosene, after which Spotted Bear lugged a wood-burning stove to the open doorway of the freight car.

Finally, Cameron began to understand. Everything was loaded into the carts in reverse order of its need, when setting up camp. The last items to be put on board the first cart were two tents, enough wood to keep the stove going for the first night, and implements for clearing their campsite of brush or snow.

Cameron's companion had so far been a man of few words, so unsurprisingly, when the time came to fill the second cart he just stood back, and pointing at Cameron said, 'You now'.

For a moment, Cameron stared at their stack of surveying equipment, and the other various piles of wood lying about on the floor of the second freight wagon. It never occurred to him that the order in which these were loaded would make any difference, after all, they were mainly just long poles, cross pieces and a few tools. However, after a few minutes contemplation, it did strike him that the theodolite and its spare were pretty important, so after first wrapping them in a few spare blankets, he carefully placed them under the driver's seat.

By the time they moved the loaded carts back to the warehouse, the sun was low in the sky and it was becoming very cold. After saying goodnight to Spotted Bear, Cameron began to amble his way back to Mr Van Horne's private railway car. Before long, his ears began to sting, and his eyelashes to stick together, as the sweat from his previous exertions dripped down his forehead and froze. Picking up his walking pace, Cameron realised he'd just learned another salutary lesson.

Nobody ambles in Canada during the winter – unless, of course, they're partial to freezing to death!

Twenty Six

The following morning, the weather was magnificent, and not a cloud marred the vast expanse of aquamarine sky.

Cameron stood on the car's rear platform, casting his eye over the clean, fresh world around him. Yesterday, he'd been too busy to pay much attention to anything outside the yard, and today one could see for miles. Mind you, the glare from the sun was almost blinding, he thought, as his hand automatically lifted to shade his eyes.

His final briefing from Major Rosser had been short but succinct.

'Mr Van Horne is relying on you. He expects to be achieving four to five miles a day next year…so the more you can get done before winter shuts you down, then the better the head start you'll have next spring.'

'I appreciate that…and you can be sure we'll do our best.'

'One more thing. I've had the yard manager load up two new rifles and a box of ammo on your cart. They're a gift from Mr Van Horne. I think you'll be quite impressed as they're the new Martini-Henry Mark 111s…and from what I've heard, they're the best guns in the world. I've also got one of those new Colt 45 handguns here for you to try out,' he said, handing Cameron a shiny, hinged box.

'I'm afraid I've never had a reason to use either before,' Cameron replied, rather hesitantly.'

'Don't worry about that. I'm sure your friend will give you all the instruction you need. Anyway, best of luck… and we'll see you back in Winnipeg.'

There was a buzz of excitement in the air as Cameron headed across the tracks towards the office. Looking to his right, the yard engine was already moving down the yard to pick up the Major's car, while all around him men scurried about the yard, happy to complete their final tasks before shipping out for the winter.

Nearing the main building, he spotted his fellow adventurer, leaning against the log pile at the side of the front door. And besides his strange dress, he now sported a large deerskin pouch, hanging at his waist by a long strap over his shoulder.

Maybe he's packed lunch for us, Cameron mused, breezily strolling up to him.

'Listen, Spotted Bear. We're going to be together for a long time, so…my name's Cameron. Now, what do you want me to call you?'

'George…good. Most white men call me that.'

Reaching into his pouch, he then produced what appeared to be a pair of wooden glasses, with a small slit in each, in place of a glass lens.

'Here…take…you need. '

An hour later the two carts left the yard, following the line of stakes left by the previous crew. Initially, there was nothing in the distance but a wavy white line forming the horizon, but as time passed, an occasional irregular smudge would appear, which, as they neared, would become an area of brush or small copse of trees.

The poles marking the previously surveyed roadbed soon ran out; but when George did not stop as expected, Cameron said nothing – having already learned not to question the actions of his guide.

As the sun climbed overhead, the day's first lesson was absorbed – the reflected glare from the sun would probably have blinded Cameron, had it not been for George's strange glasses.

Four hours later, they finally stopped – at the edge of a partly-frozen stream bordered by sheltering trees; and by the

238

time they had applied the finishing touches to their campsite, the sun was near the horizon.

The day had really been just one big lesson, thought Cameron, as his mind went over the last ten hours. Making camp had reminded him of his first few minutes with George, when he had stood in the warehouse not knowing where to start. On arrival at the campsite, they had positioned the wagons to provide two sides to their shelter, with the copse of trees making up a third. Then, the horses had been fed and watered, before being led into a temporary corral constructed with poles cut from the trees. Only then did they start to organize their own accommodation.

To Cameron's surprise, the two tents were not meant as separate accommodation – one tent being placed inside the other to provide a degree of thermal protection from the weather. The stove was then positioned onto a granite slab in the centre of the floor, followed by its chimney being fed through a specially lined collar sewn into the roof of both tents. Conifer branches were then laid against the outsides of the tent to provide more insulation, and lastly, smaller boughs were put on the floor of their two sleeping areas – primarily as insulation from the cold ground, but also to provide some comfort beneath their sleeping bags.

In the end, what had at first seemed to Cameron like an awful lot of work for just one night made sense when, on questioning George, he discovered that these encampments were to be much more than just an overnight resting place.

The intermittent beat of flapping canvass broke into Cameron's dream, wrenching him from his sleep. At the same time, a freezing gust of air struck him in the face when George, half covered in snow, re-entered the tent with an armful of wood. Rummaging about in one of the boxes stacked against the rear wall of the tent, George finally grunted with success, as his hand emerged with a worn deer-skin bag. Soon, the aroma of freshly brewed coffee permeated the air; and Cameron sprang out of bed – quickly donning his clothes and boots.

For the next thirty minutes, he and his companion sat drinking their coffee. To Cameron's ear, the wind seemed to be increasing in strength, and now, along with the continuous beat of the tent's walls, he could make out swishing sounds, as the nearby pines swayed back and forth in the stiffening breeze.

Swallowing the last of his coffee, Cameron got up, readying himself to go out and get on with their job.

'No work today! Too much wind…snow come.'

'Oh. Well…If we have to stay around here all day, it might be a good time for you to teach me how to use those new guns we've been given.'

Two cups of coffee later, the men were sufficiently motivated to go outside. Cameron headed towards his cart, and after digging around below the seat, and carefully moving aside his instruments, he retrieved the rifles and ammo. Meanwhile, George headed into the nearby woods to find suitable trees on which to carve some targets.

The two of them met at a fallen trunk, in a clearing about two hundred yards into the trees. Cameron opened the catches on the face of the long wooden case and, as he lifted the hinged top, two gleaming rifles were revealed. Hefting one out, George placed the stock against his right shoulder and sighted down the barrel. This was the first breech-loading gun either man had seen; but within a few minutes, George had worked out the difference between these and the old muzzle-loading guns like the Snider-Enfield.

The Martini-Henry was fitted with a modified rear sight, which George soon got to grips with, hitting the centre of the targets on nearly all of his shots. Cameron, on the other hand, was another story. He'd never fired a rifle in his life.

Three times that day, they ventured out onto their improvised firing range, where Cameron continued to practice until the cold made his hands useless. By the time the light began to fade, the student was not exactly what one would call a crack shot, but he could confidently handle the firearm and was regularly starting to hit the medium distance targets. George reckoned his 'eye…not bad' and arm 'almost steady' and 'maybe with much practice become hunter'; which, coming from an Indian, was probably as good a compliment as he could expect.

The following morning, as the sun began to rise, an insistent push on the shoulder woke Cameron. The coffee pot was already on the stove, belching its tainted cloud; and moments later, a metal cup arced its way towards Cameron from the other side of the tent, awakening him fully as he was forced to dodge out of its way.

'Come!…wagon ready. Lost much time.'

'Since when did you become so talkative in the morning?' Cameron yawned.

'Since I know…only way…get you out of bed.'

For the first time, the Indian's eyes appeared warmer, and Cameron thought he may even have detected the glimmer of a smile, before George quickly turned away and busied himself tidying up his sleeping space.

Over the next two weeks, a routine was established which saw good progress towards the west. Each day they would ride out to the survey line at daybreak, returning to camp just before sunset. Then, after a meal, usually prepared by George, they would retire to the tent – where Cameron would complete the task of updating the survey map before crawling into bed.

If the weather held, every fourth day would be spent moving camp another twenty miles. However, after the third such move, it was becoming obvious to Cameron that problems lay ahead. As if reading his mind, George interrupted Cameron's thoughts, late one afternoon, as they were bedding down the horses for the night.

'We need…take break. Now, no meat… almost no wood. Tomorrow we shoot deer…then cut more poles.'

The glimmer of light in the awakening sky was barely sufficient to change the blackness of night into a dark shade of grey, allowing the top of the bank on the other side of the stream to become just visible.

The two men lay motionless under a hide of branches and conifer boughs. Cameron slowly traversed his rifle from left to right and back again, willing a target to show itself over his sights. They had been in this position for over two hours, to ensure they were well hidden before the deer came down for their early morning drink. Most of the snow had melted the week before, but the mornings were still frosty and the ground cold and wet. Cameron was sure his toes must be frostbitten, as they no longer felt attached to his feet. His hands and fingers were still warm, thanks to his fur-lined mittens, but they wouldn't remain so for long because George had just signalled that it was time to prepare for the shot, forcing both men to discard their hands warm protectors.

A few minutes later, George's finger pushed against the breech of Cameron's gun, making it traverse towards the right. At first Cameron saw nothing. But then, a subtle change in the shade of grey on the far bank drew his attention. As he concentrated on that spot, the almost imperceptible slurp of a hoof sinking into the mud at the water's edge gave away the position of their prey.

'Get ready,' George whispered.

Cameron lined-up his rear sight over the small post at the front of the barrel.

'Three…two…one…fire!'

As the two guns fired, the noise was tremendous. At the same time, the birds – who only seconds before had begun their early morning chorus – screeched, rising into the air as one, madly flapping their wings to get as much height and distance as possible from the danger lurking below. The thunder of galloping hooves then became the dominant sound, as the resounding crack of the rifles drifted away down the valley.

The two men rose from their hide, hurrying down the bank as fast as their stiff legs and numb feet would allow.

'Well…somebody missed.'

George said nothing, as the two of them stepped carefully from stone to stone across the stream. Lying on its side, obviously dead, was a white-spotted buck bearing a large set of antlers.

'Ten points,' George remarked. 'Buck five years old … so good food. I skin and prepare meat…you take axe… and cut trees for poles. Plenty small tree in wood…there,' he said pointing back across the stream. 'I shout when need help to carry meat.'

Cameron knew he was not the most experienced of hunters, but when he bent over to look at the wound in the deer's side, it was blatantly obvious that two bullets had penetrated the animal behind its shoulder.

'Want to make sure buck not run…then die bad,' George said guiltily. 'Not do next time…you make good shot.'

By the end of the day, the survey wagon was again refilled with stakes and the wood supply for their little stove had been fully replenished. The antlers had been cut off the head of the buck and the hide rolled and tied into a large bundle – to be dealt with at a later date. Their large leather meat bag was once again full, and was back in its usual position, suspended ten feet in the air by a rope attached to a stout branch. Cameron still found it hard to believe bears might be around, way out here; and in hindsight, really should have known better than to express those doubts to George.

That night, the two men gorged themselves on venison. At the same time, strips of meat were being smoked outside in George's special oven built from branches and conifer boughs. According to him, the resulting dried meat would then be beaten together with fat and berries to form a nutritious, leathery food called pemmican – which provided a nourishing emergency food supply.

The following morning, as Cameron was finishing off his morning cup of coffee, George stuck his head in the tent.

'Come!'

Returning to the site of the previous days kill, George pointed to the mud at the side of the stream. Cameron didn't need to be told what animal had footprints almost a foot in length, with five worn pads and claws to match.

The rest of the weeks leading up to Cameron's Christmas deadline followed their established routine; and in what seemed like no time at all the day had arrived to head back to Brandon.

They had reached the eastern edge of a wide valley, and as far as the eye could see there was nothing but the endless plain. By his calculations, he and George had staked out the route for a further one hundred and thirty miles – which, hopefully, would prove to be more than enough to keep the General Manager happy.

The following day, Cameron and George packed up their camp and headed for home. On the first night of their return journey – after quickly setting up just one tent – neither seemed ready to go to sleep after crawling into their beds. This was the beginning of eight days conversing long into the night; and by the time they reached Brandon, Cameron's partner and guide had become his good friend.

One night, they talked about families: Cameron discovering that George's wife was called Lomasi – which in English meant pretty flower – and that he had two young boys, called Running Deer and Swift Antelope; while in return, Cameron told George about Catherine, and his first wife Mary – but for the time being, did not mention he also had a son, who's name was Alex.

On another night, Cameron learned some of the history of the Blackfoot tribe: how, in the beginning, they had welcomed the arrival of Europeans and their horses, but had been made to pay dearly, as thirty years ago their population had been decimated by a white man's disease called smallpox.

George listened with interest, as Cameron explained how he and his countrymen had lost their land to invaders from the south. And how he had left his home to try and find a better life for himself in Canada. Strangely similar, thought George, to what the Blackfoot nation had done, when their lands had been taken from them in the U.S.A., and most had fled to Canada.

Four days into their return journey, they were overwhelmed by another blizzard and were forced to seek shelter on the edge of a forest. When the weather had still not improved by the end of the following day, George decided it was time to catch some small game, as, once again, they were running short of food.

'Maybe we should bring some traps with us when we come back next year. My father used them all the time, and he had no trouble catching rabbits, grouse and even geese.'

George fixed Cameron with a stony eye, signalling his disdain at such a suggestion.

'No need metal trap. Tomorrow...I show.'

The following day, while the blizzard continued to blow, Cameron learned the Indian method of snaring rabbits, how to turn them into a tasty supper, and how to prepare their fur for their main use – as linings for mittens and boots.

Three days later, they finally arrived back at the depot. Their carts were battered and worn, and were now being pulled by two tired-looking horses. All the next day was spent in the yard, disposing of what few supplies were left, returning serviceable equipment to storage and filling out work orders for the company carpenters and blacksmiths. While in the office, copies of the survey maps were made, and then stored for future use.

Late that afternoon, the two men left the office.

'In spring...we use ox to pull cart...ox much stronger...

pull more weight. Still take horses…we need to ride out to work…and for hunting.'

'Okay…sounds fine to me. Well, it's too late to go anywhere now so we may as well go down and check in at the hotel for the night.'

'No, me sleep warehouse…then go when sun rise.'

'But that's stupid, George. The railway will pay for your room.'

'Indian no can go in white man's hotel.'

George turned away, walking towards the warehouse, while Cameron remained rooted to the spot. He was dumfounded, and felt ashamed and saddened by his friend's sudden revelation. He couldn't believe that, now that they were back in what was supposed to be civilisation, their ethnic differences would impose limits on their friendship. They had just spent nearly two months working together and sleeping in the same tent. And yet now he was supposed to treat George like some lower class form of human being, not deserving of a place in the white man's world. Shaking his head, Cameron slowly wandered back to the office, for the first time realising that maybe he hadn't left the class system behind after all.

Late the following morning, Cameron walked up the main street in Brandon – killing time as he awaited the arrival of the train taking him back to Winnipeg. Even though the weather was miserably cold, the town was bustling. Since the day that he and Catherine had been here, two new hotels had opened, along with a hardware store, two saloons, a butcher's, post office, grocery store and of course, four new real estate offices. According to the Brandon Daily newspaper, the McKendry brothers were in the process of building a new lumber yard on the eastern edge of town, and a new blacksmith's had already opened for business.

Within just a few months, Brandon had changed from a tent city to a proper town. Already workmen were putting the finishing touches to wooden sidewalks on the main street, while other teams followed along behind, installing gas street lamps.

Although passenger traffic between Brandon and Winnipeg was not yet reaching the Company's target, the freight loads more than justified the C.P.R.'s enthusiastic forecast of profits. Every train arriving in Brandon was made up of fourteen to fifteen cars. Normally, three of these were for passengers, while the rest was made up of freight wagons carrying bulk goods, and flatcars hauling materials for the railway's expansion.

Cameron reached the station; and after standing on the platform for half an hour watching the yard engine shunting freight and flatcars onto various sidings, his train steamed in from Winnipeg.

The grey, overcast sky foretold of bad weather to come, and as the cold, gusty wind increased, it scattered the grit from the loco's funnel in all directions. Cameron rubbed at the irritant with his sleeve, before finally, turning up his collar and wandering back towards the waiting room. As he did the first flakes of snow began to swirl around the yard; and looking out to the west, no longer was there a divide between the earth and the sky, as a white wall of snow approached, flattening everything in its path.

By the time his train approached Winnipeg it was late afternoon. For the last hour, they had been paralleling the Assiniboine River, but as the river began to slowly ease its way towards the south, the outskirts of the city came into sight.

Cameron stared intently out the window, willing Catherine to be waiting for him on the platform. A few moments later, a grin broke out over his face, as standing beside one of the green metal pillars supporting the platform's canopy was Catherine – anxiously searching each of the carriage's windows.

247

With a loud snake-like hiss, and the screech of metal on metal, the train drew to a halt. Cameron smiled out the widow, before reaching into the overhead luggage rack to retrieve his bag; after which, unseen to her, he almost fell flat on his face as he tripped over his own feet in his haste to exit the train. Jumping down from the car, Cameron dropped his bag onto the platform and opened his arms.

'Don't you leave me again,' Catherine sobbed against his shoulder. 'I missed you so much! I didn't know whether you were alive or dead until yesterday, when I got your telegram.'

Cameron laid his cheek on top of her head, as she continued to sniff and weep. Then, easing her away, he placed his arm around her shoulders.

'Come on, Cath. Let's go home.'

He'd barely had time to kick the cabin door shut, before Catherine threw her arms around his neck, pulling his head down to smother his lips. Cameron began to feel the tightness in his stomach edging upwards, as his hands grasped her hips. When their mouths parted, he picked her up, carrying her to their bedroom and throwing her on the bed. Standing over her, he tore off his clothes. And then, lying down beside her, hurriedly unbuttoned her tunic and blouse, while at the same time lovingly running his tongue around her ear and down her neck. For a few minutes, his fingers circled her breast, before gradually wandering further down.

They made love furiously. And when it was over, started again – only this time slower, and with tenderness. Sometime later, when the world outside their home was dark and hushed, the two lovers fell asleep – their lust satisfied.

At midday the following day, they stood at the entrance to the stable yard, alongside the river, near Donald Street.

'What are we doing here, Cameron?'

'Well, you said not to leave you behind again. So, if you're going to come next year, you've got a lot to learn.'

A tall, moustachioed man wearing an ankle-length leather coat walked out of the office.

'You must be Mr Stuart…I got your telegram yesterday and everything's ready for you. Just follow me.'

Thirty minutes later they were headed for home, with Catherine desperately trying to get to grips with driving a buckboard. Cameron stood behind her, balancing on the balls of his feet and holding the back of the seat. They hurtled down Cumberland Avenue, pulled by a beautiful brown and white pony who had made up his mind that he was in charge.

'Aren't there any brakes on this thing?' Catherine screamed.

People, who only moments before had been sedately crossing the street, madly scattered. Mothers with young children gathered them in their arms and ran for safety, while men who were about to step off the sidewalk suddenly had second thoughts – and then raised their fists as the couple sped by. Cameron laughed, and then reached passed Catherine's body from behind and gripped her hands, while slowly applying rearward pressure to the reins.

'You've got to let the horse know who is boss,' he yelled. 'If you hold the reins too loosely, and give 'em their head, they'll assume they're in charge and take off.'

That evening, after Catherine had stopped shaking and Cameron had stopped chuckling, he finished telling Catherine about George and their life on the prairies.

By the time he'd finished, she began to realise that following her husband into the wilderness was probably not quite as simple as she had thought. In fact, she now began to wonder if maybe she was being just a little foolhardy. But then, it couldn't be all that hard. After all, hundreds of women settlers were doing it every day.

Christmas came, and with it winter set in. The streets were now constantly covered with snow and ice; and Winnipeg's two main rivers were once more frozen over. Cameron swapped their rig for a sleigh, allowing them to go much further afield.

Now, on Sundays, assuming the weather was good, they would pack a lunch and head out into the woods, north of the city. Soon, Catherine became quite adept at handling their new form of transport, and seemed to enjoy taking on board some of her husband's newly discovered bush craft skills. By the end of January, she was already a competent marksman; and her bread, baked in an iron pot over an open fire, was becoming legendary – well, in the Stuart household at least.

Twenty Seven

The day was remarkable on account of two events – both natural – but nevertheless important to people who had grown weary of the misery of winter.

The first passed unnoticed by all but a few learned people who made it their business to record such phenomena. The sun as usual rose in the east and set in the west. But what made this day noteworthy was that the length of daylight hours equally matched those of darkness. Throughout history many cultures celebrated this day by giving thanks to whichever God they believed made this possible. But, in these more modern times, if it was noticed at all, it was only given credit as the official first day of spring.

The second event, beheld by all but the deaf, occurred when, with an almighty crack like the explosion of a canon, the ice in the Red River began to break up.

In Winnipeg, there was no cheering or celebrating – in fact, quite the opposite. Most faces took on a more serious look; and throughout the city everyone now seemed in a hurry to get from place to place. Each morning, worried managers of river-front businesses could be seen carefully studying the water before opening their front doors; while at the same time, queues built up on both sides of the pontoon bridge, as most drivers felt the need to approach the crossing with much greater care.

It seemed most inhabitants of Winnipeg were aware that, in 1826, the combined mass of ice and water in the Assiniboine and Red Rivers had raised its level until it had burst its banks, destroying the town. And since then, flooding to a greater or lesser extent had occurred at least every ten years.

That morning Cameron's eyes flew open, and for a moment his arms froze at his side. His heart quickened; and then, as his memory also awakened he recalled hearing a similar explosion one year before.

'What is it? What's the matter?' murmured a sleepy Catherine, before rolling over and staring at her husband with her half-opened eyes.

'Sorry if I woke you, Cath. The ice on the river has just begun to break up and the noise woke me up.'

A few seconds later, the morning's tranquillity was once more shattered by a resounding crack, as Cameron's firm hand landed on Catherine's bare bottom.

'Come on sleepy…you'd better get up. I'm going into the office early today, and you have to take me in,' he said, quickly jumping out of bed, and narrowly avoiding her retaliatory swing.

When Cameron stepped through the front doors of the C.P.R headquarters, he immediately discovered that he wasn't the only one who'd been rudely awakened. To his surprise, nearly all of the staff were at their desks. Muted conversations and the clicking of the keys on the new Remingtons greeted him as he strolled down the corridor. Along the way, he responded to the occasional 'Good morning, Mr Stuart', with a smile and witty remark about the "ice", before finally reaching his assistant's desk at the far end of the hallway.

While he and his secretary went over his agenda for the day, the hubbub suddenly ceased, and through the door marched the General Manager. His heavy-lidded eyes scanned back and forth under the over-hanging brim of his Homburg-style hat, and even he couldn't disguise the slight look of surprise on his face at the sight of so many of his employees so early in the day.

Midway through the morning, a quick knock sounded on Cameron's door, and as he looked up in walked Cornelius Van Horne.

'Please...don't get up,' the boss said as Cameron started to rise. 'I just wanted to let you know I'm going to need certain facts and figures for my meeting with the directors this afternoon. So, when you have a moment, would you bring the registers and order books up to my office? I know it'll take you some time to get them together, so shall we say...in about twenty minutes?'

That spring, in preparation for the building season ahead, Winnipeg had become an enormous supply depot. The railway's requirements for this year were almost unimaginable. Two main contractors had been signed up, who between them had promised to complete five hundred miles of track before the next winter. They in turn were hiring three thousand men and two thousand horses, as every stick of timber for the bridges, and all provisions for the total workforce of seven thousand men, would have to be hauled across the prairies by wagon. Lumber was arriving from eastern Canada and the northern part of the United States, while rails, fishplates, and spikes were coming by ship from England and Germany.

Nothing could be left to chance, and all of this was being co-ordinated by Cameron and his staff of four men. It was hardly surprising his boss was concerned. If any mistakes were made, or shipments of goods delayed, it could put the whole project in jeopardy, leaving thousands of men sitting around idle while still being paid. Mr Van Horne had made many promises to the C.P.R. board of directors, and no doubt his head was now well and truly on the block.

This was probably the reason why, two weeks before, the General Manager had again stamped his authority on the railway by firing Major Rosser. The chief engineer's lack of interest in his job, coupled with his burgeoning enthusiasm for real estate, had finally become much too public. Barely a day had gone by in the last month without press speculation concerning the amount of money being made on property by those with inside knowledge of the route of the railway.

'Please, just take a seat for a moment, Mr Stuart, while I have a quick look through these.'

Cameron's eyes gazed idly about the room, while his heart pounded noisily in his chest as he awaited his boss's approval.

'Well, it appears you and your men have things well in hand. Before you go, though, I'd just like to bring up one small area of concern. Two weeks from now the graders should be able to head out and start preparing the track beds, and a week or so after that, the track laying will recommence. As you know, the ice has started to move. What concerns me is this. If the rivers were to flood again, and we subsequently lost any of our bridges, we could end up with half of our construction materials stuck here in Winnipeg.'

To Cameron the solution was simple. At the moment, the marshalling yard in Brandon was underused, and as far as he was concerned, with a few modifications could easily be turned into a gigantic supply depot.

Orders were immediately issued, and by the end of the week trains were running twenty-four hours a day until all supplies had been shipped out of danger.

At the end of April a destructive wall of water did move down the Red River from the Northern United States. In its wake, the C.P.R.'s brand new bridge connecting the line from the east into the city, and the pontoon bridge allowing access to the marshalling yard south of the river, were both destroyed. From that day, until a new bridge was completed nine months later, all subsequent goods once more had to be shipped via St. Paul – over a hastily rebuilt pontoon bridge.

Cornelius Van Horne could not understand why Cameron would not accept any recognition for the vital contributions he had made to the success of the Company. Twice, the General Manager had tried to have him presented to the board of directors. First, for his clever inventory system – the

254

likes of which no one had ever seen before – and now for his foresight in moving the supplies from Winnipeg before the floods, which probably saved the railway from financial ruin. Van Horne greatly admired his young surveyor's conscientiousness and humility, and he was now more determined than ever to see to it that Cameron was properly rewarded, once the crossing of the prairies was complete.

Twenty Eight

Just after sunrise, on the first Wednesday in May, 1882, three red river carts set off from the Brandon depot. Leading the way was Spotted Bear, his wagon full to overflowing with all the equipment needed to make camp for the next six to seven months. Next in line came Catherine. She was the least experienced, and like her husband, had only been given minimal instruction on how to control oxen. So, her load was made up of stakes, crosspieces and firewood, which if worse came to worst, could easily be replaced. Last in line was Cameron. Like Spotted Bear, his cart was loaded to the top of its canvass hood and contained their food supplies, his delicate survey equipment and other necessities such as cooking vessels, guns and ammunition. This time, tools such as shovels, axes and fire tripods were all secured in special racks attached to the outside of the carts; while other modifications completed during the winter months included such things as the permanent fixing of water barrels to the rear of the wagons, under seat storage fixings, and leather encased padding on their seats.

Finally, bringing up the rear of this mini wagon train were three sturdy looking horses, tethered to the back of Cameron's cart by extended reins.

As they jerked and bounced along the rutted trail beside the track bed, a grin appeared on Cameron's face as he contemplated Catherine's next lesson in wilderness transportation – namely that of riding a horse. 'That should produce a few very special moments,' he muttered to himself.

'Get up!' yelled Cameron, followed by the loud crack of his whip as his oxen decided to test his concentration by slowing to nearly a halt.

There were only five commands used to control these steers, all of them normally reinforced with the sound of a hide whip cracking in the animals' ears. Apart from the command he'd just used there was 'Whoa!', which he expected might well become the most important, 'Gee!', which was supposed to get the animal to veer to the left, 'Haw!', to the right, and finally 'Back-up!', which, from what he'd been told, hardly ever worked.

Cameron smiled, as he recalled Catherine's frustration during their instruction course the week before.

'It's no good losing your temper with these boys,' said John Cuthbert, the teamster who was instructing them. 'Just remember...they can get more pig-headed than you can. They're not a unique animal...just a mature one, with an education... and an attitude!'

Cameron's thoughts drifted away as he thought about the huge juggernaut now sweeping its way across the prairies. The earth moving teams had moved off the week before – which was why the next ten to fifteen miles were easy, as all the three of them had to do was stay in the rutted track beside the newly constructed four foot high embankment. Tomorrow the track laying gang would once more embark on their relentless march across the plains, while the bridge building gang had left weeks before, and by now should have nearly completed their first river crossing.

At this moment, Cameron knew where every spike, rail and piece of wood owned by the C.P.R. rested. But, as of tomorrow, it would begin to scatter across five hundred miles of plain; and the only thing holding everything together was his system, and the men he had trained. If anything had been forgotten it was now irrelevant, because it was too late to stop the inertia of the massive machine that had been set in motion.

Suddenly, Cameron was yanked back to the present, as up ahead of him Catherine's rig veered out to the right. Thinking the worst, he drew to a halt, preparing to mount his horse and gallop off to her rescue. To his relief, his ears detected a faint command, followed by the crack of a whip, and Catherine's straying oxen swerved back into line.

Their long first day finally neared its end, as on breasting the top of a small rise their resting place for the night came into view. Below them, spread out over fifty acres, was the campsite of the crews building the track bed. The tents for almost five hundred men were stretched out in ragged clusters in all directions. In a central area was a huge corral for the hundreds of horses and oxen needed to power the wagons and carts, and two massive tents housing the mobile kitchens and serving tables. This camp moved almost daily, and was staffed by permanent wagon-drivers, cooks and labourers, whose sole purpose was to feed and house the men carrying out the all-important first phase.

For the first week, the weather was as fickle as a Scottish summer's afternoon – warm and sunny one day, chilly and gusty the next – but as they continued westwards, it started to become more welcoming.

The three wagons pushed on for a further ten days following the line staked out by Cameron the previous year. Finally, they arrived at the edge of the escarpment overlooking the wide valley. For a while, all three gazed in wonder at the limitless beauty before them, before George dragged them back to the realities of the present.

'We fill up water barrels in river…down in valley…then make camp for night. Tomorrow we travel west two more days…then make big camp.'

So, the routine that Cameron and his companion had instituted the previous year was once more re-established. Of course, slight variations had to be made now that Catherine was part of the team. Most days, she would remain in camp, while the two men rode out to the survey line. Cameron and George would then stay out on the line until almost dark, happy in the knowledge that when they got back the chores would be done and their meal would be waiting.

The men's diet improved enormously. No longer was their main staple baked beans, or a stew made with venison or a recently caught rabbit. As long as Catherine had flour, fat, sugar and eggs she would regularly make pies – some with fruit, as a treat, and others with meat served up with potatoes and whatever vegetables were to hand. Once or twice a week, the fatigue the men felt after a long day toiling in the hot sun was instantly forgotten when, a mile or two from camp, their noses would pick up the aroma of freshly baked bread.

The day of Catherine's first riding lesson – which both men had looked forward to, thinking it might provide them with some amusement – finally arrived. Much to their disappointment, it passed off with barely a hitch, because once she realised the same rules of authority applied to the control of a horse as to a stubborn ox she got the better of her mare.

The end of May arrived, and with seventy miles already behind them, progress had been better than Cameron had expected. The view to the west was now almost uninterrupted, and what few hills there were showed up as ripples on the horizon. Now, the only features of any note were the occasional river, cutting through the flat plains to eventually join up with the mighty Saskatchewan River, flowing towards the east.

These tributaries would certainly be keeping the bridging teams occupied, Cameron thought one day, as they forded their second river in a week. He knew that at this moment the men building the bridges were somewhere to the east of them, between him and the crews gouging out the track beds; and their actual location was soon to be uncovered, because

Catherine's supplies were running low and he and George had already decided that a restocking trip was needed.

The sun was setting behind their backs as the odour of salt pork and wood smoke led Cameron and Catherine over the brow of the hill; and below them, spread out alongside the river bank, was the encampment of the bridge building team.

Drawing to a halt on the outskirts of the temporary community, they both became aware of the staring faces focusing on Catherine's female form. Feeling somewhat vulnerable, Cameron unbuttoned his leather coat to reveal the Colt 45 strapped to his waist. Stepping down steadily from the seat of their cart, he then reached back up to take his wife's arm. On hearing the sound of rapidly approaching boots, Cameron's free hand moved inside his coat, and as Catherine's second foot reached the ground he released her arm, whipped open his coat, and swung around to face the intruder.

'Well, if it isn't Cameron Stuart! How the hell are you? Oh, I do beg your pardon, Ma'am... I...uh...I didn't...'

Cameron's stern face dissolved into a warm smile and his hand came off his weapon to reach forward and shake the man's hand.

'Sean...good to see you! I didn't realise you'd be out with the gang.'

The boss of the bridge building gang was Sean McIlvey, a man Cameron had met once or twice before at planning meetings in Winnipeg.

'You know what it's like. I needed to get away from the old...oh you know.'

Cameron and Catherine both laughed; and that evening, after a dinner of pork with dumplings, sweet potatoes and onions, they drank until almost dawn.

Two very sorry looking people climbed into their cart the next day. Catherine seemed unusually quiet, which Cameron put down to the previous evening's excesses, but as time wore on, he began to suspect there was more to this than just a headache.

'Okay, Cath...What have I done wrong? If it's because of last night, then I'm sorry...I admit it...I did drink too much, and I guess I was pretty loud.'

Catherine turned slightly towards him, placing her hand on his upper thigh.

'It's not you, Cameron. I've got something to tell you that I probably should have mentioned before. Somehow, the right time just didn't seem to present itself, so please don't be mad at me...I'm sure everything will be okay.'

Catherine stared into his concerned eyes for what seemed an eternity, and then quietly murmured the two words that throughout history have brought either incredible joy or instant consternation.

'I'm pregnant.'

For the rest of that day, and into the evening, Catherine tried her best to reassure Cameron. She knew that after the death of his first wife during childbirth he might be slightly apprehensive. But it had never crossed her mind he would be this anxious.

'Come on, Cameron. Women have been giving birth in the wilderness since the beginning of time. Besides, there's no reason to assume my pregnancy...and the birth of our child...will be anything but normal.'

'I don't care...If we were anywhere near civilisation I'd send you home.'

Catherine and Cameron were both strong characters, and this had been their first major disagreement. Neither of them was willing to change their opinion, so the rest of the evening, and the following day, were spent in silence.

George sensed all was not well, when they had silently driven into camp with Cameron and Catherine both wearing expressionless faces. Putting down the ladle with which he was stirring his concoction, he got up and wandered over to give them a hand.

'Hello, George,' Cameron said, throwing him the reins as he climbed down from the cart.

Turning back to face the cart, Cameron raised his hand to help Catherine.

'I can manage on my own,' she declared, grabbing the side of the cart and leaping to the ground. Then, standing up straight, she threw back her shoulders and marched off towards their tent.

'Wagon plenty full. You have good time?' George asked, rather sarcastically.

'The bridging crew are two days back, and apparently the track layers are about thirty miles behind them. Looks to me like everyone's right on schedule.'

As Cameron gazed about the campsite, it was plain to see George had been busy. The wagon containing all of their survey equipment had been almost empty when Cameron had left, but now it sat by the corral bulging with newly cut stakes. While over near George's tent, stretched tightly across four round frames, were four rabbit pelts.

'I guess I know what we're having for dinner tonight.'

Cameron walked over to the fire, then, lifting the lid off the pot, sniffed the air.

'By God, George! Your rabbit stew is unmistakeable. If you go and have a look in our wagon you'll find some potatoes and onions, which might go rather nicely with what's in here.'

Supper began as a very sombre affair, but before long the silence had become too much for Cameron to bear.

'Okay…enough is enough. Catherine, you may as well tell George what the problem is. He's entitled to know, especially as it could affect our routine in the very near future.'

To their amazement, George barely reacted to the news.

'I thought she having baby…stomach get bigger. Why you angry, Cameron? Should be happy.'

'It's…well…it's just so dangerous to have a baby out here.'

'Why dangerous? If you want…I get Lomasi…she help other mothers have baby.'

And so what had been seen by Cameron as such a major situation had, with George's calming influence, been reduced to nothing more than a minor consideration.

Catherine's increase in size now marked the passage of time, while Cameron's occasional lapse into exaggerated concern ensured that the subject of her pregnancy never retreated far from anyone's mind. For her part, Catherine stoically ignored any discomforts she felt, her only deference to her condition being to stop riding her mare two months before the baby was due.

Twenty Nine

The trio's relentless march towards the setting sun continued. Nearly every week another twenty-five miles was marked out; while during that time their small encampment would be uprooted twice and shifted further west.

The first week of July arrived – sunny, hot and very dry. The arid plains seemed to go on forever, and Cameron wondered if they would ever see a hill or forest again. Not for the first time he began to ask himself how the immigrants following the railway west could ever be expected to scratch a living out of this parched, featureless prairie. Oh, there was grass all right, and thank God there was, or else their progress would have been stalled a long way back by the lack of feed. But how could homesteaders be expected to survive out here, with the lack of trees and scarcity of water? On questioning George, the answer was always the same. His people had survived for hundreds of years on these plains – and there was plenty of water if you knew where to look.

One day, as their little convoy reached the top of a small hillock, a brilliant white blemish stood out against the dull landscape ahead.

'What's that up ahead?' Cameron asked, removing his floppy hat and wiping the dust from his brow with the back of his sleeve.

'That place we call Wascana. My father and his father… and his father before him…they come here. Now we make camp…next water ten days ride.'

One thing Cameron had already learned was that Natives called things as they saw them. Places were often named after some geographical feature, making them easily recognizable, or at other times given names commemorating special events. Similarly, the Native people themselves were often named after animals or objects from the natural world deemed significant by their elders.

In this case, Wascana was a Cree Indian word meaning pile of bones. That name had been used by Indians for over a hundred years, because of the great stack of bison bones lying there in the valley bleaching in the sun. For generations, hunting parties had skinned and disposed of animals here, and then left the bones as a marker to lead them back to this place of clean water. However, it was now midsummer, and this century old watering place had become barely a trickle as it meandered through the longer grasses, marking the arid plain like a bruise on a tanned hide.

As such, Cameron was a little unsure how this flow was supposed to satisfy the appetites of their three oxen and horses, never mind themselves; but, as was usually the case, he should never have questioned his faith in George.

He and Catherine watched in wonder as George took a few planks of wood from the side of one of the carts, and a couple of stakes from another, before damming the diminutive waterway; and within a few hours a pond grew out of nowhere, providing them with all the water they could ever use.

Two days later, while Cameron and George were taking a break from their labours to have lunch, a large cloud of dust appeared on the eastern horizon.

'Looks like we may have a sand storm approaching.'

George watched the anomaly for a few minutes, and then rose, packing his canteen away into one of his saddlebags.

'No…no storm. Visitor come…many visitor.'

Sure enough, what had at first appeared to be a large wall of dust soon turned into a wagon train. In the lead were four men on horseback, with a further one visible out on either point. Then, a large carriage drawn by four horses came into

265

sight, at the head of a formation of five covered wagons; while trailing at the rear, with the unenviable task of eating the convoy's dust, were four more riders.

Cameron wasn't totally surprised when the convoy pulled up, and who should alight from the carriage but Cornelius Van Horne.

'Mr Stuart...how nice to see you again,' the General Manager said, walking over to shake Cameron's hand. 'You've made good progress...I was beginning to wonder if we'd ever catch up.'

Cameron was taken aback by his boss's subtle compliment, and for a moment stood saying nothing.

The General Manager gazed towards the north, and then after scanning the horizon to the west, sighed.

'I think I'm beginning to understand why some people wanted us to route the railway much further to the north. We really do need to establish another town and depot out here, but for the last fifty miles I've seen nothing that looks promising.'

'Maybe we should move on to my encampment, Sir. Then we can discuss the various options available in a bit more comfort. Besides, I'm sure you'd probably like to clean up a little after your long ride.'

Less than an hour later, they arrived in the shady valley – where Van Horne's crew set about the task of making their boss's temporary home as comfortable as possible.

When the wagons had come into view, Catherine had hurried out of sight. But she couldn't hide forever. Cameron had only been back ten minutes – and had barely had time to update his wife on the day's surprises – when a messenger arrived bearing a formal invitation to dinner.

The sky was huge, and bathed in the pink light of the setting sun, as they arrived outside the General Manager's enormous tent. The tarpaulin was held aside by a jacketed waiter;

and once inside, the three pioneers were transported into another world. The interior walls had been hung with silk-like fabrics to disguise the harshness of the canvass, and gas lamps hanging from the internal framework cast a soft glow of light throughout the interior. Just inside the entrance was a sitting area, furnished with a settee, four armchairs, two coffee tables and a beautiful maple desk. This lounging space was separated from the dining area by a number of large, silk screens – decorated with golden dragons and ornate eastern palaces – strategically placed to give the illusion of a separate room. A white, linen tablecloth covered the dining table – properly laid out with white bone china, silver cutlery and crystal glasses.

It was evident that Cornelius Van Horne did not believe in being without his creature comforts wherever he might be; and in hindsight it was not really surprising that five large wagons needed to accompany him. Cameron thought the splendour of Van Horne's private railway carriage had been a real eye-opener, but this was almost as impressive, especially if one considered its location.

The General Manager smiled warmly as he got up and walked over to greet his guests. Catherine was momentarily lost for words, when he gently took her hand and effusively complimented her on her looks, before leading her to a comfortable chair. She had been totally unprepared for his charming personality, and found it difficult to believe that this was the same man who, supposedly, struck fear into all who knew him. But what bewildered her most was his complete lack of reaction to her obvious pregnant form.

As this little play was being enacted Cameron could not help but notice the other two men standing alongside his boss. Both were casually dressed, each holding a glass of red wine in their hands.

'Allow me to introduce everyone. To my left is John Cummings, our new Chief Engineer, and to his left is Thomas Shaughnessy, our Purchasing Agent…whose job, I might add, includes advising me on building projects. Gentlemen, I'd like you to meet Cameron Stuart, his wife Catherine, and their guide and assistant Spotted Bear…who, I've been reliably informed, also goes by the name of George. Now, shall we all take our seats and get to know each other?'

That evening, Cameron once again marvelled at the capacity of his boss's mind.

Within ten minutes of their arrival this afternoon he and the other two men had been out pacing off distances and recording facts and figures in their notebooks. There was no such thing as time off when in the presence of Cornelius Van Horne. His thirst for solutions to problems was insatiable, and woe betide any member of staff showing any lack of energy or enthusiasm.

Pre-dinner drinks were followed by a sumptuous four-course dinner, after which Catherine and George took their leave. The C.P.R. men then retired to the sitting area, and over port, brandy and cigars got down to the business at hand. By the time the session ended, the final decision had been confirmed. The route of the railway would remain unchanged, with the prairie crossing terminating at Fort Calgary on the Bow River. The problem of where to build the new town and depot had been solved. Not by university educated engineers and managers, but by Native know-how – George's small man-made reservoir providing the spark for Van Horne's imagination.

'Let's face it,' remarked Cornelius Van Horne. 'If there's water in this valley in the heat of the summer, then imagine how much there will be in the winter. We can build a reservoir by damming this valley, which when filled, will provide all the water needed for both the C.P.R. and a future city. Now, as you know, the other major prerequisite for any town or city is timber. And as Thomas has pointed out, there is more than enough twenty miles from here at Fort Qu'Appelle. With their trees, and the resources available from the nearby settlement, we will have everything we need.'

At sunrise the following day, Cameron was woken by the sound of horses whinnying and stomping their hooves. His head pounded; and as he rolled out of bed he was amazed at how the General Manager could survive with such little sleep – and so much drink!

Hurrying over to the lead wagon, he was just in time to hear Mr Van Horne handing out the last of his orders before they set off.

'Thank you again, Mr. Stuart, for your hard work and good advice. We're heading straight back to "track end", so I can get on with organizing the building of this new town and depot. Oh…and by the way…the Governor General called me the other day, and during our conversation just happened to mention how interested Queen Victoria was in our little project. As such, I thought it might be appropriate to remember her when we name this new town. So I've decided to call it Regina.'

Cameron did his best to show some enthusiasm for this announcement; but as he walked back to his tent, he couldn't help but wonder if he would ever stop being reminded of the perpetrators of all of his country's misfortunes.

Three days later the three of them re-packed their carts and set off again. Their food supplies had again been topped up, but this time with incredible delicacies such as chickens, beef and bacon, all provided by Mr Van Horne's extensive supply wagon.

By the end of September, they arrived at one of the major tributaries of the South Saskatchewan River – where evidence of a great number of previous visitors abounded. Numerous circular, flattened areas were dotted about the place – indicating the previous sites of tepees – and many stone circles, filled with the blackened remains of cooking fires, were dotted about the place.

George knew this site well – he and his tribe having camped here many times before. The water was clean, cool and teeming with fish, which in the evenings could be seen leaping from the water in their quest for tasty morsels of dragonflies and moths.

In fact, as far as Cameron could see, the only drawback would be the crossing of the river itself, as it was a torrent, crashing over rocks and swirling in eddies around the deeper pools.

Although there was already a Native name associated with this place, Cameron decided it was time for him to have his say – so on his map marked down the name Swift Current.

The dark circle of the new moon floated on the eastern horizon and the stars sparkled in the tranquil air as the three exhausted travellers relaxed near the circle of rocks enclosing their campfire. Setting up camp was always a tiring exercise, but was now made more wearing by Catherine's inability to do all but the most menial of tasks. She was starting into her last month of pregnancy, and George didn't need to be told Cameron's concern was on the verge of becoming all consuming.

Occasionally, as she winced from a stitch in her side or particularly hard kick from the baby, he would rush to her – only to be rebuffed in an increasingly brusque manner. So early the next morning George mounted his stallion. And with clods of mud flying from its hooves, galloped off in search of his family.

Over the next two hours, Cameron fussed about the campsite, going out of his way to delay his departure to the survey line.

'Cameron...would you please stop fidgeting about. I'm fine. Now get off and do your work...I'll see you this evening.'

Cameron was about to open his mouth. But when he saw the look of determination in her eyes, and the bunched fists at her side, he mounted his horse and cantered off.

That evening, the heavenly aroma of freshly baked bread led Cameron home. His wife was amazing, he thought. Eight months pregnant and stuck out in the middle of nowhere, yet she still manages to find the time and strength to bake bread.

For the next two days Cameron surveyed the line by himself, until finally he reached the river's crossing point, south of their encampment. Now he had the excuse he'd yearned for, as it was impossible for him to cross the river on his own. So, whistling to himself, he packed up his equipment and headed for camp.

Soon after rounding the jutting outcrop of rock just east of their temporary home, Cameron abruptly reined in his horse. In the distance were two Indian braves, sitting on ponies only yards from his tent. From where he was they appeared to be naked – apart from breechcloths and moccasins – while at the same time he could just make out quivers full of arrows hanging from their shoulders, and bows, held almost menacingly in their hands. With the flick of his reins, he encouraged his horse forward; and as he drew nearer, reached down for his Colt 45.

On arriving near the outer perimeter of their campsite, he slowed his horse to a walk, and casually eased his hand away from his firearm. The fearsome braves had turned into two young boys, and George's grey stallion had now come into sight, pawing at the ground and shaking its head in recognition of Cameron's mare.

'You look rather hot and bothered dear. Why don't you get down and come over and meet George's family?' came Catherine's familiar voice.

In the same moment, a young Native woman with high cheek bones and deep-set almond eyes stepped out from behind the tent. She wore a beautifully beaded deerskin dress, reaching down to the top of her moccasined feet, and her jet black hair, which was parted down the middle and held close to her head by a beaded band, was drawn into two tight braids hanging down to her waist.

Cameron tied off his horse at the corral and then, trying to appear as relaxed as possible strolled over to his wife.

'This is Lomasi…and on the ponies are George's two sons… Running Deer and Swift Antelope,' said Catherine.

'Oki,' said Lomasi, prompting the same response from her two boys.

Cameron wasn't very sure what greeting was expected from him, so he replied with the slight raising of his hand and a 'hello'.

Moments later George appeared, walking over to where Cameron was standing.

'I bring boys…to help cross river.'

By the time two more weeks had passed, the women had become quite fond of each other. Catherine had begun to learn a few words of Blackfoot, such as 'Oki' meaning 'hello', and 'giga waba mimbama', which roughly translated into 'I'll see you later'. In return, George's wife had learned a few words of English, and was taught how to make white man's bread.

It was another beautiful autumn day as the following afternoon the two men rode back towards camp after a day's hunting. Although they'd not had any success in shooting a deer, they at least each had a pair of rabbits hanging from the horns of their saddles.

The late autumn sun warmed the back of Cameron's neck under the brim of his hat; while high overhead squadrons of honking Canada Geese, with almost military precision, formed huge Vs in the sky as they headed south to their winter feeding grounds.

Cameron's horse suddenly stumbled, its left foreleg descending into a burrow dug by a prairie dog. A cacophony of dog-like barks sounded out, destroying the late afternoon peacefulness and spooking both horses into flight.

Within moments, both men had brought their steeds under control, but not before Cameron's mare had damaged her leg. After dismounting, Cameron held his mare's reins, while

George lifted it's foreleg to check the injury.

'She damage leg…behind knee,' George said, gently placing the hoof back on the ground. 'We walk now…camp not far.'

Finally, their tents came into sight.

'George…something's not right. Look! There's no smoke. The fire should be stoked up and cooking our evening meal.'

'Here…take horse,' George said, handing over the reins of his stallion.

Vaulting onto the unsaddled stallion, Cameron dug in his heels and galloped off towards their campsite.

It was a miracle he stayed on the stallion's back. Never before had he ridden a horse without a saddle; and it could only have been the adrenaline pumping through his body that had given his legs the strength.

In the end, his inexperience, and inertia, proved his downfall. And as he jolted to a halt in front of his tent, he flew over the stallion's neck.

With a feeling of dread in the pit of his stomach, he dusted himself off and hurried into the tent.

Catherine lay unmoving, on her side, her head facing the back of the tent.

'Sh…shush,' Lomasi whispered, putting her finger to her lips. 'She sleep now.'

Lomasi got up from where she had been sitting on the floor beside Catherine's cot and crept out of the tent.

Cameron threw his dusty hat into the corner, and then took over sitting by the head of the bed. Picking up his wife's small, pale hand, he placed it against his cheek, brushing his lips against her fingers. To him, her breathing seemed rather uneven, and she'd obviously been in some distress, as her hair was lying matted against the side of her face.

Not long later, Cameron picked up the sound of George leading his mare into camp.

The story that eventually unfolded did nothing to waylay Cameron's fears. Apparently, soon after the men had left that morning, Catherine had started into labour. As the day progressed, the frequency of the pains had increased. But during the afternoon they had started to diminish, and now seemed to have disappeared altogether. According to Lomasi this sometimes happened. But Cameron was not convinced. He now feared the worst. Guilt reared its head again, and inwardly he cursed himself for allowing Catherine to stay out on the trail.

After the sun had disappeared behind a thickening layer of cloud, a sudden groan from Catherine raised his anxiety further. Lomasi hurried back inside, while George, having been through this twice before, casually strolled off to settle the animals for the night. Returning to their campfire, he knelt in front of the dormant embers, encouraging them into life. Having successfully accomplished that task, George filled the iron pot with water from the river, knowing it would soon be needed.

Over the next few hours the rain began to pelt down, while at the same time lightning flashed and thunder roared as if trying to compete with Catherine's intermittent wailing. As the night wore on, her cries became more and more frequent, and with each muffled cry Cameron's look of anguish increased. Eventually, Lomasi turned to Cameron, and with her hand pointing towards the opening in the tent, ordered him to 'bring water'. Returning with the iron pot, he set it down beside Catherine's cot, but as he was about to lower himself beside his wife, Lomasi's finger this time pointed directly at him.

'You…go!'

Cameron plodded out through the opening in the tent, not even noticing that the rain had finally let up. Twice he stumbled over rocks, before finally reaching a large flat boulder on the edge of their campsite; and as he sat there with his mind in turmoil, the tragedy of the last childbirth came rushing back to haunt him.

Sometime later he sensed a presence behind him.

'Here…maybe help,' George said, handing Cameron a small pewter flask.

The whisky burned its way down his throat, and after another gulp he did the almost unthinkable, and offered it to his friend. George knew better, and after taking the flask, returned it to the bottom of Cameron's saddlebag.

After what seemed an eternity, their peaceful surroundings were shattered by a loud, persistent wail.

Had it been light, Cameron might just have seen the smile break out on the normally placid face of the man beside him. As it was, it took a few seconds before his brain placed that sound. Then, leaping to his feet he ran to the tent and stood outside the entrance – unsure of what to do.

Cameron nearly jumped out of his skin when, ten minutes later, the flap flew open to reveal Lomasi holding a wrapped bundle in her arms; and to dispel any further anxiety, she smiled.

'Your son.'

Cameron opened his arms, and as the baby was laid against his chest, a tiny face appeared from within the folds of the blanket. Momentarily, he was overcome with joy until a small dark cloud intruded into his thoughts.

'But…but…Catherine. What about Catherine?'

'I'm just fine, you big oaf!' she yelled from inside the tent. 'Now bring that baby in here and come and sit with me.'

Lomasi fussed and fretted while she cleaned up mother and baby. In her world, the men would be sitting around the campfire, bragging and talking about hunts, or whatever it was men talked about at times like this. And it would only be much later that the mother would present the child to its father. They would certainly not be in the way as this one was.

But white people were a strange race. Sometimes, like now, the men seemed soft. Almost like children. But then maybe that wasn't so bad either, she thought, stealing a glance at the parents laughing and playing with their newborn son.

Thirty

The plains had taken on a different complexion, now that autumn had faded and the nights were drawing in. The golden colour of the gently swaying grass had given way to a patchwork of rotting vegetation interspersed with small green patches. Some low-lying conifers, and other evergreen bushes such as Balsam Fir and Creeping Snowberry, did maintain their year-round lustre. But they were few and far between. And the rains had now become more frequent, flattening the long grass to allow it to embark on its final journey back to the soil.

As the railway pioneers continued west, a noticeable increase in woodland signalled a change in their surroundings. Great stands of Spruce, Cedar and Fir began to decorate the hills and valleys, filling the air with their pine-scented bouquet. All the while nature tried her best to cater to man's every need, for scattered amongst these conifers could also be found hardwoods – Alder, Maple and Birch – their denuded branches now stark in their bleak winter dress.

The new encampment had just been established on the side of a shallow valley, through which a small stream burbled on its relentless journey towards the north. Catherine had resumed sole responsibility for the running of the camp now that Lomasi had returned to her family, but there was no doubt she missed her, and at times was beginning to question her decision to be out here with her baby. It wasn't so much the increase in work since Callum's birth, but the fact that she was always so tired. Her sleep at night was continually interrupted, while during the day there were too many chores to be getting on with to allow her to get much rest.

As if to remind her of her plight, Callum began to cry. Right on time, she thought, as she removed the ladle from the simmering pot. Standing up, she slowly stretched and twisted, before wiping her hands on a cloth and then going to the tent to feed her son.

That night after dinner, Catherine lay with her head on Cameron's lap while they relaxed on a blanket in front of the fire. The dying embers shot sparks into the air, momentarily lighting up their faces before being carried aloft into the still night sky. This was their time, Cameron and Catherine's only private and peaceful part of the day.

'Cameron…Look! Did you see that shooting star? Wasn't it beautiful? The sky is so clear.'

'Yes I saw it…But apparently there's a reason the sky is like this. George told me that he thinks the wind is about to swing around to the north. And if it does, it's going to get a lot colder.'

'Never mind…I'm sure we'll be nice and cosy in our tent…now that the stove is back in there.'

'By the way, Cath. Have you got that list of supplies you need? George is going to be leaving early in the morning for the bridging team's camp.'

'Listen, George…When you get there just ask for Sean McIlvey…and then give him this letter. He'll make sure you get what we need. While you're gone I'm going to stay in camp with Catherine. I'll restock the survey wagon and then top up our firewood. We'll see you in a couple of days.'

George nodded and with a snap of the reins on his horse's hindquarters, set off towards the east. He knew Cameron was staying near camp to give Catherine a rest. And by the looks of her it was probably a good idea. In his world, a new mother would have the support of the whole village, and he now realised it had probably been a mistake to send Lomasi back as soon as he had.

In November, as the daylight hours became fewer and fewer, the mileage they were achieving began to drop significantly. And as Catherine's strength waned, it was now only a matter of time before the men would be forced to take over most of the domestic chores.

Cameron had originally hoped to continue surveying until the end of December. But as the cold added another degree of misery to Catherine's wearing existence, he accepted this was no longer feasible.

At the end of the first week of December, the three adults sat around the stove in the Stuarts' tent. The hissing sound of the kerosene lantern was almost lost in the background noise, as the ever-increasing wind buffeted the canvass of the outer shell. Although double tents were now being used, cold drafts still found their way inside; and outside, the icy grey rain was turning their campsite into a quagmire.

'George, I think we've got to decide how much longer we can risk being out here. I know the men laying the track will keep going until the weather makes it impossible, but I don't want to get caught in the middle of nowhere if a big storm comes our way.'

George sat quietly, his head down, as he carefully considered their current situation. At one point he raised his eyes, furtively glancing at Catherine before once more returning to stare at the floor. Finally, he looked up.

'In December…if it snow…it melt in few days. Bad storm not come till next month. But if want…we stop at Fort Walsh…maybe thirty miles west.'

Cameron looked at Catherine once more and then nodded his head.

Four days later, George woke Cameron at sunrise by hailing him from outside the tent.

As Cameron left the tent, the first thing he noticed was the silence. The wind had been blowing non-stop for the last three days, making the present calm seem almost deafening.

They were now camped in a hollow, eight or nine miles east of Fort Walsh – the headquarters of the North West Mounted Police. And although this site was fairly exposed, George had felt that, as their wood supply was still plentiful, the risk would be minimal.

'Look…there!' George said, pointing towards the west.

Cameron turned, his eyes focusing on the sinister-looking smudge between them and their destination. It was almost like a wide dust storm, except it was black and seemed to stretch upwards to the heavens.

George then turned and ran towards their temporary corral – which might not have seemed so disconcerting, had it not been for the fact that George had on what Cameron called his "serious Indian face".

'Come…Must move carts near tents…then take horse and ox over there…by rocks!' he yelled, pointing towards the right.

'What is it, George? Is it really that bad?'

'That line squall…worst thing there is on plains.'

Just then, Catherine stepped out of the tent. She had been woken by the commotion, and could tell from the urgency in George's voice that they were in danger. Within minutes she was on her knees, hammering in as many stakes she could find to help secure the two tents.

In less than an hour the wind began to blow.

The unremitting blasts of arctic air steadily increased; and soon the arrival of freezing rain added to their misery. By the time they had used up every last scrap of spare rope, their faces and hands were red from the pummelling of the wind and frozen water.

'Finish,' George yelled. 'Go inside…I see you when storm gone.'

As the hours passed, the fury of the wind increased. Each time a gust worked its way through their defensive wall of carts, the tents trembled and jerked. The freezing rain turned to ice pellets, peppering the outer shell like a hundred woodpeckers hammering the same tree.

Finally, the precipitation subsided, and when it did the temperature fell another ten degrees. The wind still rampaged through their world, but the previous staccato tapping on their walls was replaced by deep, irregular thwacks as the frozen canvass was driven back-and-forth by the periodic gusts.

Cameron sat near their little stove, one arm supporting Catherine as she rocked back and forth cradling Callum in her arms, while with his other he fed wood into the fire.

Hours later the wind finally abated and the previous dull flopping of their frozen tent walls was replaced by a strange muffled silence.

The voracious appetite of their only source of heat eventually necessitated a trip to the wood supply in the back of one of the carts. Cameron undid the ties securing the opening of their tent, before tentatively sticking his head out through the partial opening.

Their world was now white, and the visibility was so bad that he could barely make out George's tent, lying only fifteen feet away.

Sprinting to the cart, he grabbed an armful of firewood from under the canvass cover before hurrying back to their tent. Three times he shuttled back and forth. And then, satisfied that their cache was sufficient, stood outside their tent, lobbing snowballs at George's until he emerged.

'I only see one storm like this before. I think I know what come now.'

'Oh, come on, George. Surely, it can't get much worse?'

'Make sure you have plenty wood in tent...then maybe... pray to your Great Spirit that I wrong.'

The snow continued to fall for the rest of the day and into the night. But that wasn't all that fell. During the night the temperature began to drop, dramatically, and by sunrise the following day it was well below zero. This time, when Cameron opened up the flaps to exit the tent, he was met by a wall of snow, and ended up having to dig himself out.

Under normal circumstances, this amount of snow provided excellent insulation. But it was only part of the solution, and would only work as long as they had sufficient fuel for their stove – and their bodies.

As Cameron looked around, he could see two thigh deep trenches. One led from George's tent towards the rocks where they had corralled their animals, while the other wound around towards his left, ending up at the rear of the cart containing the firewood. Wading through the snow, Cameron eventually joined up with George's path leading towards their wood supply.

Half an hour later, George's boots could be heard crunching on the hard packed snow as he approached their tent.

'Come on in, George. Take off your coat and come over here by the stove. The coffee is hot and Catherine's about to make some breakfast.'

George's news that morning had been devastating. Sometime during the night, their three horses had panicked and run off to a certain death. And although the oxen were still alive, he feared they wouldn't last much longer without a drastic improvement in the weather.

'Plenty food...but meat frozen. Now... big problem... wood for fire. If I come in here with you...we have maybe two days' logs.'

After breakfast, the two men headed over to George's tent to recover whatever might be useful.

'Surely we can break up the carts for wood,' Cameron said, as he and George trudged back carrying George's bedding and his remaining firewood.

'Yes, but cart only small wood. No much good...burn too quick. And...need cart to stop wind.'

Even though later in the day the sun broke through the thin layer of cloud high above them, the temperature continued to drop.

Two days later, their chance of survival was dropping as fast as the outside temperature. It was now -40F. And once more, the wind began to increase in strength.

George knew that if nothing changed he was the only one who had any chance of staying alive. He and his people had seen conditions like these before. And for centuries had passed on from tribe to tribe what needed to be done to survive. But white people could never endure that kind of hardship.

He slept fitfully that night, and arose early the next morning.

Cameron awoke as George was putting the finishing touches to a pair of snowshoes that he'd been fashioning out of saplings and buffalo hide.

'What…what are you doing?' Cameron whispered, rolling away from Catherine.

His eyes were barely open, and his lips were cracked and swollen from the cold.

'You can't go… anywhere…in this weather.'

'Fort Walsh only seven…maybe… eight miles. Should be at fort before dark. You keep fire burning…I come back soon.'

He probably would have made it by nightfall, had he not broken one of his snowshoes when he slipped off an ice-covered boulder hidden under the snow. It took him the rest of the day to fashion a smaller pair from the remaining wood and hide; and as darkness closed in, George curled up in a snow hole for the night.

By noon the following day, he was wearily tramping across the blurred terrain.

The wind-carried snow reduced visibility to less than a hundred feet, and even he had begun to doubt his own navigation.

Eventually, the cold found its way through his long buffalo-skin coat, and his strength began to wane. For a while, the picture in his mind of Catherine and her child kept him moving. But as the day wore on, his own family's faces began to intrude into his thoughts. The cold became all encompassing. His face went from red to a frosty alabaster, while at the same time his fingers and toes went from a burning sensation to nothingness. Finally, as if some miracle had just taken place, the cold vanished. And then, as he stumbled and fell and his life began to ebb away, he was sure it was his father who, covered in furs, lifted him up and placed him in a sleigh for his final journey.

Thirty One

The two dog teams pulled up in front of the guardhouse at the entrance to the fort.

'Look what we found lying in the snow, just east of the tree line! We were chasing down a deer...when we came across this bundle of fur lying in the snow. From a distance I thought it was a buffalo calf, so imagine my surprise when we got closer...and it turned out to be some dead Indian?'

Sergeant MacDonald reached down, pulling aside the furs covering the body.

'That's a shame. It's Spotted Bear. I wonder what the hell he was doing out here at this time of year. Normally he and his band are way south of Fort Macleod by now.'

Just as he was about to throw the fur back over the body, he noticed a slight tremor in the Native's right eyelid.

'For Christ's sake, Corporal...this guy's alive! Get him inside and send someone for the company Doc.'

George's eyelids gradually opened. At first, he was unsure where he was, as it certainly didn't look like any happy hunting ground he'd ever imagined. Then, when a few moments later a bearded, dark-haired young white man wearing a scarlet tunic appeared through a door on the other side of the room, he realised he wasn't dead.

'Please...Need talk to Sergeant MacDonald.'

'All right...calm down. You need to rest. You're lucky to be alive...and even luckier that I haven't had to amputate any of your toes or fingers.'

'No…not understand. People out there...need help.'

Two hours had passed by the time the Sergeant managed to organize the rescue party. Three dog teams needed to be outfitted, as he had to assume they'd be spending at least one night at the Stuarts' encampment. One sled was packed with food, thick fur coverings and proper winter clothing for the Stuart family; the second contained a fresh supply of firewood, while the third was being brought along as extra transport to help bring back the hoped-for survivors.

Just before noon, the gates of Fort Walsh swung open. Many of the fort's inhabitants, having heard about the daring rescue mission, had gathered near the entrance; and with the sounds of encouragement ringing in their ears, the rescuers set off.

George was in the lead sled, cocooned in two heavy blankets topped with a bearskin wrap – having earlier been supplied with sealskin pants, a long sealskin coat and fur-lined mukluks for his feet. His musher – as the drivers were known – was Sergeant MacDonald, while Corporal Jones and the NWMP doctor handled the other two sleds.

The weather was settled and the winds light as they made their way eastward, guided by George's instructions. Normally, dogs could pull sleds at speeds of up to fifteen miles per hour, but due to their heavy loads, and the depth of snow, the best they could manage was three to four. The temperature was -30F, so, even dressed as they were, the cold still knifed through their layers of clothing, stabbing at their bodies and forcing them to draw on all their reserves of will-power just to keep going.

Three hours later, they came over a small rise, and appearing ahead of them were the irregular, snow-covered shapes of the campsite.

Rather ominously, no smoke could be seen rising above the Stuarts' tent. And as they drew nearer, no footprints were visible in the fresh covering of snow.

George feared the worst, and when his sled came to

a halt he leapt out, forcing himself through the deep snow towards the Stuarts' tent. Quickly undoing the restraining ties, he threw back the flap, calling out Cameron's name as he stepped through the opening.

When his eyes adjusted to the dull light inside the tent, he was horrified.

'Quick, doctor…come!' he shouted, hurrying over to Cameron's cot.

His friend's face was puffy and pale, his eyes shut, and his lips cracked and swollen; and as hard as George stared, he could see no sign of breath escaping from the blue-tinged lips.

Guilt began to overwhelm him. This was his fault. He was the one who had been hired to look after them, and he should have known better than to stay out on the prairie this late in the year – especially with a mother and newborn child in the party.

'Move out of the way, will you?' the doctor demanded, squeezing past the Indian to get a look at Catherine.

George turned away from his friend, moving over to the baby's cot. His worst nightmare stared him in the face. Somehow, Callum had thrown off half of his covers, and he was now cold as ice and stiff as a board.

'Quick, somebody get me as many spare blankets as we've got…and then get that fire started! She's still alive… although barely.'

'But baby so.…'

'I know…I'm sorry. The baby didn't make it. He didn't have a chance in these temperatures.'

In a trance like state, George stumbled towards the exit, along the way brushing against the corporal entering the tent with an armful of wood, and Sergeant MacDonald carrying blankets and other supplies.

'Right…once that fire's going I want some warm water. At the same time someone needs to get me some decent sized rocks, and warm them up so I can put them in their beds. Mr

286

and Mrs Stuart are both alive right now …and I'd like to keep it that way if I can.'

'Where the hell is that Indian? He could be doing that. At least he'd know where to find some decent sized rocks under all this snow.'

'Just take it easy, Corporal. The last time I saw him he was headed towards that outcropping of rocks, east of the campsite. He's probably got a lot to think about right now, so best you let him be.'

Even though Spotted Bear had almost died trying to save their lives, the Sergeant knew he would be feeling responsible for what had happened. The Stuarts had been his charges, and the Native would now have a terrible burden to shoulder for the rest of his life.

'Sorry,' said the doctor, 'but when you two have finished… could one of you wrap up the baby in a couple of blankets and put him in a corner of one of the sleighs? We should take him back to the fort for burial. I'm sure his mother and father will want to say their goodbyes.'

The doctor returned to monitoring Cameron and Catherine. Although their pulse and breathing rates were extremely slow, he was hopeful they'd got to them in time.

All he could do for the moment was keep them warm, and keep his fingers crossed that they'd make it through the next twenty-four hours.

'When you're finished your coffee, Corporal…I think it's time Spotted Bear came in and got something to eat and drink…so I'd like you to go and find him. Tell him the Doc's hopeful about the Stuarts, and that it's time we got things ready for the night. When he's warmed up, we'll get him to sort out the other tent for us…and while he's doing that you might want to get us out some grub. I don't know about you, but I'm kinda hungry.'

George had found all three oxen dead and partly devoured

by wolves. The tracks had been fresh, meaning they'd probably been scared off as the rescue party arrived. In a way it would probably turn out to be a good thing, thought George, as the predators would probably now leave the dogs and campsite alone.

When Cameron's eyes cracked open all he could see was a matt cloud-like colour. Spasms of shivering racked his body, and his teeth chattered like the keys on one of the office typewriters. A stranger's smiling face loomed into view, saying something he didn't quite understand, followed by a hand being placed behind his head and tilting him slightly forward. A warm liquid passed over his lips. Some of it dribbled down his stubbled chin, but a small amount did find its way into his mouth, almost choking him before sliding down his throat. The last thing he then recalled was a warming sensation in the bottom of his stomach before, once again, his eyes closed and he faded into darkness.

One more day was spent in that unforgiving wilderness before the doctor considered the two people well enough to be transported back to the fort. Both were still drifting in and out of consciousness, but their breathing was almost back to normal, and their pulses quicker and less erratic.

When the harnesses came into sight, the huskies required little further encouragement, and soon their excited barking was echoing down the valley. Ten minutes later, with the Stuarts lying in sleds under bundles of blankets and furs, two of the dog teams leaned into their leather straps and set off for home.

George and the Corporal remained behind, as the camp needed to be dismantled and returned to the wagons if any of it was to be saved from the elements. The survey cart had been partly dismantled by Cameron and used as firewood, but as George had already seen, the cold had sapped his friend's strength long before its wood had all been used up, and the cart destroyed for good. The perishable food that remained was dumped in a pile by the dead oxen; and no doubt by spring nothing would be left but bones, completely picked-clean.

The cold spell finally broke, and within days the temperature was well above freezing, with the snow mostly melted away.

An awkward silence filled the room. George had come to bid farewell, and nobody seemed to know what to say. Catherine took his hand in hers, and with fondness and sincerity in her eyes, looked into his face.

'George, I want you to know that neither of us think it was your fault. It was Cameron and I that made the decision to stay out on the plains after Callum was born. You're not God, and you can't control the weather.'

Cameron then shook George's hand, while nodding in agreement.

Both followed George to the door, watching as he mounted up. Then, as he turned and cantered off towards the gate, Catherine yelled after him.

'Please…give our love to Lomasi and the boys!'

But he never looked back.

Rays of sunlight slanted down from an azure sky, as a buckboard containing a small wooden box strapped to the floor behind its seat made its way through the front gate. Even to a stranger, it would have been obvious something distressing had befallen the couple sitting at the front. The driver sat stiffly, his empty, soulless eyes staring straight ahead from beneath his hat; whilst beside him, a woman shrouded in dark attire, and supported by the man's free arm, wept openly into his shoulder.

Sergeant MacDonald, resplendent in red serge tunic, beige Stetson-type hat, buff trousers and calf-high leather boots led the way astride a gleaming black stallion. While at the back of the cortege rode Corporal Jones, the NWMP doctor, and another man, dressed in black and sporting a small wide-brimmed padre's hat.

Twenty minutes later, the little troupe reached a grassy knoll framed by a white picket fence, and protected on three sides by mature Cypress trees; and a few minutes later, as the Sergeant and Corporal lowered the small pine coffin into the ground, the words said by the fort's Chaplain were lost to the winds.

Tears cascaded down Catherine's face as she sobbed, mercilessly, into Cameron's chest. His arm was wrapped around her, his hand grasping her waist to prevent her from collapsing if her knees gave way. Cameron's cheek lay atop her trembling head, as he stared off into the distance, unable to look at what was taking place before him.

Cameron's thoughts momentarily returned to that moment two days before when, inconsolable, he and Catherine had rocked in each other's arms after being told that Callum had died – and he had wondered if his life was destined to forever lurch from heartache to heartbreak.

Finally, the ritual drew to a close; and a tear slid from the corner of Cameron's eye, falling into his wife's windblown hair. For awhile no one moved. But ultimately, the cool, gusty breeze on top of the hill decreed the time had come to bid farewell. Cameron whispered in Catherine's ear, and then with the gentlest of tugs urged her to turn away. Slowly, she staggered back towards the rig, so despairing in her grief that it was only Cameron's support that kept her from sinking to the ground. The four mourners stared at their boots, wringing their hands and shuffling their feet until mother and father had passed. Cameron handed Catherine up to the seat, before turning back towards the gravesite.

Sergeant MacDonald stepped forward, placing a comforting hand on Cameron's shoulder.

'We'll put him to rest for you if you like. Why don't you and Mrs Stuart just go back to the fort and have a warming drink?'

Thirty Two

If anything, Winnipeg was more frenetic now than when they'd left. The city was sprawling out from the centre at an alarming rate; and property companies eager to get their piece of the seemingly untold riches, bought and sold real estate at ever more ludicrous prices. Frontage on Main Street or Portage Avenue was trading at prices per foot comparable to downtown New York, and towering six to eight story buildings were being constructed for some of North America's best know corporations. The first of these huge structures to be completed was the Bank of Montreal, which now housed the new corporate headquarters of the C.P.R.

Main Street itself ran for nearly two miles, and every foot was taken up by businesses such as hardware stores, haberdasheries, cafés, and real estate agents. Streets running off of it such as Lombard Avenue and Water Avenue were now becoming just as important, as they accommodated the headquarters of such prestigious companies as Great Western Life Assurance, and the first newspaper to be printed in Western Canada – The Nor'Wester.

Cameron and Catherine stared in wonder. In nine months the city had become almost unrecognizable. Even more fantastic was that, at this moment, they were sitting in an electric streetcar, smoothly making its way down Main Street on metal rails.

Workmen were everywhere. Those not involved in constructing something new seemed to be tearing something down. Electric lighting was being installed on all the main thoroughfares in the city, and on every street corner a knot of men could be seen either dismantling the gas street-lamps, or installing their new replacements.

Almost overnight the future had arrived, and as Cameron was well aware, it was all being built on the backs of the railway. God forbid the line doesn't get finished, he mused, as with the jangling of the driver's bell, their transport drew to a halt outside the Bank of Montreal.

'I'm just going in to say hello. I'll meet you at the Prairie Café when you've finished your shopping...then we can go and pick up the horse and buggy.'

Cameron walked through the impressive double-doors of the new building, and then headed towards the woman sitting at reception. Her semi-circular desk was beautifully crafted from maple, and was outlined in a light-coloured inlay of some type of pine; whilst behind her, on the wall, hung the CPR logo – a shield with Canadian Pacific Railway scrolled along its bottom edge, topped by a beaver gnawing on a branch of maple leaves.

His first impression of the woman was that she was more akin to a school headmistress, than the image one would have expected of an employee of an up and coming young railway. And as he was soon to find out, she played the part superbly.

'May I help you?' she asked, with a slightly condescending attitude.

'Yes...you certainly may. Would you tell me where I can find Mr Van Horne?'

'Do you have an appointment?' she inquired, frowning at him from over the top of her glasses, 'because, I'm afraid he doesn't normally see people without one.'

'No, I don't. But if you'll just tell him Cameron Stuart would like to see him... I'm sure it won't be a problem.'

'We'll see about that,' she said smugly, picking up the telephone.

A few minutes later, as the General Manager led him from the lobby – with his fleshy hand on his shoulder – Cameron momentarily turned his head, winking at the humbled, red-faced receptionist. He certainly had something to have a laugh about with Catherine tonight because the look on the receptionist's face, when Mr Van Horne had burst into the lobby, was a picture that would remain with him for quite a while.

One of the reasons Cameron had wanted to come to the office immediately on his return, was to get the pitiable part of last month out of the way. As expected, Mr Van Horne was effusive in his condolences, and was at pains to establish if there was anything he or the railway could do to help relieve their anguish; all the while there never being any suggestion of *I told you so* in his manner or the discussions that followed.

Thirty minutes later, Cameron raised a hand in farewell to the duly repentant Mrs Evans at reception, before hurrying out the front door to meet Catherine.

That night, the fire crackled and sparks flew up the chimney, as Cameron and Catherine lay on a polar bear rug in front of the hearth.

'You know something, Cath? I know it doesn't make it any easier…but I found out today that we aren't the only one's grieving. Mr Van Horne told me that we lost six men on the bridging gang during that cold snap…including Sean McIlvey. Apparently, he died after going for help…just like George nearly did…only Sean never made it to the "end of track" camp. The rescue gang found his body half a mile from safety; and by the time they reached his crew's camp, five other men had died.'

'Let's not talk about sad things any more. I think I've run out of tears, and my chest is still sore from sobbing. Why don't we just go to bed…and tomorrow we'll restart our lives.'

Cameron quickly settled back into the paperwork, and before long began to come across other problems created by the storm. Two of their big engines had cracked boilers from being allowed to stand idle for too long during the cold, and out on the line west of Regina two more engines were stranded due to water towers being frozen solid. Eventually, water was sent out by wagon to recover the precious engines, and new procedures were brought into force. Maintenance gangs were now deployed on a permanent basis, not only to ensure the safety of the track and its signalling gear, but also to light fires at the base of the water towers during periods of extreme cold.

Of course, these weren't supposed to be Cameron's problems, and should have been handled by operations. However, at staff meetings held over the next few weeks the merits of all suggestions were reviewed. And in the end, quite a few "Scottish" ideas were accepted and acted upon.

Thirty Three

When the spring of 1883 arrived, all seemed in place for the final push to Fort Calgary. During the previous winter, some of the men who couldn't be employed laying tracks were split up into construction gangs. And by the time spring arrived, Regina had the makings of a large town – with a depot on its western edge, to which supplies and equipment were being swiftly trans-shipped in readiness for the new track building season. The usual assortment of banks, hardware stores, food suppliers, hoteliers and real estate agents had been planned – with some already nearing completion – and rumours abounded that the government was about to confirm the building of a new headquarters for the North West Mounted Police in the fledgling city.

One early April evening as Cameron headed for home, his mind mulled over the upcoming dilemma. The raw edge of last year's grief had now worn away, but he knew from his own experience it was never far from one's thoughts. Conscious of the impending confrontation, and with a feeling of dread in the pit of his stomach, he opened the door to their little home.

'Hi, Cath.'

Catherine walked out of the bedroom, sauntering towards him with a barely disguised grin on her face. For the first time in months, he noticed her cheeks seemed fuller and rosier, and even in the dull light of the lamps inside the cabin, her eyes were bright and sparkling. This time it needed no explaining, and a grin spread across his face.

'You're pregnant aren't you? We're going to have a baby!'

As Catherine rushed over, Cameron opened his arms, sweeping her off the floor and whirling her around in circle, before gently setting her down.

'Oh…that's great, Cath!'

'Before you say anything else…No…I have no intention of going anywhere with you and George this year. So, if you're planning to go off with your friend you'd better find a way that we can meet up every now and then…so you can remind me what it's like to be held in your arms.'

In hindsight, Cameron realised his boss was probably so happy to be told that Catherine would not be accompanying him this year, he would probably have granted Cameron almost any wish. As it was, giving Catherine a free travel pass, and occasionally arranging for a hotel room for them, was still a pretty good deal as far as the Stuarts were concerned.

This time, the baby would be delivered in the General Hospital in Winnipeg, with the help of the best doctors and nurses, paid for by the C.P.R. And as near as they could work out, the new arrival was due during late September to early October, which should allow Cameron sufficient time to finish the survey and be home in time for the birth.

Cameron stared idly out the window, watching the smoke from the loco's stack escaping through the split roof over the platform. The trackside design reminded him of a similar station – Aberdeen – where he had stared out from a window just like this, so many times before. And as the train jerked and began to accelerate away, it drew his mind back to the other interest in his former life – and he reached into his travelling bag to find a pen and paper.

As time passed, his thoughts alternated between his letter to Margaret and the ever changing spectacle within his sight.

The service he was on was a milk run – so-called because it stopped at every halt along the way to pick up the local dairy farmers' output – and the more he gazed at the places they stopped, the more he was amazed at the rate with which some places had blossomed.

Brandon had already become a small city, its major employers being the new C.P.R maintenance yard, Hudson's Bay Company, Johnson's Flour Mill and the Western Feed and Grain Company. Broadview, which had been built on the western edge of the beautiful valley – he'd first seen when he and George turned back that first winter – had turned into a large town, mainly supported by hardware suppliers and a tanning mill. However, during the last few months, it had also become a major trans-shipment stop – born out by the huge grain elevators sitting alongside a siding west of the town. Next on the route, and for the moment the end of the main line, was Regina: already a city in waiting, its most noticeable feature being the massive reservoir nearing completion on its southern outskirts.

Luckily for Cameron, the railway had pre-booked a room for him, because Regina was like the Winnipeg of old. The place was bursting at the seams with entrepreneurs, businessmen and labourers, all vying for what little accommodation was available.

The din of saws and clanging of hammers trailed him as he walked down the newly boarded sidewalks, while an all too familiar smell cloyed at his nostrils.

Nowhere else in his travels had he come across what could only be described as that true Western Canadian fragrance: that unmistakeable mixture of resin from the pinewood; obnoxious fumes from the tar being slopped onto roofs, and manure maturing on the street. All mingling with the aroma of male sweat, exuding from unwashed bodies, and clinging to clothes that hadn't seen soap in weeks.

Finally, he spotted his hotel – strangely feeling an uncommon desire to have a bath before retiring for the night.

Early the next morning, a quick check at the railway's

office in town confirmed that a supply train would soon be leaving for the "end of track" camp. This year, the start point for the track layers was the other side of the river at Swift Current; and at this very moment their huge mobile village was already underway.

The sun was sinking behind the hills on the western side of the river as the train screeched to a halt.

'Thanks for the lift, Charlie. Maybe I'll see you later in the season. Keep that steel coming, and with any luck we'll be across the prairies by the end of the summer.'

Swinging his bag down from the shelf at the back of the caboose, Cameron threw it over his shoulder, and after a quick wave to the trainman, wandered off towards the teeming tent city.

Ten minutes later he looked up to see a familiar face striding up the slope towards him.

'Hi, George! How are you?'

'Busy… Where you been? I thought maybe I on my own this year.'

Cameron ignored the jibe, and as he stuck out his hand a wry grin spread across George's face.

'I've missed you, George…and so has Catherine.'

Two days later, they passed the site of the previous winter's tragedy.

George, who was as usual, in the lead, kept his eyes firmly to the front. He had already made his complaints to the Great Spirit. The previous week, he and his sons had spent a night at the old campsite, expelling their emotions while dancing around a pyre. Then, the following day, they'd cleaned up the site, recovered the wagons and equipment, and taken them back to the "end of track" camp.

Late that afternoon, the two friends stopped to make camp, high up the side of a beautiful valley in the hills north of Fort Walsh. George picked the spot well. The clearing he'd found allowed the early morning sun to help awaken them, while, at the end of the day, it reflected off the carpet of pine needles surrounding their camp – leading them home like a beacon.

Before long, the surveyed line neared their campsite, so Cameron knew that in a day or two they would be moving on.

'George…how far is it to Fort Walsh from here?'

'Not far …maybe five, six mile south.'

'Tomorrow, I'm going to head down towards the fort. So…can you top up the cart with survey stakes while I'm gone? I won't be long.'

Cameron set off early the next day. Initially his progress was slow due to the unsure footing in the snow covered valleys. But, once on higher, firmer ground, he cantered to make up for lost time. As the sun came overhead, he spotted the fort in the distance, then, getting his bearings, eased off slightly towards the east and pushed on again.

The spot where Callum had been buried was now just a small, damp patch of earth. The snow had only recently melted, and this year's growth had yet to get underway.

Cameron took off his hat, kneeling on one knee before the four-foot high wooden cross. Sergeant MacDonald must have arranged this he thought, because at the time, both he and Catherine had been too traumatized to even think about a memorial.

As he read the words his heart almost broke, and tears rolled down his cheeks.

Callum

Stuart

Born and Died in the Year of Our Lord 1882

God

Rest

His

Soul

The cross had been beautifully fashioned from maple or some other hardwood, while at its foot was a plinth made of oak, through which the cross was mounted. Affixed to the plinth was a metal plate with the following inscription:

Here lies a true pioneer - Born of these plains
May his spirit live eternally in these hills
And forever inspire those who follow

Cameron had promised Catherine he would ensure a marker of some kind was placed at Callum's grave. But he knew that what he saw written there on that day, was more than he or Catherine could ever have said. It was a tribute from men whose souls were inexorably entwined with this wilderness; and their words would be forever etched in his heart.

After breaking camp, Cameron and George headed for Medicine Hat – a town already established near the South Saskatchewan River. Of course, to call it a town might have been a bit presumptuous. For the moment, the settlement consisted of a few grubby cabins, a ramshackle building – immodestly called a general store – and a corral containing a few sorry looking nags. Coal had recently been discovered in its hills, which for the time being was being piled into a huge mound, while it awaited the coming of the railway.

Cameron and George arrived on a hill overlooking the town from the east, and when spotted by the town's occupants were overrun and greeted like long lost family.

The rest of the day was devoted to setting up their campsite, and as dusk fell they joined their new friends at an impromptu party organised in their honour.

The following morning, the area outside the general store resembled a battlefield. Men in various stages of indisposition wandered aimlessly about the town, while the smouldering

300

remains of a large fire sat like a carbuncle in the middle of the main street – surrounded by empty bottles and plates of half-eaten food.

Another month passed, at the end of which another hundred and twenty miles of stakes had been laid. Up until now, Cameron had measured their progress from the last major town or city, but from this moment on, it was measured by how much was left to go. By his reckoning, and assuming there were to be no big hold ups due to weather or terrain, they should be in Fort Calgary by the beginning of September.

'Listen, George. I'm going back down the line tomorrow to find the "end of track" camp. Then I'm going to telegraph Catherine and get her to meet me in Regina for a few days. If your family is anywhere near here, why don't you go and see them?'

'My band now near Winnipeg...I stay here...find many things to do.'

'All right... I'll be back in four or five days. Why don't you do a run back to the bridging crew's camp to restock our supplies? In fact, I'll drop off our list on my way by...then you'll just have to pick them up.'

Late the following afternoon, Cameron found the bridging crew starting the span over the river at Medicine Hat. After a quick stop for a drink, he handed over his supply request to the foreman, before once more setting off. Three hours later, the chaotic scene that was the "end of track" came into sight.

The next day, Cameron met Catherine as she stepped down from the Winnipeg Express, and after a prolonged greeting on the platform, they strolled out through the station onto Regina's main street.

The sidewalk was crowded with workmen hurrying from job to job; however, Catherine's rather obvious condition ensured that she and Cameron were always given a wide berth.

'Where are we staying?'

'Oh, I don't know…it's some hotel down at the end of the street.'

When they entered the Royal Hotel, the lobby was a seething mass of humanity. Thanks to Cornelius Van Horne, the suite permanently reserved for the C.P.R. was made available to them, and on entering their room, Cameron could barely contain his mirth as he looked at Catherine's face.

She was dumbstruck, having never expected such luxury to be available in all but the largest of modern cities – and certainly not in Canada's mainly untamed wilderness. Quickly recovering, she turned towards Cameron, and with her eyes squinting and her lips pursed, pummelled him with her fists.

Cameron smiled, folding her into his arms, before giving her a long and tender kiss.

Over the next few days the weather was perfect. They spent hours relaxing in their "suite" and walking and exploring the new city. On their third day Cameron hired a horse and trap, after which they headed out towards Fort Qu'Appelle, and its Hudson's Bay Trading Post. As they journeyed along the recently opened road, wagon after wagon, loaded with logs for the new mill at Regina, passed them by. Finally, just after midday, they left behind the last side road leading to the logging sites.

'Why don't we stop over there by that stream…and see if we can find a nice spot for our picnic lunch?'

Catherine turned to face Cameron, her fingers tapping like a Morse key on his upper thigh.

'Did you say lunch, Sir?' she replied, with a coquettish smile on her face.

Cameron sat alone in the caboose as the supply train hurried him away from Catherine. Their parting had been difficult, and was accompanied by floods of tears and concerns for his safety. All too soon, the whistle on Catherine's train had sounded; and with endearing words of love, and reassurances about his safety, he had helped her up the steps and into her seat.

He knew it was difficult for her, but hoped she realised this wasn't what he wanted either. Last night over dinner they had talked about their future, and both had agreed it was not to be with the railway. Thankfully, when he had mentioned cattle ranching Catherine seemed quite keen, so for the rest of the evening and into the night, they had talked over his plans. And not for the first time, it did cross his mind that what better way could there be for him to fade into obscurity, than to be out in the country where your nearest neighbour was miles away.

Between them, they had set aside a nice sum of money. But the problem now was that the price of land was increasing daily as speculators got wind of the route of the railway. It was clear to Cameron that they would have to start out small, but hopefully over time they would be able to increase the size of their ranch.

A blast of air and noise accompanied the opening of the door at the front of the caboose.

'We're nearly there, Mr Stuart. Hope you enjoyed your trip back to Regina. Are we gonna see you ag'in?'

'Thanks, Charlie…Yes…You probably will. How's everything going out here, anyway?'

'Just fine…Though some days I do see some strange sights.'

'Oh, really?'

'I sure do…Why just the other day…'bout four miles back…we passed a bunch of Indians. They were just sittin' on a hill…'bout fifty of 'em…starin' at us as we went by.'

'What's so strange about that?'

303

'Well you see, three hours later…on the return trip…there they were ag'in. They hadn't moved. It's as if they were scared to cross this 'ere set of tracks.'

'Yea…I see what you mean, Charlie.'

'And you know…even stranger…the week before there was a whole herd of Bison on the south side of the track. And apparently they never crossed over either…'cause three days later John says he seen them near the same spot…but this time they were headin' south…from where they came, I guess.'

'No wonder some of the Indians aren't very happy with us.'

'You know, Mr Stuart…somethin' tells me that, although we're joinin' this country from one side to the other, at the same time we're kinda dividin' it from top to bottom.'

Before Cameron had a chance to reply to this amazing insight, the train began to decelerate, and Charlie left through the rear door – signal flag in hand.

There was no mistaking where they were. The noise greeting Cameron as he stepped down from the caboose was like nowhere else on earth. The loco was already chuffing its way back to the other end of the train, with its whistle screaming its warning to the seemingly deaf workers on both sides of the track, while all around him sledgehammers rang out – their metal-to-metal contact almost painful to those not used to their symphony. In the distance, horses and mules whinnied and snorted as they strained at their harnesses; and men shouted and cursed as they struggled to position impossibly heavy loads. Yet amazingly, thought Cameron shaking his head, above all this could still be heard the bellowing of the foreman as they tried to cajole the navvies into working faster.

Gazing around him, he once more marvelled at the spectacle laid out before him. That unique mobile community, known as "end of track", was sprawled out across the plains – constantly on the move – only stopping to serve a meal or two before moving on again. Tents stretched off in haphazard groups as far as the eye could see, and in the centre of it all were the wagons and corrals – now his destination.

Over the next few weeks, the two men crept towards the horizon. The going was easier now that the plains had become rolling hills cut by much smaller rivers. But, as George had already warned, there was one more area to get through that would surely test their metal – and everyone knew it as "the badlands".

This name did not derive from some historical enmity between tribes and white settlers, but from the roughness of the terrain itself. It was mainly sandstone hills and cliffs, interspersed with small clumps of prickly brush, sharp rocks and boulders. And the only realistic way of passing through this desert-like ground was to follow the route of a dried up river bed.

So, after reaching it, Cameron and George spent days doing their best to straighten out the twists and turns of the long forgotten water-course, until finally, on rounding one last rocky outcrop, the land once again became lush green meadows; and the last great impediment to the railway was behind them.

'Now buffalo country. Every year my tribe chase buffalo here. In my father's day on foot…use bow and arrow and club. Near here…famous place…Indian call "Head-Smashed-In-Buffalo-Jump".'

'What the hell kind of name is that?'

'You listen…I tell you story my father tell me…and his father tell him.'

And so that afternoon, Cameron learned the history of how the Indians used to catch buffalo before the advent of the horse.

North of where they now stood, and close to Fort MacLeod, was a long escarpment leading to a thirty-foot cliff. According to George, his ancestors used to stampede the bison over that cliff – and then club and stab to death any surviving the fall. The story went that one young brave decided he wanted to see the whole process from the bottom. But sadly, the first buffalo over the cliff landed on top of him and smashed in his head.

Even George had to admit that it did sound a bit far fetched, but it was a tale that had been passed down from generation to generation. Of course, now they hunted on horseback with rifles, and no longer needed to stampede whole herds to their deaths.

At the end of another week, Cameron and George reached the Bow River and its valley. For once, instead of struggling to cross another river, they were able to parallel its path – the staked route now only needing to straighten out the worst of its excesses. With approximately twenty miles to go to Fort Calgary, they came across what Cameron thought was the most beautiful piece of land he'd seen since leaving Winnipeg. The area was on the south side of the Bow, where a fast flowing stream joined from the southwest. Cameron and George took the time to wander up this waterway, which at times vanished from sight as it wound its way back and forth between eroding banks, festooned with ferns and reeds. Its boundary was crowded with spruce and fir interspersed with small stands of cottonwoods – some growing as high as a hundred and fifty feet and looking like sentinels guarding the majestic forest. Overhead, light-grey Goshawks and grey-brown Prairie Falcons floated on columns of air – as they patrolled their bits of airspace and juggled for supremacy. While below them, their mates roosted on nests of twigs, one eye always on the lookout for easy meals nearby.

This is where I want to live, thought Cameron, his eyes gazing out at the almost endless meadows of grass, swaying in the gentle breeze like the surface of a tranquil sea.

Thirty Four

Fort Calgary, and the structures around it, were built on a bend, near the junction of the Bow and Elbow rivers. The settlement itself was made up of four main buildings: the NWMP barracks; the mission; Hudson's Bay Company post, and a general store belonging to I.G. Baker. Scattered in an arbitrary fashion around these buildings were a dozen or so log cabins – accommodating the permanent residents – and a large number of tents providing temporary refuge for those just passing through.

Cameron had hoped to spend a few peaceful nights catching up on some sleep and relaxing after the rigours of the past few months, but it was not to be. Fort Calgary was already another railway city in the making, with men loudly hawking land and questionable goods all day long, whilst drunken revellers staggered out of the temporary saloons throughout most of the night.

On the morning of their third day, having made arrangements for the safekeeping of the C.P.R.'s carts and equipment, Cameron and George set off on horseback. The two friends travelled light and fast, carrying only a few personal items and their Martini rifles. Cameron was in a hurry. The baby was due sometime in the next three weeks. He was determined to be there for the birth and, he wanted to look into the ownership of the piece of land he'd just seen along the High River – hoping to purchase it before the real estate agents pushed its value beyond his reach.

At the end of the first day they came across the bridging crew striving to span the Bow River, forty miles south east of Fort Calgary. This would be the last bridge required on the prairie crossing, and as they rode by, Cameron sensed the men knew they would soon be out of a job.

Mid-morning the following day, he and George were able to spot their destination from a distance of ten miles. The dust being thrown up by the mules and horses, mixed with the smoke from the kitchen fires, was like a straw-coloured storm boiling up on the horizon; and two hours later they rode into the man-made tempest, and corralled their horses for the last time.

As the supply train accelerated out of the railhead towards Regina, Cameron and George sat in the caboose in two old armchairs. Cameron's face bore the strained look of months of hard work, while George, as usual, showed little behind his steely, dark eyes.

'Well...I guess this is it.'

George continued to stare at a point somewhere over Cameron's left shoulder and, after a few minutes silence, Cameron continued.

'I would never have survived if it hadn't been for you, George...and I owe you a debt which I'm sure I can never repay. I know how you must feel sometimes...being treated the way that you are...but I want you to know that to Catherine and I you are more than equal to anyone we know. '

For a few seconds, George's emotionless character and stern visage appeared to soften, but in a short time a mask of solemnity once more covered his face.

'You need me...Sergeant MacDonald will find.'

Cameron nodded, and then leaned back into the chair. For the next little while, his thoughts were of Catherine and their future together. But then, as if poked by a sharp stick, he sat up and looked at George.

'I don't suppose you and your family would like to help Catherine and I start up our cattle ranch? I'm going to try to buy that piece of land we saw beside the High River.'

'Sorry …must go back to tribe…soon old chief die…then me chief.'

On September 30th, the new addition to the Stuart family duly arrived safe and sound.

This time the labour only lasted for three hours and, with the help of a doctor and two nurses, Anna was brought into the world. Catherine talked all the way through the delivery, as if it was just a slight inconvenience in her otherwise busy day; while Cameron stood proudly in the waiting room, puffing on 25-cent cigars and offering one to any men coming his way.

The following Monday, Cameron had only been at his desk for a few minutes when one of the young clerks from the outer office knocked at his door.

'Yes, come in.'

'Excuse me, Mr Stuart…The General Manager would like to see you when you have a moment.'

'All right, thank you. I'll be along as soon as I've checked my mail.'

'But, he said…'

'Thank you, William…I have the message.'

Cameron still found it strange to be back in the office and being addressed by his last name. However, he did have to admit that having underlings did have its advantages – at least you never had to make your own coffee.

Ten minutes later, Cameron knocked on his boss's door.

'Mr Stuart…How nice to see you. Please…take a seat.'

Cameron was still quite impressed by his boss's office, and each time he entered new artefacts of one kind or another seemed to have appeared. This time, what appeared to be a gold spike lay on his desktop – seemingly being used as a paperweight.

'Ah…I see you've noticed my spike. It's not solid gold, or else, as you can well imagine, wouldn't stand up very well to a sledge hammer. It's actually iron painted in gold

309

leaf, and is going to be used when they take a picture of us connecting up the last rail…somewhere in the Rockies. I had hoped you would join us…however…a rumour has come to my attention suggesting you may not be with us when that takes place. Is this true?'

Cameron had hoped to delay this bit of information, but by the looks of it, his inquiries at the C.P.R. land agent's department had made its way to this office.

Over the next little while, Cameron outlined his and Catherine's plans to become more settled, and start up a cattle ranch. As he talked, Mr Van Horne sat listening and nodding, his face totally relaxed, and his forearms crossed on his desk. Only once did he interrupt, and that was to reach into the ornate wooden box at the corner of his desk, pluck out a cigar, and offer one to Cameron. Finally, when Cameron had finished, the General Manager reached into his desk drawer and pulled out a roll of papers held together by a ribbon and red wax seal. Then, reaching across the desk, he laid them in front of Cameron.

'I've told you before how much I've valued your expertise, and appreciated the loyalty and energy you've put into the building of this railway. But, for some reason best known to yourself, you've never been willing to accept any recognition. Well…I was determined that one day you would get the credit you deserve…and when I heard what you were doing at the land office, I knew I'd finally found something you couldn't turn down. Those are the title deeds for Alberta section 11…which I believe you're interested in buying. That land is now yours, a gift from a grateful company.'

Cameron was dumfounded. His hand shook as he reached forward to grasp the documents.

'I don't know what to say. It's more land than Catherine and I could ever have afforded.'

For the first time in Cameron's presence, Cornelius Van Horne rose to his feet from behind his desk and put out his hand.

'I'd like to shake your hand. Your determination and foresight may well have saved this railway from bankruptcy… and I'm truly sorry you're leaving. I'd still like you to be there for the picture when we complete the line. So, if you're in agreement, when the official driving of the last spike is to take place, I'll have somebody from Fort Calgary contact you.'

Cameron rose and nodded his assent, before turning to head out of the office.

'Oh, before you go…I just remembered. You don't by any chance have a relative, or know of someone called Stewart, who might have lived in a place in Scotland called Dufftown, do you?'

Cameron froze to the spot, before slowly turning back to face his boss.

'No…I…ah…can't say I do.'

'I just wondered, because George Stephen…you know, one of our Directors… well, he comes from near there, and he mentioned to me the other day that the last time he was back, he'd met some fellow called Campbell…who told him his son had been killed by a man named Stewart who used to work for a railway. He supposedly got away on a ship to Australia, which then sank in the Bay of Biscay… which… I guess was some kind of justice. Anyway, I just wondered if maybe you'd heard of him…but then thinking about it, your name's not spelt that way anyway, is it?

'That's right, Sir…and…and I don't ever recall having been to some place called Dufftown,' Cameron replied. 'Is there anything else, Mr Van Horne?'

'No, that's all, thank you.'

Thank God for that! And from the sounds of it, maybe it's just as well Catherine and I have decided to move on, Cameron thought, as he opened the door and stepped out of the office.

That night, he and Catherine sat in front of the fireplace, talking about the day's big surprise.

'My God, Cath, a whole section of land! That's 640 acres…free! We could never have bought that much land. In fact, prices have gone up by so much that I was only planning on buying a quarter-section.'

'Well, I think you deserve it.'

'It isn't just me that deserves it, after all…'

'Never mind that…that wasn't the railway's fault.'

Anna suckled at her breast, as Catherine rocked back and forth in the new chair Cameron had bought her after the birth.

'You know…all the money we saved can now be spent building a house and setting up the ranch. And now, we can probably afford to have that extra room added to the house… in case of visitors…or other new arrivals?'

Her life was now nearly fulfilled, Catherine thought, as she sat listening to Cameron talk about their new ranch. She did have to admit, his enthusiasm was hard to resist, even if common sense told her they should be easing their way into this new way of life. Still, he did seem to know what he was talking about; and all she really wanted was her own home, with her family around her – as opposed to a temporary house provided by the nation and a family of servants paid to fill in the spaces.

The following Monday, Cameron was again requested to meet with the General Manager, and as he strolled down the corridor, he did begin to worry if maybe this meant the boss was after more information from him, to pass on to George Stephen, or if not, was about to rescind their gift.

'You asked to see me, Sir?'

'Yes…please sit down. Would you like coffee? It is quite early, isn't it?'

This didn't bode well, Cameron thought.

312

Mr Van Horne poured out their coffee from a china pot sitting on the tray on his desk, and then lifting the cups and saucers walked over to the two chairs placed in front of the windows overlooking Main Street.

'Let's sit over here, shall we? It's much more comfortable.'

After taking a sip from his cup, the General Manager set it down before turning towards Cameron.

'I trust you and your wife had an exciting weekend discussing your plans?'

'Yes we did…and she asked me to pass on her thanks when the opportunity arose.'

'I'll get right to the point. I was rather hoping you might see fit to doing me a small favour. I know I'm taking a bit of a liberty…and that you'd probably like to get started on your new life as soon as possible. It's just that…well…I've got a bit of a problem.'

For a moment Cameron sat perfectly still, and then with increasing apprehension leaned forward to put down his coffee.

'I'm not very happy about the survey that's been done between Fort Calgary and the Kicking Horse Pass in the Rockies. The route mileage and cost estimates seem to me to be wildly over-estimated. I was hoping I might be able to talk you into re-assessing the route for me.'

Hard as he tried, Cameron could not disguise the look of incredulity on his face; and then as he sighed with relief, a slight grin spread across his face.

'I do apologise if this has upset you. I'm just really stuck and don't have anyone else to turn to. I'll try to make it up to you…somehow.'

Cameron could barely stop himself from chuckling, as Mr Van Horne had so obviously misread him.

'I'm sorry, Mr Van Horne. Please forgive my apparent amusement at the position you find yourself in. It's just that…I was worried sick the railway had had second thoughts about the offer of the land.'

Cameron left Cornelius Van Horne's office with a spring in his step. Not only had he not lost the land, but in his pocket he now had a free railway pass for life – for himself and the family – and the promise of a two hundred dollar bonus. The downside was that he wouldn't be able to begin the survey until next April at the earliest. But then, the more he thought about it, the more he realised that this wasn't a problem anyway, as he and Catherine had no intention of moving out to their new property until early the following summer, by which time he should have completed the survey.

By the end of October, the track had been laid to Fort Calgary. A new station was immediately erected, and a depot and marshalling yards were well under construction. The newly named city of Calgary was in fact founded on the west side of the Elbow River – much to the chagrin of the speculators who had staked out most of the land to the east. C.P.R. management had finally realised that the only way to maximise their profits on land sales was to make the decisions about new stations and cities at the very last minute.

I.G. Baker's was the first business to relocate to the city's new location, followed by the Hudson's Bay Company; and within days, the air resonated to the hammering of nails, sawing of wood and screaming of foremen.

Wood was in plentiful supply. The foothills of the Rocky Mountains were covered in bountiful forests, and were only a short wagon ride away. Soon, one enterprising businessman opened a sawmill alongside the Bow River west of the city, and in no time at all, dressed planks began to replace the roughly sawn timbers.

It didn't take long before those representing the moneyed investors back east realised that Calgary was to become a major western city. And as had happened in Winnipeg not many years before, finance poured in, starting another property boom.

314

Thirty Five

They were only a few miles west of Calgary, following the north bank of the Bow River, when Cameron started to feel the muscles in his thighs and back beginning to rebel. He found it hard to believe how little it took of what George called "the soft life", before one's body was once more out of condition. But one thing was for sure, he had no intention of revealing his discomfort to his travelling companion!

The two men quickly passed the Old Bow Fort, and after following the waterway through the Bow River Gap, arrived at Padmore. This settlement had already been designated by the railway as the main water and coaling station for locomotives, prior to their commencement of the tortuous passage through the mountains. A small siding and depot were now under construction; and an enterprising family called Jones had already established a small trading post, just a few hundred feet from the tracks.

Cameron and George carried on in a west north-westerly direction, getting ever nearer to the majestic mountains. Cameron was still puzzled why Van Horne had wanted him to check this route, because so far, the previous surveyor had done exactly what he would have done, by following the Bow River valley.

One afternoon, as they rounded a small hill on the western side of the valley, a huge mountain loomed into view completely blocking further progress. This was what it was all about, thought Cameron, as he withdrew a leather-bound notebook from his saddlebag and consulted the previous surveyor's notes.

'We'll camp here for a while, George. We need to have a good look around.'

That night, after cleaning up their dishes – totally soiled by their gourmet pork and beans – Cameron sat warming his hands in front of the fire. As he stared into the blaze, idly kicking the unburned ends of the logs into the dying embers, his thoughts once more returned to his future plans; while above him, the moon lit up the area like a flickering light bulb, as the clouds raced by overhead.

'Cameron…why you leave soft job in city to work with crazy cows…in place south of river?'

It was then that Cameron decided to be honest with his friend, so over the next two hours told George about his real family's history, and his own murderous past.

'Well, George…you know more about me now than Catherine does…so maybe you understand why I feel I must move on.'

George said nothing for ages, making Cameron wonder if maybe he'd gone a step too far. But then, without taking his eyes from the flames, George responded.

'I not understand most white men. In my world…we do same…like you…because spirits of dead not rest until death paid for.'

Three days later, he and George found a new route by-passing the offending mountain. A small creek disappearing into a nearby wood had in fact opened out into another valley. Following that valley would still meet the gradient requirements of the railway, while at the same time negating the need for a long tunnel. That tunnel alone would have taken at least a year to build, and cost over a million dollars – as opposed to Cameron's diversion, which would increase the track distance by less than a mile, equating to a cost increase of less than fifty thousand dollars.

Thirty Six

It was unusually warm for the first week of June in this part of Canada. Cameron stood on the platform at the station in Calgary, awaiting the arrival of the express train from Winnipeg. Finally, a muted blast in the distance announced its impending presence, followed a few minutes later by its appearance between the buildings on the eastern edge of the city.

As the train drew to a halt, the screech of the brakes was the only arrival announcement required. With a loud thump, the door of the first-class passenger car swung open – clamping itself to the side of the carriage. Within seconds, a uniformed conductor stepped down from the opening, placing a metal box-like step onto the platform. Climbing back on board, he subsequently reappeared bearing two large suitcases, and carefully set them down before turning to offer a hand to Catherine.

Thirty minutes later, Cameron and Catherine were on the dusty, worn trail heading south-east from Calgary. Initially, their non-stop chatter drowned out any sounds that might have accompanied their progress, but after they'd caught up on their news, both lapsed into silence; as Nature's symphony and the scenery began to weave its magic.

To their left, an emerald-green valley descended towards the Bow River – its surface sparkling in the noon-day sun – while to their right, the track was bounded by splendid fir trees, interwoven with groups of birches and cottonwoods. As they ventured further south, the river continued to trail along beside them, but the stalwart sentinels to their right gradually disappeared from sight, giving way to grasses and foothills telling of the greater majesty to come. Finally, as the land alongside the Bow began to rise, the magnificence of the snow-capped Rockies burst into view – lying like the ragged teeth of a saw against the incandescent sky.

Three hours into their journey, they arrived at another river.

'This is it Cath.'

'Where?…Which part is ours?'

Cameron turned the buggy parallel to the new river, before reining in the mare.

'As far as you can see along this river…and then over that way for three miles,' he said, indicating with the sweep of his hand. 'Oh…and we've been on our land for about the last ten minutes as well.'

Catherine was momentarily stunned.

'My God…I didn't realise 640 acres was so huge.'

'Well, it's actually slightly more than that. Under the Dominion Land Act we're allowed to file an interim claim on each adjoining quarter section of land... so that's what I've done. That means we now have claim over another 640 acres…and the best part is that we don't have to start paying the government for any of it for another five years.'

Just then Anna began to cry.

'Well…that little noise means its feeding time. Are we near home or shall I feed Anna as we go along?'

'There's a little way to go yet, so you might as well start,' he said, snapping the reins.

Catherine did her best to feed Anna, while Cameron guided their horse along a barely visible track beside the new river. Finally, on rounding a small hill, two large tents came into sight.

Catherine's heart sank.

'What the…'

'Hang on a minute.'

As they got a little further around the hill, a small log cabin, adjoining a recently fenced corral, became visible.

Catherine said nothing as she took in what she assumed was their new house.

Pulling up in front of the cabin, Cameron reached down and tied-off the reins, before jumping down from the buggy. Turning back to help Catherine, it was obvious from the look on her face that she wasn't exactly thrilled by what she'd seen so far.

'Is everything all right, Cath? You look a little pale.'

'Is that...our...our house?' she stammered. 'It looks smaller than the one we've been using in Winnipeg…and that was just a summer home. I'm not going to.…'

Cameron could no longer contain himself, and burst into laughter.

That night, Catherine knew she'd found true happiness. They were living on their own land, with their daughter safe in a cot beside them. And soon she would have a beautiful house, which could finally be called home.

After his initial teasing, Cameron confessed that the cabin was only a temporary home and, after their new house was built, would be turned into a stable and store room.

The only niggling doubt Catherine now harboured was the distance between here and the nearest civilization. Was it really safe to be out here by themselves in the middle of nowhere?

The following morning – shortly after dawn – they heard the squeaking and rattling of wagons, and the snorting and whinnying of horses as they approached. The men sent by Baker's duly moved into their temporary canvass quarters, and then got to work on the Stuarts' new house.

The next six years sped by, and during that time, Cameron and Catherine's "C&C" branded cattle continued to grow in number. He had decided to break with tradition, and was breeding Texas Longhorns, as opposed to the more normal short-horned variety. He knew from his experience working on American ranches that they didn't put on weight as quickly as their short-horned cousins. But their ability to almost take care of themselves – especially during the long, cold winters of southern Alberta – should more than make up for the slightly longer fattening time. Their herd had now grown to ninety head, and this year, Cameron hoped would produce another twenty-five calves. It had been hard work. However, he was now making a tidy profit. In fact, the money they'd made over the last two years had already allowed him to repay half of his debt to the government, and next year he would almost certainly be able to pay off the rest.

Of course, the herd wasn't all that was growing. He and Catherine had purposely decided not to have any more children until their new livelihood was well established. And having now reached that point, Catherine was once more pregnant.

Anna seemed more than happy with her outdoor way of life; and although Catherine was doing her best to tutor her young daughter, she and Cameron both knew that a more formal education would soon need to be found.

During the last five years, two new neighbours had arrived – both within a twenty-minute ride of the C&C ranch. One family was Scandinavian. They had immigrated to Canada three years ago, and were now running a pig farm, three miles away. The other family were Irish, having arrived from County Down nearly five years ago. Their family was made up of Kieran, the father, and Colleen, the mother, as well as a son called Liam and five year old daughter named Megan. But what interested Cameron most was that Kieran was breeding shorthorn cattle, which inevitably became the main topic of conversation whenever they got together.

Of course, what pleased Catherine was not the progress of beef cattle, but the fact that she now had a good friend close by, and other children with whom Anna could socialise.

'Honey…Look who's here!' Catherine shouted one day, while standing outside hanging up her washing.

Cameron came out of the kitchen door, and then stared down the track to where four horses could be seen approaching in a cloud of dust. The grey stallion and dark brown appaloosa were horses that Cameron and Catherine both knew well – having belonged to George and Lomasi since the Stuarts had first known them – but the other two riders on Palominos were, at first, indiscernible. Finally, as the ill-defined group drew nearer recognition dawned, as George and Lomasi's sons' arms rose in salute.

At dusk, the wind had died away to nothing. They all sat cross-legged around the fire, as the sparks and smoke lifted straight towards the heavens; and apart from the occasional 'who…who' of a great horned owl, and the crackling and snapping of the blazing logs, the night was silent.

Anna spent the first few hours of the evening staring in awe at the two young men, and then, much to her disgust, had been ordered to bed.

For the next little while, the six reminisced about the old days, and their time spent together on the plains; but once the sacred pipe began to be passed around, all slipped into an almost reverential silence – not necessarily because of the rigours of the day, or sudden belief in the Great Spirit, but more likely due to the psychoactive effects of George's "special" tobacco.

'You know, Cath,' said Cameron later, as they prepared themselves for bed. I know this sounds weird…but I could have sworn I did feel some kind of spirit out there…or at least something making me feel…I don't know…kind of at peace with the world.'

Receiving no reply, Cameron turned, looking at Catherine lying peacefully beside him. She was already asleep. But maybe her reply, he thought, was the almost serene look spread across her tender, expressionless face.

Not long after the sun had begun to rise over the plains to the east, they were all sitting on the banks of the High River enjoying a picnic breakfast. A wispy breeze rose, rustling the leaves on the nearby cottonwoods, while at the same time the long grass surrounding them seemed to be constantly changing colour, as it swayed in the morning's freshening gusts.

All too soon it was time to say goodbye. George got up from the blanket, momentarily drawing Cameron aside.

'I have favour to ask.'

'Of course, George. You know I'll do anything I can for you.'

'Many night...I sit in front of fire...listening to Great Spirit. Now I understand... Indian way of life on plain almost gone. We must change...or will die. My two sons must learn new way...like white man.'

'You're probably right, George. Listen...Next spring... when you head north again, why don't you leave the boys with me? I can always use more hands during round up time.'

As they stood watching George and his family ride off, Cameron had one arm around Catherine's back while his other rested on Anna's shoulder.

'You know, Cameron...it's such a shame we don't see them more often. Life just seems...Oh I don't know...more tranquil, when they're here.'

'Yes, well tranquil it may be, but right now I've got over sixty, three and four year old steers to move to the railhead by the weekend. So, I've got to ride over to Kieran's and see if I can get him and his cowboys here on Friday to give me a hand.'

'Be careful!' said the taller of the two men, knocking the binoculars down from his partner's eyes.

'For Christ's sake, Colin...Can ye no see the sun over

322

there? It could easily reflect off them glasses an give us away.'

The two men squatted behind a large bush, on the edge of the wood behind the Stuarts' corral. Neither was in the best of moods, having just spent the night hiding in the woods, and being eaten alive by mosquitoes.

The man doing the talking was certainly not the friendliest looking person, with his acne-scarred face, thin cheeks and thick black eyebrows; while the other man, named Colin, was short and rotund, with tiny low-set ears, curved eyebrows and a broad nose.

'Thank God, them bloody Indians be gone! Now maybe we can get on wi' what we be here for.'

'Are ye sure he be the one?'

'Ah've spent twelve years huntin' him down...ever since that dumb nurse, Annie, went an opened her big mouth in the pub...an Sergeant Boyd's sister done heard her. Ah know he be Cameron Stewart, an pay day is comin',' he said, rubbing his hands with relish.

'But...surely no the woman an bairn?'

'Listen...old man Campbell said all of 'em.'

Catherine was forced from her peaceful sleep by an intermittent slamming noise from somewhere outside. Rolling over, she prodded Cameron, rousing him from his slumber.

'Cameron, wake up. I think the barn door's open. I can hear it banging.'

'What...oh, all right,' he yawned.

'Bloody door,' he murmured, throwing off his covers.

Then, after rolling out of bed, he picked up his socks from the floor.

For a moment he hesitated, hoping what Catherine had heard had been in her dreams. But, seconds later, a dull thump resounded, so he continued to get dressed.

Quietly, shuffling passed his daughter's door, Cameron

turned left, descending the stairs and then turned left again, before ambling through the kitchen to the back door. As he swung it open, a momentary bright flash in his consciousness suddenly lighted the darkness greeting him, before he pitched forwards to the ground and oblivion.

'Come over here, Colin. Hurry up…let's be gettin' on wi' this.'

'Christ…did ye need to whack him so hard? He's bleedin' all over the place.'

'Does no really matter. There'll no be any sign of that later. Now…have ye got that wee bottle wi' you?'

'Aye. It be here…in ma pocket,' Colin replied, patting his side.

'Follow me then…quietly.'

Moments later, Catherine was woken by the feel of a damp cloth being forced over her nose and mouth, followed by a pungent smell invading her nostrils. Her hands clawed at her face, but within seconds she began to feel dizzy and passed out.

'Right…come on…let's be draggin' her out of here,' whispered the tall man. 'We can lay her doon over there, at the top of them stairs.'

Having helped to arrange her body to his partner's satisfaction, Colin stood up.

'Now what we be doin'?'

'Now we go an get Cameron Stewart.'

The two men dragged Cameron's body up the stairs, leaving him lying in the hallway a few feet from his daughter's bedroom door.

'Right…ye get in there an use that stuff to make sure the wee lass is out of it, while Ah go doon to the front room an open a window.'

'Why ye be doin' that?'

'Do ye no remember anythin'? The idea is they'll find the broken kerosene lamp layin' below the window an assume a gust of wind knocked it to the floor. Now… when yer finished come downstairs…Then Ah'll drop the lamp to start the fire.

An make sure ye no leave that bottle behind. Remember this must be lookin' like a mishap.'

A few minutes later, a crash in the front room was followed by a loud whoosh as the liquid burst into flames.

'Right, that be it…Come on, Colin. Let's be getting' out of here.'

The two men rushed out through the kitchen, making sure they closed the back door before scurrying across the yard.

'Hang on a minute, Colin. I just want to be sure it goes up proper.'

As they watched, the flames erupted from the downstairs windows turning night into day.

'That'll do, let's go.'

Both men turned, heading towards the tree line behind the corral.

Suddenly, a scream filled the night.

'What the hell! Ah thought Ah be tellin' ye to put her out.'

'Ah could no do it. She looked so young an innocent. Can we no just let her go?'

'No! Are ye crazy? Now we'll just have to wait an make sure she does no get out.'

Cameron's head pounded; and after putting his hand to the back of his skull it came away sticky. Where was he? Why was he lying on the floor? A roaring and crackling filled his ears; and then, as a searing heat worked its way through to his senses, he realised where he was and what was happening. Looking down, he was horrified at the sight of flames devouring the legs of his trousers, and desperately beat at them with his bare hands.

Just then, a piercing scream broke through the confusion surrounding him. Anna's heart-rending plea stabbed at his soul, dispelling any thoughts of his own pain. Rising to his knees, Cameron inched towards her door. Smoke now filled the corridor, blinding him and taking the place of what little oxygen was left in the blistering air.

Suddenly, a crashing sound from above was followed by him being slammed to the floor – his last mental picture being the skin on the backs of his hands blistering and shrivelling, as his pain melted away.

As the two men waited in the shadows by the barn, the flames got higher and higher. At the same time Anna's heart rending cries overwhelmed the crackling and spitting of the inferno, sending shivers up both men's spines.

But in the end, it was the harrowing little face at the bedroom window – agony exhaling with each breath from her tortured mouth – which Colin knew he would take to his grave, and his certain journey to hell.

Epilogue

Alex pushed Morty on as fast as he dared. As he did his mop of unruly red hair began to freeze in disorderly tufts and his ears to sting – reminding him of his ill-advised haste in leaving home without his hat.

The leaden sky and clammy air now felt as though it was pressing down on the earth, and he knew it was only a matter of time before snow would start to fall.

On both sides of the track the fields were covered in snow – apart from the odd patch of last year's stubble breaking through the dull white surface. While in the distance, a rising column of smoke above the trees showed him the way.

In due course, Alex entered the woodland – made up of sugar maples and the odd scattered conifer and birch trees. Many years ago, his father's family had planted the trees, and their maturity now ensured a good source of extra income. The grainy wood was always in demand with furniture makers, while in the spring, the sale of maple syrup was a welcome addition to the family's earnings at a time when the farm produced little.

His progress slowed to a walk. He and Morty weaved their way through the trees, as care was required to make certain the buckets hanging from the metal taps drilled into the trees were not disturbed. Horse and rider were guided by the sweet odour in the air, until at last, the clearing came in to sight.

'Pa...Quick! Ma wants you home right away!'

John looked up, momentarily halting his stirring of the syrup in the huge, iron pot suspended over the fire.

'What is it, Alex? Is she sick?'

'I don't know... I don't think so. Constable Girarde rode over to our place, and the next thing I knew Ma was telling me to hurry and get you.'

'All right, give me the reins...I'll take Morty back. You can finish bottling up for me, and then saddle up Blackie and come home.'

John swung up into the saddle, heading back down the trail at a trot – the risk of collisions with the buckets no longer seeming so important. He sensed something must be terribly wrong, as he knew Margaret would never have sent Alex down to him without an explanation, unless things were seriously amiss.

Reaching the backyard, he reined in Morty, and then leaping from the saddle bounded up the steps and yanked open the back door.

'Maggie…Maggie, where are you?'

Holding his breath, a barely discernible response could be heard coming from the front of the house.

John hurried down the hall, ignoring the wet marks he left on their new hall carpet.

As he entered the front room, Margaret ran to him, throwing her arms around his neck and sobbing into his shoulder.

'What is it? Are you sick?'

Then, his eyes fell on the dusty old bible, and his breath caught in his throat.

By the time Alex had finished siphoning off the rest of the bubbling liquid, it was almost dark. Placing the large demijohns into the storage shack, he retrieved Blackie's saddle and hurried outside.

It had now been snowing for over an hour, and the light was fading fast. Alex galloped clear of the tree line, and it was only then that he became aware of how poor the visibility had become. The cold, snow-laden wind was whipping across the open fields – with drifts quickly building across his path.

Finding his way home was not the problem. Blackie could do that blindfolded. But what did worry him was what he would find when he got there.

The storm worsened by the minute, as he and Blackie took on an almost ghostly appearance. Finally, the farm's outbuildings loomed into view, and with an encouraging 'yee-hah' he pushed Blackie on.

As they drew nearer, the sight that greeted Alex pushed all thoughts of personal discomfort to the back of his mind. Morty was not only unstabled, but was now wandering loose in the backyard – his saddle, blanket and mane covered in freshly fallen snow. Quickly dismounting, Alex grabbed both horses' reins and, tying them off on the back rail, sprinted for the house.

Worryingly, as he stepped through the kitchen door, the house was silent. Normally, his mother would have been in the kitchen preparing their evening meal, while his father would either be passing the time of day with her, or checking their customers' orders on paperwork spread over the kitchen table.

'Ma…Pa, where are you?' he shouted, heading for the front room.

Alex's anxiety increased with each step.

'We're in here,' murmured his father, in an unusually restrained manner.

Turning into the sitting room, Alex's steps faltered.

The sight before his eyes alarmed him like nothing ever before. His father's shoulders sagged, and his hands trembled. While his face, which until now had always been strong and full of colour, was drawn and sallow.

Close beside him on the couch, sat his mother.

She was never what Alex would have called pretty, although her complexion was clear and her eyes usually sparkling and warm. She always kept her hair brushed and tied-back off of her face; and what few clothes she had were, without exception, neat and pressed.

Being clean and presentable had always been important to her, which was why the woman he now beheld seemed almost a stranger. Her face was ashen, her eyes puffy and bordered in red. Her hair lay unkempt in straggly strands all over her head; while her dress was a wrinkled mess, and stained down the front with damp patches.

For the first time in his life, Alex was really frightened. His parents, who had always been his teachers, providers and protectors, had now fallen apart in front of his eyes.

This time it was his mother who broke the stillness.

'Please, Alex…Please sit down over here,' she sniffed, patting the seat beside her. 'There's something you need to know.'